BITTERSWEET
MEMORIES OF
LAST SPRING

ARDAIN ISMA

Printed by Village Care Corp.
Village Care Publishing
99 King Street #1822
Saint Augustine, FL, 32085

Table of Contents

Brief Bio

Ardain Isma was born in Haiti, where he lived until he was 18. He migrated to the United States during the mass migration of the 1980s. He is an essayist, novelist, and the Chief Editor of CSMS Magazine (www.csmsmagazine.org). He teaches Introduction to Research Methods at Embry Riddle University. A prolific writer, Ardain has written extensively on three main issues: writers' tools for success, social justice, and multiculturalism. Ardain lives with his wife Maryse in Saint Augustine, Florida.

Also by Ardain Isma

Alicia Maldonado: A Mother Lost

Midnight at Noon

Acknowledgments

In memory of my parents, Tibince Cédieu and Anne-Rose Isma, who continue to be my main point of comfort in moments of uncertainties.

To my sister, Erna Isma Jules, with whom I spent my earlier years as an immigrant in the United States. We had nothing, but we had each other.

To my other siblings, Guyto, Compa, and Royo, from whom I also draw inspiration to write this story.

To my wife, Maryse, my children Ardine, Ardain Junior, and Ardy who are my biggest fans in this writing journey.

Book 1

Quote

*L' art haitien représente en effet le réel avec son cortège d'
étranges, de fantastiques, de rêves, de demi-jours, de
mystères, et de merveilleux.* (Jacques Stéphen Alexis)

Haitian art is indeed real because of its unique, fantastic,
dreamy, crepuscular, mysterious, and marvelous forms. (Jacques
Stéphen Alexis)

Prologue

Bittersweet Memories of Last Spring

In the belly of this crowded sailboat, the stench was unbearable. Seasickness had turned the passengers, including me, into the living dead. Stomachs churned, heads spun, and, like a furnace belching into flame, dizziness had forced many of us to heave and gush out whatever was left inside our stomachs. For the first time in my young life I came to realize how precious it is to be young and free, and how painful it could be when that freedom has been abridged. As we sailed to no end in the middle of this vast ocean, nothing short of escaping out of my skin was enough to save my sanity.

Manman told me Miami was not far off. She told me nothing came easy in life. Wallowing in this web of fear and uncertainty, I tried to hold onto my mother's words of reassurance, but the cries of despair echoing around me gave me no room for comfort. Then, there was a crack up above, and the hatchway was pushed open.

"Get ready to change ship," said a man in a husky voice. His face was that of a brown leather shoe. The people said he was the captain. "We should be on our way to Miami in the next hour." he added.

Bewildered and beaten, I looked around and, as if by magic, everyone rose to their feet, picking up their belongings. With anxious stares, they waited for the ship of salvation to arrive. Unexpectedly, a surge of hope took hold of my mind. This seemed to be shared among us all as dying faces became smiling ones. Everyone was alive again. I too sensed I had conquered my feeling of despair. Hopelessness, I thought, was the greatest tragedy to befall someone.

There, we waited. After five long minutes, we began to hear the faint rumbling of an engine in the distance, growing louder and soon full-blown. Our sailboat started shaking violently, swayed by the powerful waves from the bigger ship as it drew near to retrieve us. Then, the waves subsided and the ocean was stilled. My heart was racing. The hatchway was reopened, and the captain craned his neck forward.

"Listen, I need two at a time," he growled. Just before I had a chance to ask about safety during the change, the captain disappeared. Like obedient school children, we formed rows of two, and I was in the third row.

The journey seemed endless. Manman told me Miami was a city hidden behind La Tortue, an island just off the coast of my hometown, Saint Louis. It was where seafarers were brought in before embarking on risky voyages to the unknown.

It had been two days since we left Haiti, and Miami was nowhere in sight. I knew no one on the ship, and I confined myself inside the tiny cabin to which I was assigned. It was smaller than a jail cell. I spoke to no one. I could not. Fear crippled my mind like a caged bird in unfamiliar terrain. This ship was an engine-powered sailboat and no bigger than the previous one, but it was large enough to accommodate thirty of us; all whose faith depended on the expertise of the crew. The passengers no longer looked seasick as I watched them chat and laugh.

In the early morning of the third day, I stepped out onto the deck, and my eyes spied a seabird flying directly above the ship. In my mind, there was a renewed sense of hope.

Back home, people used to say if you saw birds at sea, it meant you were very close to land. My optimism grew as I glanced across the vast ocean, and there was land in the faded distance. It was massive, long, and gray, but the ship sailed parallel to it. The entire day went by, and that land was no closer than when I had first spotted it. At dusk, I lost track of the land, and the ship sailed on under the starry blue sky. Disappointed, I walked to one of the crew members. "Wasn't it Florida, the land we watched in the distance all day long?"

"No, my son," he replied with a broad smile. That was Cuba, but you'll be able to see Florida soon." He was a short, red-haired man like the rest of the crew. "Today is Wednesday. Do you think we might get there by tomorrow?"

"No, my son. We should get there by Saturday night." He sensed my anxiety. "*Jeannette*," he called to a tall, slim woman who sat in a low chair in the far end of the dining area. She fixed her blue headcloth, then quickly got up and walked toward us.

"Keep this young man close to you. Okay?" the crewman asked Jeannette.

"*Yes,* sir," she replied, taking my hand and guiding me to her chair in the dining room.

In a move to comfort me, she avoided her chair and pulled my hand down on the floor where we squatted next to each other. "What's your name, son?" she asked in a low voice, wrapping her arm around my neck to lessen my fear.

"Yrvin," I answered, my voice timid.

"How old are you?"

"Seventeen."

"What town are you from?"

"Saint Louis."

"That's where I'm from, too." She squeezed me in a quick hug. "Who're your parents?"

"Rose and Tibince."

"I know your mother very well. For a while, she was the one who supported me financially when my husband was sick in Miami. She fed my children when they were hungry, buying them clothes for Christmas."

Soon, Jeannette became a friend, a point of comfort, a shepherd. To kill the passage of time, we told each other stories of people and friends back home.

On Saturday morning, the captain ordered everyone to get ready as we were likely nearing Miami. Even before he finished his sentence, folks around me were already on the move as they had been during the switch from the sailboat to the ship.

Those who live in the shadow of death, though keenly aware of their precarious conditions, do not always feel frightened until their escape from poverty draws near. This was a lesson my grandmother taught me. The laughter of the previous days was soon replaced by fear-ridden faces. I was nervous as my young life was about to enter a new chapter. After the announcement, however, we sailed for another half-day, and Miami, the Promised Land, was still out of sight. Getting a glimpse of that elusive land would be the therapeutic dose I needed to temper my nervousness. It was the only time during the voyage that the blurred faces of friends and relatives who had embarked upon this similar journey before me started to trickle into my consciousness.

Jeannette and I sat close to the glass windows, trying to be the first to spot the mysterious land. But all we could see was the vast empty water; wavy and dark blue. The engine-powered boat sailed on. My hope to finally escape began to wane, but I concealed my disappointment.

Suddenly, the ship stopped. Jeannette and I held each other's hands, praying that we would make it to Miami safely. The crew ordered everyone to remain in their cabins. It was a stern order. We all had memories of dead bodies floating in the shallow. Adherence to captain's orders was key to survival. To disobey the captain's orders was risky and foolhardy. Before long, the captain's reassuring expression was replaced by an unapologetic, devilish look. The officers only spoke in authoritative terms. Uncertainty consumed us. It did not take us long to learn the reason for such a dramatic change in the captain's attitude. Many of the passengers, myself included, had no passport. If the ship reached its destination before dusk, everyone would be arrested and the ship would be seized by the authorities if found out at the time of inspection.

It was eight p.m. and finally dark when we started moving again. Darkness had already arrived. We were alone in this immense ocean. An hour later, we began to see twinkling lights in the distance, which grew brighter and more glamorous as the ship edged to the land. What had started as a tense dreary day was now bright and playful. We sailed past a myriad sailboats, white and beautiful. I had no doubt in my mind that we were at last entering paradise, the dazzling place Manman always told me about. I now understood why so many folks had risked, and still continued to risk, their lives to get to this city. Golden lights sparkled inside tall buildings that seemed to soar as the ship drew closer. Jeannette's jaw dropped in astonishment.

Then, there was the dreaded voice of the captain again. "If you don't have a passport, go down and wait to be called. The rest of you, move up to the deck to get ready for inspections."

A good number of us, and Jeannette and I, were herded down inside a small, dark room with an iron door. There, the captain ordered everyone to remain silent until someone returned for us. It was hot. I was sweating and scared. Jeannette held me tight, sheltering me under her long, skinny arms and, to ease my pain, whispered "Hang on. We're almost there. We'll make it through."

From the belly of the ship, we could hear people laughing, ship horns blowing, and of the captain's throaty voice speaking strange words we could not understand. Then, the commotion stopped, giving way to an eerie silence. Finally, the iron door was unlocked and a short man in dark uniform stood right outside the door. He held a toothpick in the corner of his mouth and ordered five of us to follow him. Jeannette was among the five. She tried to bring me along but was quickly stopped. I stretched my hand like a starving child begging for food. Tears welled up in my eyes. My heart sank. She was gone. I would have to face the final leg of this journey on my own. The chatter of those left behind pounded in my ears as I waited. When the man in the uniform returned, he took another group of people. But I was again not part of it.

When I finally walked out along with four other passengers, Jeannette was gone. The other refugees, who had also left before me, were nowhere in sight. On the deck stood the captain, the man in the uniform, and my group of five, bewildered and disoriented after such a long voyage.

"Do you have an address?" The captain asked. He looked tense. He knew the stakes were high for all of us. If spotted, he would lose his ship, and we all would be arrested for an eventual deportation.

"Yes, I do," I replied along with the rest of the group. Each of us handed our respective address. He read them carefully.

"Stay here, young man," he said while ordering my other four boat-mates to follow him behind some shipping containers and soon disappeared. A short moment later, he returned and instructed the man in the uniform, who was still standing next to me, to walk me down a narrow alleyway that led to a deserted street where a taxi was waiting.

"Get in," the taxi driver said, pushing the door for me to get inside.

"Goodbye, young man," the man in the uniform said as he hurried back to the ship.

Relieved, I yanked a piece of paper from my back pocket. Written on it was the address of my uncle Philippe's home. He was a longtime Miami resident and my older sister, Lorna, currently lived with him. I handed it to the driver.

"I don't need it. I already know where you're going," he said with a lowered voice, which provided me no comfort.

In the car, inside of me there was a feeling I could not describe. I knew I was close to my final destination, but I was nervous, thinking about the nervousness that showed up on the captain's face few minutes earlier. The driver, a chubby man with a jet-black face and untrimmed beard, looked through the rearview mirror and saw how anxious I was. "Stay calm and don't look back. We'll be at your address in the few minutes," he said, trying to reassure me. He had a funny Creole accent like the American missionaries that I used to see in my town in Haiti.

It was a midsummer night, hot and steamy. The streets were deserted. As we sped away in the still of the night, I was shocked to watch block after block of rundown buildings with groups of homeless folks sleeping on the narrow porches. I began to question the Promised Land Miami was supposed to have been as Manman used to tell me in Haiti. Of course, I kept my thoughts to myself.

The taxi turned and we entered a grand boulevard with strip malls, shops, and boutiques with signs written in French as it was customary in Haiti. It was late evening, but few cars drove by with Creole music blasting away. On the sidewalk, few men and women strolled along, speaking Creole. Their demeanor, their laughter, and their melodious speech quickly made me understand that these folks were compatriots from home. I knew we had rolled into Little Haiti. Five minutes later, the taxi veered to the left and exited the boulevard. The driver pulled in front of a giant, yellow apartment building.

"You have arrived," he said with a grin. I asked him to wait while I went to get the money from my sister. "Go. There's no need to," he said with a smile. "I was once in your shoes."

Anxious, I walked toward the front door and knocked. A young boy of about six years of age promptly opened the door and walked away. I could see my uncle and a friend sitting on the living room couch watching television. His eyes slanted toward the door and he recognized me. "*Yrvin!*" he exclaimed. He was gleeful. I went in without replying. The cab driver, who was waiting for me to get in, drove off. I never saw him again.

My sister, who was upstairs, hurried down and we all converged into the living room for an impromptu celebration. Uncle Philippe, a middle aged man of a medium height with a shiny bald head and firm features, grabbed me by the arms and pulled me against his chest for a prolonged hug. His skinny, six-year-old son, Phillippe Junior, in the bewilderment of joy, came crashing into me, making funny stares out of excitement, looking at a cousin until now he had known nothing about. My sister was in tears, but they were tears of joy, knowing I was finally safe in her arms. She had known I was at sea, for Manman had phoned her few weeks before to let her know about the voyage.

"You must be hungry. Look at you. Let me go make rice pudding, your favorite. I remember," she said, pulling my chin up close while peering into my sleepy eyes, taking a closer look at my careworn face.

"Yes, I am. But I'm more eager to tell Manman that I'm now safe in Miami," I replied, watching her bare brown face aglow and her short, slim body running to the kitchen in total elation.

"Do people now have phone service in Saint Louis?" my uncle asked curiously.

"No. There is a central office where everyone goes," I replied, looking exhausted.

"But I'm sure it's now closed. Isn't it, Vinco?" Nana said.

"Yes."

"We'll do it in the morning, Vinco," Uncle Philippe said.

The days at sea had taken its toll. I was tired and overwhelmed from my journey filled with uncertainties. They surrounded me, asking questions about my journey, my hometown, my mother, and my siblings. I wanted to reply to every question, for I had so much to share. But my body would not cooperate.

They lived in a townhouse apartment with a tiny kitchen and a small living room downstairs. Nana went to make rice pudding. Uncle Philippe took me upstairs to take a much-needed shower. When I came back, I joined her in the kitchen. About a half hour later, the food was ready. All four of us now congregated around the kitchen table to continue the celebration over rice pudding.

Though, the food was delicious, I only took a few spoonfuls. I was tired. They understood. Surrounded by loved ones, I was convinced a new chapter in life had just begun.

Chapter 1

Early the next morning, I woke up around 6 am after a long, quiet night, away from the high seas' turbulences, from the occasional wind gusts that forced the ship to tip sideways, and then pivoted upward in rapid motion as we sailed through an endless ocean. My first morning in America was a worry-free, peaceful Sunday morning. I slept through the night in a room that I shared with Phillippe Junior, but he was still sleeping and snoring when I tiptoed out of the room and made my way to a small balcony, taking aim at the neighborhood, watching few cars driving down the noiseless street and some small cottage homes on both sides that lay dormant against the giant housing complex that had become my new home. When I went back inside, Junior was still in bed. I strolled to my sister's room and knocked. She did not answer. So, I ran downstairs, where I found her in the kitchen, making breakfast while Uncle Philippe still in his pajamas sat in the couch in the living room, a cup of coffee in hands, watching television.

"Bonjour Uncle, Bonjour Nana," I greeted them.

Nana looked at me with adorable eyes filled with sisterly pride. "Did you have a good night sleep, Vinco?"

"Of course," I said, edging closer, landing a little kiss on her rosy cheek. Then, I went to talk to Uncle Philippe.

"How was your first night in America," he said, teasing me.

"It was great," I replied, taking a seat next to him. I wanted to enjoy the moment, but I could not understand what was being said. English was alien to me.

"What time is the phone office in Saint Louis open?" He asked. He was as eager as I was to let my mother know that I was indeed under his care. He was my father's younger brother. The two brothers had developed a strong bond, even though my dad lived in the Bahamas and had yet to visit the United States. He knew about the voyage, for he was the one who made payment arrangement for the voyage.

"At 8 am, Uncle" I replied, evermore reassured that I was home.

"We'll call Haiti, and then the Bahamas," he said, sipping in his coffee.

Later after breakfast, Uncle called the central office of Saint Louis, leaving a message to go and get my mother who lived a short distance away. As I waited, neighbors started coming in, having learned about my arrival the night before. They were all Haitians from the Saint Louis region, and many of them knew my parents. For the moment, I thought I was still in Haiti. They all surrounded me, bombarding me with questions about the town, about its progress etc.

In the middle of this euphoria, Phillippe Junior called me. "Vinco, your mother is on the phone."

I left everyone and ran toward the phone. "Manman," I cried.

"Yes, Vinco. I'm so happy that I can hear your voice," she said. She was delighted.

"Me, too, Manman." Tears sprang from my eyes.

"I had been fasting since you left, praying day and night."

In the middle of the excitement, the phone went dead. We lost communication, just as Nana was about to talk to her. We tried again several times to get reconnected, but the line was busy. Still, I was happy to the fact Manman now knew, through my own voice, that I was safe. When Uncle Philippe called my dad in the Bahamas, he was not home, but he left a message for him to call. Later in the day, he called, and we had a blast over the phone.

The following month, which was August, my sister took me to enroll in school for the upcoming academic year. There, they placed me in eleventh grade because of my age. All my courses, including math, were self-contained taught by an ESL (English as a Second Language) teacher. Although I liked the setting, a portable classroom filled with students from many parts of the world, especially from Cuba, the Dominican Republic, and Haiti, I always felt a sense of isolation. It was located outside the main building, and it was only on the playground that I could mingle with other Haitian children who went to mainstream classes. When I left Haiti at seventeen, I was in my last year of secondary school. So, my academic background had helped a lot in my performance in high school.

Like any immigrant, I had to go through the tedious process of cultural integration and second language acquisition. In the fight for immersion, I was on stage four, meaning I had become a Haitian-American boy, fully integrated into mainstream society. From the honeymoon period of the early days to the

17

unforgettable cultural shocks, I suffered as I struggled to get adjusted. In the early days, I used to feel frustrated for not being able to understand gestures which often resulted in miscommunications. I was afraid of going alone to fast food restaurants like Burger King or Kentucky Fried Chicken, which I loved. It was a fast-moving environment, and I was expected to order fast, which I could not. My English was in its infancy.

Now, I became confident that I had transcended my old self. There was a downside, I missed Saint Louis, the enchanted Haitian country town where I first saw the light of day, where everything dear to my heart was deeply rooted. I missed Régine, the girl who stole my heart and to whom I hoped to return someday.

Despite my feeling of nostalgia, however, I felt a bit luckier than many other refugees I knew. The Little Haiti environment in which I was living was far less unfriendly than other communities. That may have saved my Haitan roots, keeping me from totally becoming Americanized. I could still enjoy a delicious *griyo* at home or at any Haitian restaurant around. I could get my old favorites like rice and beans and chicken, red snapper or strawberry grouper, Creole style, anywhere in town.

On Saturdays, I loved going to Northeast 2nd Avenue around 59th Street to buy mouthwatering pastries while the delightful Haitian konpa music blasted from the shops and restaurants.

At school, I used the playground to fast-track my English acquisition. I befriended many classmates from all ethnic and cultural backgrounds. Some were refugees like me, others were kids who were born in the United States from Haitian parents. There was also a group we used to call Haitian-Bahamians because they were born in the Bahamas. All of them spoke a slurred, northern Haitian Creole, and when they switched to English, I got intimidated and downright confused. Some of the words they used were slang taken from their islands. My classmate and good friend Suzette lived on the same street as me, but was born and raised in the Bahamas. She would come up to me and say in her charming Bahamian way, "Man (mun), me want some *switcha*."

"Some *switcha*?" I would reply, perplexed.

Then she would switch to Creole. "*Mwen vle bwè limonad.*" And she would land a kiss on my lips to tame my anxiety and allay my confusion. "*I want some lemonade,*" was what she meant.

Suzette was a coffee-colored girl, short and curvy, and strangely enough, she always wore blue jeans, a white t-shirt, and flat tennis shoes. Her hair was always brushed back and held together by a blue barrette. "Mudda sick!" (Are you kidding!) she would say to me, bursting out laughing, expressing her excitement during our afternoon strolls at a nearby park whenever she wanted to show off her ladylike capriciousness in islander fashion.

In class, my teachers found my sociable and cognitive styles quite enjoyable. There was never a silent period in my pre-production stage as an English language learner. It has been said that personality style has a lot to do with the building of cross-cultural awareness. My friends called me a social interactionist who blended charms, survival instincts, and exquisite fair play to sway his interlocutors in a linguistic environment he wholeheartedly loved. In two years, I was immersed.

19

At the end of my twelfth grade, I graduated, not with honor, but with impressive academic achievements for which I received the "Most Improved" award. Meanwhile, the growing influx of refugees from Cuba and Haiti coming to Florida almost daily had pushed the immigration debate in Washington to a new level. As the debate dragged on, Democrats and Republicans remained deadlocked, but only agreed on a provisionary immigration act called the "Cuban/Haitian Entrant Act of 1980." Qualified immigrants, including me, were issued a temporary card which established their temporary, legal status and with which they could apply for social services, looking for jobs, and even going to college should they decide to. Immigrants who had decided to go to college were even qualified for the federal Financial Aid program.

#

Three years had passed since the dreaded night at the Port of Miami. Then, I was already a student at Barry University, majoring in computer science. I dreamed of graduation day, when my sister would be cheering in the audience and exploding into uncontrolled joy and laughter as my name is called to walk on stage. A Catholic institution located in Miami Shores, Barry was not far from Little Haiti. In fact, I only had to stand in front of the school, crane my neck, and Little Haiti would be in full view. I had an afterschool gig, working as a dishwasher at a salad restaurant making $3.25 an hour in the upscale suburb of North Miami Beach. The need to get my own room had convinced my sister to move out of our uncle's apartment. We rented an apartment right in the heart of Little Haiti, about a block away from Notre Dame d'Haiti, the most important Haitian Catholic church in town.

Everything seemed to be moving along nicely. I reconnected with old childhood friends whom I had lost long ago after they migrated to Miami to join their parents and relatives. I was not so lucky. My father lived a precarious life in The Bahamas, finding work wherever he could to support the family in Haiti. My mother could not migrate to the United States to join my sister; nor could she go to The Bahamas to be with my father, for she did not want to leave us behind to be raised by relatives. Among the children in Haiti, I was older. Consequently, when the opportunity to migrate was presented, my father insisted that I be the one to do so.

At school, I played a vigorous role in social activism. I became an important figure to both the Haitian Students Association and the International Students Association. On Friday afternoons in the cafeteria where we held kickoff weekend parties, I was the impresario every student, especially the girls, could not do without. In a cacophony of joy and laughter, we blended Soka, Merengue, Bachata, Salsa, Konpa, Zouk, and Brazilian Bosanova to create a dazzling medley of Caribbean and South American music.

Due to my meager salary, I had to learn fiscal responsibility. My sister and I created an effective budget to deal with paying the rent, buying groceries, doing the laundry, saving money for allocations for bus fares, and most importantly, providing financial support to our relatives back home.

Chapter 2

Although the memories of my childhood had remained vivid, I was no longer nostalgic for my teenage years on the island. I now had a lofty goal, and just being an American would not take me there. I wanted to become an educated American who would someday turn out to be a productive citizen, playing a pivotal role in the community, helping the other immigrants as they sought to immerse into the new society. I spent most of my time at the university campus outside of home and work; and it suited me well.

One Friday afternoon in early summer, I walked into the university gym for my regular exercise. As a young man, feeling and looking fit were two things of profound meaning to me. Consequently, I and a couple of classmates had devoted three days of the week to workout in a newly built fitness center that attracted many students. That day, however, it was unusually empty but for a young woman in her workout outfit jogging on a treadmill and listening to music through her headset. I came and stepped on a machine next to her. I greeted her and she acknowledged my presence with a single nod. But I could sense we both welcomed the unspoken company. Her music earpiece soon fell, and I stepped off my machine, grabbed the earpiece from the floor, and handed it to her.

"Thank you," she said with a coquettish lift to her voice.

"You're welcome," I replied with a grin. "What's your name?"

"Judy, Judy McCarter."

"I'm Yrvin Lacroix. But my friends call me Vinco."

She slowed her speed, and I brought mine down almost to a halt. "Are you a senior?" I asked her, trying to keep the conversation going.

"No. I'm a sophomore," she replied in a smile that lit up her oval face.

"I'm just as you, but I've never seen you around campus," I said.

"I've been here—in hiding, buried under books, term papers, and other homework assignments." She laughed, self-conscious.

"I hear you, Judy."

"Sometimes, I miss home, and just getting away from this stressful college life," she said in an expression of sullen self-confidence.

"Where's home?" I asked, hoping she was going to say Haiti.

"Freeport, Grand Bahama," she proudly said with a persistent smile that shone her flawless visage.

"Really, Judy? When I was in high school, I had a few friends who were from that part of the world."

"Is that right? And you, Vinco. Where's home?"

23

"A small town on Haiti's northern coast."

We both now stopped the treadmills, facing each other. We started talking about the school environment, the Catholic institution, and the urge to graduate. I noticed her distinct form of intellectualism, mixing blunt, slurred island speech with refined language like that of a grammarian. Maybe it was because she wanted to impress me. She spoke with a mellow voice that quickly captured my attention, and the sweet look in her eyes was, to me, like a magic wand that weakened my Caribbean machismo and blurred my vision.

Two weeks later, we met again during a birthday party at a mutual friend's home in an upscale suburb of Hollywood, Florida. It was a venue filled with out-of-control, spoiled, rich young folks from school. I was standing in a line near the punchbowl, waiting to be served a piece of the birthday cake when she walked behind me. She was in a knee-length, strapless, sweetheart dress. One hand was on her hip, the other held a clutch purse.

"Vinco, what a *gift* to see you here!" She giggled in a kittenish fashion that set my heart aglow.

I told her about my friendship with the birthday boy, a young man named Richard, the son of a wealthy Jamaican businessman. She chatted about her longtime association with many of the rich young people in attendance. I no longer needed the cake, for she was the cake I wanted most. I had the best of time as we danced our night away. At the end of the party, I walked her out to her car, a flashy red BMW convertible. We exchanged phone numbers and she left, speeding away under the wan light of the early morning.

I had always been a one-girlfriend boy. So, dating multiple girls at once was never part of what I sought in my ever-complicated existence as an immigrant. Most of my peers at school did it. I never knew how, for between school and work, there was hardly any time left for me to play this tricky and disingenuous game. But somehow Judy had caught my eyes in a profound way. She was a girl with a slender outline and velvet skin enhanced by the radiance of her youthful, flamboyant posture. Boys went feverish as she strolled behind the bloomed rosebush, sprawling along the ficus edge near the library on her way to and from classes. Since that night at the Hollywood party, we had become friends, and sometimes we behaved like unadventurous friends, but other times, during our regular chat at dusk sitting on a bench behind the university chapel, we would hug and kiss like lovers do.

Judy was an uptown girl with all the mannerisms commonly found in upper-class children: extraordinary, unconcerned, and well aware of her sculptural beauty. She had an intimidating stare, which served as a repellent that kept many of my friends at bay. With me, however, she was different. Though proud and intelligent, she was loving, sweet, enthusiastic, and accommodating in my presence. My female Haitian friends never liked her, not because she was not a Creole, but because of her high-class demeanor. They said she was too "bougie" and therefore did not fit the profile of a girl I should be dating.

One afternoon after class, she was in a different mood when we met as usual behind the chapel, where she would sit on one of the outside benches, eyeing the path that led to the chapel's backdoor, waiting. As I fought hard to get a smile from her, I asked, "What's wrong, Judy?"

"You made me wait, and you never came yesterday."

"I'm so sorry. I had to leave early, and you were still in class."

There was a brief silence as we sat side by side. Abruptly, she rose from the bench. Her eyes slanted, as if chasing the crepuscular sun ray slowly sinking behind the heavy clouds in the distant sky. "Vinco, I wanna share something with you, something I've never shared with anyone before."

"What is it, my dear?" My heart leaped suddenly, and to suppress this unexpected nervousness, I stood right up, facing her while pulling onto her, my arms wrapped around her waist.

"Every time I think of you, there's always this awed feeling I can never fully describe. But yesterday when you didn't show up, I realized how much you mean to me."

"I myself have been trying hard not to overplay my hands and break through the boundaries that hold a friendship, but I just can't. I must admit, Judy, that I've succumbed to your ravishing and irresistible charm…."

She smiled, finally. "If this is love, I don't think I'll be able to sustain it," she said sharply.

"And why? Is it because of some invisible barriers that stand in the way?"

"What barrier? I hope you don't misunderstand."

"Judy, I'm well aware of our unusual situation. I know our friendship has crossed a threshold, but if you're willing to give me a place in your heart, however small that might be, I can assure you that you won't be disappointed. I promise." I held her both hands, trying to soften her heart.

"Vinco, there can be no barrier standing in our way. I'm just scared you might leave me along the way. I've been deceived before. Most men are like hunters, hunting for sexual pleasures, not love. Honestly, I'm afraid I won't fall into your trap."

"I'm no love trapper or catcher; I'm falling in love naturally. I would agree that some men are dishonest, not most because love can't be trapped—true love that is. In any case, I can only speak for myself. I can proudly say I'm not like *them*. I want you to know what's keeping me awake at night, what sends my heart aglow when I'm with you can in no way be described as mischievousness." She freed her hands from mine, refusing to make eye contact.

"Baby," she said faintly, as if diving into a warm and sweetened spring of love and affection. It was the first time she addressed me this way.

"Yes, my love."

"I have something, a very serious thing I wanna tell you, but not now."

"Why not now?"

"Because it's not the best moment. I'll tell you in due time."

We said nothing more while staying folded into each other's arms until it was time to leave. Then I walked her up to the library's front door, where she had to go meet her older sister, who was also a student at Barry University. For a minute, I stood there contemplating her suave, unconscious elegance, and the rhythmic motion of her strides, a secret which only a young woman from the tropics knows. But Judy's lifestyle intimidated me, preventing me the sentimental comfort that any man seeks from his beloved girl.

At twenty-one, a young man is still at the spring of his life. This thought dawned on me each time Judy came to my mind, especially in my little bedroom at night. We both were young and preoccupied with school. This girl had played a critical role in keeping me focused. We helped each other with homework assignments, although we never shared a class. My main goals were to graduate and to someday become a software engineer. I was committed to making my parents feel honored, proud of the young man I would someday become despite the odds.

My biggest hurdles were the tuition fees. I had a scholarship, but it only covered a portion. My meager salary from the dishwashing job could barely meet my basic needs. But I was determined to make my dream come true. This was a secret I could never reveal to my peers, not even Judy. The excitement that had always boiled into my friends' hearts at the end of each semester was always absent in my life as a refugee struggling to secure a decent life in America. While all my friends bragged about their upcoming vacations in resort islands in the Caribbean or weekends in Europe, I was thinking of finding a part-time job so that I could save enough money to pay for the rest of my tuition.

My nights were long and sleepless. My mind was caught in a slew of thoughts, thinking of problems for which I had no immediate solutions. I took comfort in the fact that I had already secured two years in the program, and I had the upcoming summer to find a second job and save for the following year. I had just purchased a used Volkswagen, which was an important component in my plan. Twice, I had missed the transit bus for work and was late, for which I was reprimanded. Many times, I sacrificed lunch at school to save for tuition and books. To keep me from starving around campus, I started bringing my own lunch, leftovers from the night before, and I would eat in the parking lot, away from the always frenetic ambiance in the cafeteria.

No one but my sister knew of my struggle, our struggle. When she realized how painful it had become for me to get the nutrition that college studies require, she started preparing my lunch to spare me the time and the stress of doing it myself, and missing lunch would certainly mean spending a day without food, for I had to drive to work straight from school. One Monday morning, I left my lunch on the kitchen counter and I did not realize it until I was about to get into class. "Oh well," I muttered to myself. "Another day...."

"Another what?" my friend Pedro asked.

"Another raining day," I lied.

"I think this final exam is driving you *nuts*," he said, mocking me. "This is clear blue sky."

We went in. On the way out after the class, I met Laurette, one of my Haitian friends, below the steps. "Your sister's outside, waiting for you."

"For what?"

"How do I know? She asked me to come get you."

"*Where* is she?"

"Near the back entrance."

I ran almost out of breath, thinking something terrible had happened. By that time of the day, she should have been at work. When I reached the entrance, I saw her, short and thin, standing by the side of the street in a calico dress, looking just like Manman. My lunch was wrapped in a plastic bag. She crossed the quiet street to meet me. "*Nana,*" I cried. "I thought you were at work."

"How can I work when I know you're at school with an empty stomach?"

"Oh, Nana, you didn't have to do this. I was going to be okay." I could see the unmistakable worry on her sweaty face as the early summer heat beat down on her.

"Here, eat," she commanded like Manman used to do when things were rough in Haiti.

I took the bag but wanted to stay with her for a few more minutes because my next class would not have started for another thirty minutes. "Go eat inside. It's too hot here," she insisted. "Besides, I have to catch the bus, and I don't wanna miss it."

To her disapproval, I walked her to the main street and stayed with her until the next metrobus arrived and she got on. I stood there, watching her silhouette as she handed her pass to the driver. I could feel the pain that must have been in her heart when she realized I left my lunch on the kitchen counter, and I could see on her face the joy, the pride she could not conceal when she was able to spare me a day without food.

As I walked through the cafeteria, some of my friends, joyful and playful, waved and I waved back. They invited me to join them at their table. None of them had the tiniest idea of my unrevealed hardships, for I had learned to live with an unfilled stomach. The way I managed to beat back agonizing hunger was by putting heavier concentration on my study, knowing it would all be over someday and only a good education could make it possible. Some of my friends, especially Pedro, could have treated me for lunch that day, but asking for a treat at lunchtime was never part of my character. Judy could cheerfully treat me also or even shower me with money; but asking the girl I love such favor would demean my dignity. Endurance is the best weapon against adversity, Papa used to teach me, and living those precarious moments had convinced me of the fundamental truth that empowered his lessons. I had become more resolute in my pursuit of higher education.

Although Pedro and I rarely discussed money, let alone tuitions, he overheard me on the phone talking to my sister about my worries. Pedro, a fine young man I'd been friends with since my freshman year, was born in Bronx, New York, the son of a Puerto Rican mother and a Venezuelan father. He was fair-skinned, tall, and built with an indigenous feature. He was well-versed in both English and Spanish. He despised the notion of colorism, which he considered a fabrication with no scientific merit fomented by Europeans to divide and conquer weak-minded individuals. Easily noticeable, his peers, including me, admired him for his energetic, assiduous character. Girls around campus dubbed him a bold prince for his striking sense of clothing and his unique, polished behavior around campus. We had an algebra class every Wednesday afternoon, and one day before class started, he pulled me over. "Vinco, I'm gonna try to find a part-time job during the summer."

"I think I should do the same, Ped."

"Why don't you go with me this Friday? I know a Cuban guy who owns a furniture store on 79th Street in the shopping plaza across from the immigration building. He plans on hiring college students for the summer to work in the sales department."

31

"That's interesting," I replied, but I was quite disengaged, knowing how Cuban business folks in the city thought about employing Haitians. Cubans hired their own, as my Haitian collegemates used to say, which would make a lot of sense because Cuban immigrants believed in community empowerment, and having the means to make big acquisitions was the best way to flex that power.

"You don't wanna go, Vinco?" he asked when he realized I was uncommitted.

"I do, but I know he won't hire me."

"What makes you think so?"

"Cubans don't like Haitians enough to let them work in their businesses. They falsely accuse Haitians of being supportive of the Cuban revolution, and because of that the two communities don't get along."

"Listen, I'm not Cuban."

"But, you're Latino."

"You're Haitian and you speak Creole. It would be stupid for this man not to hire people who could relate to most of his customers."

"Okay. But we have to get there before or exactly at three p.m.."

"So, let's meet at the Burger King on the corner of Biscayne Boulevard and 79th."

I came home that day, thinking about the job, and my chance at being hired. What Pedro said made a lot of sense. I spoke Creole, and I would be a good asset for the furniture store. I had concluded that I would concentrate on my Haitianism, my ethnolinguistic advantage to get the job. But the cold strife between the two most vocal ethnic groups in South Florida could still be an unwanted obstacle. Or so I believed.

Chapter 3

A month earlier, tensions had flared between the two communities, reaching the tipping point over the arrest and beating of a Haitian man who went into a Cuban-owned clothing store at the plaza. He was falsely accused of stealing a polo shirt, although he pleaded his innocence. The man, short and stocky, was later shown in the six o'clock evening news. His face was swollen and bruised from the multiple blows he suffered at the hands of a security guard at the store. In a chilling account, the man explained how he was knocked down by the security guard who held his boot on his neck while the store owner alerted the police. Two police officers soon arrived at the scene but were not interested in listening to his plea as dozens of shoppers watched in horror, despite the fact he kept telling the officers he had proof to show his innocence. Instead, he was handcuffed and hauled off to police headquarters downtown. The Haitian Refugee Center and its lawyers were notified and instantly intervened. The man was released three hours after the incident. At a press conference in front of the refugee center, the Haitian man by their sides, the lawyers displayed the receipt before a legion of local journalists.

Rage and indignation swept Little Haiti. The next day, responding to calls for a mass protest, thousands of Haitians poured into the streets shortly after midday. They made their way to the shopping plaza. Emotions ran high, and dark faces filled 79th Street and stretched out for several blocks. When they reached the main entrance of the plaza adjacent to the immigration building, they were met by stone-faced cops determined to keep them away from the shopping plaza, citing that the protesters were disrupting traffic. The officers then had to pull back for fear of being submerged, for there were too many demonstrators.

Like a rushing river after a heavy downpour, the Haitians and their sympathizers broke through the main entrance and invaded the parking lot, which was full of cars and shoppers. Some angry protesters threatened to storm the clothing store. A line of police officers moved in and cordoned off the store entrance to protect the frightened employees trapped inside. Then the Haitians raised the stick. Community radios in coordination with the protesters launched a total boycott of Cuban businesses across Little Haiti.

For weeks, Haitian shoppers stayed away, and businesses dwindled, including the furniture store that was now hiring. Four weeks after the incident, boycotting Cuban businesses remained one of the hottest topics in Little Haiti. Although the anger that fueled the boycott and its early success in the campaign began to show signs of waning. This was not because of physical fatigue, but because of the community's political and socioeconomic realities in Miami. Haitians had no fair representation in the city's power structure. Their struggle for social justice through immersion and assimilation was seen as a threat to the entrenched establishment of well-connected, wealthy white men whose racism was an open secret.

They studied the Haitians' weaknesses- a community that lacked the solid economic foundation to sustain a prolonged boycotting campaign. Prudently they waited; and through a series of financial hoodwinking, mea culpa on Haitian radios, bribing radio commentators to change the narrative. These were followed by several rounds of "seventy-five percent off" and "buy one, get two free". They had succeeded in weathering the Haitian storm. These deals were too sweet to resist. Haitian businesses, small and operating on the fringe, could ill-afford to compete against conglomerate, powerful retail chains owned by Cuban American corporations.

Wednesday morning, I woke up with an awful migraine I had only slept for three hours. I spent the rest of the night thinking about the job interview and its implications if I were to be hired. I was afraid some of my friends would see my action as unforgivable disloyalty. I tried to get up, but an early morning rain shower over the rooftop pinned me down.

I was about to drift into sleep when my sister opened my bedroom door. "Vinco, get up, get *up!* Don't you see what time it is?"

I took a quick glance at the clock, and it was ten minutes to seven. "Nana, I had a rough night," I said, still struggling to get out of bed.

"How come?" She came and sat next to me.

"My friend Pedro told me about a part-time job. He told me they're hiring college students for the summer. He's been encouraging me to apply, but I'm having second thoughts."

"What do you mean by 'having second thoughts?'"

"Because it's in Las Calinas, a Cuban furniture store in the 79th Street Plaza, not far from where the incident at the clothing store took place."

"I see. So, you don't wanna go?"

"I do, but I'm not sure if I'll be comfortable working with Cubans."

"Vinco, you should go, and you'll need to put on your best face when you get there. If they give you a job, I'll be happy not just for you, but for me and for the rest of the family."

"Really, Nana?"

"The tuition keeps me awake at night. Believe me, Vinco. So, finding a part-time job this summer will be a blessing. You and I will only have to worry about the books and other materials, and I'll pay for them. I already started saving for that."

"Nana, every time I think about the way they smashed the man's face—"

She put a hand up to silence me. "I'm shocked, Vinco, to see that you have yet to learn how to be a *man*. I thought you already did—with surprising courage. The days you spent on the high seas in that sailboat alone with strangers were proof to show you can survive without Manman and Papa. You were only seventeen. If they give you a job in Las Calinas, it won't destroy your dignity. You'd be working at a store they say belongs to Cubans, but it'll be a give-and-take. You won't work for anyone for free, not for Cubans, not for Haitians or any other…."

She hardened her face and stared coldly with tearful, anguished eyes. The anguish for being unable to shelter her brother from the difficult and exploited life of immigration. The aching for being reminded once more of her boundaries in an unfair world. One that did not permit her to take her beloved brother's hands and lead him unharmed along the rocky road to success. I pushed my pillow aside and sat up, next to her, my body tilting toward her. She wrapped her hands around my neck. "Will your friends pay for the courses for you?"

"What kind of question is that?"

"I bet many of those people who were expressing their anger would take this job in a heartbeat if given the opportunity. That's the irony of life. It's not because they don't have any shame. It's because they *must* live. Having a paycheck, even out of the worst, most humiliating conditions, is far more important than not being able to pay your bills. Besides, this would be a summer job. By September, you'll be back at school and no one will remember your time at the furniture store. Self-pride won't save our community. Remember that, young man."

She abruptly got up and pulled me along. "Nana, I'm still sleepy."

"Now, go take your shower. I'll fix the bed."

While I was in the shower, she walked in. "Vinco, I'm leaving. Your egg is on the stove. Hurry and eat before it gets cold. I already put your lunch in the car."

"Love you, Nana."

"Love you, too, and be yourself at the interview." She shut the door behind her and left.

Later, I arrived at the plaza fifteen minutes before three p.m. I did not see Pedro, and I figured he must have been looking for a parking spot just like me. On any normal day, finding a spot in that vast parking area was no easy task. After weeks of total paralysis, businesses had resumed to full capacity, creating a traffic mess. The shoppers were back despite the sweltering heat.

Although its official name was *Seventy-Ninth Street Plaza*, it was an imposing strip mall. Shops and boutiques stood side by side in a long line that curved around a huge parking lot. From mom-and-pop stores, to nail salons, to supermarkets, to restaurants, you found all you would need, even immigrations lawyers' offices competing against each other for new and old clients - refugees applying for their green cards in order to live legally and peacefully in this little corner of their own they called Little Haiti. Luckily, as I navigated around, I found a spot a few feet away from Las Calinas, next to a taxi stand.

A rash of eagerness took hold of my mind. I did not want to be late. Pedro told me to be there at three. I walked out of my car, passing a group of cab drivers, all Haitians discussing politics back home. I paid no attention to them as I remembered what my sister told me that morning. Soon, I came across two men in rags begging in front of *La Belle Creole*, a Haitian restaurant near the furniture store well-known for its Caribbean delicacies. I pulled out my wallet and gave each a one-dollar bill. "God blesses you, son," they both said at once. I welcomed their wishes, which felt like a spiritual gift I needed to boost my chance. Manman always said feeding the poor brought you rewards in times of uncertainty.

At last, I stepped into Las Calinas. Folder in hand, I checked my pressed blue shirt to make sure it was well tucked inside my neat, starched khaki trousers that my sister and carefully ironed the night before. A bull-necked, heavily built Hispanic man in a black security uniform greeted me. "Wait for Maria. She's with a customer," he grunted, handing me a catalog filled with low sale prices. Some of the prices were written in big letters on two giant glass windows to lure potential customers.

"I'm here to see the manager," I said in a calm but firm voice.

"Maria *is* also the manager," the security guard said in a much stronger, affirmative way.

I looked around, hoping to see Pedro coming. He was nowhere in sight. "I'm interested in the sales representative position, and I'm here to apply for it," I said.

"Wait here." He then went and talked in Spanish to Maria, a petite Hispanic woman in a tailored dress and with straight dark hair sitting behind a desk in a small room, speaking to a gentleman in a dark suit. The security guard came back and asked me to sit on a brown leather sofa. "You'll need to speak to Lopez. He's coming." He retreated to his post.

My heart raced, my nervousness mounting, but I fought back to put forth an easy posture, like a comfortable young professional. Twenty minutes later, a stout, middle-aged man walked in from the back door, wearing a wrinkled brown blazer over a tight, collared, button-down shirt. Bald headed, his face was round, swelled, and oily. Clipboard in hand, his belly sprawled and swayed at each step as he moved in my direction. "Good afternoon, sir," he greeted me.

"Good afternoon," I replied, standing up to speak to him.

"Are you Yrvin Lacroix?" he asked, which left me puzzled.

"Yes, I am, and I'm here to apply for the sales representative position," I replied with a subdued grin.

We shook hands. "I'm Lopez, and I'm sure you're wondering how I know about your interest in the summer position."

40

"Yes, sir."

"This morning, I received a phone call about you," he confirmed in a sonorous voice.

"Really?" The racing inside my chest lessened.

"Follow me."

I trailed him to a back office where he handed me a form. "Fill it as much as you can. Don't worry about what you don't know," he said while instructing me to sit in a chair in the corner. Meanwhile, he got on the phone with a banker, speaking with grandiloquent expressions while stroking his thick, untidy mustache that had upturned ends. So, I thought he was well aware of his unconventional posture and was doing his best to untwine his personal adornment with his business savvy. After all, behind the telephone, physical appearance is meaningless.

Ten minutes later, I raised my hand to signal him that I was done. He then said goodbye into the phone and turned to speak to me. As requested, I handed him the application. He took a quick glance and put it aside as if filling out the form was more of a formality in the hiring process rather than being a deciding factor in his decision. "Mr. Lacroix," he said. His voice growled a bit, but he quickly cleared his throat. "What makes you interested in this job?" he asked, looking straight at me with unblinking eyes.

"Because I'm a people person and I'm always eager to learn new tasks."

"Do you speak Spanish?"

"No, sir."

"What other language or languages do you speak besides English?"

"Creole and French." He grabbed the application and flipped it, giving it an up-close look like when searching for the golden catch.

"I see you were born in Haiti."

"That's correct, sir."

"That's interesting. We're in urgent need of a Creole speaker for our sales department, and I've already interviewed several other candidates. So, what makes you think you're the one I must choose?"

"Mr. Lopez, I think any of them would do a good job because Haitians love to shop where there're people they can identify with. In addition, I don't know who the other candidates are; nor do I know their skills in human interactions. But I know I can get the job done to your greatest satisfaction."

He smiled briefly, stroking his messy mustache once more.

"Are you saying you don't think you're the best candidate, Mr. Lacroix?"

"I'm not saying that, Mr. Lopez. I'm simply saying I don't know them. If I may add this: Language alone should not be the determining factor in hiring. I'm not a businessperson. But if I were one, I would consider other factors."

"Like what?"

"Cross-cultural awareness, the ability to connect with potential customers, educational backgrounds to name a few."

His oily face now brightened; he was visibly impressed. At that point he stopped asking questions and went on to explain the nature of the job, the salary, the work schedule, and a bunch of other things related to the job. In the end, he walked me over to meet Maria at the other office. There, we talked a little bit about Haiti's history and its culture. I thought this whole interest in learning about Haiti was a way to raise the profile of Las Calinas as a place where Haitian culture is highly valued.

Before leaving, Lopez promised to call me but did not offer me a job. I then walked to my car and drove back to school. I wanted to know what had happened to Pedro. I met him near the bookstore, sitting on a bench studying. He immediately rose to his feet and threw a silly smile when he saw me coming. "Where the *hell* were you, man?" I asked, clearly disappointed.

"I've been right here on this bench waiting for another hour to call you at home."

"But we were supposed to meet at the furniture store."

"I've decided not to go anymore, fearing I could ruin your chance."

"How?"

"Don't be naive, Vinco. Cuban people hire their own, at least someone they can relate to. You were right when you made the reference earlier. So, how was the interview?"

"I think it went well. The man who interviewed me said he'll call me. We'll see."

"I hope he keeps his words. What's the man's name?"

"Lopez."

"I know him. His full name is Santiago Lopez. He's my parents' neighbor. I told my mom about your interest there, and she's talked to him. I didn't want to tell you. By the way, Judy was asking for you. She told me she can't wait for the end-of-the-year party Friday night."

"Is she still on campus?"

"I don't know, but I think she went home. Last time I saw her, she was making her way behind the cafeteria."

Pedro and I chatted a little bit. Then I walked him to the parking lot where he got in his car and drove home.

After Pedro left, I ran to the back entrance, hoping to see Judy. As soon as I strode into the cafeteria on the way to the backdoor, I saw her with her Bahamian collegemates, and she immediately drifted away when our eyes met. We rushed toward each other, grabbing hands, and threaded to the side of the room as her friends sniggered at her.

"I looked for you all afternoon," she said, eyes turned feverish, starving for an answer.

"Sorry, I had to leave early for a job interview." I pulled her up close and delivered two slurpy smooches that sweetened her heart.

"Vinco, you have such a shrewd way of disarming a girl in the trench of her resistance," she smirked.

"My princess."

"Yes, darling."

"Can't wait for the Friday night party."

"I want it more."

Her sister Ella then walked in, and she called to her. Our hands parted, and she left. "Call you tonight," she tittered. I threw kisses without replying.

Later when I came home, I saw the message notification on the telephone flashing ceaselessly. I thought it was Judy. I hurried and listened, but it was the voice of Mr. Lopez. "Mr. Lacroix, I'm pleased to let you know that you have been hired. Welcome to Las Calinas! I have your schedule here. You'll start on Monday. You'll be working from nine a.m. to one p.m. Try to get here at eight-thirty to get all paperwork done." I was delirious. My sister was away, so I called Pedro and delivered the good news. Oh, he was happy.

"I had no doubt you were gonna get the job, *man*," he kept on saying. We chatted for about a half hour, and I went to my room to read my favorite novel, when Judy called.

"Baby, for the first time going home for the summer doesn't make me feel good. I'm not homesick. I'm lovesick."

"Me, too. I'm sad already. But we can take comfort in the fact that we have Friday night to enjoy ourselves."

"I wanna dance now."

"You can do it over the telephone. Just describe the moves to me."

"You're *so* funny. I'm good at showing, not at describing."

"What do Bahamians dance? Calypso?"

"We dance a little bit of everything, including Reggae and Soca."

"How about Haitian konpa?"

"For that, I'll have to wait for Friday night. You'll teach me."
She laughed.

"Konpa is as groovy as Soca. You wind up the body—waist
and hips—but a bit slower. It gives you a romantic feel."

"*Wow!*" she groaned.

My sister then walked in. "Baby, I have to go. My sister's
here. Tomorrow."

We said goodbye, and I turned my attention to Nana, eager
to give her the good news.

"How did it go?" she asked anxiously.

"I got the job!"

"Hallelujah!"

I filled her in the whole process and she listened with a jolly
face. She was in a festive mood. She ran to the kitchen to make
rice pudding. When the pudding was finished, we sat at the table
to eat. "Vinco, let's pray."

"Yes, sister."

We closed our eyes and rested our hands on the table, and
she began to pray. "Heavenly Father, we thank You for
everything You've done for us, even when we least expect it.
You've opened doors for us when we thought it was impossible
to do. Thank You, Lord, for providing Vinco the health and the
intelligence he needs to continue his education. Oh God, protect
him against all pitfalls and evil spells that would prevent him
from graduating. We know we're not worthy of Your special
attention, but we also know You're our sole protector in a world
that can sometimes be very unfair. For that, we want to remain

faithful to You in the name of the Father, the Son, and the Holy Spirit, amen."

When she opened her eyes, she realized my eyes were half open. "You need to *concentrate* when praying."

"I did," I picked up my spoon and started eating. She grabbed her spoon, too.

"I bet you were more focused on the food."

"Why do you need to close your eyes when you pray?"

"Because it shows God that you're really serious in your relationship to Him. Remember, you're seeking spiritual guidance as well."

"Nana, I think God doesn't need me to close my eyes to know if I'm making a fool out of myself. He's God, omnipresent, the Creator of our universe."

"I'm not gonna argue with you. Next time, you close your eyes." She dragged her spoon down her big bowl and pulled out a spoonful of that delicious pudding.

"You're gonna choke yourself." I teased her. Mouth full, she nearly suffocated herself.

"You see what you make me do? Stop playing. Eat."

We ate and joked until bedtime.

Chapter 4

Mid-June, the schoolyard was swamped with students in a jolly mood. The last exams were behind us, and the summer vacations were on everyone's mind. Soon, the school would be empty as students flew home. In every one of my classrooms, classmates were in a festive mood, exchanging well-wishes during multicultural activities, showcasing their distinct traits with infinite pride. It was Friday, the last day before we went our separate ways. As usual, in the cafeteria, preparations for the end-of-the-year party were a joy to watch. It was the last gathering—the party a student could not go without. Balloons of all colors floated in the room.

On that classic summer day, Miami was hot and steamy, and at school, the festivities had already begun. A feeling of nostalgia crept in my heart. I only had one more day with Judy before she flew home to Freeport. This had provided a moment of awakening, forcing me to take a closer look at our relationship. For the first time, I was able to measure the depth of my love for this girl from the tropics whose love and affection I could no longer live without. I needed her love while I wrestled to suppress my anxiety over the new job on Monday. I did not see

Judy all day. I called her at home, but she did not answer. To keep my mind afloat and save my sanity, I joined classmates in impromptu discussions about girls and their desires to be pampered.

By midafternoon, I had decided to go home to be ready for the party. On the way, I met Pedro near the library, heading toward his car. "I'm going home, *man*, to rest and get prepared."

"Me, too. So see you in about four hours." We got into our separate vehicles and drove off.

It was seven-thirty when I pulled into the parking lot. The sun was long gone, and it was dark and hazy. Rich boys in fancy cars with tinted windows played low-tone music amid feminine laughter. As I walked by, some of the half-open windows were quickly pulled up to shield their girls and block my view of their shenanigans. I quickened my steps to stay away from the haze.

In a few long strides, I reached the cafeteria's back door and walked into a festive sight. I had never seen the room so flooded with partygoers. Even before the DJ got set up and the music began, the room was already filled. Early birds sat at tables scattered around. A few sneaky lads took their seats on backless high stools near the counter-now-improvised-bar, behind which a square-faced, enthusiastic woman served soft drinks and secretly sold reefer to those who had fallen in love with Mary Jane. In the middle of the dancefloor, impatient girls in tight blue jeans waited for their dates, eyeing the double doors. In the midst of the crowded room, wide-eyed players with no girlfriends wandered aimlessly, hoping for a catch. I sauntered in, looking for Pedro. He was nowhere in sight. Amid yells and laughter, I moved around, ambling past groups of young women with flushed, radiant faces that sprouted before my eyes like frivolous buds.

"*Goddammit,*" I said to myself. "Where the *hell* is Pedro?" I turned around, and there came the Haitian bunch, hawks and doves alike, moving in my direction. Trailing them but moving astray from the group was Arianne, a mixed-race girl, aristocratic in all of her mannerisms. But I almost fainted when I saw a freckle-faced, blond boy with a Dixie flag draped around his shoulders, holding her by the waist while leading her like two wildfowls going to bushland. I turned my face away and blended in a haze of Brazilian classmates.

"Vinco," a boy named Thiago called to me. "Two girls were busy looking for you," he told me.

"Were they Haitians?" I asked.

"*Not* sure," he said, jerking his head pensively. I was about to leave, but he stopped me. "Wait, Vinco. One of them was that Bahamian girl, Judy McArthur, who wanted to make out with you behind the chapel," he said, teasing me.

"No *way*. You know she and I...."

"There she is," Thiago preempted me, pointing out to the main door that opened to the bookstore.

I turned around and saw Pedro entering the room flanked by two girls. I jogged along to meet them. One of them was a very drunk Chinese girl I had never seen before. She was having trouble opening her eyes, her head leaning on Pedro. The other was Judy in a flashy dress and bathed in a crowd-pleaser perfume. She was quite stylish. Flexing her arms, she pulled me to the side and whispered to my ear in a slurred Bahamian tone, "Tonight, *mun*, I'm yours." Suddenly, a slim, whey-faced boy showed up and grabbed her by the arm just as the DJ struck the room with *Sugar Boom, Sugar Boom, Sugar Boom Boom, I love you so. You dance all right*…. a sweet Caribbean ballad. Judy twisted her head and squinted her eyes. "I'll be back," she muttered. She and the boy then weaved out of sight.

"Ped."

"Huh."

"Who's this flunky with her, now?" I was disturbed.

"Vinco, that's her old boyfriend. He goes to UM—the University of Miami."

"Really? She never told me."

"And don't you know why?"

"I know where you're headed, Ped. Don't even go there."

"But you heard what she just told you."

"You eavesdropped on us. I can't believe you heard that, too."

"What do you mean? She was going stir-crazy looking for you when I met her by the parking lot. She told me tonight she wants to be with you. She wants you all the way. That girl is losing her mind."

"How the fuck she wanna be with me when that whitish boy is hooked on her?"

"Don't worry. You know Judy. She'll do anything for you."

The Chinese girl finally lifted up her head and widened her sleepy eyes, indigo and glary, and in a quick reflection of acknowledgment, waved to me feebly as she propelled Pedro to the dancefloor. Before they disappeared in the middle of wild young folks, Pedro halted his move and turned to me as the girl tried to pull him toward her. *"No te preocupas. La chica tiene que regresar,"* he said in Spanish. (Don't worry. The girl has to come back.)

There, I waited with mounting impatience and restless eyes. I was stunned. Never once did she mention a boyfriend, old or new, who was a student at UM. I felt wrecked. The music ceased, and Pedro and the Chinese girl came back to standing next to me. Then, stepping a foot away from the girl, he pulled me over. "Vinco, do me a favor," he said between clenched teeth.

I lowered my voice. "What is it, Ped?"

"Let's meet here again at three a.m. If you don't see me back by then, I have to be rescued."

"From where?"

"I'll be in dorm six, upstairs, room eighteen."

"You got it. But listen, I no longer have the appetite to stay here."

"Why? Because of Judy being with the boy? Honestly, I thought you knew."

"No, Ped."

"Vinco, don't do this to me. Stop being the pontificator. When she returns, play along with her. You have to score tonight. You *hear* me?"

Then he and the girl vanished. Now, alone by the door, a feeling of sadness trickled into my mind. The images of Judy cozying up with a boy I never knew paralyzed me. Baffled and feeling betrayed, I wanted to go home. I glanced across the room, and on the deep end, I spotted some of my Haitian buddies congregated at a table, drinking beer while waiting for the DJ to roll their sweet konpa. I did not see Arianne, and I thought she must have been with the redneck boy. It hurt me to watch a Haitian girl being dragged by someone whose symbol of hate was unmistakable. I was about to walk toward them when a girl's finger poked my cheek, and she threw me a silly grin.

"Judy!" I exclaimed. "You left me stranded."

"Vinco, I *told* you I was gonna be back," she said coyly. Her charm knocked me down, at least for the moment.

"And who was that *boy* whose arm you clung to and disappeared with?" My mood changed completely.

"Baby, it's a long story. I'll tell you in a minute."

Face hardened, I didn't reply.

"Vinco, please. I'm gonna tell you, but not here in this room." Her eyes moistened.

"Vinco is the lucky *star*. You look *so* beautiful tonight, Judy," said one of the boys pushing his way through to go meet his girlfriend waiting on the dancefloor. We both smiled.

"This beauty is now folded in your arms—all for you, Vinco." She pulled on me, and I raised her stunning oval face, stroking her golden hair. She looked at me, scrutinizing the man on which she was now melted. "I've never seen you look so handsome. Look at your jacket. It matches well with your nut-brown skin, and you look like a Hollywood star inside these blue jeans," she meowed, like an exotic kitten yearning to be petted. Still wrecked inside, I did not reply. The vibe of a few minutes earlier had all but disappeared. She was in my arms, pulling on me, soft and melted. Then, I could hear Pedro's voice saying to me, "You have to score tonight. You *hear* me?"

The music resumed, this time in the slow, romantic beat of sweet konpa love. Our arms about each other's waist, we threaded to the center. A flicker of light soon ran across her face, and her tropical, polished, sherry-finished tan beamed. She threw a smile, and between her sexy lips and shiny teeth, her pleasant tongue stuck out, and I leaned in, pressing my mouth to hers. She folded her arms around my shoulders, and we began to follow the steps. I was astonished to see how skillfully she moved along in her sexually charged, heartrending manner.

"Vinco, I wanted to have this dance with you *so* much," she muttered in my ear.

Still unsure how to play this game of love and betrayal, I avoided a direct reply. Instead, I pulled her tighter against my chest, lurching for a kiss, which she delivered easily. "And where's that guy now?" I asked, throwing a tortured grin.

"I had to put him out of commission," she said, then burst out in uproarious laughter.

"How, Judy?"

"Two quick booms and a couple of puffs of Mary Jane with whom he is madly in love—"

"I need no further explanation, my Caribbean queen." That appeared to sweeten her heart.

"I'm wet, already," she confessed.

"You *are?*" I asked. Without replying, she dragged my hand under her dress and crept it up to her panties where my fingers ran across a wet, slimy liquid like the same clear goop found in okra pods. *My gosh! She's hot,* I said to myself.

"Vinco, I want you *now,* in my room," she commanded.

"Baby, let's wait for the dance…" I said, trying to stall her.

"To be over? For *what?*"

Next thing I knew, she was in the lead, hauling me along as young men and women with giddy eyes looked on. We headed for the exit, shoving our way until we reached the back door. We pushed it open, and a gust of foggy wind slapped us in the face. It was drizzling. She clung to me and I shielded her with my jacket. We hastened our steps to get to her place.

She lived with her sister in a fancy home bought by her parents just outside the school, on the next street in beautiful Miami Shores. We got there in less than three minutes. From the front porch, we could still hear the sweet konpa, rather weakly. One lone squeak in the keyhole opened the door and we strolled into an imposing living room lavishly decorated with contemporary artwork and glamorous pictures in golden frames.

"Where's your sister?" I asked.

"She and her boyfriend flew down to Treasure Key for the weekend," she replied, leading me to the kitchen where she took out two glasses from one of the cabinets. She then paced to a fridge and took out a bottle of red wine. She instructed me to follow her to a grand hallway that led to multiple bedrooms. Hers was the third one near a cabana bathroom. We went in. She poured some wine in both of our glasses. I took a couple of sips, but she emptied hers with one gulp. She then placed the bottle on top of her dresser. I took off my jacket and lay it on the side of the bed, but she quickly removed it and hooked it on a stand on the corner.

"We want this bed all for us. Can't share it with any clothes," she said with a voracious smile. My heart pounded. I could not erase in my mind the picture of her and the young man, hand in hand, disappearing amid the crowd on the dancefloor. But I fought it off for the moment. I had to perform.

She took off her flashy dress and her bra, leaving only her moist panties over which she put on a clear pink nightgown. Her voluptuous, feline features and firm, tangerine breasts set my heart on fire. She took out the bun that held her hair and let it fall over her shoulders and about her face. The air conditioner in the home was set at sixty, and my naked body shivered in the dim room. She wanted to turn the heat on, but I objected, saying the heat of our bodies would soon fill the void. We then went under a king-size matelassé coverlet comforter that rolled up to our chests. Her head tilted toward me, almost leaning on my chest.

"Vinco, I've never felt this way for any man before."

I held her tighter, trying to calm her down through kisses. "Vinco, I know you weren't pleased earlier when you saw me with someone you'd never seen," she said feebly.

"I'm not gonna lie to you. When I saw you earlier with the gentleman, my heart was in shreds."

"Oh, baby. I'm so sorry."

I was going to tell it all. Then, I remembered Pedro's words. "Don't be sorry, *chouchou*. It's not the time."

"*Chouchou*? What does that mean?"

"It's a cutie way to call someone you love in Creole."

"Ah!" she laughed. "My chouchou," I want you to know that I love you naturally, but my relationship with Mark is purely circumstantial," she admitted.

56

"That's his name—Mark?"

"Yes. He's the son of one of the richest folks on the island of Abaco. His father, like my dad, is a real estate tycoon. There's no chemistry between us, and I think we're both suffering. In my country, rich folks manipulate and sometimes coerce their children to marry individuals of the same class of origin to preserve what they call 'the world of between themselves.'"

"I see."

"Vinco, I hope you don't think I'm a bimbo."

"I would have never dated a bimbo. I love you, Judy, and that's why I'm hurt. This would not have been such a shock had you told me in advance. You're smart, you're articulate, you're charming."

"You, too, my prince."

I now felt tenderized. "Here, we are, alone and naked under this comfy sheet. Let's celebrate, chouchou."

Without saying anything more, we went for several salvos of French kisses, licking each other's body through waves of lacerating moans, which catapulted into multiple rounds of lovemaking. When it was over, we showered together, giggling and tickling each other like children do in the schoolyard. After the shower, I put on my clothes, ready to leave. She had on her nightgown. As we stood by the bed, she begged me to stay for the rest of the night. "Vinco, you don't know how it feels to breathe in the smell of your sweat. Stay with me, my love."

"Chouchou, I'd love to, but you know I have to go home. I can't call my parents now without exploding their hearts."

"Please, baby."

"Chouchou, you're asking me to do something that's impossible."

"Vinco, I hope you know I'm suffering."

I sat down again, and she widened her legs and wrapped them around my waist as if she was trying to pin me down. I started caressing her hair. She held me and did not want to let go. Tears sprung out of her eyes, and through showers of hugs and kisses, she fell asleep. I discreetly walked out and locked the door behind me. By then, it was three in the morning. I had to rescue Pedro. I stepped down from her porch. It was peaceful outside. From some distance away, a stray dog snarled and broke the silent night. My heart thundered furiously. With hurried steps, I crossed the street and went back to the party in the cafeteria. The room was near empty when I walked in, except for a few recalcitrant night cruisers still enjoying themselves on the dancefloor even as the DJ was losing his balance, dozing off behind the music stand.

"Vinco," Pedro called to me, sitting at a table by the entrance door.

"Here you are, man! How did it go?" I asked.

"Man, we never made it to room eighteen."

"*What?*"

"Yep. Her roommate was there with her boyfriend. So, we ended up going for a ride to nowhere and came back to a cozy spot in the parking lot for the shenanigan."

"Wow!"

"I'm sure you had the best night."

"You bet."

"Listen, Vinco. You'd better get out of here quick."

"Why?"

"Laurette and her friends spotted you going in with Judy. They were very upset."

"Let's get out, Ped."

We walked out, surveying the parking lot. It was still. We ran to our separate cars and left. Later that night, in my room, I could not stop thinking about Judy. My experience with her had reinforced my conviction that money is not everything in life. Her behavior and suffering were no different from many of my rich Haitian folks at school. They were being forced to marry someone of their privileged clan, regardless of how they felt, to preserve wealth and influence. As Judy told me earlier in the night, her parents were wealthy Bahamians, and so were the parents of the young man chosen for her to date. Still, I was not ready to forgive her after hiding this shocking truth from me. As a disclaimer, she should have laid out everything on the table ahead of this wild ride. I felt totally bruised.

Chapter 5

Eight a.m., Monday morning, I showed up at Las Calinas. Shirt well tucked inside dark trousers, and folder in hand, I was ready for work. The minute I arrived, I met Mr. Lopez in the front office right where I met the security guard when I came to apply for the job.

"Good morning, Mr. Lacroix," he said with a big smile and a strong handshake, inviting me to his office located in the back.

"Good morning to you, sir." I smiled back, standing relaxed, but it was just a facade, for deep within me, stress and nervousness reigned supreme.

I knew the expectations were high. I felt like I was walking on an icy roadway. I had to deliver. To emphasize the urgency of the moment, we did not sit in his office. He simply wanted to go over the order of the day, the people I would be meeting, paperwork that had to be completed, and the population to which the store mostly served. Mr. Lopez then led me to the store showroom, it was vast and filled with all kinds of furniture sets, from living room, to dining room, to bedroom, to patio. Modernist crystal living room sets, including shiny stiff plush leather sofas—*Considerable Massive*, a brand I knew many Haitian immigrants loved, foretold the story of those who could afford them.

The Considerable Massive topped the list when Haitians felt the urge to decorate their homes. I would visit my friends, and the gigantic set wrapped in clear plastic covers, a shield against wear and tear, would fill the tiny living room, leaving me little space to walk around.

"Mr. Lacroix, you'll be working here along with Pito Fuentes, our other salesman. You'll be shadowing him today, and I'm positive you'll learn the business pretty quickly."

I did not reply. Instead, I smiled and nodded in agreement. A lady soon walked in, and Mr. Lopez briefly left me to go speak to her. Alone in the showroom, my nervousness seemed watered down, easing up a bit. Through the glass window, my eyes caught early shoppers perambulating the sidewalk, the troubadour musicians, a couple of Trouvères, and the old jongleurs dressed in Medieval, buffoonish outfits setting up and getting ready for another day in the streets' entertaining business. Trails of cars trickled in and began to fill up the plaza's parking lot. Mr. Lopez soon returned and instructed me to follow him to a modest office across the room where a short-haired woman sat behind a mahogany desk.

"Melissa, I'm pleased to present to you Mr. Yrvin Lacroix, our new employee."

"It's a pleasure to have you here, Mr. Lacroix," said the woman, adjusting herself behind the desk and smiling forcefully in an abrasive, self-confident manner.

"Get his paperwork done," Mr. Lopez directed her.

"Sure," the woman replied and then asked me to take my seat on a couch adjacent to her.

"Mr. Lacroix, come join me in the front when you're done."

"Yes, sir."

Mr. Lopez left and shut the door. It became all quiet in the room, albeit the wince-inducing, popping sound of Melissa's fingers flipping through papers, busying herself in gathering and organizing them in an orderly fashion while making sure she had the right forms she needed me to fill out and sign. Then, with a brusque gesture, she called to me. "Mr. Lacroix, here fill out the form and sign wherever there's an 'x.'"

Her non-cordial attitude did not please me. But it did not bother me, for she was not the person who hired me. She rose from her desk, walked toward me, and handed me a manilla folder within which were a dozen forms I had to fill out. "Thank you," I said, anxiously beginning to complete the forms so that I could go back to Mr. Lopez. Melissa returned to her desk and buried her face behind piles of papers. Halfway through the forms, she craned her neck.

"I need both your employment authorization and your social security cards," she said in an authoritative manner, staring at me like an immigration agent screening foreign migrants.

"Sure." I pulled out my wallet, retrieving the cards and handing them to her.

"You're Haitian, are you?"

"Yes, I am. And you?"

"I'm Cuban. Cuban American. Mr. Lacroix, you can go ahead and sign the remaining forms. I'll get them filled out for you."

I did not react to her offer. Nor did I give her any more chance to throw another interrogative sentence at me. I had always felt uncomfortable signing papers without reading them. So, an uneasiness seized up my mind but on the first day on the job, I wanted to start on the right foot, establishing myself as a friendly and approachable individual. Besides, Mr. Lopez was waiting. I quickened my fingers over the signature lines, signed, and handed the forms back to her. She gave me back my cards and I made my way to the front. I found Mr. Lopez by the main entrance talking to a wiry fellow, beardless and boyish-faced, who dressed like an unconventional businessman—sleeves rolled up to his elbows, tie loosened around his button-down shirt, and hands folded inside black jeans.

"Mr. Lacroix, I'm delighted to introduce to you Pito Fuentes, your coworker. I reached out to him, and we shook hands like bold and energic professionals do.

"A pleasure to have you at Las Calinas, Mr. Lacroix," Pito said with a fictitious smile.

"The pleasure is also mine."

"Gentlemen, I have to get to my office. Call me if you need anything." Lopez then retreated to his office.

Before the shoppers started to arrive, Pito Fuentes used the quiet moment to give a brief introduction about the business culture. "Mr. Lacroix, it's quiet now, but this could be the calm before the storm."

"Really?" My fear heightened, and he noticed my brows furrow.

"Relax. Don't worry. I remember my first day here. I had no one to guide me. Two salespersons had resigned a few days before."

"Is that right?"

"Mr. Lacroix, the first day in any job is never easy. I'll share with you some strategies I've developed over the years to transform potential buyers into real ones."

I laughed to ease my nervousness, my churning stomach. "How long have you been here?"

"This is my fifth year," He jerked his head, trying to be funny. "Let me show you where our VIP quarter is located."

"Mr. Fuentes, are we expecting a lot of people today?" I asked curiously.

"Not sure. But this business is very unpredictable," he replied with a laugh while leading me to my yet undiscovered office.

"Being busy is something I look forward to because it keeps my mind preoccupied as time flies."

"Then, you have a strong partner in me. By the way, Mr. Lacroix, can we call each other by our first name?"

"Sure, why not." I could not agree more. That 'Mr. Lacroix' was too formal for me, and it started to weigh me down. I had never been addressed this way so many times by a group of professionals, and Pito Fuentes sensed the uneasiness.

"Call me Pito, as everyone here does."

"And you call me Yrvin."

We then went into a small room. Two tiny wooden desks almost filled the space. One of them stood empty on top of which placed two paperless, iron trays. I instantly figured out it was mine.

"Yrvin, this is where you'll store sales-related files and other documents, including payroll checks," Pito said with a smile as he pointed to a mail divider built onto the wall.

"When you say, 'other documents,' like what? If I may ask."

"Client folders, purchasing forms, and more. You have to keep record of all your sales before transferring them to Melissa who will then classify them. The number of sales is a leading indicator in evaluating progress or lack thereof."

"I see."

"Don't you worry. We're a team. Your success or failure is mine as well."

"And I would assume your coaching, on which I'll heavily depend, will be essential to bringing about that desirable productivity level." My eyes, unblinking, fixated on him.

"I like that, Yrvin." He seemed impressed hearing my formal articulation.

"Like what, Pito?"

"You sound like a successful salesman already with that formal speech."

I grinned.

"Let's go back to the showroom, Yrvin."

I was glad to be out of the minuscule office. We returned to the showroom just as Maria, rawboned, gaunt-faced and dressed in a business outfit, walked in. She was the manager to whom Mr. Lopez had already introduced me back on Wednesday.

"Good morning, gentlemen," she said, rushing to get to her office. "Happy to have you, Mr. Lacroix," she shrieked like that of a distressed bird.

"Thank you!" I replied.

Pito called to her. "Hey, Maria, the married couple from yesterday called earlier."

"They want to reconsider?"

"I'm not sure, but the husband says he loves the set."

"Let's see. Oh, wait!" Maria uttered in a prolonged, high-pitched cry like that of a puppy howling in agony. Both Pito and I startled. "Mr. Lacroix, maybe you can help. The couple is Haitian."

"I'll be glad if I can," I said, perplexed and anxious, not knowing exactly what the couple's main choice was and why they did not purchase the day before.

I knew Haitians negotiate pretty much everything they desired, including fixed-price items in high-end stores. I refrained, however, from asking too many questions. I had learned on the first day in any work environment, new hires must go with the flow, control their eagerness to take on an unfamiliar task while studying the atmosphere, and more importantly the articulated positional hierarchy. Sometimes, what's on paper does not necessarily reflect the reality in practice. Maria was the office manager, but Pito was my immediate coach. In this crucial stage, I needed him more than I needed Maria. After all, selling furniture required unspoken rules and tricks that a salesperson must grasp.

66

"Don't worry, Yrvin. Your first try will come soon." He nodded toward the window, and my eyes followed.

By now, it was ten-thirty, and outside the sun rose to its full strength, but the piercing rays seemed to have done little to temper the commotion. In astonishment, I watched a myriad of boisterous people, young and old, moving past each other in quickening speed, heads skewed to one side, all in a race for the best deal. Groups of spiky-haired teenagers and tattooed arms rambled about from stores to stores, ice cream in hand, window-shopping. Then, in waves, came retired women and married couples pushing their way to T.J. Maxx on the south entrance, swayed by the discount banners.

Early summer in Miami meant the sale season had arrived, and average folks seized on the moment to acquire their dreamed-of commodities—fancy cologne, that priceless gold necklace, or that fashionable dress easily noticed in Saturday night parties. Those were items priced beyond their means in other times. And one by one, the shoppers began to trickle into Las Calinas in mounting intensity. Pito and I stood on the opposite side of the room. The moment of truth had arrived. A gentleman with his splendid fiancée, arm in arm, stepped in, throwing glittering smiles behind their trendy spectacles. They walked around the vast room, vetting the furniture before making their choice.

I sauntered up to Pito. "Can I help them?"

"Wait a little," he commanded.

He seemed pressured by the growing crowd for just the two of us to deal with. I returned to my post. Then came a group of people, asking for Pito, but before I could point to him, they had already spotted him. These appeared to be regular customers.

They talked in low tones and very quickly, making it difficult to discern what they were saying, but one of them, a slim brunette who wore Coco Chanel glasses moved away and strolled toward one of the living room sets made out of sleek faux leather wraps, which were enhanced by chenille seat cushions. That set seemed to have stolen her mind. Lost deep in her contemplation, she did not realize the rest of the group had left the showroom, following Pito to the back.

"Can I help you?" I asked.

She turned around and found out she was alone. Puzzled, she did not appear to know which way to go. "Where did they go?" she asked, startled.

"To the back with Pito Fuentes," I assured her.

"Thank you."

"But do you like this set?"

"Oh! This is gorgeous!" she shouted.

"I can get you a thirty percent discount if you purchase today." She now turned around, facing me. "And I'll make sure your warranty is expanded to two years," I added.

My offer had stalled her, preventing her from reaching the rest of the group. She took off her glasses and wiped them out a bit, but failed to put them on again, her big bright eyes now glued on the set, which was priced at two thousand dollars.

She turned to me again. "Are you sure you can get me what you just said, sir?"

"I'm positive."

For a minute, she was pensive. Suddenly, she dug into her purse and yanked out a calculator, and after doing the math, she concluded she had more than enough to pay for the set. A triumphant smile beamed upon her face. Her mood now switched from reluctance to glee.

"You want it?" I asked.

"Yes, yes," she replied. "Be back," she added, making her way to the back in long strides.

My hope for a first deal grew. She came right back with the rest of the group but without Pito. She firmly held hands with an older woman in a black dress, pulling her along deliriously until they reached the living room set. She then released the woman's hand and dove into the sofa. The rest of the group followed with strange stares.

"Let me call my supervisor, then," I said.

"Yeah, yeah," she replied, her amused giggling building into full laughter, preempting all unwanted questions and disapproval from the group.

Stunned, the group obviously did not share her apparent inexperience and naivete in shopping at furniture stores where out-of-control desires to purchase were usually met with salespersons' overconfidence and unwillingness to compromise on the asking price.

In the back room, I met Pito behind the desk in his little office, purchase form in hand, busy wrapping up the sale. "How many sets these people are buying, Pito?"

He raised his head, held off his pen, and faced me. "Just one, and I'm almost done. Why?" He looked puzzled.

"I think you might want to stop and go ask." He rose from the desk and hopped out of the tiny office.

"What the *hell* they want now?" he said furiously.

"I think they just made a new choice."

Dumbfounded, Pito could not believe his eyes. The young woman lay on the sofa, head resting on the back cushion, becoming awkwardly restive like a crazed girl diving into a wild restless ride. A pimply-nosed lad in the group stepped forward and mumbled some words I could not understand. His face hardened and eyes bulged, he seemed poised to grab the young woman by the legs and throw her out of the sofa.

"It's her wedding. Leave her alone. She has the right to choose whatever pleases her," said the woman in black. The rest of the group looked on, horrified. I knew then the reason for such frenzied behavior.

"You wanna buy an additional set?" Pito asked.

"I don't think so," said a tall, middle-aged, salt-and-pepper-haired man. He looked as disturbed as the rest of the people. The man, who appeared to be the young woman's father, was as baffled as Pito, who thought he had secured a sweet deal for the family on a brown leatherette with intricately carved trim, chipping away almost fifty percent off the asking price.

The young woman sprinted out of the sofa. "I've changed my mind. I want this set instead."

"That's okay. But this comes without a discount," Pito said.

"How much is it?" asked the young woman.

"Let me see," Pito replied, looking for the price tag. "It's two thousand dollars," Pito affirmed.

"But the young man just told me he can get me a thirty percent discount if I buy it today."

"Sorry, he's our new employee and he was mistaken. He's still learning."

"That's okay. I'll take it anyway," the young woman asserted, preempting her mother, totally feverish like fishermen going gaga after a wild catch.

"No problem. You all can stay here while I go change the order," Pito said, returning to his office. I followed him. When we reached a small hallway, out of anyone's view, I watched in shock as Pito jumped with joy. My jaw dropped in confusion. "We made five hundred dollars today out of these fools," he said, patting me on the back.

"I don't understand, Pito." My confusion deepened.

"Besides our regular paycheck, we also make fifty percent as a bonus for each overpriced deal."

"So, what is the regular price for this new set, then?"

"The actual price is fifteen hundred."

"But, Pito, the tag says two thousand dollars."

"Although it says two thousand dollars, they could have bought it for fifteen hundred."

"So, you just made two hundred and fifty dollars."

"We'll have to share it—your first catch, Yrvin!"

Still in shock, I left Pito, and he went on to write the new purchase order and I went back to the showroom where the group, in resignation, congregated near the living room set, chatting. Meanwhile, the store had gotten rowdy as waves of shoppers poured in, swayed by the ridiculous prices written on the window. Some looked around, stopped, touched a little, asked for clarifications on the exact price, and left. Others were interested in a layaway program in which they could give a down payment on a furniture set of their choice to secure a deal, and the rest would have to be paid in several subsequent payments until they finally paid off the set. But there were folks who walked in with plenty of cash, and they spent without even looking at the prices. Many of them were wealthy individuals from the southside of town; others were corrupt government officials from Latin America. They walked around surrounded by maids, butlers, and security attachés who were closely attentive to their wants.

It was in the middle of this slew of would-be buyers that an athletic gentleman in a polo shirt and a short lady in chic afro ponytail and fashionable eyeglasses rushed in hand in hand. Their eyes surveyed the showroom and zeroed in a classic cherry wood bedroom set. "*Se sa-a!*" (This is it!) the lady cried in Creole.

"*Mwen ka edew?*" (Can I help you?) I swiftly asked likewise in Creole.

"*Wi!*" (Yes) replied the gentleman.

"So, let me go call my Mr. Lopez," I said.

"No, *no*, we prefer to be with you, a brother from home," they said at once.

"You seem to love this set. Don't you?" I teased them.

"I *love* it." The lady tee-heed like a spoiled child.

"Whatever the woman says, the woman gets," the gentleman sighed in resignation.

"Otherwise, you're in trouble," I said, mocking him with a grin. "So, this bedroom set is listed for five thousand eighty-five," I added.

"Yes, we know. We were here yesterday."

"Ah, you must be the Haitian couple Mr. Lopez was telling me about."

"Yes, we are, but Lopez didn't want to budge on the price."

"I see. This is my first day here. Let me talk to my boss. You stay here." I ran to see Pito and told him what the people wanted, but with a discount. He was busy with the group, writing the new purchase order. He lifted his head.

"If they truly want the set, go speak to Lopez. I'm sure he'll say yes." As I was leaving, he called to me, and I turned around. "Help those people as best as you can," he said with a twinkle in his eyes.

I knew what he meant. "You know the trick. Don't let them go." I did not reply. I simply smiled, a forced smile, for I began to get the sense of how the world of retail business in immigrant communities operated. Preying on people's ignorance and emotion was the cornerstone in the scheme to maximize profit, and that unfair practice did not sit well in my subconsciousness. I felt powerless to make a difference, especially on my first day in Las Calinas. A faultless performance was what I sought, not to antagonize the very person who hired me.

I went to Mr. Lopez as instructed, and told him the Haitian couple would love to buy the bedroom set, but had fallen short on the price, and they were not interested in the layaway program.

"Mr. Lacroix, do what you can to secure the deal." He gave me a thumbs-up. I hurried and rejoined the couple.

"I can take off two hundred dollars," I said gently.

The woman looked at the gentleman who nodded in agreement. "Yes, we'll take it." She leaned against him, kissing him to tenderize him, disarming all vestiges of resistance.

"Okay," I said with concealed excitement.

"By the way, what's your name?" the lady asked as we were leaving to execute the purchase order.

"Yrvin," I replied. "And yours?"

"Mirlène, and he's my husband Justin," she replied like a woman in command. In pure Haitian tradition, in a marriage, the iron lady wears the pants while *he* wears the skirt, swapping the roles.

"You speak Creole with an accent I'm used to. Are you from Saint Louis?" the lady asked.

"Are you, Ms. Milène?"

"Yes, but it's more than ten years since I left."

"It doesn't mean much," Justin interjected. "Folks from Saint Louis control a big chunk of Little Haiti. I'm from Saint Louis, too, and I'm never nostalgic for my hometown."

"Same, here, sir. I don't miss the town. I miss my mom and my siblings. I dream of the day we can be reunited here in America."

"Do you go to school, young man?" Justin asked.

"Yes, I do."

"Which one you go to, Lindsey Hopkins?" Milène asked.

"No, I go to Barry University." They both looked at each other, surprised.

In the 1980s, Haitian immigrants who wanted to pursue a professional career, went first to Lindsey Hopkins, a school that offered several programs including English as a Second Language and job development programs to prepare immigrants to enter the workforce. I spent a semester there and then quit because I didn't want to go the trade school route. I had always dreamed of a college education.

"We're proud of you, Yrvin."

While chatting, I was also completing the purchase order. "Thank you. I appreciate your business. Take this form to the office behind us. A woman named Maria will take the payment. I hope you come again."

"We certainly will."

In all, the day ended on a positive note. I knew there was still a lot to learn, but in my mind, a sudden optimism grew. Perhaps I could soon stand on my own, away from Pito's shadow, and work honestly. Since hired, I knew my unspoken role was to lure the Haitians back into the store. If done right, I could solidify my position in Las Calinas. But using disingenuous means to make money off an already marginalized population was not part of my character. My success depended on how the immigrant customers reacted to my sales practices. I had to build a good rapport based on trust, not necessarily on cultural and linguistic similarities.

As I was leaving, Mr. Lopez was unable to hide his satisfaction. "Drive safely, my son," he said with an unrestrained, hearty laugh.

Although tiredness threatened to paralyze me, my day was yet to be over. My afternoon dishwashing job awaited me. Life had become stiffer to navigate, but nothing could be tougher than the inability to pay for my college tuition, and that was enough to reenergize my exhausted body.

When I came home later that day, my whole body ached, especially my feet, which needed a rest. Putting food in my mouth felt harder than the pressure I had to endure earlier in Las Calinas. That experience, however, had reinforced my conviction and done away with all lingering doubts about my swift crossing to manhood. My sister was in the kitchen fixing supper when I came in.

"How was your day, my baby boy?" she asked, smiling.

"It was great, Nana." I avoided making eye contact, but the ache it caused me to put on a happy face quickly revealed the pain I tried to suppress.

"Vinco, you don't need to tell me. That stubborn little body has finally been tamed," she chortled as I tried to muster up a tired smile.

"I'm fine, Nana."

"No, you're not. The human body can only endure so much, even for a young body at the spring of his time."

I wanted to let her know I was up to the task, and the pride of being a man came with it the burden of daily sacrifices and the unflinching will to overcome all obstacles standing in the way. But Nana knew her little brother, still babyish in her presence, and when a hug and a kiss were her only gift of the day, she went into a panic. She stopped cooking and turned off the burners, understanding at that moment that I needed her sisterly love and affection more than anything. From the living room, I watched her moving in slow, unsteady steps, tottering toward the sofa where I sat, dozing off.

"This is life in America, Vinco." We now sat side by side, my head resting on her shoulder. She patted me on the head, poking my face, like Manman used to do when we were kids.

"Nana, don't worry. My body is tired, but my mind is not."

"Look at you, baby boy."

"How do I look?" I asked with a shrug.

"Dog-tired, like people in bondage after an awful day in the field."

"Nana, you've gone too far."

She laughed, a laugh of renewed confidence and unmeasured pride that her brother had overcome his fear of the unknown in a world overwhelmed by pitfalls and invisible barriers, which only men of ambitious minds and deep convictions could break through.

"So, how was Las Calinas?"

"Busy, and I made my first sale."

"Bravo, my prince!"

I smiled.

"Vinco, you need a business card to give to your customers. You wanna build your own base. At least, that's what I heard people in the business say."

"I'll have the card next week. My boss promised me that."

"Did you see a lot of Haitians coming in?"

"Not really, but it was a Haitian couple who bought a furniture set from me."

"Wow!"

"But I'm uncomfortable with the way they do business there."

"What do you mean?"

"They use all kinds of tricks to make the maximum profit."

"That's the nature of things, Vinco. In the race for money, *seul les plus justes seront sauvés.*" (Only the fairest will be saved.)

"That's Manman's line."

She laughed. "But keep your mouth shut. You need a job."

"I know, Nana."

"Now, go take your shower. You smell like a wild goat. I'll fix your food."

"No, Nana. No strength."

"How about your favorite rice pudding?"

"Oh yes, but that takes forever."

"It'll be done in twenty minutes. By the way, your Bahamian girl called earlier."

Startled, I asked, "Did she leave a message?"

"Yes, she asked me to tell you to call her when you came home."

"Okay, I will."

That was enough to keep my mind away from the grueling work that still awaited me the next day. Thinking of Judy, however, had become an unsustainable pain since the Friday night party, and I had been trying hard not to let her ruin my nights. The images of that young man fleeing with her in the middle of the crowded room were tough to digest. Deep in my broken heart, I felt her action underscored a prior assumption that I would be fine with anything she desired, including flirting with other boys, even if it were in one of the most unconventional ways. Perhaps in her wild and reckless reasoning, she must have been convinced that a shadowy love affair could do no harm to our burgeoning romance. So hurtful was her action that I began to think it was a mistake to make love to her that night. I did not want to cheapen my character, being any girl's little secret. I was no longer interested in that relationship. I made several attempts to pick up the phone and call her, but I could not. Concentrating on school was my top priority.

Chapter 6

Sunday morning in mid-August, in the heart of the Miami summer, my sister was busy making special dishes and getting ready to go to a picnic in Virginia Key on the island of Key Biscayne. It was to kick off a two-week celebration to honor Saint Louis Roi de France, my Haitian hometown's patron saint. The festivities were held every August in Saint Louis. My sister belonged to a group at her church made up exclusively of people from Saint Louis. Those who had the means to travel flew to the island to enjoy the tropical ambiance, but those who could not make the journey due to travel restrictions or lack of legal papers celebrated in South Florida. These included churchgoers, voodoo worshippers, and non-committed balladeers, nostalgic to the old days.

Having been busy with school and work, I had little time to stay connected with friends from home as well as with social activities in Miami. Sunday was my only free day that I could spend some extra hours in bed, but the sound of spoons clattering in the kitchen had ruined my early morning sleep. I got out of bed and walked to the kitchen. There my sister was in her white apron, making blackened rice mix with lima beans. A giant cake lay in an aluminum tray on the dining room table along with multiple ingredients in preparation for making *cremas*. All feelings of laziness now vanished. I was fully awake. Cremas, cake, and blackened rice were my favorite dishes. "Nana, why didn't you wake me up?"

"What for? You forgot all about the picnic?"

"Oh, my God. I totally forgot. Sister, you know these days I'm not my old self anymore."

"Tell me about it." She grabbed a large wooden spoon from the kitchen cabinet and began to stir the rice in a big pot.

"Can I help?" I edged closer, throwing a little kiss on her cheek.

"You mean stirring up the rice?"

"Uh-huh."

"I didn't know you knew how to make this special rice?" She laughed, and I took the spoon off her hand. She grabbed it right back. "Get ready. I'm sending you to the store."

"What for, Nana?"

"I need some additional ingredients for the cremas and the icing for the cake."

"What are the ingredients you need?"

"Go take your shower and put on your clothes. I'll have them written down on a piece of paper when you're done."

Ten minutes later, I was back. "Ready!" I exclaimed.

"So fast? I bet you didn't take your shower."

"Go, look, Nana, and the bed is fixed, too."

"I have no time for that." She then led me to the table to review what was there and what was missing for the cremas.

I surveyed the ingredients. "You have the lime zest, the sweetened condensed milk, the coconut milk, the evaporated milk, sugar, and vanilla extract. I think you have all you need."

"Poor little brother, that's what you think," she said, ridiculing me. "Here's the list of what's missing."

She read it along with me. "Almond extract, a bottle of Haitian rum Barbancourt (three stars), nutmeg, and a couple more condensed milks."

"How about some cinnamon and some vanilla extract, Nana?"

"No. The nutmeg and the almond extract will do."

"Manman used to include them."

"I know, but it's not necessary. Now, go and hurry."

Just when I grabbed the car key and was ready to leave, she called to me, "I forgot to include the icing for the cake."

"Don't worry, I won't forget."

I came back almost twenty minutes later. She was on the couch, dozing off, exhausted after being up since three a.m. to get the food ready. The entire group heavily counted on her for every major event. For that, she was meticulous in every task, and hers was to prepare desserts for the picnic. The minute I stepped in she was on her feet. "What took you so long?"

"I had to go to the supermarket on 82nd Street. There was a long line in front of Cayard's Market. Too many people from

Saint Louis buying patties. Besides, I didn't want them to see me."

"Why?"

"Folks from Saint Louis are gossipers."

"You're still worried about do-nothing people, going around, and telling lies?"

"I'm not worried about them. My hair was not properly combed, and I'm worried about what they would say to Manman once they travel to Haiti. Having my hair in such a mess, my shirt a bit wrinkled—their story wouldn't be a made-up one. Believe it or not, I saw Altéon and his fat wife Clorette standing in line, waiting to be served. Claireline and her crazy daughter Cocotte stood right behind them. I had to run. Remember how they almost tore Manman's heart into pieces after they told her we had become panhandlers in the streets of Miami?"

"I have no time for empty-headed fools who have yet to understand their mission as refugees in this country. While they lie, you're at school, empowering yourself with education."

"You're right. I overreacted." I placed the ingredients on the table, watching her with dismay. She was unable to open up her eyes. "Why don't you go lie down for at least an hour. I know how to get the rest done."

She turned off the stove burner but left the rice on the pot. "Vinco, after you put in the remaining ingredients, you'll have to stir it until it becomes very creamy."

"What about the icing?"

"Leave it here, I'll decorate the cake when I wake up." She went in, and within minutes, she was snoring.

#

Virginia Key Beach Park was one of the nicest beach parks in Southeast Miami-Dade County. It was not far from downtown and was the prime destination for Haitians and every person of color. It creates an emblematic footprint in the ethnic and cultural diversity that makes up historical sunny South Florida. Along with other Caribbean festivities taking place almost every weekend, konpa, Haiti's famous contemporary music genre, especially among young people, could be heard loud and clear on a breezy Sunday afternoon when popular local bands performed. Beachgoers went crazy, grooving to the konpa beat. It was the place where romance began and sometimes ended, where hearts were broken, where sentimental overtures foretold the dawn of long and lasting relationships.

My sister, in a one-piece swimsuit and a denim skirt, and I, wearing sunglasses, a t-shirt over denim shorts, arrived at the park around eleven a.m.. A few group members made it before us. Park-built open shelters were lined up all the way to the edge of the beach where timid waves landed in the white sandy shores. We wasted no time setting up. We had brought in a portable table that was long enough to display our food under one of the shelters located on the eastern side. Nana put the rice in a large to-go food container overlapped by aluminum foil to keep warm. She displayed cake and cremas on the table under a clear plastic box to protect them against the sea breeze. We also had brought in Haitian colas, paper cups, and plates; all were laid out on the table to make a perfect impression.

Soon, others came and set up their stands next to us. Though all those people came from the Saint Louis area of Haiti, we knew none of them. Nana's churchmates had yet to arrive, and a tinge of worry popped on her face. By midday, group members started trickling in.

"What took you guys so long?" Nana asked.

"An accident at the entrance of the Rickenbacker Causeway slowed all traffic going into the island," said Lavanie, one of the group leaders and a close friend of my sister.

Within minutes, our shelter had transformed, exhibiting the best stand filled with food and party drinks. Our stand had the perfect ocean view, with calm blue water under a cloudless turquoise sky. Some families were busy setting up their tents and laying out their blankets while children played around down on the sandy beach. Farther out in the water, couples on jet skis and wave runners interweaved in a race against the shallow currents.

By early afternoon, the park and beach were very much alive. Music blared, and expatriates from Saint Louis swelled the area. What we anticipated had awesomely come true. *La Saint Louis* had arrived. Nana's group, deeply religious, stayed away from the live music and dirty dancing. Instead, they focused more on jokes, laughter, and food. I left the group and ventured away with some childhood friends I reconnected with at the picnic.

Periodically, I would return to check on Nana and the food. I noticed that while her friends sat chatting and eating, she was in a different mood, and she would shrug me off each time I asked about why such a change in attitude. But Guylène, a young woman, who wore a straw hat and fashionable spectacles to shield her face against the sun, told me Nana just caught her boyfriend Lucien flirting and kissing with a hot, sexy girl from lower Saint Louis. Devastated, all her appetite for food had disappeared.

"Vinco, we had been telling her to dump him for months," Guylène said, stamping her feet down in anger.

Charming and good-looking, Lucien seemed irresistible in the eyes of many young Haitian women in town. A sweet-talker, he was clean shaved and well-built. He had big black eyes that twinkled as a ploy to disarm and trap women who inclined to resist his cunning overtures. Like many of his prey, my sister could not resist, and somehow, she thought her persistent prayers and faultless demeanor would eventually morph him into the sincere and dovish boy she had wanted him to be. She was wrong. There, in Virginia Key, reality had set into her torn mind and threatened to shred the lingering fibers of her broken heart. I never liked Lucien, and I had warned Nana.

Clarine, another close friend and a vocal member of the group who watched in horror at how upset I was, told me Lucien hid behind the line of a cactus bush under a blue tent framed by two women. I went for him with my camera. Clarine went with me. We tiptoed down a tiny weed-covered pathway and halted our steps on the other side of the bush. We craned our necks and peered through the holes. There he was French kissing and interlacing with a lady in a crop top and bikini bottoms. I took several snapshots, and Clarine and I secretly retreated to our stand. Nana still stood there, hoping for a glimpse of Lucien.

"Nana, you need to get rid of this loser or you'll be miserable for the *rest* of your life," I sternly said.

"Vinco, you're overreacting like always," she replied, trying to water down the seriousness of the situation.

"Nana, I wished Vinco was overreacting," Clarine ensued. "You don't have to go see for yourself. We have pictures for you," Clarine continued, looking at my sister straight in the eyes, seeming to search for any remaining sense of acceptable reasoning. Nana avoided looking, and I did not insist, preferring to wait for when we got home later in the evening.

My sister's struggle to free herself from Lucien's love trap and my inability to help her reach salvation had paralyzed me. I saw her pain through the lenses of my own predicament with Judy. Love does not die overnight, but when it dies, it dies. It took me a long time to realize that dwelling in lopsided or unfaithful love affairs feels like living on a cliff edge, and any attempt at retrieving that love will simply prolong the inevitable.

I had also learned that biased love can never be sustained. It is like a sinking ship in which the endangered passengers refuse to vacate in the hope the tide will sway their way. Unfortunately, fake love deeply rooted in deceptions and lusty adventures cannot be endured nor reversed when fading, for adulterous behavior is not conducive to any serious relationship. Obviously, if Lucien were serious, he would have been with my sister, not with these other women, just a few feet away from where my sister stood in longing. My sister must let go, I thought, or she will fall off that cliff and plunge to her demise. I had to help her.

I urged the group to stage an impromptu celebration in her honor, thanking her for her tireless leadership and efforts in keeping the group together, for her religious passion, and for being compassionate in helping the most vulnerable in her church. We all then vacated the stand and strolled down the white sugar sand beach amid hundreds of partygoers, and we sang and danced to the beat of konpa. Slowly, she began to return to her old self, singing along, making jokes, and even presenting me to members who did not know me before as her proud brother, now a student at Barry University. A few girls in the group shouted out loud, "I'll marry him after graduation!"

"For that, you'll have to wait for two years," she shouted back sarcastically.

"Is that right, you'll graduate in two years?" Clarine asked me.

"If all goes well, yeah. I'll be a junior when school resumes in a couple of weeks," I replied, moving next to Nana, my hand wrapped around her shoulders. "Let's go back to the stand to get rid of the cake and the cremas I helped prepare," I bragged while urging the group to follow us. In less than ten minutes, the food was gone. I then hurried and took out the stand, folded it back into the trunk of my car. Nana and I exchanged hugs and kisses with the group members, and before the evening crickets began to chirp and interfere with the music still playing a few meters down the beach, we pulled out of the park and drove home.

Chapter 7

In May, when the refreshing air of spring transitioned to the dreaded, sultry winds of summer, I was down in darkness, fighting my inner worries on multiple fronts, and the most frightening of all was the uncertainty over my college tuitions; but as the summer nights gave way to the autumnal mornings of September, hope and optimism had once again dawned in my young immigrant journey.

On the first Friday of September, I showed up for work in Las Calinas for the last time. My goal had been reached and my mission accomplished. Getting the Haitians back into the store, the prime reason why Mr. Lopez hired me, was achieved. For two long months, Haitian customers had never stopped coming into the store and were happily purchasing furniture. New faces showed up every day, asking for Mr. Lacroix immediately after they walked in. Each knew, by word of mouth, that I had always ensured that my customers were awarded the discount they sought before making a deal.

There were times when Pito refused to lower the asking price for fear of losing his commission and I agreed to give up mine so the customer could still buy and go home a happy camper.

Consequently, in many transactions, I found myself constantly engaged in dual negotiations with both Pito and the buyer. I did the best I could to hide this practice from Mr. Lopez. Unfortunately, he knew Pito more than I did, and Pito's elation after each deal for which he did not negotiate did not help me. Soon, his cheerfulness had caught the attention of Mr. Lopez, who secretly reprimanded him for taking advantage of me.

For average folks, however, money is like blood, and without it, no one can survive. At least that was a common theme among immigrants in South Florida. For Pito, the temptation to go home with some extra cash was greater than Lopez's shallow warnings. I could have easily stopped Pito's disingenuousness, but I feared doing so could damage our friendship.

On my last day at Las Calinas, no feeling of nostalgia seized me, but with a tinge of chagrin, an annoying ache stemmed from the fact that I was going to miss working with professionals who treated me fairly and serving my Haitian expatriates who heavily counted on me for a reasonable deal. For the first time, I watched Pito look sad when I walked into the little office that we had shared for two months, telling jokes while we worked, negotiating with weary customers, and talking about the difficult life of refugees in America. He had learned firsthand from his parents, who immigrated to Miami many years earlier from the town of Bluefields on the Caribbean coast of Nicaragua, fleeing the dictatorship of Somoza. Besides his unreasonable thirst for money, Pito was a fine young man who had mastered the art of retail business and who wholeheartedly taught me how to be successful as a salesman.

"Bro, I miss you already."

"Me, too, *man*. I'll never forget our camaraderie, your great sense of humor," I said, dropping my little suitcase on my desk and emptying the drawers.

"But I completely understand your departure. A man must have a higher goal, greater ambitions. Your strong will to graduate from college impresses me a lot, as well as your positive attitude. Even in the most difficult moment, you always find a way to keep a customer engaged until the deal is secured. I have no doubt you'll graduate and become not just an asset for your immediate family but for the community at large. I'm not sure, Yrvin, if I'll ever have the pleasure to work with a fine young man like you again."

"Don't make me feel guilty for leaving, Pito."

"Not at all, my friend. Because of you, I'm now seriously thinking of going back to college."

"What will be your major?"

"I have an associate degree in Business Administration. So, I plan on going back for my BS."

"That's awesome. What university you plan on attending?"

"Not sure yet, but it might be University of Miami. I heard UM has a fantastic business school. My sister graduated there two years ago."

While chatting, we heard clattering footsteps in the showroom. I left Pito and returned to the front. A silver-haired, mustachioed man dressed in a gray suit with a pocket watch held by a golden chain walked around the furniture like prospective buyers do. His strange feline eyes caught a versatile, elegant two-piece living room set, and he paused to give an intimate look.

"How can I help you?" I asked with a broad smile.

"I'm looking for the price tag," he said with a tiny stroke on his mustache, imperial and bushy.

"It's down on the left side by the foot."

He bent down a bit and saw the price tag. "Seventeen hundred. It's pricy," he said, moving to the next set. I noticed he was anxious and edgy. He took an up-close look at the pocket watch as if scrutinizing the time and mumbled a few words I could not hear. "*Mais où est-elle?*" he said in French suddenly. (But where is she?) His befogged eyes now fixated on the walkway outside where the crowd of shoppers had grown.

"*De qui parlez-vous, monsieur?*" I asked. (Who are you referring to?) Surprised, he turned to me. "Are you Haitian?" he asked.

"Yes, I am."

"I am Maurepas de Vaudreuil," he said with an aristocratic, old-fashioned gesticulation, stressing the importance of every word.

"I'm Yrvin Lacroix, and I know Marie-Alice de Vaudreuil, a student at my university," I replied.

Astounded, his hands, until now rested in the hips, dropped as he approached me to shake my hand. "Marie-Alice is my lovely *daugh*ter, impeccably intelligent. She is in her last year and will graduate at the top of her class. She was in South Hampton for the summer. She called me this morning from Vienna, where she is spending the week with her fiancé." Then he switched from English to French. "*Elle a, comme son père, toutes les bonnes manières des gens de la grande société.*" (Like her father, she possesses all the good manners like people from high society.)

92

He spoke in peculiar utterances, obtrusive, and meticulously designed to show prominence, like those from the Haitian elite who were educated in Oxford and in Paris, who spoke the refined English of the exclusive hilltop of Port-au-Prince, and who believed they were born to shamelessly lead some of the most deprived people on the planet; for their nobility made them superior and distinguished.

"Marie-Alice has a proud father," I said, laughing in an incongruous form of mockery. "If you decide on a set that you like, let us know, sir."

I left, leaving him standing in the middle of the showroom, returning to my office to ask Pito to deal with him in case he wanted to make a purchase. When I reached the backdoor, I turned around to get a glimpse of the man who had fathered one of my collegemates and whose demeanor in style and mannerism I disapproved of. He seemed astonished that a young man who fit the profile of many of his subalterns in Haiti was not interested in his pontificated words.

Feeling helpless, he called to me. "I'd like to buy this set," he said, pointing at the same two-piece he was looking at a few minutes before.

"I'll get someone to help you. I'm already busy with a customer." I lied.

"Can you, *please*?" he beseeched, and I could see how he struggled to address me in such a pleading way, a vivid reminder that Miami was not part of his bubble, the world of men whose desires were always executed without contest, a surreal inheritance which made them calm, absurd, serene, and arrogantly indifferent toward the misery of others.

"All right give me a few minutes. You sit in the waiting room," I commanded. I went back and filled Pito in, and I told him that I was going to start the process, and he would have to finish it. He agreed. By then, it was already half-past ten a.m. I had to leave early due to a meeting at school. When I returned to the showroom, I found Vaudreuil now standing by the living set with an imposingly elegant woman, tall and strong, leaning against him, hands intertwined.

"Voilà monsieur Yrvin," he said with a burst of laughter. The woman, whose youthful appearance did not fit the category of a lady he should be dating, lifted her head and acknowledged my presence.

"Cheri," she said with a little laugh, short and half-suppressed. "Yrvin seems a fine young man who will help his fellow countrymen." She had her arm around Vaudreuil's waist like a proud concubine. Vaudreuil, old, vulnerable, and defenseless, caved into his lover's want without any form of resistance, agreeing to purchase the same set he believed was too costly an hour earlier.

"Do you want it now?" I asked.

"Yes," affirmed the woman, eyes twinkling seductively.

"Okay," Vaudreuil said, turning his face sideways, embarrassingly capitulated.

"Stay here, my coworker Pito is coming to serve you." I called Pito, who came immediately. I presented him to the couple.

"Mr. Vaudreuil, Madame, Mr. Fuentes will take good care of you. It was a pleasure to meet you."

94

I made my way to Mr. Lopez, who was in his office. "I come to say goodbye and to thank you for giving me the opportunity to work with professionals like you," I said.

"We're going to miss you, Mr. Lacroix." He was visibly saddened.

"Me, too. I'll be missing all of you. You were incredibly generous to me," I replied.

"Can you work for us at least on weekends? I know you're going to be busy with school," he uttered as if pleading a lost cause.

"I wish I could. Unfortunately, my weekends will be my busiest days because I'll have group studies with my collegemates."

"How about next summer?" Maria asked, walking out of her office next door to let me know how much she was going to miss me.

"That's a long way off. I'd love to, and I'll let you know when the time comes."

They all walked me to the front door. Pito left the Haitian customers and joined us. We hugged each other goodbye, shed a little tear, and I left a proud and happy young man. With the money I saved, I was able to pay for my tuition, buy my books without my sister's help, send some much-needed cash to Manman in Haiti, and put aside some money for the spring semester.

#

September had arrived, and BU was alive again. From the cafeteria to the library and along the walkways leading to and from classes, jolly shoppers wandered around like uncaged birds in wonderland. The first day back was the most dazzling, when the happy memories of the past summer were told, when hugs and kisses, deep and shallow, seemed endless. Amid this fevered atmosphere I was busy finding out my new classes, meeting my new profs, scrutinizing courses' syllabi, and eagerly ready to start. At last, I was a junior, a proud one deep in a trench warfare against the uncertainties of life. Halfway through the journey, I grew more confident that in a not-too-distant future I could see the daystar, still burning bright at the tail end of this long struggle.

Luckily enough, Pedro and I shared a Humanities class, one of my last general education courses. I met him right at the entrance. We greeted each other in our usual, warm brotherly hug. He looked a bit taller. Maybe that was how my eyes caught his polished features, clean shaved, shorter-haired, wearing flashy new Adidas and polo shirt.

"Man, is this the new *you?*" I joked, laughing.

"That was what I missed greatly during the summer, Vinco."

"What was that?"

"Your good-natured *chaff.*"

"I also missed your cunning ways at seducing the girls."

"I'm not sure about that anymore."

"How so, Ped?"

"One girl has put a stop to this game of chicken."

"Which one?"

"Chen, the Chinese girl. She has stolen my heart, man."

"Really?"

"I finally found a girl whose maturity and intellectual probity are mind-blowing. Since the night at the party, we've been not just boyfriend and girlfriend, but soulmates. We can now finish each other's sentences."

"I'm happy for you. Settling with this girl will spare you the time you'll need to concentrate in your studies."

"Yep. But Vinco, how is Judy?"

"I don't know, man. Remember, she went home to the Bahamas shortly after the party."

"She never called you?"

"No. But, I'm fine with that. In fact, her silence has helped a lot. My main focus is my courses, and girls' torments are the last thing I need."

"How was your summer, Vinco?"

"It was no fun, but productive. I spent two months working at Las Calinas, and I quit last week. We all cried. The management wanted me to stay."

"And what did you tell them?"

"I told them no, of course, Ped. As long as I can pay for my classes, and my sister's fine, I'll be fine."

I knew I was not telling Pedro the whole truth about Judy. I still loved her, and I ached from the fact I did not hear from her. I wished I had never met her, or at least I had not gone to bed with her. After class, I met Arianne, Élodie, Paul, Gregory, Eugenia, Christine, and a few others of my rich, spoiled Haitian collegemates. They were all happy to be back and be friends again, enjoying the college life and sharing the same desire to succeed with all the pain associated with it.

On that first day, they complained about their strange new dorm on the opposite side of the cafeteria, their new roommates, freshmen who could barely relate to them, to their extravagant lifestyle—especially Élodie, a golden honey with almond-shaped eyes and asymmetrical lips, slightly fuller on the lower side. I liked her a lot, and I imagined how sugary those lips must be. Though I was tempted several times to make a move, her girlish giggles when we were together kept me at bay. I thought she was too immature.

Like the rest of my peers, I went through the day with the same collective readiness to take on the tasks necessary to achieve academic success. By midafternoon, the school hours were behind me, but my day was not yet over. I had not seen Judy. So, I decided to walk down the path that led to that little bench behind the chapel, our usual spot. There she was in a floral dress, wearing chic oversized sunglasses with the allure of a Hollywood star, her purse and books in hand, waiting as if she had rendezvoused me. She rose from the bench as I reached her. We hugged each other with the same old gaiety, falling once more into each other's arms like wading across a river of love.

"*Vinco*," she said like a happy child in a theme park. "How come you never answered my calls?"

"Chouchou, when did you call me?"

"It wasn't just once. I called many times and multiple times a day."

"I screen my phone every day. Maybe you were calling a wrong number."

"How could I?" she said forcefully. "There's no one in the world outside your family who knows your phone number better than I do." And then she emphatically rattled off the correct phone number.

I knew she was right, and my sister usually told me she had called and left messages. I avoided the telephone every day after work for fear I would not have to feel the urge to call back. I only reacted to the phone messages when the message box was full. The light flickered, and I emptied it.

"Chouchou, you didn't leave me a number to call you. Was it a coincidence?"

"No, Vinco."

"And why?"

"Because I—" She stumbled, unable to find the right word to justify her action.

"No need to explain. I get the message."

"Vinco, I thought it would have been better to call you instead of you calling me."

"Really. So, your butlers wouldn't find out and tell on you?"

"Vinco, I'm no baby. I'm just trying to avoid unnecessary problems. If my dad knows about us, he will undoubtedly send me to school somewhere else, and that would be my worst nightmare."

"Chouchou, I can't play this love game. It's not part of my character."

"Oh, Vinco. You're the only man I love."

"If so, prove it."

"Maybe I'm not strong enough to stand up to my parents' selfishness."

"The truth is that fear of the unknown cripples you."

"I fear losing you, only you, and I'm not sure our relationship is rooted enough to survive a long-distance scenario. I'm not gonna lie to you. I'm afraid, and I need you to help me overcome my fear." She edged closer, her eyes twinkling, and I leaned toward her sensual lips. Until then, we stood few inches apart.

"Look at you. Looking so sharp under your jacket, your blue jeans. You're dressed just the way I've imagined you would be when we meet again." We both laughed at once.

Hand in hand, we walked down the walkway that threaded up to her home across the street. She invited me in, but I refused, saying it was getting late and that I had to go home to go over my syllabi and start working on new assignments. We stood by the front steps and chatted for few more minutes. I left, but I promised to call before bedtime.

I genuinely wanted to give my relationship with Judy a second look, but that would have required sacrifices I was unable to make. If she were mine and mine alone, things would have been different. Schoolwork took precedent. Although I started the new academic year with a great sense of optimism, I understood the difficult days that lay ahead. My junior year would be the toughest yet.

As time crept by, the days had become longer and heavier as the nights were short and often sleepless. At least three times a week I had to pull an all-nighter for weekly exams and other work assignments. Maintaining a grade point average above 3.0 was vital to me. Ahead of midterm and final exams, Pedro and I and other classmates would spend a lot of time, especially on weekends, in the library studying, and we would eat Jamaican patties and drink Haitian colas on break time.

I had been so busy and so stressed with school that one day, my sister told me she was looking for a part-time job so that I could quit my afternoon gig to concentrate solely on my college obligations. I refused, saying it would not have been fair to her as she had already picked up the bulk of the bills. My precarious condition, however, had hardened my resolve: graduation was the only road to salvation. To alleviate my stress, I squeezed one hour out of my schedule every three days after class to go workout in the university gym, which was crucial to preserving my sanity and self-confidence as a young man.

There were moments I missed my sophomore year's routines immeasurably—friends congregating around the bookstores or in the cafeteria, telling jokes over sandwiches and iced tea, weekend parties in a little nightclub on Dixie Highway, where I would take center stage to the gleeful and envious eyes of the girls who wanted to have fun with us.

Judy and I rarely saw each other. She herself had been busy with schoolwork, but we made sure we met every Friday afternoon. We would go to a cozy Bahamian restaurant in South Miami, near Coconut Grove, where we ate fried conch with french fries. Though it looked like the perfect arrangement, it was mostly a romantic struggle. Judy wanted more quality time, which I could not deliver. As a defense mechanism, I would remind her of her "official" boyfriend, and we would go back to the car frustrated and hopeful that next weekend might be better. Since the night of the end-of-year party, we had been interacting only loosely, managing what was an unmanageable love that had gone astray.

When we met, we were never alone because I knew how she felt, and being together where no one was around could trigger another heated moment. I was tempted sometimes to go home with her, but her unfaithfulness paralyzed me. I knew she was suffering. I knew she yearned for something I could never deliver. One day, I was leaving the financial aid office when I ran into her. She looked disturbed, wan, and bleary-eyed. She looked as if she wanted to tell me something she knew would not please me. She stood right below the front step, a foot away from the door.

I edged closer and grabbed her hand, trying to cheer her up. "Chouchou, what's going on?" I asked.

"Vinco, I have something to tell you. Can you walk me home?"

"Sure, why not?" I avoided the cafeteria altogether.

Meeting my nosy Haitian friends terrified me. We walked east toward NE 2nd Avenue and on to the next street, her street. I noticed she did not have her school materials, although she wore her usual sexy trademark of Calvin Klein blue jeans and low-heel footwear. When we reached her front door, we met her sister Ella, a girl with a slim figure who walked with a unique form of elegance and unconscious prudishness. She was very polite and quite different from Judy, who was outgoing, fun-loving, impulsive, and seldom walked away from any challenge. Nonetheless, both sisters shared almost identical physical traits: light-skinned of mixed races, long golden hair, and hazel eyes. Binders in hand, Ella was on the way out, going to some group study at the library.

"Hey Vinco, how are things going?" she asked, wriggling like a chirping songbird while stepping down, ready to leave.

"Nothing much, Ella. You know the drill. Studying hard to boost the GPA."

"You got that right." She turned to Judy, who freed her hand from mine but still stood next to me, almost leaning on me. "Mommy just called and wanted you to give her a jingle when you came home."

"Okay, I will."

Ella stepped down, and I reached her for a hug. Wrapping her long, golden arm around my neck like my sister always did, she landed a kiss on my forehead. "See you guys later," she smirked, leaving an echo of a laugh in her wake. It was unrestrained, hearty, and blissful. Judy and I then went in and shut the door. We strolled past the living room, the family room and stepped onto a back porch that led to a screened-in patio garlanded by fancy patio furniture, broadleaved indoor plants, and multicolored South Florida impatiens. Hands folded about each other, we paced toward a loveseat futon where we sat, our bodies entwined.

"Judy, here it's so lovely and peaceful," I said, poking her creamy oval cheeks.

"But its natural beauty only serves to deepen my solitude."

"Why are you saying this, Judy?"

"Vinco, it's hard for me to come here without thinking of you."

"Judy, I can imagine."

103

"Vinco, don't tell me these little lies. I'm sure you can imagine yourself being in a place like this with someone, certainly not with me...."

"And with whom, chouchou?"

"Vinco, you know I'm not a child. I'm a young woman with a broken heart, a heart so shredded that I'm afraid it will never be put back together. It hurts me each time we're together, and I watch how you struggle to avoid the only conversation that could perhaps heal my suffering. But I understand. Sometimes words left unsaid are the most painful to endure." Her body shivered, and I held her tighter.

Crushed by her act of disloyalty, I knew I could never recover. I felt I had hit a wall; the way forward for our relationship had stopped. Knowing the circumstances, I never questioned her love for me, but I despised her duplicity. Born and raised in the opulent world of upper-crust bourgeoisie, Judy's attitude and demeanor at first glance shed the dull and repulsive manner commonly found in the spoiled, aristocratic offspring of her island nation of the Bahamas. She was well aware of this inheritance, which she fought hard to suppress. Although many girls at school, especially my Haitian friends, shunned her and dubbed her self-centered, egotistical, and sluttish. I, who beheld how she lived with a secret relationship, saw in Judy a girl with a dovish heart and a victim of her class of origin.

From the get-go, I doubted anything serious could have come out of this relationship because our lifestyles were too different, too far apart. What seemed natural to her was like an enigma to me. As our relationship developed, I started to believe she was the girl of my life, a priceless gift from God that I was not about to trade for any girl in town. There on that loveseat that afternoon, we painfully reviewed our short and shallow romance. I felt helpless, for I could not offer the perfect amorousness she wanted.

"Chouchou, believe me, I know how you feel, and that's my greatest pain," I uttered. My heart was broken and contrite.

"*No*, Vinco. You *don't*." Her voice rose on a long, tearing wail, pulling away a bit from me. Her eyes sparkled under the weight of her emotion. "I'm not sure you have the slightest idea of a young woman's dreams, her hopes, and her unrevealed desires, especially a girl like me who has been forced to wallow in a web of pain and rejection, whose love will never reach its well-deserved destination. Vinco, it's not that I don't understand our predicament. It's just that sometimes I feel life has cheated me, putting me on a path to love a man who will never be mine. There're times I think my pain, my endless suffering will last forever." She covered her face with both of her hands and turned her back on me.

I trembled in panic and embarrassment. I truly understood the upsurge of her romantic desire, her inability to suppress the lust that ran through her veins, and her bizarre and frantic expression of boundless affection that had always escaped her sensual lips each time we were together. I had never felt so helpless. I sat there, listening to her words, piercing and indignant.

"Chouchou, please forgive me," I said softly. She turned to me again, her hands still covered her face, but I quickly removed them and wrapped her arms around my neck. I pulled her against my chest, and we began to sob into each other's arms.

Across the vast courtyard, the sun sank sluggishly behind gray, mushroomed clouds that blocked the turquoise sky. A wind gust swept through, pushing mango leaves to flutter around like a tornado. Darkness trickled in. We both got up at once and strolled back inside where we sat on a couch in the family room, facing a giant television screen we had no interest in watching, even as the evening news was on.

"Vinco," she said faintly in an agonizing voice, "what if tonight is our *last* one together?" she asked in a quivery voice, like she was burying the memory of a vanquished love.

"Not sure I understand, chouchou." My anxiety deepened.

"I'm saying this might be the last time you see me."

"Where're you going?" My eyes burned tearfully.

"Back home."

"But Judy, this is September."

"Vinco, I can no longer live like this. I know it's a sacrifice, but sometimes a sacrifice is what one must do to save one's sanity and restore her dignity. I've already talked to my parents. I'll lose the semester, but I'll join my brother in Britain in the spring, where he's already a senior at Oxford."

"Judy, I know it's painful for the two of us, at least you could have told me about this plan."

"Because I never thought this could be a concern for you. But, I'm telling you now, Vinco. I would've never left without telling you. Despite our terrible situation, you'll always be the man who's given me the gift of love. Before I met you, love and affection were two words of equal meaning to me. Now, I know the difference."

"Judy, please forgive me. Believe me, the pain is not one-sided. But I can't reciprocate the way you feel because there are huge barriers standing in the way. I know you're seeing someone, even if he's not the person you've always wanted. You just said sacrifice is sometimes necessary, but I'm not sure you're ready to give up everything, your class of privilege and lavish lifestyle in exchange for me, someone who has nothing to offer. I'm from the fringes of society, and I know my boundaries."

"Oh Vinco, don't say this." Her sobbing now exploded into an outburst of crying and rage. "You're saying this because you've already written me off your heart," she growled.

"You know that's not true, chouchou. But dwelling in an unsatisfying, temporary love is not what both you and I want. We deserve better than that."

She was no longer interested in listening to my morally repugnant statements. I tried to put on my best face, but she bought none of that. I attempted to calm her down, tempering her emotion, but that only inflamed her rage. There was not much I could do, and I blamed myself for having intruded upon the innermost part of her life: her heart.

On that couch, we kept on crying into each other's arms. I wanted to leave her there and walk out. Fear crippled my legs, as tears sprang out of my eyes. It was getting late. We now huddled under a large multicolor throw, licking each other's face. I stayed with her until Ella came back. Then, Judy walked me outside. As we reached the driveway where she had parked her BMW, we held hands one last time, leaning on the passenger door, reliving the rosy moments that we had spent together, slow dragging on dancefloors, swimming in the crescent beaches of Miami, dining in fancy restaurants and making love in the wee hours in the morning. Finally, a little drizzle forced us to let go.

"Goodbye, chouchou," I murmured.

"Goodbye, my love," she muttered.

I walked off, back to campus, and she retreated to her front porch. When I reached the corner, I turned around to get a last glimpse. She was still on the porch, watching the man she had loved fading out of her sight, out of her life.

Chapter 8

Judy left, and with it our shared memory of a short and intense romance. Weeks after her departure, I stayed away from the usual spot behind the chapel. This unintended consequence, however, was an opportunity to focus more on my studies. Academic performance preceded everything.

Some classes were easy to manage; others, however, required intense practices to keep up with the pace, especially computer languages like Formula Translating System (Fortran) and Common Business Oriented Language (Cobol). I found Fortran to be my toughest challenge because of its numeric and scientific computing. It was designed for engineering applications. My main goal was to become a software engineer. In those days, the computer lab was a busy place. Students milled around the room, some standing in line with their assignments written on coded cards to be read by huge PC machines and others sat at their computer desks trying to finish up their assignments.

There were times that some of my assignments would keep me awake at night thinking of possible solutions, and when I thought I had the answer, I would jump off the bed and head straight to the bathroom to take my shower. I would leave early for school before Nana woke up to be one of the first students in the computer lab, and I would celebrate when my answers proved to be the right ones. Because of situations like this, Nana would prepare lunch for me the night before so I would not wake her up in the morning. I would call her from the lab to let her know that I had arrived safe and sound at school.

"Did you eat?" she would ask.

"Of course, I did," I would reply with laughter.

Although Pedro and I had one course together, we could rarely find time to joke around, except for when we went to the gym for a workout. Some collegemates would join us in the jokes, including some of my Haitian friends, then we all would head for the cafeteria to eat delicious sandwiches over iced tea. The academic year ended on a positive note. My grade point average rose to 3.5. I shared the good news with my sister, who rewarded me with special breakfasts of Haitian patties, chocolate milk, and bananas. She did not understand the GPA concept. All she wanted was for me to advance to my last year.

"You'll be a senior next year, and I dream already of graduation day and the beautiful dress I would wear," she would say while poking my face like Manman used to do.

I spent the summer working at the little restaurant, and sometimes with overtime, saving for the last year. I never returned to Las Calinas, although I was tempted to do so. I had applied and was approved for the students' assistance program. All summer long, I spent time with some of my cousins and Pedro, going to the Saturday night parties and picnics on Haulover Beach Park, having fun.

Summer was over, and the new academic year had begun. I felt no major challenges, studying. Maybe it was because I grew more confident about my cognitive ability, and graduation was no longer a distant dream. One Friday afternoon, I sat in the cafeteria, head bent down, studying for a math midterm exam. In my mind, there was a race to grasp the final chapter of some difficult math concepts that were keeping me awake at night.

Abruptly, a girl ran past me. She ushered a sharp shriek like that of a mockingbird, and swiftly disappeared behind the wall that divided the cafeteria from the bookstore. Her giggling— piercing, silly, and brisk— left an indelible mark in my heart, and my brain felt like it had just been struck by lightning. It was on fire. The breakneck noise brought back the memory of Régine, a girl I had been madly in love when I lived in Haiti. Before I left, I had made a vow to remain faithful to her. It was a vow on which I swore never to renege. I promised that I would return, and like the fairytales end, we would live happily ever after.

In the early days, we kept a loose form of correspondence that faded over time as reality set in, and Haiti was no longer the place for me to find and secure the love of my life. My love for Haiti and its subjects was reduced to the patriotic malaise from which most Haitian immigrants suffered. It was a feeling of intense nostalgia, self-inflicted punishment, and a dull sense of resignation. A strong sense of guilt suddenly wrapped my soul. I lifted my head to steal a glimpse, but she was gone. I jumped out of my chair and zipped down the vast hallway leading to the front steps. I pushed the double doors open, but I could only catch the faint reflection of a tall, slim girl in an overall garment and white t-shirt, moving speedily. She soon disappeared amid the cars in the parking lot. Her hair was short but wavy. The nape of her neck was textured in the hue of a café au lait, like that of my Haitian girl.

Was it Régine? I wondered. It was not impossible, for the streets of Miami had long been taken over by two groups of refugees: Haitians and Cubans. From the Overtown section of Miami to the very edge of the university, one sensed his universe was reduced to the dimension of those who lived in the land of the zombies. Every sidewalk was filled with dazed onlookers walking aimlessly, chirping like stray birds, in a suppressed, clamorous mix of Spanglish, Creolglish, and Frenglish. "*Régine,*" I screamed out of desperation.

My scream caught the attention of Pedro, with whom I shared this story before. He was standing by the entrance of the cafeteria. "What's wrong, Vinco?" he asked.

"Nothing," I muttered. "By the way, I'm not feeling well this afternoon. I'm going home," I added, going back to the cafeteria to retrieve my studying materials.

"Do you want me to take you home?"

"No. I can drive."

"You look disturbed, and your eyes are red and moist. Are you sure you can drive? You can leave your car here, and I can drive you home."

"Don't worry. I'll be fine." Pedro walked me to the parking lot and waited until I got in the car and drove away.

#

I was not a coward. In fact, I braved my fear all the time, testing how strong I could be in the face of adversity. Even my

112

sister recognized this fact, although she rarely admitted it. Lately, though, she seemed to have been quite preoccupied with my sense of gloom. One morning at dawn, before the first woodpigeon chirped and flapped its wings outside my window, there she was, sitting at the head of my bed, by my pillow, stroking my hair. To acknowledge her presence, I widened my eyes. She smiled, sending her rosy cheeks radiating under the first ray of daylight, which trickled in through the windowpanes. Her beaming smile greeted me, and I stretched like an eagle, spreading arms and legs, seeking the strength needed to face the brand-new day.

Her softly tender hands soothed my hair with a sisterly care that I had not felt in years. She then tightened her lips and landed a kiss on my forehead. "Bonjour, my young prince," she uttered, patting my back as I was sitting up. Her hair, unkempt and bedraggled, was a complete mess. Still in her nightgown, her tiny frame made its way into our small kitchen to make breakfast. I quickly jumped off the bed, put on my jogging suit, and headed for a few laps at a nearby park.

I gently closed the door behind me, but I could not stop my sister's hum from following me to the front porch. She used to like mumbling old folksongs from the tropics while making an omelet.

"Don't be late, you hear? Or your egg will be too *cold*," she reminded me. There was no need for me to reply because her warning had long become an early morning tease.

I jogged along, nudged an edge of Mexican Heathers, and veered toward 62nd Street. Along the way, I caught a glimpse of Mr. Jackson, pacing up and down his long back porch, his hand folded inside his robe, as usual.

"Where ya finin' go? You ain't gonna *comb*?" he yelled at Travon, his chubby teenage boy on his way to the bus station to catch an early ride to North Miami Beach High School, where he was a senior. Insensible to his father's jab, he kept on going, his hair truly in a mess.

"I *done* told you twice, I ain't *tell* you no *more*," Mr. Jackson forcefully reminded his son.

I laughed uproariously. He was a middle-aged man, maybe in his early fifties because he had gray dots sprawling all over his wavy hair. A Creole from Baton Rouge, Louisiana, he spoke in a funny way that amused me so much. Like many times before, he did not notice me watching with unshared awe.

I jogged on, and Notre Dame d'Haiti Catholic Church appeared across from me. I waved to Larémise and two other women going in for an early morning prayer. Larémise was overweight and ambulated like someone with prosthetic legs. Larémise had a daughter who was very close to Régine, and that was enough to bring back my anxieties of yesterday. I hid behind a music studio on the edge of the street and let her walk until she reached the church's back door.

Chapter 9

"What time is it?" My cousin Jean-Dennis growled from the base of his throat.

I never bothered to reply, for the alarm clock hooked onto the wall was adjacent to his bed. He came down from Fort Lauderdale due to a job offer and was staying with us temporarily. I simply strolled to my room and shut the door, leaving him to wrestle with the time. From the warm quietude and serenity of my bedroom, I heard him bolt out of his bed, sniffing the air as if looking for the strength to face another day. I could hear him stretching and flapping his arms like wings of wild birds in the morning twilight. Then I heard him tiptoeing toward the bathroom. Within seconds, he switched on the shower, which sounded like a river in full fury. Then the shower stopped as abruptly as it started, and the whole place turned cold until his hums came in to perturb the dull stillness of the apartment.

Five minutes later, he was gone, and I was left alone in my self-absorbing solitude. I lay in bed, eyes closed, and in my mind, Régine, the girl with whom I was madly in love, was all over me. She was tall, slender, wearing an expression of sentimentalism.

Her ginger lips twitched as we ambled hand in hand down the sugar sand beach of L'ester Dere near our hometown in Haiti. Régine still lived in a far-off land, some one thousand miles away, and she could not be the girl I vaguely saw at school. I had no means to reach out and hug her, to squeeze her in passionate, bewildered embraces. I began to dream about the good old times, wishing I could morph into a migratory bird and fly to her. These sentimental stirrings only enflamed my suffering.

Jean was both a cousin and a close friend, the only person I could share my sudden misfortune with, but he was hardly ever home. When he was not at work, he was at Augusta's, a sleazy, oversized woman who lived on 55th Street and who managed a nighttime flourishing *fritay* business. Jean was always on the go. Like domesticated chickens, when he finally came home to roost, it was already the wee hours in the morning. Each night I waited in vain just to drift into the misty fog of sleep, dozing on the couch until my sister came and dragged me into bed.

But I was not a namby-pamby bald head—an expression I learned from Mr. Palotay, a neighbor, when he was disciplining Mathieu, his troubled young man. Never was I going to let myself be consumed by the purplish-blue of outright melancholy. Dwelling in the fog of elusive love was an experience I never wished to have. I believed nothing could better drag the sanity of a man into moral and intellectual bankruptcy than his awkward habit of romanticizing his vicissitudes.

The next day was a holiday. I woke up early. After eating breakfast, I got dressed and ready for a morning walk. The sun had already risen behind the lofty buildings across the street when I stepped onto the front porch. Hordes of pedestrians crisscrossed each other down the sidewalk, going in both directions. Chatting and laughter echoed in an uproar of

116

idiosyncratic sounds, mixing Spanish, Creole, and English. It was a scary dissonance. I made my way west toward North Miami Avenue and then south to 59th Street to see my friend Robert. In gigantic strides, I walked down, passing a few cottages built off the ground, which looked ostentatiously out of place for a fast-moving boulevard like North Miami Avenue.

At the edge of where North Miami Avenue intersected 59th Street, a tall young lady with an exposed belly and tanned skin suddenly grabbed me by the arm and planted a kiss on my left cheek, leaving a stamp from her fat moist lips on my face. My heart jumped, feverishly spooked. I peered into her eyes to get a good glimpse of the stranger. She did not let go of my arm, nor did I want to wrestle with her.

"*Vinco*," she castigated. "So glad to see you. Look at you! Still have this cutie, handsome face." She finally set my arm free, but now started poking me in both cheeks like children do to their baby dolls. I did not know what to say. "How's Nana doing?" she asked. I was now reassured. She knew my sister's name.

"Nana's doing great," I replied with a broad smile.

"You live around here, Vinco?"

"Yes."

"Do you have a phone number?"

"I'm afraid I don't. But if you give me yours, I'll make sure I pass it on to my sister."

She quickly wrote it down on the back of a business card and handed it to me. I folded it into my shirt pocket without looking. She then strolled north, but just before she reached the next block, she called to me, and I turned around to face her.

"Tell Nana my sister Nadège would *love* to hear from her," she said, throwing kisses to me.

The reference to Nadège helped me solve the puzzle. She was Caroline, an empty-headed bimbo who lived in some community near Miami's Overtown. Later, Nana told me she had befriended her because Caroline had an eye on me. But Caroline was related to Régine, and that was enough to reactivate the deep sadness that I thought I had just left at home.

I decided to forgo Robert's. Instead, I sauntered toward a little park just off the road. There, I sat on a rough, rusty bench, head bent down, and Régine's shadow once again took a nosedive to land in the deepest level of my heart, sweeping my soul. I could see her and me on a romantic promenade near the shorelines of Saint Louis, where L'Ile de la Tortue loomed in the distance. Beneath a clear blue sky and over turquoise water, seabirds flew in stunning formation. Régine's oval, golden-honey face rested against my chest as we sat below the sea grapes, contemplating the shallow waves, near and far, sending foam to crash against our naked feet. I could hear the whimper of her suave voice making the infinite vow to win against the odds. I could feel the tenderness of her smooth hand stroking my hair.

Suddenly, some children on a swing set behind me made a sharp scream, which brought me back to reality. I leaped off the bench and left in a haste. Dodging the avenue, I meandered east toward Northeast Miami Court, which stretched all the way to 54th Street. In the distance, I saw a huge crowd of dark profiles, growing steadily in slow motion as I marched on. This prompted my attention. I then took aim at the crowd. I quickened my steps, and at every intersection, a legion of people mostly dressed in red and blue, the color of the Haitian flag, herded down toward 54th Street.

Groups of home dwellers congregated in front porches on both sides of the street to watch the proceeding. Petrified toddlers held onto their parents, who, with blazing eyes, watched the long lines of Haitians heading down to where the main event was taking place. These parents looked no different from those who live at the raw edge of poverty. As I reached the site of the events, my eyes began to lurch in restless glances, watching a sea of politically charged people stretching to more than a mile, singing patriotic songs, and throwing insults at the Duvalier regime in Haiti.

In an instant, a feeling of *joie de vivre* took hold of my body. I had never been in an ambiance like this before, where everyone converged into one location to express their anger, their emotion, and their determination to get rid of the Creole fascists in Haiti. A tall woman everyone called Jésula, who wore a knee-length, high-collared blue dress held at her waist by a red leather belt, suddenly rose from the center of the gathering and pushed her way toward a makeshift stand and then took up position, facing the crowd. A pair of large hoop rings adorned her coffee-colored face. She kept a firm grip on a cordless microphone and, like an imposing songstress, began to twist and stir. She sang:

Haiti Chérie

You're like the old bamboo

You can only be bent

But never be broken....

I felt completely thawed. That song had kindled my heart and built a deep trench in it. A kind of patriotic romanticism suddenly descended in my fragile being, bringing with it feelings of awe

119

and shock, love and hate, along with an instant thirst to avenge the thousands of victims of the Duvaliers' brutal regime.

The gathering was the latest reaction to news reports coming out of Haiti confirming despicable atrocities being committed by the *tonton macoutes*, the Duvaliers' secret police, against an increasingly emboldened Haitian people now unafraid to take on the fascists from their niches. When Jésula was finished, Father Gérard Jean-Juste, head of the Haitian Refugee Center of Miami, walked up the stage under showers of applause. She handed the microphone to him. Father Jean-Juste was a real enthusiast with an unflinching stare who spoke expressively and critically. His oily face was aglow under the harsh, piercing rays of the late-morning sun. Wearing a black jacket over his Roman-collared shirt, he was preaching a kind of Renaissance humanism while leading the fight against immigration officials on behalf of thousands of Haitian refugees, myself included. I was fired up. The father spoke for about fifteen minutes. The crowd's energy soon resumed. It lasted until the sun went down, and the crowd dispersed. Then, I reclaimed the road back home.

Chapter 10

Tu m'avais dit un jour que seule la mort pourrait nous séparer. Ce soir, alors que nous sommes en train de vivre nos derniers moments avant que tu partes pour ce long voyage, je veux que tu saches que peu importe le temps que cela prendra, je serai là, à t'attendre.

J'espère que tu reviendras dans un avenir qui ne sera pas trop lointain. Comme tu le sais, Vinco, c'est dur de vivre dans une solitude sans fin. N'oublie-pas que tu es mon sublime amour, un amour pour lequel je suis prête à sacrifier la plus belle saison de ma vie: le printemps.

Once you told me that only death could do us part. Tonight, as we are living our last moments before you set off on this long journey, I want you to know that no matter how long it takes, I will be here waiting for you.

I hope you will return in the not-too-distant future. As you know, Vinco, it's hard to live in endless loneliness. You are the love of my life, a love for which I am prepared to sacrifice the most important season of my existence: the spring of my life.

The last time Régine and I met under the starry sky of Saint Louis, she folded these lines written on a golden piece of paper. In the heat of wild caresses, she slid it down inside my shirt pocket. Then, my sadness was too deep to take a serious aim at the narrative displayed on the wrinkled paper. We said goodbye more than a thousand times, and each time was reinforced by a barrage of kisses that further deepened my gloom. That night was exceptionally fluorescent under the glow of the moonlight. A faint breeze blew just enough to fondle our faces, which were coated in the trademark of innocence. I held her firm against my chest, tickling my hands under her beige garment and desperately trying to find a pair of imaginary wings to fly with her to the unknown.

Régine was a girl with an oddly stoic form of resistance and an admirable sense of kinship. Once she told me that the feelings she harbored in her heart for me were indescribable because she always felt small and vulnerable in my presence. It was something she had never experienced before. Every time we were together, she felt *so* softened, melted in sweet surrender, and that her suddenly furrowed face was just a farce, a weak line of defense in the game of love and chivalrous romance.

"I can't believe I'm revealing this to you," she muttered timidly.

I said nothing. I was too moved to utter a word. I thought I was in a dream. I was in flushed delight!

There was a quick silence after such an amazing revelation, these passionate words that escaped her mouth. Then I started to lick her face, clumsily trying to wash away the tears springing out of her eyes and streaming down her golden cheeks. But these were tears of mixed emotions, ushering a sense of liberation, despite the ever-present caution of optimism that shaped her character. Since then, her capriciousness had faded.

#

It was early Friday afternoon in mid-December, and I had just come home from school. The Christmas carols were blasting on the airwaves. I stepped out into the backyard, taking pleasure in watching the neighborhood children caroling around. This reminded me of the old country during holiday seasons and how Régine and I used to go promenading around the town's square, eating ice cream while gazing at dozens of children parading up and down Main Street with their thin, bright, multicolor lanterns in hand. It then became too much to absorb, and I drifted back inside.

My sister had not yet arrived from work. Being home alone terrified me and going to my room did not bring comfort. Régine's picture was displayed in a bronze frame on top of my end table, and the minute I stepped into the room, her anxious stare greeted me. It was a constant reminder of our vow, despite the odds. To be consumed by solitude is the most nightmarish of despondencies.

After so many sleepless nights, I decided to deal with Régine in expeditious gallops. The pain was too raw. I paced over the picture, grabbed it by the frame, and dove under my bed where I kept an old suitcase. I violently pulled the lock and, in a swift gesture, buried Régine in effigy, along with my French poetry collection and other sentimental missives.

"I'm a free man now," I muttered to myself.

Or so I thought. In the process, the frame was broken, the picture went adrift and carried away by the wind gust from the

123

ceiling fan, which forced my poems and other important letters to scatter around the room. I stepped backward and snatched the floating picture. Then, a quick glance put me face-to-face with *"Tu m'avais dit un jour que seule la mort pourrait nous séparer."* (Once you told me that only death could do us part.)

Guilt-ridden, I could not stop the tears from streaming down my cheeks. Nor could I wrestle with the selfishness sprawling within me. Régine may have been a thousand miles away, but her words still hurt. Every word pounded my heart, like a double-edged dagger, oozing its way into the deepest end of it. Beaten, I collapsed at the foot of the bed.

A few minutes later, the phone rang. It was my childhood friend, Tipous, on the other end.

"*Sak pase*, man?" (What's going on?) I asked, stretching out of bed.

"Nothing, man. Listen, there's gonna be a meeting at a house on 2th Avenue, near Pastor Robert's church. I'm told Sansaricq is expected there. You wanna go?"

"Sure, why not."

"See you there, then."

Tipous's call saved me. It shifted my mind into something new, more concrete. Since the large demonstration in front of the Haitian Refugee Center, politics had begun playing a pivotal role in my young life in Miami. Second only to my school obligations, I was always present in most afternoon gatherings there. The crowd was not always large, however, no matter the day, small groups of Haitians would be found assembling either on the sidewalk or inside a small room next to the refugee center's office; where Father Jean-Juste shared the latest news from immigration officials or news from Haiti.

In a rush, I took my shower, got dressed, and walked out. Sansaricq would be there at six, so I decided to maneuver toward Liline's. She was a cousin of mine who had been in Miami *way* before I had arrived. She was a true Haitian American girl with all the skills to blend into both cultures. I liked her very much, and we were very close, but she was too unreserved. She could never keep a secret. For that, I never shared my inner demons with her. She was short with a strong frame, but downright stylish with sparkling black eyes. To supplement her height deficiency, she wore high-heeled boots into which she folded her tight blue jeans. Her hips swayed at every step, and young men flocked to her trail.

She lived five blocks down with her parents, but her room extended from the main house, in the back end. A little pathway led to it. When I arrived that afternoon, for some odd reason, I did not bother to knock. Instead, I snuck toward her room. I heard the soft pitch of feline moaning as if in romantic distress. The closer I got, the louder the moaning. I glanced through her window and I was stunned to find Liline naked from the waist up, her breast was in Jean-Marie's mouth, sucking it. Jean was a friend from school.

A shrewd young woman, Liline tightly folded both hands between her legs, leaving Jean-Marie no chance to unlock them. I laughed. Despite her easy-going attitude, she was skillful in the game of courtship. She knew how to lure a man to her niche and keep him there. As she told me later, "He gets no piece of the pie until he does what's right."

"And what's right?" I asked.

125

"He can only get it at the wedding night. I'll never be an extra toy in a man's collection," she proudly replied.

"You sound so clever, like a pro in the game, a bit cunning too," I teased her.

"I may be cocoonish, but not cunning," she replied in her usual triumphant manner.

And she was right. They got married a few years later.

Disappointed, I decided to go back home. Along the way, I ran into a group of expatriates from my hometown in Haiti. "*Ti kouzen!*" exclaimed a boy named Bertin. *Ti kouzen*, Creole word for little cousin. It was how young folks from Saint Louis called each other. With him were Ronel, Lanlan, Guy and some others. I was thrilled. We chatted all the way to 65th Street, where Bertin was seeing a girl named Doudoune.

Bertin was very athletic and jovial, molded in a chocolate tan. He loved to stroke his wavy hair, which was combed backward to make him look like an intellectual. Bertin was different from the pack, for just like me, he was struggling to find the perfect balance between revolutionary fervor and school obligations. We found common ground in discussing politics, our great disdain for the fascist regime of Haiti, and our fired-up attitude guided by an extreme sense of patriotism.

He and I, and the rest of the lads joked all the way to the front door of Doudoune's place, an imposing white building that housed four apartments. Doudoune lived upstairs. As we walked through the iron double door, Doudoune met us at the bottom of a stairway built in the middle of the building. She was jet black with squinting eyes, thin lips, and long glossy hair that waved down toward her shoulders. She threw a subtle smile as Bertin presented her to me. A light-skinned girl with strange purplish-brown eyes stood a pace behind her. Doudoune pushed her forward. She smiled timidly, and Lanlan drifted apart while instructing her to follow him. Later, Ronel told me her name was Monnette, and that she was Lanlan's sweetheart. We chatted there until it was time for me to join Tipous at the Sansaricq's gathering.

It was early evening, around six p.m., when I arrived at a small house fenced in by a chain-link fence on Northeast 2nd Avenue. I met Tipous and Abner, another childhood friend, standing by the fence eyeing the road, waiting for me. When they saw me, they quickly opened the gates and let me in. We hugged each other, and went inside. About a dozen folks were also there, but Sansaricq was nowhere in sight.

A chubby man with a scarred face was entertaining the group. Tipous told me the man's name was Paul Sylvestre; he was Sansaricq's spokesperson. Fifteen minutes later, the front door pushed wide open and a tall mixed-race gentleman with a trimmed beard and dark mustache waltzed in. He wore an olive-green uniform and black shining boots. He held in his hand an M-16 rifle. Four well-armed men guarded him, all dressed in military fatigues—two on each side. Sansaricq seemed to tower over everyone in the room, which stilled as all eyes now glued onto that mixed-race man, who was moving around the room in an authoritative manner.

"Brothers, I'm here to let you know that within a few days, the Duvaliers will be history. We've just led a successful 'drop' over Port-au-Prince. The entire population was showered by thousands of leaflets telling the people that Duvalier will be arrested on January first."

I rose to my feet and everyone followed with rounds of applause. Sansaricq spoke for about an hour. He told us stories about his history of rebellion against the regime in Port-au-Prince, about his well-armed fighters, and about how he was going to put Baby Doc on trial for crimes against humanity. After that bombastic speech, he spent a few minutes taking questions from the elated group, and then, in a theatrical exit, he walked out of the room as mysteriously as he came. The audience dispersed, and Tipous, Abner, and I went home.

I spent the remaining days leading up to the new year suffering from an unexplained anxiety, like living on the edge, waiting for news from Haiti confirming Baby Doc Duvalier's arrest. It was wishful thinking. I was naive, and I believed the man. On New Year's Day, no such news came out of Haiti. Extreme sadness took hold of my mind. I got on the phone and called Sansaricq's operation headquarters. A gentleman named Richard Brisson, another of Sansaricq's spokespersons, picked up the phone.

"Don't worry young man," he said with an air of profound assurance. "In a matter of hours, Jean-Claude Duvalier will be under arrest."

I knew Brisson, a mixed-race man who was expelled from Port-au-Prince in November of 1980 for being part of a leading movement headed by journalists who were not afraid to take on the brutal regime in Haiti. A few weeks later came the shocking news of his death along with several other expatriates who followed Sansaricq on a failed mission to overthrow the government of Haiti. I was devastated. So too were most Haitians in Miami. I soon learned Sansaricq was merely a mercenary, a Haitian Rambo, who took these men on a suicide mission. In Haiti, hope had turned into despair. The memories of my relatives and the townsfolks living like zombies under the watchful eyes of the Duvaliers' secret police came back to hunt me. For the moment, freedom and democracy would have to wait.

Chapter 11

It was Saturday. Normally, I would call my friend Tipous for a stroll down the streets of Little Haiti, visiting local bookstores to buy new releases by Haitian authors, but it was raining. Tipous would not join me. So, I decided to drive downtown for a little Christmas shopping. Despite the rain, shoppers swelled the streets, looking for bargains. Luckily enough, I found a spot right in the heart of downtown, where the place was the busiest—not far from the courthouse and a block away from Macoris, Miami's famous bazaar where delicious pastries could be found. My stomach growled, as I had not had lunch, so I headed straight to Macoris. I stepped in, and the place was swamped with buyers laughing, chatting, eating, creating an unwanted, distracting commotion.

Standing in line, which stretched all the way from the main entrance, served no purpose to me. I decided to forgo the pastries and walked next door to a shoe store, hoping to get a fashionable pair. Like the rest of downtown, bargain hunters packed the place. There were so many good deals, I could not believe my eyes. A girl of medium height walked up to me. She worked there, and she wanted to help me find the perfect size for a pair of a Pierre Cardin shoes. Although we exchanged words in English, her filtered voice quickly triggered long-repressed memories. Another episode of that stubborn remembrance struck me, and I began to take a frantic aim at this girl, searching for Régine through her hazel eyes, her shapeliness, her delicate features—voluptuous, coquettish, and flawlessly exuberant. She was a fair-skinned mixed-race girl with a divine sense of humility. I struggled to maintain my composure.

"What's your name?" I asked.

"Michaela," she replied, widening her eyes as if taking a deeper look at me. "And yours?" she queried in a kind of an interrogative rebuttal, turning her face sideways.

"Vinco."

"Vinco, do you still want the pair of shoes?"

"Yes, but I want something more."

"What's *that?*"

"Your friendship."

"Sure, why not? I've seen you before."

"*Where?*"

"At school, in the cafeteria chatting with your Haitian buddies." She burst out laughing and led me to the cash register where I paid for the shoes.

I was ready to leave, but another round of heavy downpour pinned me down. Then, for some reason, she stood in front of me as if vetting my big, black, and nervous eyes. "This stupid rain," I muttered.

"Don't worry. I'll walk you outside," she tittered, grabbing an umbrella from behind the counter, unzipping it to shield me from the pelting raindrops, and she walked me all the way to my car.

"See you at school," I said.

"You bet," she replied and turned around, heading back inside.

Her act of humbleness coupled with her exotic features paralyzed me. From my car, I watched her feline movements, sharp and assertive, as if she was trying to walk between the drops. Régine had been resurrected through Michaela, and I was as happy as a child waiting for Santa's sleigh.

On Monday, I was with my friends in the cafeteria for lunch as usual. She then walked in, molded in a pair of blue jeans and a dark jacket. She did not notice me, instead she seemed preoccupied, looking for something. I pulled away from my friends and sauntered off, moving toward her. She glanced across the vast room and saw me coming.

"*Here* you are," she chuckled.

"So glad to see you again!" I said, totally overjoyed.

"Me too," she said with an awesome stare, peering into my eyes. "I knew I was gonna meet you here."

"Is that right?" I asked, inviting her to join me in line to order lunch.

She smiled and edged closer. I understood. She did not have to reply. So, we trailed in line side by side. We both ordered tuna. I offered to pay, but she refused rather politely. The weather was nice, and we agreed to take our seats outside at an isolated table under a coconut tree. There, we sat facing each other, and I took pleasure contemplating her beauty, her suave voice, her seductive smile.

"Vinco, *Vinco*? Am I pronouncing it right?"

"Perfect."

"Michaela," I said briskly.

"Yes, Vinco."

"I have to admit. I've never been in front of such a unique beauty."

"Don't embarrass me. You *also* have some unique traits that impress me."

"Really? What are they?"

"I never share my thoughts and feelings with someone I barely know. But I will say this: You're very handsome."

"Thank you for letting me know. That reassures me."

"What do you mean, Vinco? You never believe in yourself?"

"Of course, I do, but hearing this from a girl like you pleases me tremendously."

"What's your major, Vinco?"

"Computer Science. And you?"

"Business."

"I hope next semester we're classmates."

"Vinco, we don't have to share the same classroom to maintain a friendship. The fact that we sit here talking…."

"You're right."

"Listen, I have to go. I can't be late."

"See you after class?"

She did not reply. She was in a hurry. I sat there, taking a last glimpse of her curvaceous figure undulating through waves of students, rushing to get to class. Then, I got up and walked off. I did not see her after class, and I had failed to ask for a phone number. The next day, I was the one who went to look for her. I found her at the bottom of the stairs as she was about to go up for her early morning class. She could not stay and talk, but we agreed to meet again for lunch.

At lunchtime, she showed up right on schedule with the same enthusiasm as the day before. Always punctual, she seemed sincere like Régine. I surprised her by buying lunch for both of us. Reluctantly, she accepted it, but with the agreement that she was going to be the one to treat me the next day. All week long, we kept our punctual and delicate rendezvous at lunchtime, unconcerned about the emerging gossips. Our mutual emotions grew stronger at each meeting, and it was with a bittersweet chagrin and shivering lips that we said goodbye after lunch.

Before long, Friday had arrived, and I did not know what to say. I knew spending two long and painful days without our lunchtime chat would ache, but I hesitated to ask for her phone number. Surprisingly that day, she arrived before I did, waiting at our usual place outside under the coconut palm. As soon as she noticed my shadow weaving up to her, she walked out of her seat and met me halfway.

"What *took* you so long, Vinco?"

"Are you saying I'm being tardy?"

"Yep."

"Look at your watch."

"Do I need to?"

"No, my dar—" I stumbled on the other syllable. She understood but made no attempt to reciprocate. In the middle of the courtyard, we held each other's hands, our fingers intertwined.

"Let's go order our food," I commanded.

"No, I've already ordered," she replied. She was excited.

"Okay. Just wait for me there, and I'll try to order as quickly as I can."

"No need to, Vinco. I've ordered for the two of us."

I was about to thank her for the treat, but she preempted me. "Let's go sit," she giggled, pulling my hand along the way.

So, we strolled to our little spot and sat adjacent to each other, as normal. This time, she ordered a large tuna sandwich in a golden wrap. She unwrapped it, and I noticed it was not cut in half. We both then held the sandwich on each end and began to bite and chew, **looking into each other's eyes. Each bite,** emotionally charged, seemed forced us in a dazzling race to **meet each other's lips. Midway, she burst out laughing** out of excitement, letting go of her end of the sandwich. I also dropped mine. I was nervous, not knowing if her laugh was a demonstration of a spark of love she could no longer conceal, a show of the chemistry now taking hold of her heart and mind. I grabbed her hands, intwining my fingers with hers in a loose grip.

"Mica, it's Friday already," I said suddenly, peering into her hazel eyes; they had turned purplish-blue under the high noon sun.

"Yeah. But it'll be Monday soon," she reassured me.

She directed her attention to the vast courtyard, taking aim at a goose honking in the midday air as she led her goslings to the edge of a small pond behind the cafeteria. Michaela jumped to her feet, and ran after the babies, trying to catch one. I also got up and ran after her.

"Be careful, Mica. Mother goose will jump on you!" I shouted.

On the warning, she halted her run and turned around to rejoin me just as her leg hit a rock and she stumbled, about to fall. I lurched forward and grabbed her by the elbow, trying to steady her. Mica stirred in my arms, and her yellow floral skirt twirled and fluttered about her knees. We both lost balance and collapsed on the grass near a flowerbed. She lay on top of me, and I held her by the waist. A breeze came through and forced dry leaves to scuttle into the air. Some of them landed onto her soft, golden wavy hair, and I released my hands from her waist to chase away the falling leaves. Our lips met, and she closed her eyes. What followed was an avalanche of ardent kisses.

There, we remained, interlocked, mindless of the world around us. Only a distant honk from the geese across the pond brought us back to reality, and we realized we were alone. The students were gone. The cafeteria was emptied. We got up and strolled back to our small table. She was blushing in embarrassment. I now sat near her and let my arm rest around her shoulders to mitigate her uneasiness. For the first time, she did not seem to mind being late for class after lunch, and I was thrilled to have been granted some extra minutes, golden for a boy who had just secured the greatest of catches: winning the heart of a princess. We managed to finish our sandwich and once more our lips met, finishing the sandwich. I then walked her to the front door of her classroom.

Since that day, Michaela and I became so attached to each other, symbiotically linked, that only a thin blue line remained before we were morphed into two wild turtledoves like the legendary characters in the old French *comédie musicale, Pierrot and Colombine*. Convinced, most of my friends at school thought she had become the girl of my life. Between classes, we stayed together, chatting, and promenading along the rose garden near the cafeteria. On weekends, we were at the movie theater inside the Omni International Mall. Then afterward, we would go for a romantic stroll near the bayside, amid groups of other couples, contemplating the Biscayne Bay and the waves, extending all the way to the crowded shores of Miami Beach.

An amorous twosome, inseparable, always entwined in each other's arms—life, in an unexpected twist, had new meaning. Yet, I never formally expressed such unexplained feelings of awe. All that changed on a Friday afternoon at school. It was gray, windy, and cold, like the typical South Florida weather in December. Consequently, we decided to take shelter inside the library before going home. We went in and found a quiet seat at the deepest end where nearby conversations could not disturb us. As usual, she looked relaxed and had her long arm wrapped around my neck, but she refused eye contact. Instead, she squinted her eyes toward the glass window adjacent to us, through which she seemed to be scrutinizing the wild lilies tossing in the wind.

"Vinco," she said abruptly, turning around to face me this time. "I had a sleepless night," she added.

"Why was that?" I asked. My eyes grew feverish.

"What are we?" she questioned in a low but firm voice. Her piercing eyes fixated on me as if hungry for an answer.

"What do you mean, Mica?" Mica was now how I lovingly called her.

"Are we fiancés? Are we simply opportunist lovers, intruding into each other's lives?"

My lips quivered as I tried to come up with an honest answer. After almost one long minute, I uttered timidly, "I don't know how I could live without you, because words alone will never be enough to describe what I'm feeling inside, right now."

"*Really?*

"I swear, Mica. But don't believe my words. Watch what I do."

She smiled, a smile that was about to burst into explosive laughter until I stopped her, reminding her of where we were. I lurched forward, going for her lips, and she dissolved into my arms.

"Mica, you know?"

"What is it, my love?"

"We've been more than just friends for some time, sharing each other's ups and downs. We've entered the forbidden land where regular friends are not permitted to venture. From kissing, to squeezing, to enjoying moonlit promenades, we've done it all. I know I'm not perfect, and neither are you. I could be a nuisance sometimes because I could sense it in our *unique* friendship. Irresistibly, I hound, urge, pinch, and your monosyllabic replies hurt me to the core. But I think I can now safely say these childish attitudes that we all find in human behavior truly define the bond that we share," I confessed.

Her eyes turned watery. "Vinco, do you really mean everything you just said?"

I did not reply. I simply pulled her toward me and pressed her hard against my chest. I had never felt her so melted. We sensed the whole world was reduced to our own little space inside the library. We did not care whether we were being overheard. Michaela gave me the sensation that we had entered the rosy stage one of every romance.

I trembled in fear because I knew I remained halfhearted. I loved her, but only as long as she continued to remind me of Régine. My heart sank. I found myself wrestling against the fox I swore never to become in any romantic relationship. How selfish I was, I felt. There was a long silence, but we were still interlaced. Suddenly, she pulled herself out of me. Our hands intertwined, while she stared at the long lines of bookcases filling the library.

"I'm going to the Dominican Republic this month," she said faintly.

"Are you *sure*? How come you never told me?"

"I didn't know, Vinco. My mom only told me last night."

"When are you leaving? Do you know?"

"Yeah. December fifteenth."

"Are you spending Christmas there?"

"Yes. And that's what killing me inside. Spending Christmas without you feels…"

"This is my greatest shock in a while."

"I'm sorry, *mi amor*. Forgive me, *por favor*. I could've stayed with my sister, but she's going, too."

"Where in the D.R. are you guys going? Santo Domingo?"

"No, we're not from there. We're from the town of Las Matas in the province of San Juan de la Maguana, not too far from the Haitian border. I was only three when I left the town, although I've always returned to visit relatives."

"I'm surprised you still have relatives there. You never told me this part of your story."

"Well, I'm telling it to you now. I'm not a hundred percent Dominican. I also have Haitian blood running down my veins. When I was little, I used to listen to my grandparents talking in Creole."

"You're *kidding*."

"Why? Mi amor, you're the last person I would be lying to."

These last words struck a chord. I knew she was sincere, but I was not.

"My grandmother, Mercedes Montoya, was born in the border town of Dajabón, where she grew up and met a man named André Dimanche. According to my grandma, he was very handsome, and he was from the Haitian town of Ouanaminthe, right across the border. Dimanche was a successful businessman who managed a sugar-and-cotton business with offices in both Ouanaminthe and Dajabón. They fell in love and got married. They had homes in both places, but their main home was in

140

Ouanaminthe. There, my grandma learned to speak Creole and French. My grandpa was equally fluent in Spanish, French, and Creole. In 1938, Generalissimo El Jefe ordered the massacre of thousands of Haitians. My grandparents lost everything they had and moved farther inland to Las Matas."

"Who was Generalissimo El Jefe?"

"Rafael Leónidas Trujillo Molina, a feared man like Papa Doc in Haiti."

"I understand now. Many historians wrote about the historical hatred between Haitians and Dominicans. Haiti dominated and even occupied the eastern side of the island of Hispaniola for many years during the nineteenth century."

"Vinco, yes, it's true. My dad told me all about it. He also told me the Haitians then mistreated the Dominicans, and that's where the hatred comes from. And Trujillo used that hatred to order the massacre of thousands of Haitians who were living in the Dominican Republic for his own cruel and selfish interest."

"So, what happened to your grandparents when they arrived in Las Matas?"

"Some folks in town had denounced my grandpa for being a Haitian, and he and my grandma had to flee again in the middle of the night along with their three children—my mom and her two brothers. They took the road south toward San Cristobal, near Santo Domingo. My grandfather, although his skin has darkened now due to old age, was a man of a fair complexion. He used a dark wig and he disguised himself like *un compañero Español*. They paid a guy a fortune to take them there. Halfway through San Cristobal, they were stopped by secret police in plain clothes near the town of Sabana Yegua. The undercover

141

policemen separated my grandpa from the rest of the family and the driver." She paused for a moment to catch her breath.

"So, what happened?" I asked in horror.

"Then, they led him at gunpoint down a twisty road that snaked to the bed of a deep, wooded ravine. One of them pulled the trigger, but no bullet came out. They were drunk. They had killed so many Haitians earlier in the day, and they didn't realize their guns were empty. My grandpa seized the moment to give his life a second chance. Out of desperation, he jumped on both men and strangled them to death. When my grandpa walked out of the woods, he found my grandma lying face down in the car. She was unconscious. He wrapped his arm around her and was licking her face until she regained consciousness. They ordered the driver to make a detour and to maneuver toward the town of San Jose de Ocoa, where they stayed for a year in hiding at a cousin of my grandma's. When things died down, they returned to La Matas. They're very old now, but they still live there."

"Why didn't they go to San Cristobal ?"

"It was too risky. They feared the road down might have been swamped with hitmen."

"Something puzzles me in the story. Why didn't they cross the border to Ouanaminthe in Haiti, which was closer than Las Matas?"

"I asked that question myself. But my mom told me that she and her brothers were in Las Matas with their grandparents. So, they felt they had an obligation to go there to rescue their children they loved so much."

"Baby, you have quite a story. I wish I could have an opportunity to meet your grandparents someday."

BITTERSWEET MEMORIES OF LAST SPRING

"I'm sure you will. But let's go now. It's getting late."

We left the library and strolled down toward the parking lot, where we got into the car. I drove her home that day in a quite unusual manner. We exchanged a few words, but the joy and laughter that often characterized the ride were obviously absent. She leaned on my shoulder as I drove. Her eyes brimmed with tears, but they were tears of joy that lovers shed after reaching a milestone. My heart was racing as I remained tightlipped. A painful feeling of guilt took ownership of my broken heart. I had never felt so remorseful in my life. It was almost impossible to utter a word. Two blocks from her home, I slowed the car, and she straightened herself. When we finally reached the front gate of her home, she turned to face me and held my hand.

"Promise me that you'll never leave me," she voiced.

"Mica, I believe I've already said it, back at the library," I replied feebly. "I'm not sure I can ever live without you."

I took out my handkerchief and wiped the tears from her eyes. We walked out of the car and I led her up to the sidewalk. There we said goodbye, my legs anchored to the ground as I watched her unlatch the gates. Then I walked back to the car and drove home. That day was the first time I was able to measure the depth of my love for Michaela. Before, my eccentric behavior left me no room to rationalize love in its truest form. I never thought, even for a quick second, the prospect of losing her could have had such a profound effect on me. The firmness of her words and the dramatic story of her grandparents stirred up in phenomenal fashion the dormant fibers of my heart, the love I desired since I left Régine back in Haiti. Without warning, this love, holistic in its form, had struck an awakening—awesome, dazzling, but also nerve-racking emotion.

143

Chapter 12

Since that day with Michaela, I ceased to believe my relationship with Régine could be rekindled. There was irreparable guilt that I had to learn to live with, perhaps for the rest of my life. More and more I was entering the icy cave of sentimental ruthlessness. On December fifteenth, Michaela flew with her parents to her island of the Dominican Republic, and I was left alone to wrestle with the sin that was eating away my soul. From Las Matas, she called me whenever she could, but she wrote soulful missives every day about the newfound happiness that kept her heart radiated. Some of those letters were mailed to me. However, she kept most of them in her diary, to share with me when she returned home to Miami.

Every day, I grew more and more sorrowful and sometimes chagrined by this unexpected, dazzling vibe. *Can Régine be replaced?* This question haunted me. As my emotion for Régine faded, my amorousness for Michaela flourished like red roses in the mornings of spring. When I did not hear from her for a day or two, I transformed into a withered hibiscus waiting to be watered. I craved her smile, her voice, her magic touch that set my heart on fire. I went to sleep each night with her sentimental postscripts from Las Matas wrapped under my pillow.

To keep my mind from sinking into a state of despair, I became further involved in community activism, spending most of my afternoons on 54th Street near the Haitian Refugee Center, talking about politics and pondering the latest news from Port-au-Prince. For Haitians in the diaspora, there was a two-pronged struggle: The battle against immigration officials to gain work permits for the thousands of refugees who arrived every day on the shores of Miami, and the fight against the Duvalier regime and its secret agents scattered all over South Florida.

That famous street had become the center of the Haitian struggle for equality and human rights in Florida. It was Little's Haiti's main business district which contained doctor's offices, restaurants, shops, and boutiques. Invaded by Haitian immigrants every afternoon, that part of 54th Street was off-limits to regular traffic, for the Haitian Refugee Center was located right in the middle of it. Understandably, business owners were feeling the pressure as sales dwindled. Their echo had reached the city police department, which always dispatched a contingent of police officers to clear the street, putting barricades on both sides of the road to allow traffic to come through, effectively keeping Haitian demonstrators on the sidewalk and threatening to arrest anyone who dared jumping over the barricades. As always, the police presence did little to intimidate the demonstrators. The barricades were overrun as the cops were submerged under the weight of hundreds of politically charged individuals swelling the street.

The holiday season, however, had caused many of the demonstrators to focus their attention elsewhere. Their main aim now was to find a little cash to send to their relatives back home.

Only the true believers still came, myself included. The cops had the upper hand.

Two days before Christmas, on a Wednesday afternoon, I showed up as usual. To the east, the sky was still gray, as foams of clouds ballooned in the distance. There was rain in the forecast, but no rainfall could scare us away. We numbered about a dozen and were led by a daring preacher named Pastor Jean, a muscular man about six feet tall who spoke with such a rage that it was impossible to overlook the depth of his conviction. The doors of the center were closed, and Father Jean-Juste was nowhere in sight. We congregated on the sidewalk, kept at bay by the barricades and the stone-faced cops who stood firm in the middle of the street, regulating traffic.

Pastor Jean led us in a prayer that was soon followed by patriotic songs, denouncing the daily injustices perpetrated by the fascist regime in Port-au-Prince, supported by the United States. A few more people joined us. Emotions ran high. All of a sudden, Pastor Jean raised both of his hands and ordered the singing to stop.

"Now it's time to jump over the barricades," he growled in Creole. "I'm gonna count to five. Then, we jump."

I glanced across the street, and the firm stand of the police officers and their sidearms frightened me. For a split second, I saw my parents and Michaela, to whom I swore never to let down. That fear quickly vanished when Pastor Jean began to count. "One, two, three, four, *five*." He jumped first without any hesitation, and the rest of us followed. My heart raced to 150 beats a minute when I realized what I had just done. Swiftly, the cops moved in, raising their batons to take on the demonstrators. We held each other's hands and formed what they used to call a revolution cordon. Stoically, we maintained our position. The police captain seemed reluctant to lead the charge against us, and our confidence grew. A standoff emerged, and an imaginary line of demarcation was imposed. Hundreds more residents in the neighborhood joined our ranks. The cops retreated, and we won the fight.

The day was at its twilight when I came home, exhausted. My blue and red t-shirt, the color of the Haitian flag, got soaked from a river of sweat still streaming down my body. No children played hide-and-seek on my neighborhood street that late afternoon. Even Mr. Jackson usually in his white robe, smoking his Cuban cigar, had already vacated his back porch. As I was about to step onto my front door, I heard rapid footsteps coming from behind. I turned around, and there was Travon. He was as sweaty as I was, smelling like a wild goat. His hair in complete shambles, weltering in the evening breeze; he looked quite nervous. He wore a white undershirt folded inside his blue boxers visibly exposed by his sagging blue jeans. When he reached my front door, he dropped his unzipped backpack, inside which I could see his wrinkled and dirty shirt in the middle of a slew of torn papers and a few disorganized books.

"*Travon*, what the hell are you doing here at this hour?" I asked him in a firm, low tone.

"Shhhh," he muttered. "I was in an afterschool football game. The game was so exciting that I lost track of time. Could you please walk me home? Otherwise, I'm dead meat." Twisting his big black eyes, he tried and failed to wipe out the heavy drops of sweats still welling down his sun-tanned cheeks.

I asked him to wait. I went in and quickly returned with a paper towel and handed it to him to clean his face. Then, I walked him home. We knocked on the door. Sitting in his divan, Mr. Jackson immediately rose from his seat and made a giant leap toward the door. I preempted him before he had a chance to say a word.

"It's me, Mr. Jackson. Travon was with me. I was helping him with some math concepts he was struggling to understand."

"Huh, okay," he replied, opening the door to let Travon in.

Then, I rushed back home. As I stepped into the apartment, I saw a brown envelope on top of the kitchen table. At first, I thought it was a letter from Michaela. Then, I became suspicious because it did not look like the envelopes from the Dominican Republic. Wrinkled and bruised, this envelope looked like those from Haiti. At first, I ignored it, and like a stealthy chameleon, I crawled to my room.

As soon as I stepped in, the mellow voice of my sister called out to me. "Vinco, didn't you see the letter on the table?"

"No," I replied. Little white lie.

"It's from your *anmourèz*, I'm told." (Your little girlfriend.)

I did not reply, for I could not. My heart was beating so hard and so fast. I sat at the foot of the bed, grappling with my fear. There is not anything in the world that is more nail-biting than the feeling of guilt. When I finally mustered the strength, I pushed the door open, walked to the table, and grabbed the envelope, but still lacked the fortitude to open it. With unsteady legs, I ambled back to my room. Once there, I managed to rip the envelope open and pluck out the letter. A small photo of her was clipped on top of a folder. She was in a lovely floral dress, sitting alone on a rotten branch under the old sea grape tree, facing the island of La Tortue. I could see the foam on top of the waves in the distance, under the colorful splendor of the tropical sky.

When I unfolded the paper, it was a copy of the note she gave me the last night we met. Feeling like a beaten man, all my energy unraveled. Régine will always be Régine: the girl with a pristine character. After I read the letter, I began to think maybe the girl I saw at school could have been Régine. Perhaps, I thought, I overreacted.

Chapter 13

The holiday season was finally over, and Michaela was back from Las Matas. We were once more the amorous twosome, always on the hunt for evasive, sensuous pleasure. It was now early January. At school, everyone was busy, trying to get adjusted to the new semester. Graduation moved ever closer. Understandably, few of us could be found chatting, gossiping around the bookstore and in the cafeteria. Even the folks from the Haitian upper-class, who maintained a passive attitude toward school obligations, rarely congregated on the long sofa across from the bookstore.

These young men and women from Haiti, mixed-race and Arabs alike, constituted an exclusive group, arrogant and clannish, from whom most of us dark-skinned Haitians shunned. Victims of their upbringing, these kids manifested a grotesque form of nonchalance vis-à-vis their fellow Haitian students because they knew their Caucasian features could easily hide the African blood that ran down their veins. Consequently, to conceal their identity, many of them pretended to be Hispanics. Ironically, when they gathered among themselves, their Creole could be heard loud and clear all the way from the parking lot.

When a fellow Haitian with an ebony complexion tried to address them in Creole, however, they quickly replied in French with the aim of dominating and intimidating as they do in Haiti where roughly fifteen percent of the population can claim to be fluent in French.

One Thursday morning, I was running late for a philosophy class, and a girl named Chantale came from the opposite direction. "Vinco, Vinco, *Vinco*," she called to me almost out of breath.

I abruptly stopped. "What is it, Chantale?" My hand was on the exit door, for Dr. Cassini, my philosophy professor, accepted no excuse for being late.

"It's something I'd like to share with you, and I'm sure you'll be so happy," she said, lowering her voice to throw a bombshell. "Régine is *here*," she added. And she left, pushing her way through a crowd of students rushing to class.

"*Where?*" I shrieked.

"Let's talk about it later at lunch," she shouted and speedily faded behind the walls.

She spoiled my day. Tussling to regain my fast-dwindling strength, I managed to make it to class just before Dr. Cassini shut the door. My heart was racing, and I could not even hear him when he ordered the students to take out their notebooks for an important lecture on the Bolshevik revolution, a subject that had always been of great significance to me.

My head bent down, and my mind was now off the classroom I could see Régine making her emotional reproach. Already I could feel her punchy words of rebuke perforating my guilty heart. Self-inflicted guilt can only bring the harshest of pain

151

in any relationship. When Dr. Cassini finally dismissed the class, the commotion that followed drifted me back to reality.

"Did you take notes, Alfredo?" I asked a classmate and a friend sitting next to me.

"Yes, I did," he replied, throwing me a worried look because he had never seen me in such a distracted state of mind.

Before he had the chance to express his concern, I was gone, pushing and shoving my way through the crowded hallway. Out of breath, I reached the bookstore area, and Chantale was already there. Her gigantic hoop earrings seemed unsettled as she moved with restive glances, looking for me.

"There you are!" she cried upon spotting me coming. She burst out laughing when she saw my nervous shaking. "Calm *down*, Vinco," she said with a sarcastic utterance that further exacerbated my pain.

"Come on, Chantale. Tell me if this is true."

"You think I'm kidding?"

"No, I don't. I'm just hoping this is a joke, an early April fool."

"I know why."

"Why?" I asked, trying to be evasive.

"Because you're too afraid of facing the truth and you're too tied up with your Dominican girl." In a quick twist, she turned on me, taking aim at the coming and going of students buying schools supplies from the bookstore. She soon turned to me again, raising her arms, pulling up her ponytail to secure it with a brown elastic band. "Follow me," she ordered, grabbing my hand when she realized I was hesitant.

She led me outside through the back gate where we then crossed the street and walked down North Miami Avenue and onto 111th Street. At the intersection, she abruptly stopped and pointed to a little white house in the middle of a shaded courtyard.

"This is where she lives," she said, lowering her voice to make sure no one overheard her. "I'm told she arrived last month, and now learning English at an ESOL program for new immigrants at Lindsey Hopkins Technical School downtown."

I made no comment. I could not as I shuddered. My guilty feet searched in vain for the perfect rhythm to stroll along with Chantale. I tried to put forth the deceiving posture of an invincible macho boy, but my repressed, cold stare certainly unmasked the image I was trying to project. Chantale, who sensed my sensitive dilemma, said nothing . She held my hand like a concerned parent walking her dazed child to school. We went back to the cafeteria. There, she hugged me goodbye and went off to class.

I drifted to the couch, pondering my next move. "How do I face Régine when I'm so tied up with Michaela?" I muttered to myself. "What kind of a selfish young man am I?"

I had promised Michaela that I would never leave her, and she reciprocated by offering her heart in the purest form of honesty. She despised those who lied over strategic and sentimental matters because, for her, the trait of lying always revealed a soul predisposed to betray its soulmate. For that, I vowed to remain true to the end. The last thing I wanted was to make her feel deceived, shunned, and ultimately abandoned by the only man she had ever loved and for whom she was ready to face the toughest challenge in life.

153

The news felt like my heart had hit a grindstone. When someone is at the spring of his life, love takes center stage, and in every courtship, pristine romance is the dazzling prize to win. Unforeseen circumstances, however, can be the unwanted murk that strains and blurs the way forward. These thoughts kept racing through my mind.

#

A week later, it was around six-thirty in early evening when I got off the bus on my way home. My car was at the garage mechanic that day. At the entrance of 67th Street, the gateway to my neighborhood, I met Soledad, a restless filly, whose sole dream was to be a cabaret dancer. That day, though, she was not on her front porch, retooling her dancing skills. I rather found her a bit farther, leaning against the chain-link fence of her cottage home.

"*Soledad*, what's going on?" I asked.

She did not reply. Instead, she pointed to a large group of people who lined up on both sides, two blocks down the street. Her cousin, Henriette, a stone-faced young woman, suddenly came running out of the house with tears springing from her eyes. But Henriette too would not say anything to me. My sister, who befriended her, once told me she had been in an infinite novena, invoking all the saints from heaven to go rescue her boyfriend trapped in Haiti. I thought it might have been why she was crying.

So, I pushed forward with a more focused aim. The closer I got, the louder the crowd grew. Those who were not in the congregation simply stood by on the edge of the street, like bewitched zombies in the evening twilight. They stood with their jaws dropped and their hands folded behind their heads. Rodrigo Lopez, a grocery store owner, who liked to hum like an early songbird in the morning to herald the neighbors and let them know that he was already open for business. Mrs. Chang, a Jamaican-Chinese woman, who moved like an insomniac sleepwalker, that most of the neighborhood children were afraid of, thinking she was fiendish. Abboud Rashid, a Libyan nomad who finally settled here because, he said, Northeast Miami was going to be his final refuge in life. Yvan Yakimono, a retired sumo wrestler, whose goofy posture had made him the neighborhood's number one celebrity, and who dressed as Santa every Christmas Eve to sit in a homemade sleigh filled with gifts for the children.

My immigrant neighborhood came alive that evening, for all the wrong reasons. Everyone was speaking in low tones in their native tongues to ensure no one eavesdropped on their conversations. Tobacco chewers, slum dwellers, unwanted gossipers, dirty-foot vagabonds, and even stray prostitutes, who came all the way from 79th Street, had poured in to watch the ugly quarrel between a sleazy mambo and a greedy mother. I was still clueless when I walked through the crowd. It was not until I reached the intersection between 64th Street and Northeast Miami Court that I saw a thin, leather-skinned fellow named Onès, shaking his head and laughing at the same time.

"Oh God!" he said. "Why didn't she tell the man she wasn't a virgin?"

"What happened, *Onès*?" I asked.

"Esmeralda Rojas got caught in a big lie."

"Esmeralda, *who*?"

155

"The pretty girl who lives in that red house." He pointed to the house.

At first, I did not believe him, for Onès, a sacristan from my church, Notre Dame d'Haiti, was a heavy drinker, a polluted sinner who was always groggy from alcohol intoxication. Consequently, I edged closer to the house. There was Esmeralda, crying in a high pitch. Her white skirt was in rags and her face was awfully red, like a ripe tomato. This was the first time I saw this girl in such attire and in this deplorable state of mind. For as long as I had known her, she had always dressed in one specific fashion: low-heeled footwear, a black dress, and a church shawl. Folks on my street thought she was enshrined by the powers of divination, a kind of living saint, a devoted Catholic, and no one dared to question her immaculate character. However, beneath her tidy knee-length dress like that of an altar girl's lay a deep secret only she and her mother, Susana Rojas, a crafty woman from Panama, knew.

For years, both Susana and her daughter never worried, because they believed most men do not make a splash when they go to bed for the first time with a sexually experienced woman, even on the wedding night. Like most womenfolk in this immigrant neighborhood, Susana believed in coaching her daughter to wed highly professional men, their best chance at making what they called "the giant leap from Purgatory to Heaven."

In the quest to get rich and rich fast, Susana, who was tired of living the precarious life of a refugee, had succeeded in grooming Esmeralda to marry Panamanian millionaire businessman José Blandon, who only agreed to the deal on the condition that Esmeralda was a virgin. Her daughter, however, was anything but a virgin, and in fear of bringing shame to the family, she violently rejected the idea. She pleaded with her mother, begging her to forgo the deal because she could not imagine herself going to bed with someone she barely knew, let alone to allow him to penetrate the most sacred part of her body. Understandably, she hated Blandon, a man twice her age and a former pimp turned millionaire.

After intense pressure, Esmeralda reluctantly agreed, and to get rid of her reluctance, Susana reassured her daughter not to worry, for the stain of honor will be displayed first thing in the morning after the wedding. Susana then went next door to Fosia, a Haitian mambo, a voodoo priestess, and con artist, to help her stage the coup against Blandon. After a long night of invoking the African gods, Fosia gave Susana three spoons of permanganate folded in a plastic bag. Along with the permanganate, Fosia also gave the Panamanian woman a small plastic bottle of holy water that she stole from Onès, the sacristan. Fosia told Susana to go mix the permanganate with the holy water at the front gate of a nearby cemetery at midnight and then to go home and wait. Fosia finally told Susana not to hand the bottle to Esmeralda until after the newlyweds received the holy sacrament of marriage and they were on their way to their hotel room. To reassure a hesitant Susana, Fosia told her that most men suffer from a performance phobia on the wedding bed. They are so paralyzed by anxiety to the point that it is almost impossible to perform anything unless the bride comes to the rescue.

The wedding took place at a five-star hotel in the exclusive Miami section of Coconut Grove, inside the grand ballroom where more than a hundred fancy guests wined and dined over delicious Panamanian gastronomy. Susana was head-over-heels elated after she had scrupulously followed Fosia's instructions.

Now, she was waiting to extract the juice of her dirty Machiavellian work. After the guests left, Blandon took his wedded wife to a lavish suite on the seventeenth floor overlooking the stunning Biscayne Bay to spend the night in the pursuit of the stain of honor. Susana went home but left two men to secretly monitor the situation and to report anything deemed promising. She was playing her last card in the fight to get out of poverty, regardless of how cunning her action was and how cruel it was to sacrifice her daughter in the hope of getting rich. Understandably, she spent the night waiting with bated breath. The night came and went, and she heard nothing, not even from the men to whom she had paid a fortune to spy on Blandon's moves inside the fancy suite.

It was six a.m. the morning after when a taxi pulled into Susana's driveway. The driver walked out, opened the passenger door, and literally dumped Esmeralda, still in her nightgown, to Susana's front door. Blandon, an underhanded *chulo*, had foiled the coup. The news spread throughout the neighborhood like a tornado that struck without notice. When I finally managed to reach Susana's front gate, I found her and Fosia almost at each other's throats, blaming each other for the coup's failure while gleeful spectators looked on. To get a better grasp of the story, I went to talk to Laurette, Fosia's eldest daughter, who was a classmate from school. The second I stepped into the house, I came across a young woman dressed in blue jeans and a red t-shirt. Her hair, tightened by a visored cap, was combed in straight pigtails floating over her shoulders. Her back turned on me, she faced Laurette. It had been almost four years since I left Saint Louis, and meeting who I was about to meet was the last thing even remotely possible in my mind.

Upon seeing me, Laurette rose from a low chair and leaped forward to greet me. "*Vinco!*" she uttered. The young woman then turned around, and there she was, feet anchored to the ground, staring at me. I was speechless and numbed, only for a nanosecond. I stared back.

"*Régine!*" I yelped.

She showed no emotion as she began sizing me up from head to toe. I tried to step forward to hold her hand. She gave me no chance. Rejecting my presence, she headed for the door in quick, hurried footsteps, pushed it open, and strolled toward a black Toyota with tinted windows. I ran outside, but she was gone. I could not see the person in the driver's seat who drove the car off, bending around the street corner and soon fading amid the groups of onlookers still enjoying the ugly and peculiar story of Susana and her bitter quarrel with Fosia.

My heart was in shreds. I started to touch my face, my clothes to make sure that I was not in a dream. I went back to Laurette. "Why didn't you tell me Régine was here?"

"What for?" She replied interrogatively. Back in Haiti, Laurette and Régine were close friends.

"What do you mean 'what for?'"

"Listen, Vinco. As much as I like you and as much as I would love to see that you and Régine are back to normal, I will never be the facilitator. Contributing to Régine's suffering is something you should never expect from me."

"Why are you saying this? Wasn't it you who managed to convince her to click with me?"

"That was then. Now, the world has new meaning for her, and for me, too. Because of what you did to her, I was able to learn the tricks, the little white lies, the backstabbing and raw deceptions that push lovers to their dark alleys of no return. You promised her the world, and most importantly you promised to return. She believed you, and you betrayed her trust. I never shared with you my own personal struggle and the pain that always strikes me each time I watch you at school, parading around with the new princess in your life."

"You mean, Michaela?"

"Don't *play* with me."

Tears welled down my cheeks, and I turned sideways, facing the wall. She did not believe me. "That's the crocodile cry," she teased me. "*Ou kwè-m kwè-w?*" (Do you think I believe you?)

I said nothing more, but I hugged her goodbye. Then, I walked out. The golden, crepuscular rays of earlier in the evening were washed out to give way to total darkness. Going home, I moved through the crowd like a beaten young man after a school cafeteria fight. My mind was in turmoil. I felt ashamed, still bearing that irreparable guilt, a self-reproach I was now convinced was going to trail me as long as I lived. I wished I had gone straight home instead of going to see Laurette. Never in this fashion did I foretell such a dramatic encounter, braving this raw truth, facing Régine.

As I was about to get into my apartment, I met Travon and his mother, who were enjoying the show along with the rest of the neighbors. I asked for Mr. Jackson, and with a little nod, Travon told me his dad was inside, and his mother Mrs. Jackson instructed me to go in. I ran up the back porch. The door was ajar, but still made a little squeak when I pushed it wider to get in. A bit startled, I met Mr. Jackson outside the bathroom door, which was closed behind him. He had just finished shaving, and he held a small white towel in his hand. He wore a cotton shirt folded inside his khaki pants held by elastic suspenders. He seemed a bit unconcerned about the commotion outside.

I asked him if he was unaware of what was going on. He said he knew, but that was none of his business. He then inferred that many of the women outside may have committed worse than this poor girl. Edging closer to the window, he peered through the blinds to take a quick glimpse of the people outside. With a subtle smile, he turned around, facing me.

"The reality of it is, we may never know how they would react if they were in a similar situation like Esmeralda, nor will we ever know about their unreported secret dealings," he uttered vaguely. "You can strike water more than a million times, it will never spill blood, even with a machete," he added, dropping the small towel into a laundry basket and tapping on his suspenders to ensure they were tightened.

"You're right, Mr. Jackson." I gave a repressed smile. I knew this metaphor too well in my Haitian Creole. "*Kout manchèt nan dlo pa make.*" This means without catching a sexually active woman in the act, the odds of forcing her into an admission of guilt are next to nil.

"Obviously," he went on, "most men on the wedding night simply forgo the virginity issue, and if the bride is caught to have been sexually active before marriage, the groom just brushes it aside, as long as no one knows about it. This José Blandon must be a psychopath."

Usually, I would laugh deliriously, but this time I felt subdued. He sensed that I was tense, and he did not think it was because of what was going on outside. He led me to a little sofa

161

in the family room covered by neat tapestry throws. There we sat on opposite ends, facing each other.

"What can I do for you, son?" he asked, tapping on his bushy mustache to be sure it was properly trimmed.

"When you were young, did you ever find yourself entangled in difficult love stories?"

"I'm not sure I understand the question, son."

"I mean were you ever involved with more than one girl at the same time?"

"I see. Yeah, of course. Isn't that what young boys do?" He took an up-close look at me. "Back home in Baton Rouge, girls used to call me a playboy aficionado." He burst into an uproarious laugh.

"I'm not a player, but unforeseen circumstances in life have put me into some very unwanted predicaments. Before I left Haiti, I promised a girl I was madly in love with that I would return to marry her. But—"

He stopped me right there. "No need to continue. I've heard these stories more than a million times. Unsettled hearts can't keep promises on strategic matters. Romance in the teenage years are like seasonal flowers that sprout, grow, bloom, shed their leaves, and bloom again in the spring but always with new buds—different from the last season."

He got up and strolled toward the kitchen to fix some green tea. "I'm sure you truly loved that girl back in Haiti."

"I did, very much so. She's here now, but I'm already involved with another girl at school."

"Do you feel you still love her the way you did back then?"

"I'm not sure."

"You see, pure love can't be second-guessed. If you're unsure now, that means you've already turned the page. How about this new girl you're now seeing?"

"My passion for her grows daily."

"Young man," he said. "Follow your heart."

"Thank you, Mr. Jackson." I left.

Later at home, I started to rationalize what Mr. Jackson had told me. I realized there are issues in life that are easier to express than to solve. It is true my heart now gravitated toward Michaela, and her mannerisms continued to be the catalyst behind why I wanted to be with her so much. Now that Régine was in town, I had to wrestle with the reality of someday facing her, somehow.

Chapter 14

There is nothing rosy in the life of a foreign immigrant trying to break the cycle of despair without a good social support system. In my case, I had one, but my financial support system was weak, and I needed a job to sustain it. Like all young men of my age, dreaming played a key role in my daily living, and turning those dreams into realities was the toughest hurdle. There were a lot of objects I desired, and money was scarce. I was saving to buy another car because my little Volkswagen Dasher was getting old and had become more and more difficult to maintain. Half of my meager savings was used to pay for repairs. Having a job, however small it was, gave me a sense of socioeconomic empowerment, and for the first time I began to feel confident in my ability to help my relatives back home in Haiti.

"There is no life in one way," my mother used to say, because there are always pitfalls and setbacks on the road to success. If life could be unfair for average people, it is no doubt cruel for an immigrant struggling to establish a foothold in the host country.

I learned this when I showed up for work at the modest salad bar restaurant one afternoon, and my boss told me he was closing shop and that I had to find work elsewhere. At that moment, I felt like someone who had just fallen off the steepest cliff. Never had I anticipated such devastating news. Graduation took place in a few months, and getting another car would have been the best self-reward. The day before, I had high hopes for the upcoming summer: new outfits, sending money to Mom and siblings in Haiti, buying a used car, and money for my home obligations. I started throwing insults to an unfair life. It was goodbye new car, money for relatives, buying summer clothes. The bills? My sister would come to the rescue.

I stepped out of the restaurant, trying to stomach this latest blow. I got in my car and took off. When misfortunes befall someone, only courage, clear vision, and determination can bring back the sudden loss of happiness. For those who live at the raw edge of poverty, their existential realities are precarious at best. As these thoughts raced in my head, I made a bold move. For sure, my hopes for the summer had been unraveled, but my petty bourgeois aspirations were still strong. I intended to fight this latest wave of setbacks with all my might. A few blocks down, I pulled into the lot of a newsstand. I bought the Sunday edition of the Miami Herald, scavenging for employment opportunities in the classified section. Finding a new job was my top priority.

When I got home that day, I found my sister in the kitchen preparing dinner. Her usually cheerful face fell into a stormy glare.

"Why are you here so early?" she asked, keeping a firm hold of her wooden spoon as she halted the stirring from the rice pot.

"I lost my job," I muttered while walking to my room.

"Really?" she wheeled about and stood motionless, her wooden spoon frozen in mid-air, with grains of rice dropping over the stove burners.

165

Her face was tightly drawn. I did not reply. Instead, I continued on to my room where I lay on my bed face up, digging through the paper for a job I could do. There was nothing. Disappointed once more, I dropped the paper onto the floor and turned sideways, pondering. I was just about to drift into a much-needed sleep when my sister burst into the room.

"I forgot to tell you. Your Dominican girl called earlier and left a message for you."

"What did she say?"

"She wants you to call her as soon as you come home. By the way, your food is ready on the table."

Less than a minute later, the phone rang. I picked it up just when I was about to take my seat at the table. "Mi amor, you got me worried. I went crazy searching for you after class."

"But I left you a note with Jahaira, your cousin."

"Really?"

"Yep."

"You know, Jahaira is a hot-headed girl. Listen, Vinco, I wanted to ask you something special."

"What is it, Mica?"

"I'm still at school. Can you come?"

"Baby, I'm afraid I can't." My voice quivered.

"You sound awful. Is everything okay?"

"I don't know. I'm not sure."

"Mi amor, no need to explain. I can sense you're not all right. Can I come to see you?"

"How?"

"Though it's a long stretch, I can walk."

"No, Mica. I can't put you through this painful walk. I'm okay."

"See you soon." She gave me no chance to reply.

Fifteen minutes later, she was at the door. My friend Ronel stood by her side, hands folded inside his blue jeans, smiling.

"Here is your sweetie pie. You owe me one," he said in a gentlemanly fashion.

Michaela stepped in and landed a kiss on my lips. I then asked her to sit on the couch while I walked outside to talk to Ronel, who had to go.

"I'm so sad, man. I just lost my job," I whispered.

"*What?* I hear you, man. You'll bounce back, man. I've been there before. Remember, we're Haitians. We're like bamboos. We can't be easily broken."

"Talk to you later, man."

Ronel left and I shut the door to go join Michaela, inviting her to the table to have dinner with me. She hesitated. She then glanced across the kitchen and her eyes met those of my sister, who smiled at her reluctance.

"I made it, not him. Try it. You won't be disappointed."

"I'm used to Haitian food. I've just never had rice mixed with lima beans before."

"Trust me," Nana pleaded.

I then took a full spoon of rice and I slipped it between her sensual lips. On the first bite, she was overjoyed. Besides the rice, that afternoon my sister had made deep-fried red snapper, well-seasoned and breaded, a fish she knew I loved so much. My sister, who seemed to have had a great admiration for my girlfriend, seized upon the opportunity to make Michaela know how well she was appreciated. On top of the delicious meal, she made fresh-squeezed lemonade for us. Then, she left us for an early evening church service.

Shortly after my sister left, we retired from the food and went back to sit on the couch. I sat upright while she leaned on me, her hair, golden and wavy, sprawled about my face.

"Mi amor, I overheard what you told Ronel, and now I understand why you were sad."

There was no need for me to reply, so I did not. She raised her arms, entwined her fingers around my neck, and forced me down. We both lay facing each other. "Losing a job is not the end of the world."

"You're right, *mi querida*," I murmured, poking her reddish cinnamon cheeks. "Losing you would be a devastation," I added.

She laughed, and her eyes flickered. "Don't even think about it, mi amor." In a quick change of mood, she sat right up. "By the way, there's going to be a job fair at school tomorrow."

"Job fair?"

"Well, it isn't for the general public. It's only for students in the financial aid program. Since we both are, why don't we go together?"

I felt a bit relieved by that information. "Can we go back to the table to finish the food?" I asked her, but she was not interested. She began caressing my cheeks. "I don't think I can live without you."

"Me too, *mi querida.*"

"Listen, mi amor. I talked to my parents about us, and they're eager to meet you, but I told them I would have to discuss it with you."

Like a lightning strike, I bolted to one side. "That's a giant leap for me to take. You know that, don't you?"

"No, mi amor, that's not what you think." She pulled me toward her. "Last night, my mom asked about you. I don't think they're seeking a wedding engagement. Obviously, we're in no way ready to be married. I think they're anxious to see who I'm dating, and I'm confident they'll like you," she added.

How could I say no? She was fast becoming my guardian angel, attentive to my objectives, and committed to sharing my worries, my pains, my desires, my joys, and my misfortunes. I could sense the uncertainty in her struggle to grasp the depth of my commitment. I learned for the first time that affection is far from being in love, although no love can flourish without it. From that point on, there was no doubt in my mind that, like Régine, Michaela had mastered the sixth sense of human behavior. I knew her latest move was a strategic and sentimental charge to place me before a *fait accompli*, to get me to the point of no return in our romantic journey.

After she left, I began to think of my predicament: a young man with a divided heart, one half pulled toward Régine and the other solidly entrenched, with every bit of it embedded in my lovey-dovey entanglement with Michaela. I felt I owed a great deal to Régine, with whom I grew up and shared my childhood reveries. Since the night of our dramatic encounter, I had been trying to avoid being dragged into a semantic discourse ushered by a mutually inclusive nostalgia. I knew she was right to scold my presence after having crushed her heart when I reneged on my promise to return, or at the very least to uphold the intense relationship we had shared back on the island. More and more, I was becoming the lone romancero who moved through life, dwelling in the thickest fog of love. I needed to be myself. I knew I had a choice to make, and I had to do it quickly. Otherwise, my sanity would be as elusive as ever, my search for a new job would be tempered and my authentic engagement at school would be damaged.

#

Although Michaela was a business major while I was a computer science student, some of our general education courses happened to be the same. However, we never had the chance to be in the same class. I guessed she did not like the idea of sharing the same classroom with the man with whom she was madly in love. In fact, both of us agreed that it would not be a smart move, because our emotions would have interfered with the authentic engagement that was required to succeed. Between each interval, however, we would meet under the coconut trees right outside the cafeteria. Whoever came first would wait for the other, and we could not go to our next class until we had a quick chat, then kissed each other and went our separate ways until the next interval.

This had become a romantic routine, a sentimental boost I could no longer do without. Neither could she. Once, she confessed she was unable to grasp any instructional strategy without our little chat between classes. Henceforth, she did not have to explain how bad she felt when I went off to work the day before without checking in with her.

The next day around ten a.m., I met Michaela near the entrance of the library, halfway between the auditorium and the coconut trees. It was right after our first morning class and I was rushing to meet her. All of a sudden, I felt a hand dug into my shoulder. I whirled around, making an abrupt stop. There she was, in a taffeta outfit. She grinned and her lovely smile sent my heart soaring. She leaned forward, and I landed a kiss on her sexy lips. Her rouge lipstick coated my lips. We held each other as if we were alone, oblivious to the sea of students moving around us. Even the piercing sun rays were unable to chase us away.

"You got me so scared, *mi querida*," I uttered, stroking her twisted ponytail held together by black bobby pins while searching for her hazel eyes hidden under fancy Chanel glasses.

"Let's go. Some folks' eyes are glued on us," she muttered. She soon propelled me to the front of her and she followed behind as we navigated our way toward the cafeteria.

"Remember the job fair?" I asked.

"Of course. We have to be there in fifteen minutes."

This was just in time to order a tuna sandwich, which we did, wolfing it down in few giant bites. Off to the fair we went. In those days, Barry University constituted only three main buildings for instructional purposes, supported by the library building on its southern edge, noticeable for its decaying colonial windows. The bookstore and the cafeteria were in the same building, anchored in the middle of the schoolyard. Oblique from the bookstore and adjacent to the library was the university chapel, inside which the job fair was being held. Sandwiched between the chapel and the bookstore was the courtyard. Lush, green Saint Augustine grass dotted by a multitude of iron benches and a network of walkways adorned it. As we reached the yard, the line of job hunters stretched all the way to the main entrance on Northeast 2nd Avenue.

"Honey, we don't stand a chance," I said with an air of hopelessness. I was disappointed.

"We need to have faith, Vinco." She tried to put on her best face, despite knowing it seemed to be a lost cause.

Michaela knew I needed a job even more than she did. To put weight to her words, she asked me to wait right there. She did not want us to lose our spot as more students came, swelling the line. She said she saw some people she knew among the officials in charge of the reception area where they handed out the applications. I watched her pushing her way through the thick line of anxious job hunters, going to the bursar's office, which buffered the chapel and was separated only by a low concrete wall. Behind that was a back door, left swinging in the wind, that the job fair organizers used to interview prospective candidates.

It had been more than a half hour since she left and still there was no sign of her. The line was moving, and I was forced to move along with it, keeping my head high above the crowd, eyeing the path leading to the chapel across the courtyard. I fought hard to suppress both my fear and hope, holding them firmly on equal footing. I did not want to raise my hope too high, for fear that if Michaela's effort turned out to be fruitless I would not have to feel browbeaten.

Every ten or fifteen minutes or so, one of the organizers walked out of the chapel to allow more students to get in as others were leaving the building after their interviews. The scene was far from reassuring. The sullen faces vastly outweighed the few-and-far-between happy ones, which further exacerbated my worries. Every call for a new wave of students to come in brought with it an unbelievable commotion—heads turned, eyes widened, and feet thumped the concrete walkway in mounting anxiety. Ahead and behind me, some half-committed, sleepy-eyed students whispered among themselves. They wanted to give up.

Suddenly, I spotted her coming. She was walking fast. A big smile beamed on her face. My anxiety then lowered, and as soon as we made eye contact, she motioned me to join her. "What about the line?" I shouted.

"Don't worry. Come," she insisted with a smile that was dazzling and hopeful.

I leaped forward, and I ran to meet her halfway through the courtyard. "Follow me," she instructed.

"Did you get a better spot?" I asked.

"No."

"Then what took you so long?"

By then, we had already reached the bursar's office. She pulled me to the side of the main concrete porch. "I think we got a good chance at getting a job," she uttered almost out of breath.

"What makes you believe so?" I was perplexed.

"Well, I offered to volunteer, and they said okay. Sister Jean was there, and she and I interviewed more than fifteen candidates. That was what took me so long. Then, I told Sister Jean my friend and I wanted a job, too."

"What did she say?"

"She went to a room next door where they processed the applications. I watched her talking to Dr. Bernstein. She came back a minute later and told me to go to him."

"Doctor *who*?"

"Bernstein, the chemistry prof."

"I don't know him, but that's not important." I gesticulated in a pessimistic fashion. "So, what did Dr. Bernstein say?"

"He was very skeptical at first. Then, I told him Sister Jean sent me, and that I've spoken to her about a spot for me and my friend."

"Any guarantee?"

"He told me he can secure a spot for me at the library and one at the financial aid office for my friend. So, I'm not one hundred percent sure, but I think we got a good shot."

I could not hide the anxiety on my face. Before I could open my mouth to throw another question, she grabbed me by the hand. "Let's go," she said, cheering me up to suppress my skepticism. So, we held each other's hands and jogged down the porch to get to the chapel. As soon as we pulled the backdoor open, we came face-to-face with Dr. Bernstein, who was about to leave for a break.

A bald, bushy-faced man, perhaps in his midforties, Dr. Bernstein looked like a specimen from prehistoric times, like a caveman. Salt and pepper hair totally covered his face. "You're back already?" He cleared his throat and threw a distorted grin, but only at Michaela, ignoring my presence. His feline eyes

174

fixated on her as if I did not exist. He seemed disturbed as we were intruding on his cigarette break.

"Yes, sir," Michaela replied. I stood there, looking relaxed, showing no signs of eagerness or desperation for a work-study job.

"Come with me," he said, rolling his sleeves and loosening the knot of his necktie.

We followed him to his office, where a mountain of papers scattered all over a mahogany desk in an ugly, disorganized manner. On top of a pile of manila folders, a pocket-size container filled with snuff tobacco, which he quickly grabbed and dropped into one of his open drawers in a clumsy move to get rid of the strong and unpleasant scent.

"So, where's the friend you were supposed to bring?" he asked, still ignoring my presence.

"What do you mean?" Michaela replied. His eyes then squinted to my side as a sign of acknowledgment, but he made no eye contact with me as if I were an unwanted sunray that made him squint.

"I thought you meant a girlfriend."

"No, this is he, and he is multilingual, which would be a perfect asset for the financial aid office—I think."

"And what's your name?" he asked me this time, turning to me.

"Yrvin Lacroix." I was calm and serene.

"Are you a student here?"

"Are you talking to me?"

"*Yes.*" His face hardened, and for the first time I noticed a little bit of hair skewed to the side of what was left off his bald head.

I showed him my ID card. "I thought you were supposed to be a student here to even qualify for work-study here," I said in a calm but firm voice. "I didn't know if anyone in this town could come and apply," I added, looking at him straight in the eyes.

"You sound very sarcastic, boy."

I did not reply, and Michaela seemed relieved. She knew what I wanted to tell this man because once I told her that I allowed no one to call me "boy," except my parents.

"Do you understand *me*? Do you speak *English*?" He yanked out of his back pocket a tanned white handkerchief to wipe out dark traces of the snuff that coated both nostrils of his thin, pointed nose. Michaela and I looked at each other. We then became convinced he was a tobacco sniffer.

"Is this part of the job interview questions? My professors and my friends never ask me such questions, nor do they ever ask me to repeat when I speak to them," I replied. This time I was clear, precise and I kept my face neutral and relaxed, but I wanted to leave. No more was I interested in what was shaping up to be an embarrassing, shortsighted, or even a prejudicial semantic dialogue with Dr. Bernstein. His negative attitude was displayed only when he had to address me, which left no doubt in my mind that he was hoping I understood what he did not wish to articulate.

I took two steps backward, ready to walk out of the room. "I'll see you outside, Michaela."

She grabbed my hand and seemed also ready to leave. "Sorry, Dr. Bernstein, for disturbing your break," Michaela said, following me.

We strolled out of the office. He may have been stunned by our reaction. When we reached the backdoor, Michaela suggested that we go and speak to Sister Jean, who stood by the main entry door, supervising the application process. I refused.

We were about to push the door open when Dr. Bernstein called to us. "I never told you to *leave*," he crowed. We halted our march and stood still. When we saw him walking toward us, we walked back, meeting him halfway. He handed each of us a pass to go to our respective site. "I've already spoken to both the library and the financial aid office. Young lady, you report to work tomorrow after school. Young man, you go the FAO now. A lady name Joanne is waiting for you." He then returned to his office and closed the door.

Chapter 15

At the financial aid office, we met a young man with robust shoulders under his tight, button-down shirt. He stood behind the counter. "How can I help you?" he asked with an odd grin, raising the collar of his shirt to show off his muscles.

"I'm here to speak to Joanne. Dr. Bernstein sent me to her," I replied.

"You mean *Sister* Joanne." He stressed it out to make sure we were talking about the same person.

"I believe so."

"Here she comes," Michaela muttered, pulling away her arm that was wrapped around my waist.

"Sister Joanne, here are two students coming to see you," the young man at the counter called out to Sister Joanne. He spoke English in an arid, rusty way, rolling the "r" the way native Spanish speakers do.

In a quick glance at an open door behind the counter, I saw a petite woman, maybe in her late thirties or early forties, wearing a black monastic apostolnik. She was moving toward us, and when she reached the counter, she stopped.

"Pablo, go to your break now," she told the young man, who immediately walked toward the back room and disappeared.

She then turned to us and grinned. "Are you Yrvin Lacroix?" she asked in a polite and professional way which, in an instant, made Dr. Bernstein's acrimonious fashion a thing of the past. I was relieved.

"Yes," I replied.

"And you, young lady?"

"I'm just with him. He's my friend." Michaela smiled nervously.

Before I had a chance to explain why I was there, she preempted me. "I know. Dr. Bernstein called me."

She then told me to wait. She returned to the room and came right back with a folder in her hand. She flipped the folder open and took out a form. "Fill this out and hand it back to me when you're finished. And ring this little bell in the corner to let me know," she instructed me. Then, she was gone, shutting the door behind her. What she had handed to me was a form all students who had been hired were required to fill out.

In five minutes, I was done. Just when I was about to ring the little bell, she came through the door. Apparently, she was looking for something behind the counter. "You're done already?"

"Yes, Sister." I handed her back the paper.

"Come back tomorrow, anytime between classes to get your work schedule."

"Thank you, Sister Joanne."

As soon as we stepped out of the office, Michaela and I burst out in delirious laughter, hugging each other.

#

I returned home in the early afternoon feeling at ease, and for the first time I realized how stress and anxiety can literally steal someone's appetite. An urge to celebrate my new job took hold of my being. Like a hungry dog, I was sniffing the air, searching for the aroma of my sister's delicious Creole cuisine, which I had shown no interest in the day before. She was not home—away at work as usual around this time. I opened the refrigerator. The shelves were filled with uncooked food, except for loaves of bread, some peanut butter, and orange juice. I was not interested in any of those. I wanted solid food, Haitian food. I walked out again, got in my car, and drove off to Belle Fourchette, a Haitian takeout just off 82nd Street on North Miami Avenue.

Like every afternoon at this early hour in front of the restaurant, long lines of hungry folks filled the lot. Men, women, and children all came for their favorite *griyo*, a deep-fried marinated pork shoulder-cut into small cubes and served with fried plantain and a hot chili pepper called *pikliz* or pickles as a side dish. This was the dish I came for.

I pulled into the busy parking lot. Like the rest of them, I got into line, starving and impatient. This small restaurant had no seating area. It was a ramshackle cabin, a kind of outpost anchored in the middle of a vast empty lot. People were being served through a window. For each plate being handed out, the aroma filled the air and intensified my hunger even more. It was also a safe refuge for immigrants to talk about their ordeals, trying to make a living in the host country while struggling to support relatives they left behind in Haiti. Their stories were painful to listen to, and I, who could not dissociate their tales from mine, fought to hold back tears pouring out of my eyes.

Lamartine, a frail-looking man standing ahead of me, was talking to himself about his back-breaking job as a tomato picker in a vegetable field in South Miami-Dade County. He mumbled about his painstaking effort to send money to his wife and children back on the island and then save enough to pay for a room he rented from a friend. On top of that, the stooped man was trying to digest the latest news from home. His eldest daughter had wandered off with her eccentric boyfriend, and his sober wife had no clue of their whereabouts. He was blaming it all on his absence.

Behind me was a short woman with a solid frame in a long, blue garment that drew her bosom to giddy heights. "Germaine, *pitit*," (girl,) cried another woman driving an old Datsun. "How've you been?" she asked the woman behind me, edging her car close enough so they could talk.

"I'm okay, living day by day," Germaine replied with an embarrassing grin.

"You know, cousin, life in America is never easy, especially for womenfolk like us. How're the kids and husband?"

"Okay. Jean-Marie is now enrolled in a trade school. The girls go to Miami Edison Junior High. Finding a job here is the toughest thing, cousin. My husband just got laid off from his factory job in Hialeah. He's looking, but there's nothing yet. The hotel where I work on Key Biscayne is sending people home every day. My manager said business is slow now. They only give me three days each week, now, cousin. I want to apply for food stamps, but my neighbor Lucienne told me yesterday they don't give the stamps to new refugees. With all these problems, cousin, I got a letter from Haiti, from my sister Saintamise. Her man left her for a mambo in Bassin Bleu. She is now alone to feed four children, and my mother who is sick...."

Despite her gut-wrenching description, Germaine's tale drew no attention, except for mine as I stood next to her and the lady in the car to whom she was talking. Everyone had their own load, and Germaine's story was music to their ears. Everywhere in town, in this immigrant community, the tales were almost identical, tales of wayfarers and their struggles to survive, their gloom, their fear, their humiliation, and their hopes for an uncertain future. The lady in the car simply shook her head in disgust and threw a little nod.

"Hold firm, girl. Keep your hope high. Life will get better." She then sped away, making a U-turn and soon disappearing amid heavy traffic down North Miami Avenue.

After the long wait, I made it to the window, bought my food, and went back to my car. I could not even wait to get home. I ate the food right there. I was ready to drive off when I heard sounds of horn blowing. A group of jubilant Haitians were driving down, celebrating news out of Haiti, claiming the departure of Jean-Claude Duvalier, Baby Doc, had finally happened. The news came after twenty-nine years of a brutal dynasty that left a trail of blood too heavy to dilute. More than fifty thousand citizens of Haiti reportedly disappeared under the fascist regime. When the news reached the restaurant's lot, the lines melted like morning frost after sunrise. Everyone rose in a delirious state of mind. Foot-stamping, hand-clapping, and waves of happy cries filled the lot.

One by one, they vacated the restaurant, singing *La Dessalinienne*, the Haitian national anthem. Everyone headed for the Haitian Refugee Center. What started as a line of about a dozen vehicles, in which drivers and riders raised the Haitian flag in a cacophony of euphoria, quickly turned into a steady stream of cars, a caravan of gleeful riders, paralyzing traffic on their way down toward 54th Street. Stunned and spellbound, I followed them. I could not believe my ears and eyes.

In an instant, Little Haiti had completely transformed into a revolutionary land of free men and women. They came from every corner of that section of Miami to fill the main boulevard running down to the refugee center. From 82nd Street, it took me more than a half hour to get to where the main action was taking place. On a normal day, it would take me no more than five minutes.

Approaching 54th Street and seeing the commotion ahead of me, I swung toward 56th Street, two blocks off, and pulled into the driveway of a cousin of mine. No one was there. So, I got out of my car and jogged forward, pushing my way through an increasing, impenetrable crowd. People danced and sang patriotic songs while folksinger Kiki Wainwright kept the elated Haitians on their toes. Suddenly, a tall, fleshy woman in a vintage madras dress was propelled to the middle of the crowd where Kiki was performing. Her eyes were scarlet red, and a blue scarf wrapped around her swollen waistline. Kiki then halted the performance, and the crowd went still. I had never seen that woman before, but I could hear the folks around me whispering about her.

"Haiti is now liberated!" she shouted, raising her right hand up while tapping on the white headcloth wrapped loosely around her hair.

Many of my comrades and friends rushed to take position next to her. I saw Hervé, tall and slender, hand a microphone to her. Maxo, poet and revolutionary, stood right behind Hervé. He was ecstatic. Gérard and Rony were at the zenith of their moment of joy, despite the fact their frail ebony frames were tossed in the afternoon wind as they stood on the stand near the performers. The party dragged on for more than three hours. It ended only when conflicting reports out of Port-au-Prince started pouring in, and it became clear the celebration was premature, and Baby Doc did not flee the presidential palace as it was earlier reported. Later, Baby Doc released a video saying he was living and that he was standing firm as a monkey's tail.

The mood switched and faces crumpled; the crowd dispersed. On my way to the car, someone from behind called to me. "*Vinco.*" I turned around, and there were Chantale and Laurette, hurrying to meet me.

I was jubilant. It was the first time I saw Laurette since the crazy night when her mother, Fosia, and neighbor, Susana, were at each other's throats over the wedding scam. At school, I stayed away from them out of embarrassment over my estranged relationship with Régine. "*Where* have you been hiding, lover boy?" Chantale teased me.

"Well, lover boy has been too busy with his *mulatta?*" Laurette added without giving me a chance to reply to Chantale.

I avoided the conversation. I moved to the right side of the car and opened the doors to let them in. Laurette sat in the front seat next to me while Chantale sat in the middle, legs spread between the two backseats, neck craned forward so we all could talk together. "When did you girls learn about the false rumor?" I asked.

184

"It was around three o'clock when a friend called me and gave me the news. I called Chantale immediately. Within minutes, she was at the door, tellin' me about so many people already in the street," Laurette replied, adjusting herself in the front seat in a ladylike fashion.

"Why didn't you girls call me too? You know how passionate I am about Haiti," I said with a soured grin.

"I tried to, but…" Chantale mumbled, halting her sentence when realizing the gaffe she was about to commit.

"But *what?*" I raised my voice a little.

"I told her not to call you. And you know why, I presume," Laurette castigated. Her earlier smile now vanished.

"Let's not talk about this, Laurette. I've already confessed my guilt, and you also know how sorry I feel…"

"No need to feel guilty, Vinco. Things happen, and love can sometimes be circumstantial," Chantale interjected.

"What do you *mean?*" Laurette asked.

"Well, I think it's hard to nurture a relationship when you're so far away. Haiti is a long way, *girl.*"

"No, I screwed up with Régine not because of the long distance, but because of my own selfishness, and that's what makes my pain so unbearable," I replied with guilt-ridden caution.

"I understand, Vinco," Chantale said.

"*Shut up*, spoiler," Laurette chastised her.

"I mean I was too busy trying to survive, to learn English…."

"To *be* an American," Laurette said, shutting me up, too.

185

"You know, let's not let this sad story destroy our solid friendship. We have a lot more to lose in bickering," Chantale sighed. "Vinco's story is no different from so many others I know in my six years in this country. Just last night, I heard Eliannise dumped her fiancé in Haiti and went off with a white dude. As we speak, no one knows where she is. Simon, the boy on 71st Street, moved to New York last week to go living with a buxom girl he met through a mutual friend. Even his parents were stunned because he was scheduled to marry Alexandrine, his longtime girlfriend in Port-au-Prince. The worst news was the one from that wild turkey named Michou, who was caught sneaking out of a North Miami motel with a man twice her age. That news spread like wildfire last Monday. Despite her stinky moves, she still talks to that guy in Gonaives every day. Her cousin Nicole told me last night."

"I know like everything else in life, love is subjected to changes. But I'm not goin' to lie to you. Vinco's betrayal is harsh to swallow," Laurette admitted.

"I've been tryin' to reach out to her without success," I conveyed, attempting to prove my innocence.

"Since *when?*"

"*Stop* it, Laurette," Chantale shrieked.

"Listen, girls. There isn't a day going by without thinking of Régine. At first, I wrestled with myself. I wanted at all costs to maintain the relationship. As time went by, I grew distant. I rarely got a letter from her, and I didn't write to her either."

While chatting in the car, we had reached Laurette's front door without realizing it. Fosia stood on the front porch, a broom in her hand. Her eyes bulged as if they were ready to

186

escape their sockets. "Good afternoon, Aunt Fosia," Chantale and I greeted her with one voice.

"I'm fine, kids. Look at you, boy. Rose would be so happy to see her prince in Miami," she gaily said. I smiled, but I gave no reply. Fosia went back inside but left the door half open for Laurette, who was still in the car with us.

"Wait for me, Vinco. I have something for you." She rushed inside but came right back out with a small wooden box in her hand. Chantale's eyes widened in innocent bewilderment. She edged closer to me to get a better glimpse of what was in the box. Laurette got in the car. Her eyes surveyed the front yard, making sure no one was watching, as though she were about to hand me the hidden treasures of Saint Louis. "This is what Régine sent you last week, Vinco. She entrusted me to hand this to you."

I took the box and pulled its top. A mountain of letters was inside. Each missive was sealed in a brown envelope. As it appeared, there were more than a hundred of them, each addressed to me. My heart sank. My hands shivered out of emotion. Laurette kissed me goodbye, hugged Chantale, and exited the car. I lay the box on the passenger seat next to me while Chantale, inquisitive, kept staring at the box. I drove her home, a few more blocks down on the same street.

"I'm not gonna ask you to read them now. Go read and give me a summary tomorrow at school."

I didn't reply. I simply dropped her off without kissing her goodbye and drove home. My sister had just gotten home when I opened the door. She was on the phone and seemed to be engaged in an intense conversation with someone, but she lowered her voice and demeanor when she saw me. I walked over and hugged her with a brotherly kiss. She threw a broad smile and patted me on the back as I made my way to my room.

"Don't you want your food now?" she asked.

"Not yet. Don't worry. I'll get it myself when I'm ready."

I got to my bedroom, shut the door behind me, dropped my bookbag, and opened the box. The letters were arranged in sequence, from the oldest to the most recent ones. I took out the first one, ripped it open, and started to read. On the first line, I began to vibrate. I went through the letter like a hungry wolf. The lines were written with an unimaginable, feverish passion that left me bemused, wondering whether it was indeed my little Régine who penned these words, so sexually charged and with a raw and terrified paroxysm of desire. It was twenty-five pages long and designed with unbound descriptions, which made me sense her mind, body, and soul were somehow merged and buried in a trench that was built in my selfish heart. Everything she wanted to do the last night we spent together was enshrined in this sentimental narrative. She wrote of her endless and uncontrollable lust, of her urge to climax as soon as I kissed her lips, of her wildest feeling to go naked from the waist down and offer her pristine body to the man she will forever love....

The second one was nineteen pages long, a watered-down version, but it was just intense as the first one. The graphic design, however, was blurred in a poetic narrative crafted with a tenderized vibe of explicit, boundless emotion. I kept on reading, letter after letter, each jotted down in a progressive adulteration until they started morphing into romantic courtship messages. Then the letters turned into a collection of notes from a conspiratorial lover. Soon they became diaries of untold stories from a chagrined and abandoned girlfriend hopelessly yearning for the prince of her life to return.

One letter was an acrostic poem, blending my name with hers, fashioned in flawless rhymes, showing off her creative eloquence. That poem was written on a perfumed white paper dotted with kisses from her rouge lipstick that served as the backdrop to show that her dovish heart could still love, even as the passage of time threatened to assuage her unwavering faith.

In all, there were three hundred letters. The last ten, however, were simply replicas of each other. There were a few different words here and there, but the essence remained constant. They were tied together by a rubber band. A piece of wrinkled parchment separated this group from the rest of the bunch, and a small divider was taped on its top edge with the title Defeated Heroine labeled in bolded and cursive letters. It took her three years to amass this gut-wrenching collection. At the bottom of the box, there was a tiny note addressed to me. "It's all yours, now." And mine, it was. My heart was on fire.

By the time I finished reading, it was already four o'clock in the morning. I folded the letters back into the box and covered the top just as Laurette had handed it to me. I got out of bed and walked toward my dresser, where I buried the box under my undershirts in the bottom drawer. I then gently opened my bedroom door and tiptoed toward the table, and like the stealth of a sneaky cat, I took the food off the table and buried it inside a small supermarket plastic bag, closed it with a twister, and dumped it in the garbage can right outside the backdoor. I was in trouble if my sister realized I did not eat.

I went back to bed, lying face up, raising my pillow from the head of the bed, both hands folded under my head. I was deep in thought. Thinking about the first letter, a frenzied lust took hold of my mind. In a blur, faded souvenirs came back with a vengeance. The urge to reciprocate was unbearable. I grabbed my pen and let my heart and mind guide my hand to the wilderness of explicit romance.

So, I wrote these lines:

Régine,

I never question the depth of your love, and that's what's killing me inside. I know you have all the reasons to fight off every trace of sympathy that might still be lingering in your broken heart. Romantic backstabbing is one of the worst misdeeds in human interactions. Understandably, I make no apology for my selfish behavior. Régine, despite what you've come to believe, I want you to know my love never wilts. I acted this way not out of self-centered egoism, but because of some circumstances of life that most immigrants face in their first arrival here in this country. In the quest to survive, I lost track of time and, most importantly, I betrayed your trust. I know I'm no longer worthy of your pristine love.

Your collection of sentimental missives crafted out of the deepest of emotions left me speechless and plunged me into even deeper anguish. I know your profound and uncharacteristic feelings—pure, honest, vibrant—are long gone, and I don't deserve your forgiveness. Régine, I know I'm unfit to be the one at the receiving end of your good heart, but I also know hatred harbors no place in your soul. For sure, my actions have shattered your heart, but I'm convinced it is not yet filled with intolerable loathing. I have acted badly, and I'm sorry.

Sincerely, Vinco.

Chapter 16

The next morning, I showed up at school feeling groggy after spending such an unbelievable sleepless night. The stress was blatant on my face. As usual, Michaela was waiting in the far corner of the cafeteria. As soon as she saw me, her face beamed with pride. I walked down to meet her, and just before I reached her table, she rose from her chair and craned her neck forward. I landed a kiss on her sensual lips. She edged closer and wrapped her arms around me. I struggled to flash a smile, I failed because I could not hide the obvious fatigue on my face.

"Are you okay, *mi amorecito?*"

"I'm fine," I replied, turning my face sideways.

She walked me down the path that led to my classroom and there, we kissed each other goodbye. Just before I pulled the door open to get into class, she called to me and I turned around.

"Vinco, remember you can't look sleepy on your first day on a job. Fight the tiredness, okay? I'll meet you after class."

I did not reply. Instead, I threw a grin, raising my two fingers to make the victory sign.

Everyone was already at their seats as I strolled to the back and took my spot. Professor Cassini was very upbeat that morning. He stood tall in his unique manner, wearing a down vest and blue jeans. He was pacing up and down in front of his desk, one hand folded into his pants pocket and the other was stroking his unkempt hair. The lecture was on Marxism and its role in the Bolshevik revolution.

"The Russian revolution was one of the most powerful events in modern times," he began. "When a deprived people have run out of options in their quest to break free from the chokehold of exploitation, revolution becomes the course of last resort," he concluded, just as a boy named Mario from the front row raised his hand. In acknowledgment, Professor Cassini took two steps back and sat on top of his desk.

"Are you saying a revolution is an act of desperation?" Mario asked.

"No, it's an act of unbelievable courage. It's daring, stoic, with a laser-guided focus on bringing radical changes, overthrowing the current order in favor of the vast majority of the population, the deprived masses. That's why it's called a revolution," he replied with such an intellectual fervor that I almost believed he himself was a revolutionary.

"Can we say the State Duma introduced by the Czarist regime in 1905 was an attempt to beat back the revolution?" Inquired another student.

"Absolutely, but that move was met with a stronger resistance that ultimately led to the downfall of the last autocratic Czar, Nicholas II."

In a blur, the last vestige of my tiredness vanished. This was my favorite topic. I could not resist. "If the revolution was glorious, we must agree that the Marxist revolutionaries who led it were powerful men, and their heroism deserved to be honored. Right?" I asked.

"I beg your pardon?" He was unprepared for my question.

"Vladimir Lenin should be recognized as a Russian Toussaint Louverture, as the leader of the Bolsheviks. No?" I rephrased my question. This time, I was unequivocal.

"No, he was not. His Marxist ideology was incompatible with Western democracies."

"I thought Marxism was a science, not an ideology. Isn't it a fair assertion?" I asked. The class was still. All eyes were on me, for they had never seen me in such a focused state of mind, posing what seemed to be complex questions.

"Yes, Marxism is a science because it's based on scientific studies of society, describing the reasons and the danger of class antagonisms. Marxism fails, however, in its attempt to create a communist utopia, a society where everyone would be equal. The proponents of this idea in Russia failed in their attempt to uphold Marxist values. Instead, they used social contradictions, pitting poor against rich. They ended up creating a proletarian dictatorship."

"But if the new revolutionary government favors the working class and, as we understand it, the word *democracy* means power to the majority, then we can also call the new order a proletarian democracy. Right, Dr. Cassini?" questioned a young woman named Suzie who sat in the middle of the class, looking Professor Cassini straight in the eye, searching for an answer.

Professor Cassini began to sweat. Feeling besieged, his answers took an erratic, evasive nature. The questions kept coming, sharper and quite sarcastic. In the end, I could see the disappointment on his face. His intellectual charm failed to sway the class, and the students remained unconvinced. When the bell finally rang and the class was dismissed, there was a sense of liberation visible on his worried face.

I walked out of class, and Michaela was right below the steps. She was surprised and happy to see a rejuvenated "me". Gleeful, she moved up one step to greet me, wrapping her arm around my waist. Obviously in love, we strolled across the schoolyard and headed south toward the library. Just before we pulled the front door open, she halted my step while inviting me for lunch at the cafeteria. I told her I was not hungry, but she reminded me of my new job at the financial aid office. I was scheduled to start at two p.m. Earlier in the morning, I had gone to pick my schedule as Sister Joanne told me the day before. I shrugged it off, reassuring her I would be fine. So, we stepped inside and wandered down toward the back to take our seats as usual.

That day was anything but business as usual. The collection of letters from Régine had paralyzed me. There Michaela was, looking so innocent, so pure in the sincerest form of dovish romance. Mica wanted to share it all with me—her smile, her hazel eyes, her intellect, her boundless honesty, and, above all, her promising future. We sat there, interlaced like a pair of lovebirds ready to go on a morning flight. In a brisk move, I straightened and pulled her oval face toward me, peering into her eyes as if to rediscover once more the rarity of her charm. A thrilling and unexplained sensation suddenly took hold of my mind. Mica was a Caribbean beauty queen that every man would lust after, and I felt so lucky to be the one at the receiving end of

194

her love. That morning, I struggled to be the Shakespearean hero she had always desired of me, but I felt pinned down, trapped in a childhood fantasy. Could I trade this all for the Creole girl that continued to remind me of a time long gone?

With a timid bounce, Mica released herself from my embrace. "Why are you looking at me like this?" she asked. Her eyes widened as if insisting on an answer. Obviously, I could not deliver what she was seeking.

"You're my charming princess," I said, and she burst out laughing.

"You told me that yesterday." She threw a smile with an odd mixture of wariness and girlish capriciousness.

"And I will say it again this afternoon, tomorrow, and the day after...."

"*Amorecito,* you know something?"

"What is it, *amorecita?*"

Our fingers intertwined, she squeezed my hands. "I believe I was born to love one man."

"Baby, who is that?" I was quite derisive.

"It's a man named Yrvin Lacroix. And the day he leaves me will be the day that I love no more."

My heart sank. I was about to make a vow, but the image of Régine just flashed across my mind and my lips went numb. I lurched for a hug, searching for her lips. Eyes closed, she met me halfway in a delirious urge to have it all. I loved her, but I still could not free myself from the main reason why I had first approached her. I wanted to love her for who she was, not because of an invasive remembrance of a childhood dream, and what happened the night before did very little to lessen those invisible boundaries that had been keeping my heart from leaping wholly toward her.

In the quest to be free, I held her tighter. In my embrace, she seemed to have found the sentimental shelter that every woman dreams of. I could feel it. So, we stayed there, interlaced. In the stillness of the library, only the pounding of my heart punctuated the silence. I never felt so miserable, so slavishly submissive to the love of two young women, one of which I must choose. There in my arms, the tenderness of my hands and the beat of my heart simply transported her to the purple haze of sleep. We remained there until it was time to go. I walked to the financial aid office and she went back to class.

When I stepped inside the financial aid office, Pablo was there behind the counter. A young man about my age, he was tall and slender, skin hued in a light brown tan. He had big black eyes that threw precision-guided stares. He was in clean, starched khaki trousers, and he wore loose, straight-cut, short-sleeved shirts framed around the neck by cutaway collars raised up to the back of his dark wavy hair. He was very handsome, and he seemed to know it.

"*Here* you are!" He smiled. "I was waiting for you to go on my lunch break," he added, strolling out from behind the counter and asking me to take his seat.

"But you can't leave me on my own in my first day on the job. How do I answer questions from students who come in?"

"Tell them to wait for me."

"Why? I'm an employee, not a helper." I was very serious.

196

He stopped, pondering. He then turned around, quite disturbed. "Usually, they come in to learn about the status of their financial aid applications. What you do is to ask for their names and social security numbers. Then you type their names to look for the information from the computer."

Before I got the chance to say something more, he was already at the door, pushing it open and disappearing into the middle of a crowd of students on their way to the cafeteria. About ten minutes later, the back door squeaked, and Sister Joanne waltzed in. "Good to see you again." She grinned.

"Me too, Sister."

She edged closer, glanced over the computer screen as if to survey the work, and then walked toward the shelves where a multitude of papers, financial aid-related forms, and other office materials were stored. After a quick reflection, she walked right back to me. "Where's Pablo?" she asked.

"He went out on his lunch break."

"How long ago?"

"He just left, about ten minutes ago."

"When he returns, make sure he shows you where things are."

"He was doing that, but he was hungry..."

She laughed and quickly made the sign of the cross. "Poor boy. He'll never change," she mumbled. "We need to pray and ask the Holy Father to save his soul," she added, taking her rosary off her long black tunic and rolling the beads.

"What's wrong, Sister?"

"His soul needs to be rescued before the girls steal it from him.…. He always finds every excuse to get out of this office, and he's the first one to come in for his check on Friday morning."

I said nothing, but the suppressed smile on my face seemed to have made Sister Joanne understand that I took her words literally and was unexpectedly amused.

"This isn't *funny*," she crowed and then burst out into hilarious laughter. Just then, Pablo walked in, framed by two young women who quickly retreated out the door when Sister Joanne threw her pontifical stare at them.

"Sister, the papers were signed and mailed out this morning," he said, trying to pinpoint Sister Joanne's motive for being in the office at this hour, but the sister did not reciprocate.

Instead, she was sizing him up. A smile of guilt soon wrapped his face, and he sauntered toward the front desk and took position near me. The sister still stood there, giving him a motherly look full of pity. "You know what, Pablo?"

"Yes, Sister."

"There's only one thing you need."

"What's that, Sister?"

"You urgently need contrition. I'll send you to Father Ramirez's confessional this Saturday. I'll instruct him to impose penance on you and then give you the absolution. In my view, this is the only way to cleanse your heart from the demon that dwells in it." Sister Joanne then walked to the far end of the office and slammed the door behind us.

"What did you do?" I asked Pablo.

"Don't worry. Sister Joanne is very strict. She was only talking to me but was also talking to you."

"How so? She doesn't know me that much."

"Precisely. She thinks all young men are the same."

As we were talking, Laurette walked with two other friends who came to get their financial aid results. They seemed to be Hispanics. I had never seen them before.

"You work here now?" She asked.

"Yeah, since this morning."

"Good for you, Vinco. You need to tell me…."

"I know, Laurette. By the way, I have something to give you for her." I stepped backward, retrieved my note from the night before, and handed it to Laurette in a white envelope. With reluctance, she grabbed it from me and walked away with her friends.

I performed my duty on the first day as best as I could, despite my sentimental ordeals. I was a fast learner. I kept Pablo on a tight leash, forcing him to show me where forms and records were as Sister Joanne told him to. The sky was blue-gray, reddish at the edge when I left the school to go home.

#

The next morning was Saturday, and for Haitians and other immigrants from the Caribbean, it was market day. One venue, which attracted many Haitians in the Miami area, was the Hialeah Flea Market, an open marketplace sprawled between the western fringe of the city of Opa-locka and the beginning of Hialeah, a town in northwest Miami-Dade County with a large Spanish-speaking population. For Little Haiti residents, two major arteries led to that flea market: North Miami Avenue and 103rd Street, which ran like a clogged vein, extending all the way down until it hit a secondary street that gave way to the market's main entrance.

I always had mixed feelings going there, in part because of my sister who loved to shop at the Caribbean market but who systematically refused to carry the goods. I had to do it, and they were heavy. Worse of all, there were no shopping carts and the unpaved parking lot was not close to where the vendors were. If there was one place, however, that reminded me of the open marketplace back home in Haiti, it was this one. Logically, despite the traffic jam on 103rd Street, the horn blowing, and the heavy load I had to carry, I stood ready for Nana's first call on Saturday mornings.

It was a very windy morning, and the sun fought sluggishly to break through the gray clouds mushroomed in the far-off distance when my sister and I entered the marketplace. Hordes of bargain hunters roamed the place amid a disharmony of sandal clapping, yelling, laughing, and selling. A stew of brown, black, yellow, and red faces crisscrossed each other like pilgrims who had just been heralded to the Promised Land. Some folks seemed at the zenith of their joy, others looked dull, betrayed by their concerned faces soaked in salty sweat or caked by filth and grime as each wind gust sent clouds of dust into the air. I trailed after my sister's fast pace, trying to keep up with her. With nervous eyes, she cast her glare about for the best deals.

Many times, we were there not just to buy Caribbean groceries. A blousy dress, a pair of tennis shoes for me, a pair of blue jeans, all could be found at the Hialeah Flea Market for half the price of what they were selling at regular department stores.

A few steps down, we ran across a young man selling Native American garments. His eyes roved around as he looked for the prospective buyer. "How much is this quilt?" My sister asked, eyeing the multicolor fabric.

"*Quince pesos*," he replied, face aglow while pulling the quilt aside in full display.

My sister turned to me. "What did he say?" She asked.

"Fifteen dollars," I answered. I was not happy, knowing that my ordeal had just begun. I was simply resigned to another round of hard work. Without hesitation, she handed the money to the street vendor, snatched the quilt from his hands, and dumped it on my back like they do to baggage handlers in Haiti's pen stations.

The path soon curved around a thin alleyway filled with Haitian merchants, selling fresh vegetables, live hens, and multi-flavor colas. Like vultures descending upon roadkill, my sister dove into the stands, buying carrots, pigeon peas, plantains, coco malangas, sweet potatoes—enough to fill three grocery bags. Adjacent to the grocery stands, a woman named Mathilda, better known by her nickname Tilda, was busy selling fresh, hot Haitian patties stuffed with smoked fish. To keep my mind off the increasingly heavy load, my sister drifted to the other side and bought three patties and a banana cola. She then left me with the bags while she went off to chat with some old friends from back home. To better enjoy my Haitian patties, I took a seat on a rough wooden bench that was nearby.

I was on my first bite when a girl called to me from behind. "*Vinco.*"

My mouth froze in the bite. I turned around, and there was Carona, Laurette's chubby little sister. Her mother Fosia owned one of the vegetable stands on an alleyway before the turn of the curve. She was moving up in rapid footsteps.

"Do you want some patties?" I asked.

"No." She grinned, handing me a square envelope with Régine's name imprinted on it as the sender. "My sister saw you coming. She thought you were gonna stop by my mom's stand, but you went the other way," she added.

"I might before I leave," I replied.

Carona went back to Laurette, who usually worked with her mother every Saturday. That first bite on the patty was my last one. My appetite was gone, totally gone. I left the patties on the bench, grabbed the bags, and leaped to the back of Mathilda's stand, making my way to a remote corner away from the crowd. A decaying balustrade kept the noise from perturbing the quietness I needed to make sense of the note I was about to read. It was Régine's response to my plea.

Vinco, I read your note with utmost attention. Despite their mischievous undertone, I couldn't brush aside those carefully worded lines. You have to forgive me for using a third party to send you this collection of notes because they had become too heavy for my broken heart to digest. They were the main flashpoint of my suffering. So, I entrusted Laurette, a good friend, to hand them to you. They had turned into a manageable disease that could never be cured. I knew, perhaps as much as you did, that our love story was doomed since the very last night you left my mom's front porch and kissed me goodbye. I was too naïve to believe that our romance could have survived despite the unimaginable distance. My biggest problem, Vinco, is that no matter how hard I fight, I'm still unable to get rid of the bittersweet memories, the story of the man who stole my heart and then dumped it in the shallow grave of betrayal.

Vinco, I must admit, it's going to be extremely difficult if not impossible for me to love again. After I read your words, I spent the whole night thinking about you. They rekindled moments I thought were long buried in the shadow of my past. We've known each other since the moment we learned to play hide-and-seek in my grandmother's courtyard. I was only six. And you? Probably seven. Back then, I only saw you as the lone boy who could shake the deepest end of my soul. I shrugged off this feeling every time it came to haunt me. The truth was that I had always wanted to be with you, loving you with such an unbelievable thirst for affection that even my old grandma would have found it impossible to comprehend.

I still remember the little excuses to get to the river source, so we could be alone—away from the rest of the crowd. The memories of our frantic walks down the sandy riverbed in search of freshwater crawfish that we would later grill in my grandma's old Chinese pot flash across my mind from time to time.

Forgotten memories are never truly forgotten. They simply lie dormant until they're forced to come back. Love hurts, and I find it hard to believe that I still love you. I never thought one heart could love and hate the same person at the same time. It was that bittersweet feeling that kept me wide awake until the wee hours in the morning last night. I truly want to be with you, but I think it's too late—unless you want to prove me wrong.

Bye, Régine.

Régine's response was not reassuring to me. I was hoping that she understood what I would rather not say—that I could not go back to her, that I could not repair those wrongs despite our mutually shared pain. It was truly painful. Her collection of romance writing did not help either, for it had further deepened my suffering. Bewildered, I folded the note into my shirt pocket and ran back outside just as my sister was making her way to the pastry stand.

"You're already *done?*" she asked, looking quite surprised.

"I've *been* done," I replied, holding the bags tighter to show my readiness to go home.

"Do you wanna go now?"

"Yeah, I just remembered I have a group project for my computer class. It's due Monday."

"We need to hurry up, then."

She took the lead as always, waving goodbye to old friends and expatriates from Haiti. In gigantic steps, I followed her. It wasn't until I nearly reached the exit gate that I remembered to stop by Laurette's. "Oh Lord! I'll catch her later," I muttered to myself.

Later that afternoon, I drove north to the university via North Miami Avenue. I chose that route because I knew Régine lived on 111th Street, a couple of houses off the road and a few meters away from the university's library. Although I lied to my sister earlier at the flea market about the group project, I usually went there on Saturday to study with classmates. That afternoon, however, only one thing was on my mind: meeting Régine, or at the very least, catching a glimpse of her.

When I drove past her street, I saw no one. Just when I was about to veer toward the university parking lot, I took a last look through the rearview mirror, and there she was. Standing by her side on her front porch was a tall gentleman. She stood firm and lustrous under the afternoon sun. She was quite developed, like a hibiscus in full bloom, a bit taller, almost as high as the young man on whom she leaned. Her milky, coffee-colored face, adorned by a pair of hoop rings, beamed with a dazzling smile when he began to stroke her dark wavy hair. His dominant posture and his bushy mustache fit the profile of a conquistador at the prime of his adventure. From the front porch, they stepped down toward a young mango tree in the middle of the courtyard. Their fingers intertwined while holding each other's hands, she was throwing subtle smiles in the capricious and precocious fashion of a roguish woman at the height of her stratagem.

I felt crushed. I wanted to scream to the highest heaven. A mixture of fear and rage took hold of my mind. I hurried and parked the car. Then, I leaped toward the backseat to get a better glimpse of this horror story unfolding before my eyes. I wished it were a dream.

Who is this young man? I asked myself. He had a fair complexion and smiled like a wicked *chulo*. He wore a long-sleeved, button-down white shirt that was folded inside his patched blue jeans. He had a muscular frame, built like a young boxer. I could not hear what they were talking about. From his body language, however, I could tell how triumphant he must have felt. He was manning a submissive Régine with victorious glee, like a fisherman with a great, unexpected catch. She threw coy smiles in the presence of this macho man as she quivered in his arms and cooed like a dove.

About fifteen minutes later, a lean young girl stepped out and called out to her. "*Régine*, Mommy needs you," she crowed. She then stepped right back inside and shut the door behind her. He held her by the shoulders as she craned her neck to kiss him goodbye. Before their lips met, I turned my face away. The blow was too harsh. I leaped back to the driver's seat and drove off, heading straight home.

With hands shaking and legs trembling, I made it inside my front door. I was breathing hard, unable to retrieve the key to the door from my back pocket. I resorted to knocking. The first knock was so hard that my sister, who I could see through the window was sitting on the couch, jerked bold upright.

"Who the *hell* is it?" She growled.

"It's me," I replied. My voice was breaking.

"What's *wrong*?" She asked, opening the door to let me in as if trying to shelter her little brother from imminent danger.

"I have a major headache. I couldn't stay at the group study."

"You want some Tylenol?"

"No, I'll be fine. I just need to rest." I walked to my bedroom and closed the door.

I went straight to bed, trying to make sense of what I just saw, which was totally at odds with what was in her note. I never thought she could be so deceptive. I was now trapped in a thick fog. There at the edge of the bed, I was forced to face a truth that I had been working hard to ignore. I still loved her, and her action had reinforced my conviction that new and solid foundations could not be built from the shallow ground of childhood reveries. Another sleepless night loomed.

I flicked off the light to confront my fear. I lay face up, hands folded under my head and fingers intertwined. I felt the sensation of a vicious struggle raging within me, pitting my mind against my racing heart. From the living room, I heard the jolly mood of my sister on the telephone, chatting and laughing with her friend. In her sweet Creole, her filtered voice was raised in uproarious pitches, then quivered, faded, and silenced. I wished I were someone else. When emotion has been withered and romance worn off, the dark hours in a dwindling relationship are the most painful to overcome. Right here in my solitary room, I was living it and fighting it at once. My sister hung up the phone, and the night became soundless, motionless. The deathly hollowness that followed was only penetrated by the claps of her footsteps when she retired to her room and closed the door.

I wanted to go join her and rest at the foot of her bed, playing the baby boy I was back in Saint Louis when she would tell me stories in the *Cric Crac* hours, tales of revolting slaves in the mountains around Saint Louis during the colonial era—their hums, their grief, and their fights for freedom against the French. She would tell me stories of our great-great-grandpa, a mixed-race, who was a cattle rancher, a windmill owner, and who, in 1888, was an influential member of the Liberal Party and a close adviser to President Boisrond-Canal. Reaching the echelon of influence enabled his womanizing ways; he fathered over three dozen children throughout Haiti.

I chose not to join my sister. "No, not tonight," I murmured. I wanted to stay in my dark room and face my fear. The sudden roar of a passing vehicle across the street broke the silence. It zoomed, hummed, whispered in the distance, and then vanished. Unnerved, I got out of my bed and strode toward the window.

I peered through, taking frantic aim at the garden. Nothing was moving, except for the sprawling blooms of the Mexican Heathers, the timid rustling of the hibiscuses floating in the night breeze, and the full moon's glow waning behind the thick mushrooms of clouds in the distant sky. I shuffled back to bed, drowsing somewhere between sleep and waking; seeing Régine—her eyes turned scarlet red—dressed in a red garment running away from me as I tried to hold her hand. I bolted awake, calling her name, surveying my bed as if she were beside me. The night dragged on. So too, was my suffering. I longed for the woodpigeons. I yearned for their morning hooting outside my window, heralding the coming of a brand-new day.

Chapter 17

The next morning, I woke up feeling tired, for I had lain face up all night. There was no end in sight for my self-inflicted suffering. In vain, I searched for elusive comfort. My heart and mind were edgy, and the night came as dreadfully as it went. It was Sunday morning, and usually I would get up and turn on the radio to get the latest news out of Haiti from the local Creole stations. That morning, however, I was in no searching mood. Life was a dark-blue blur. My sister had already left for church. So, I stepped out of the room and headed to the kitchen to make breakfast. I pulled out the cutting board and the frying pan from the kitchen cabinet, grabbed a couple of eggs, some green onions, cherry tomatoes, and other green vegetables to make delicious Haitian omelets. I laid everything out with the cutting board and snatched up one of the green onions.

The minute I retrieved the sharp-edged knife to begin slicing, the images of Régine molded in the arms of that man came back like a ghost. Both energy and appetite were now gone. I simply ate a little bit, leaving the rest for later on the frying pan, and going back to my room where I remained under the bedsheet. I wanted to cry, but I could find no tears. I wanted to fly, to escape out of my skin. I wished I were in the library with my classmates and away from that unwanted scene, but it was too late. I already saw it. I saw everything. To regain my sanity, I decided to reply to her note, which I intended to do anyway. The turn of events, however, had placed me before a *fait accompli*.

Despite the golden memories and my lingering feelings for Régine, I now felt the moment had come for me to turn the page. Michaela was now the young lady with whom I felt the manifestation of true love. She had become the girl I could not live without. The way we gravitated toward each other felt like a commercial airline a few minutes after takeoff where she, as the skillful pilot, used her mastery to circumvent early turbulence, the massive foam clouds of the uncertainty of love, to reach the sweet romantic altitude where we could now cruise in the calm. She wanted me for who I was, just like Régine, seeking nothing in return but a love that was genuine, pure. Our relationship had already passed a major milestone, for I no longer desired her because she reminded me of Régine. The vibe was obvious each time we were together.

It had been more than five years since the last time Régine and I had held each other's hands romantically. I was not sure I could gather the strength or the skills, like all Machiavellian *chulo*, to keep her in my nest.

I knew exactly what the Haitian girl was going through. I had been there. As with all new arrivals, her interests, and more importantly, her survival agenda were clear. Establishing a foothold through immersion in the new country had no doubt topped her list of goals. In a quest to make sense of it all, I concluded she no longer saw me as part of the solution to her mounting problems. She was alone. She had no financial stability. She was living with people to whom she could barely relate. She no longer trusted me, for I had betrayed her trust, shattering her hope, and left her stranded on the riverbank of love. Perhaps she may have succeeded in suppressing those childhood memories that continued to haunt me day and night. In essence, she had moved on. Falling into the arms of another man was the biggest proof of that.

For sure, I still loved Régine, but my emotions had substantially dwindled, especially after what I had seen the night before. Still, I blamed myself for pushing her into the arms of a stranger. But, I knew Régine to be a girl with a strong character who never acted out of frivolous, lighthearted emotions. She thought situations through before making strategic moves. "Love is the most painful trade-off. It's like inviting someone into the innermost part of your heart in exchange for promises that may never be kept," she once told me.

I then began to take frantic aim at the facts of life. The existential realities of a refugee are full of scary intervals, like a roller coaster that never offers the straight, unaltered ride to Blissland. Behind the breadth and depth of human intelligence lies that unaware, unconscious survival instinct that we all shelter deep in our both heart and mind, from which we always draw strength in times of great uncertainties. Maybe I was lucky to have succeeded early on in winning over my worries and my anxieties to once again find love—pure and unfettered—in Michaela.

How many others were not so lucky? They took a gamble with their lives and lost. Perhaps Régine belonged to this category of folks who left home, beating what seemed to be unbeatable odds to push their way here in America, seeking a decent way of life. The first few days and weeks in immigration, commonly known as the honeymoon stage, are usually marked by a fierce, ignorant upsurge of joyous arrogance that will undoubtedly be short-lived as reality sets in and finding the road to financial success remains as elusive as ever. Being here alone does not guarantee a spot in paradise. Régine may have fallen victim to this dull form of innocence and naivete.

This odd reality had dawned upon me like an alarm bell that I could not ignore. Though an immigrant like her, already I could see light somewhere in that foggy tunnel of hope, and despite her reproachful attitude about my unacceptable actions, I was still hopeful she would someday forgive me. Perhaps, her coyness in the arms of this man may have been a push for survival rather than an act of simplemindedness.

Years before our love story began, Régine was a little girl, tall and puckish, with a dry oval face and cheeks with famished hollows and who seemed to have been born to be an integral part of my life. "Let's go," she would urge me when other girls in the neighborhood shunned her out of some unexplained prejudice, something I later understood was because of her parents' situation in life, which did not allow them to provide in abundance what other parents would for their children. The precariousness of their living conditions, at the raw edge of poverty, could not be hidden.

I would follow her blindly at her first order to leave, not out of some odd pity, but because within me, there was an indescribable, awed feeling that naturally gravitated toward her. I was always friend-sick and perhaps lovesick when she was away on trips to the countryside with her parents. I knew this amazing sensation was mutual when we danced, cheek to cheek, for the first time one Sunday afternoon during a teenage party at the Coquillage. Then, the bones of her milky coffee frame were long gone, sheltered deep beneath the now radiant, glossy skin of her youthful glow. We were both sixteen, at the spring of an ascendant life. Her lustrous, feline eyes darted, flashed, and twinkled when her young firm breasts were rubbed against my chest as we danced and danced to the beat of a sweet konpa love. Her arms wrapped around my neck and mine around her waist; we were oblivious to the world around us.

I knew Régine was right to have taken such a strong stand against my unacceptable behavior. Worse of all was my inability to muster the courage to tell her that whatever we had was over and that I was seeing someone. I feared doing so whould have shattered her dignity, knowing her precarious situation in the new country as an immigrant. Still, I had to find a way to make it clear to her that our lost love was irretrievable. So, I felt compelled once more to reply to her note.

Just like you, Ginou, I read your note with utmost attention. The meticulousness of your recollection and the precise wording used tell me how much those unforgettable memories meant and still mean to you. With a bitter chagrin, I read your account, and for a moment my desire to be with you was uncontrollable. I am now convinced that all these years, we have been nothing but stray lovers on an impossible mission to re-conquer a dazzling past. I wish I could turn back the clock, going in retrospect just to relive those happy moments that will forever remain hidden deep in my heart.

Sincerely, Y. L.

This time, in two folds I crinkled the note and placed it inside a white envelope on which I formally wrote her name as if ready for postage. I then stuck it under my pillow and went to the bathroom to take a shower. A few minutes later, I felt refreshed but somewhat anxious. I was not sure if this latest note would be clear enough to make her understand we can no longer rescue from the shadow of our past what was already, in my view, a dying love story. My heart and mind were fluctuating between hope and anxiety. Perhaps if I did not see her in the arms of that man, it would have been extremely difficult to heal my self-inflicted wound. Nonetheless, I became restless, on the brink of losing my mind.

I got dressed, grabbed the envelope, and walked out. The sun was still rising when I closed the door behind me and stepped down. With a few long strides along a lush garden of kaleidoscopic flowers and swollen blooms, I reached the sidewalk and then paused. I gazed at the street, which stretched down like the dry bed of an urban canal until it died on 68th Street where Soledad and her cousin Henriette lived. It seemed vast and bare, naked amid the haze, colliding with invading shades of overhanging tree branches that rose behind chain-link fences that enclosed overgrown front yards of tiny cottages on both sides. That Sunday morning, the breeze was quite feeble. The nearby trees stood almost motionless, except for some twiggy branches shifting . Glancing east, I saw Mrs. Jackson in a blue dress, disappearing as she turned around the corner on her way to the Catholic church for Sunday Mass. Travon was trailing her.

Facing north and taking aim at the croton edge that crafted the landscape of Soledad's home in the distance, I strolled onward. Halfway through, a radio played "Matilda, Matilda," Belafonte's classic, which reminded me of the very night Régine and I had danced for the first time at the Coquillage. The music blared piercingly from inside Mr. Yakimuno's home. An unforeseen flicker of sadness seized upon my deprived mind, which was soon followed by an upsurge of rage and lovesickness that ultimately dwindled into shallow grief. My eyes burned as tears welled up, as I struggled in erratic fashion to hold back

BITTERSWEET MEMORIES OF LAST SPRING

unwanted tears of self-inflicted defeat. It had been five years, away from that Haitian girl, and it felt like an eternity that had come and gone while I was left to wrestle with remembrances from a distant land—a land that continued to feel so ingrained in my mind and so close to my heart. Dwelling in the mist of deceptive love tasted like drinking the deadliest poison from a golden cup.

Soon, I dashed off. Two blocks down, a boy called to me from one of the homes nearby. My eyes drifted, and there was Cedric, Soledad's twin brother, a tall boy of an extremely light complexion with unusual gray eyes, red-hair, and a pinched frame. Most folks in the neighborhood doubted his biological relationship with Soledad, who was also slim, but black eyed with a golden undertone. "Are you going to see Henriette?" he asked, running in the middle of the street and stopping abruptly before me.

"Yes," I replied, grabbing his little red hand into a big brother's handshake.

"She ain't home. She's at church. Soledad's also with her. I heard them say Father Guy was going to speak about what's going on in Haiti."

"Father Guy?"

"Yeah. I saw Berline and her baby sister Marlène just a few minutes ago returning from the diocese. They said traffic was jammed, backed up all the way to 59th Street. People knew he was gonna be there this morning. Yesterday, he was all over the radio, announcing his visit to Miami and his homily at the Notre Dame."

"Why didn't you go with your sister?"

"I don't know. I guess I'm not fired up like many folks in this community. Haiti is the only conversation in the house, and my mom and dad can't seem to get enough of it."

"Really?"

"Yeah. My dad was on the phone this morning with his cousin who lives in Gonaives. My dad put him on a speaker phone, so my mom could listen too. He said last night, demonstrators burned down several police stations in that city. In defiance of the *tonton macoutes*, they raised the red and blue flag as soldiers stood by and did nothing. A young man named Jean Tatoune was leading the resistance movement in the city."

"Wow!" I was overjoyed.

I grabbed him by the arms and lifted him into the air while dancing and jumping. Then an old man just happened to walk by, carrying a radio out of which a Creole voice boomed. A reporter from the city of Cap-Haitien was giving a blistering account of the latest developments on the island. The Duvaliers' days were numbered. According to the reporter, Haiti had finally risen to give its own verdict to the Creole fascists.

"Let's go to Notre Dame!" I told Cedric.

"Only if you promise to take me to soccer practice next Saturday."

"You *got* it."

His little gray eyes lit up, sparkling under the ascending sunrays as we raced in total jubilation to Notre Dame. Within minutes, we were already in the church parking lot. We were stunned when we saw the size of the crowd, filling the vast front yard. Despite the excruciating heat, no one wanted to leave. Lines of cars came from all directions, swelling the corner between

62nd Street and Northeast 2nd Avenue to merge their way into the church's main gate.

Before it became Miami's Little Haiti Catholic Center, Notre Dame was just a little Catholic school run by orthodox nuns, and like all Catholic institutions, it had a chapel. With the arrival of new refugees, the demographic picture of the area profoundly changed. Soon, the school was moved away, and that chapel was converted into a full-blown Haitian church, exclusively Creole, that served the new arrivals in Northeast Miami. Father Thomas Wenski, a young priest of Polish descent, led the small diocese. A robust gentleman who spoke flawless Creole, Father Wenski gained fame among the immigrant population for his staunch anti-Duvalierist position and for speaking to the press on behalf of the refugees. The school building itself was transformed into a major center where they provided social services and ESL classes to the immigrant population, regardless of their origins.

The very tiny chapel could hold no more than one hundred people. It was easy to understand the commotion that morning, as everyone tried to get a better spot to listen to Father Guy, a mixed-race man whose family was nearly wiped out by the Duvalierists. Despite the sea of people amassing in front of the church, Cedric and I were determined to get in. I placed him ahead of me as he squeezed his way between people's legs while I put on a stony face, yelling at him, pretending he was my little brother who went astray, and I did not want to lose track of him. Like speedboats breaking ocean waves, the parishioners were shocked as Cedric and I shoved them aside. We pushed our way to the very main entrance of the church. Before I had the chance to make my final step, someone grabbed my arm and forced me back. I turned around, and it was Chantale.

"Look behind me," she snarled, still holding on to my arm.

My eyes lit up, and there they were: Henriette, Soledad, Laurette, and a group of other young folks, boys and girls, from the neighborhood. Soledad dashed off, going after Cedric, who did not realize that I had been forced back. She managed to seize him by the collar of his shirt just as he was about to disappear in the midst of the overcrowded church.

We all sat on top of a backless wooden bench that gave us a perfect perspective of what was going on with the altar in full view. On it were two boys dressed in white robes tied at the waist by blue and red ribbons. Hands rested in their laps, they sat in the back seats. Next to the altar boys was Father Guy. He was framed by flamboyant Father Gérard Jean-Juste, the head of the refugee center, and Father Karl Levèque, a mixed-race man and a fervent liberation theologist following Camilo Torres's style. On the far left, next to Father Karl Levèque and to my shock, was the infamous sacristan Onès in a red liturgical cassock like that of a Trappist monk. He was stroking his drooping beard. No one had seen him since the great feud between Fosia and Susana over Esmeralda's failed marriage. He was the one who stole the holy water from the altar and sold it to Fosia to build the magic charm that was supposed to trap Esmeralda's husband, José Blandon, on their wedding night.

"If it wasn't for this historic moment, he could have been stoned—this F—sucker," Laurette screamed in anger.

"*Stop* it. Onès is not the enemy right now. Baby Doc and his band of thieves are," growled a red-eyed, heavyset woman who stood just ahead of us.

Just then, Father Guy rose from his seat and walked toward the microphone. The stage was set for the revolutionary message.

"My brothers and sisters," he began, "Luke 4:18 tells us that 'Jesus comes to preach the gospel to the poor.' Jesus's Gospel, although it's foregrounded on the basis of strengthening the soul, we cannot ignore its materialistic aspect. Let's not forget that Jesus came to a land that was occupied by the Roman Empire. So, His preaching to the destitute made Him an instant threat to the occupying masters. Jesus understood that human dignity can only be upheld through the lens of social justice. In our beloved country of Haiti, the concept of freedom, democracy, and justice for all is totally nonexistent. For too long, the word 'poverty' has come to be the perfect 'etiquette,' it seems, to describe the dehumanizing conditions in which millions of our fellow Haitian countrymen live in.

But the enemies of Haiti have long told us that when Jesus came to preach the message of God to the poor, His message was intended to *only* strengthen the spirituality of the sick and the poor, not to help them improve their social conditions. Their misinterpretations—or their own interpretations, if I may say— of the Holy Bible seem to tell us our sins are at the roots of our hellish conditions, whether they are venial or mortal. Because of our sins, they say, we must be born, grow, and die in poverty. And those who rise against their spiritual order *must* be condemned to face the ultimate punishment.

"My brothers and sisters, they are wrong because Isaiah 61:1 tells us 'the Spirit of the Lord is on me, because He has anointed me to proclaim the good news to the poor. He has sent me to proclaim freedom for the prisoners and recovery of sight for the blind, to set the oppressed free.'

"For almost three decades, no country in the Caribbean has suffered more than Haiti. For twenty-nine years, the *tonton macoutes* did all they could to break our will to live in dignity. They

219

raped, beat, and killed our children, assassinated our parents, and destroyed everything and everyone who posed a threat to their repressive rule…. My brothers and sisters, the recent massive demonstrations in the country have confirmed Haiti will soon be free from the venom of Creole fascism. The Duvalierists have entered the final hours of their sadistic rule…."

The message lasted about an hour, and the Father ended his homily by reminding the parishioners to remain vigilant until Baby Doc Duvalier and his henchmen were removed from power.

Everyone was mesmerized. All around me, it was like deliverance had just dawned upon us. Amid church bells ringing and patriotic fever, the politically charged parishioners streamed out of their seats and made their way to the courtyard, forever resolute to keep the pressure on the dying regime down in Port-au-Prince. I had not seen Laurette so happy in months, at least not with me. Ecstatically gleeful, her cinnamon, feline bearing moved with grace inside of a red t-shirt and blue jeans. She and I took the lead of the group from our neighborhood, singing along with the rest of the churchgoers on their way to their cars:

Lè-n a libere
Ayiti va bel O ya tande
Ala yon ti peyi mache
O ya tande…
When we're finally free
Haiti will be pretty
Oh yeah, they will see
What a wonderful little country
Oh yeah, they'll certainly know…

Like a church procession, we sang all the way home. As the group reached my front door, I pulled Laurette aside and gave her the note for Régine.

"What's this?" she asked, snatching the envelope away from my hand, throwing a peevish stare, an expression of pointless confusion even while pretending she did not know what was inside the envelope.

"You *know* what it is," I replied. My eyebrows raised.

"Am I the mailwoman?" Her eyes drifted toward the rest of the group, who continued to sing and hum while waiting for her. Soon Cedric walked out of the group and grabbed Laurette's arm.

"Bye Vinco!" he shouted. "Let's go, Laurette," he said, trying to pull her away from me.

I did not reply. Instead, I edged toward her, held her by the shoulders, and landed a kiss on her forehead.

"You'll *never* change," she muttered while rushing to join the other young folks in the distance, all in red and blue, the color of the Haitian flag, still singing their favorite Haitian revolutionary song.

#

My sister greeted me with an indescribable elation when I unlocked the door and walked in.

"Haiti will soon be free, *free* as a bird!" she cried, grabbing me by the shoulders as if she wanted to lift me up into the air just like she used to when I was a toddler.

She was jumping, and I jumped right along with her. I never realized how deep her patriotism was. Before that festive morning and the encouraging news from Haiti, her expressed thoughts were always short and weirdly shallow. When I would press her to go deeper, she would stop me with a little pinch in my face like mothers lovingly do to soothe their children during anxious moments. "Vinco, things are bad, but there ain't anything we can do. They're beyond our control," she would say with a vague expression of subdued concern, a carefree attitude that would soon catapult into ridiculous, satiric, and even unpatriotic laughter.

That morning, though, I came to understand how wrong and disrespectful I had been to question her love for her motherland. We kept on singing and dancing, and in the middle of this euphoric moment, the phone rang. I edged closer to pick it up, but by the time I reached out and grabbed it, it turned silent, but soon rang again. With no sense of urgency, it picked it up again.

"Hello," I answered feebly.

"I'm sure my Vinco is the happiest man on earth this morning," Michaela's voice tittered on the other end, like a tropical songbird, sounding quite blissful.

"You bet I am, Mica," I replied, singing the same Creole revolutionary song from earlier at the church.

"You know I don't understand the words," she giggled. "But I surely understand the essence. I'm happy for you, too, mi amor."

"I'll teach you tomorrow at school."

222

"Yeah, *right*. That will be the last thing on your mind. Baby, don't forget I'm waiting on you this afternoon at home. I already talked to Mom."

"No, no, Mica, I didn't forget. But didn't you tell your dad, too?"

"No, I didn't have to. Mom already did. Don't worry."

"I'm not worried, just wanted to know."

"What time you think you might get here?"

"Let's say around five."

"*Besitos, amorecito.*"

"Love you, *amorecita*."

We both hung up the phone. My mood suddenly changed. A wave of anxiety seized upon my mind, and I could not hide it from my sister who was now in the kitchen, retrieving vegetables from the fridge to make a salad.

"What happened?" She asked.

"Nothing. It was Michaela."

"And why do you look so disturbed?"

"She wants me to meet her parents this afternoon."

"Really? Is it going to be a formal presentation or—"

I preempted her. "She simply wants her folks to get to know who I am since she'd told them she's seeing someone."

"Be careful, Vinco. If they press you to commit to something formal, tell them, politely though, that you're not ready and that your parents aren't in town."

"I know, sister. Believe me, no one can tighten the noose around my neck unless I allow them to."

"Don't get me wrong. Michaela is adorable. She's very respectful and she sounds very intelligent. She would be the perfect one for you, but I don't think either of you is ready for anything formal. Besides, graduation should be your main priority."

My sister walked outside to water the flowers from her little garden, and I walked to my room, where I sat on the carpet, head resting against the bed, pondering. I had never met Michaela's parents before. I never came across any of her relatives. The only thing I had as reference to her folks was the anecdotal accounts of her grandparents' story. Even though I was nervous, however, I was in total control of my anxiety because I knew at some point, I had to face the people whom, besides me, she loved unconditionally. Between nervousness and self-assurance, my heart finally rested on her sweet, melodious voice from which I could hear an expression of infinite bliss, an indescribable tone of innocence beyond which love at its purest could be found. That played well in suppressing my fear.

In my twenty-three years on this earth, I had never felt such uneasiness. Until then, I thought I was the Machiavellian macho, the Caribbean fox with all the ruses to trap and keep a girl in his hidden den. The last call from Michaela, however, brought me back to reality. Now I knew all I was doing was trying to stall the inevitable. How could I say no to the girl I loved when she invited me to visit her parents? More and more I felt a sense of urgency to tell Régine about my relationship with Michaela. In my last note, I should have found a way to tell her that I was seeing someone. This would have removed the feeling of guilt that continued to dwell in my mind each time I was with

Michaela. The moment of truth was upon me. I picked the phone and called Ronel, a trusted friend with whom I could share my ordeal. The moment I started telling him about my painful situation, he stopped me.

"Vinco, I thought you knew Régine was seeing another man. Laurette told me that story a month ago."

"Really? How come you never shared it with me?"

"Like I said, I honestly thought you knew because Chantale, Laurette, all of them knew. That's not all. I learned last week Régine and the young man are getting married. In two weeks, I'm told. But I'm leaving now. We'll talk about it at school tomorrow."

I dropped the phone and went to my room, confused by how ruined I felt. Early afternoon, Chantale walked to my door, knocked, and my sister let her in. I was in my bedroom, but I made a hasty hop when I heard her voice.

"Vinco, here is a note from Régine." The note was folded inside an envelope. Before I opened up my mouth to say a word, she was gone.

"*Chantoutou*," I called to her.

"My mom is waiting on me. See you tomorrow at school."

I went to my room and dropped the letter onto my lamp table, having neither the courage nor the appetite to read it. I had to muster all my strength a couple of hours later to grab it off my bed and begin reading.

Cheri, Régine wrote, *your last letter struck a chord in my veins. It has awakened and enlightened a feeling of nostalgia I thought I had long overcome. I was wrong. Deep in my subconsciousness, something unimaginative but dazzling, pure, nostalgic, graceful, splendid, breathtaking, and magnificent dwelled on for years. For a while, I thought my feeling would have been shunned, ignored or brushed aside if I were to tell my story to friends and strangers alike—a lopsided love story rusted in time. So, I suffered in silence.*

But our conspicuous correspondence has rekindled the scowl, the frown, the glare, and the ultimate bright light I clumsily searched for a long time. Yes, our childhood memories are golden—a heavenly prize to cherish until the end of time, and beyond. They make us love-bound, but also slave-bound—slaves of our own inherited love story crafted in a holy innocence and in a lustrous but profound conviction. I sat in my bedroom, at the edge of the foot of the bed to be precise, pondering what to do.

After I wolfed down your note, I could picture both of us in Saint Louis, wandering up and down the seaside as we used to on Saturday afternoons. I could still feel your giant hand, quirky but pliable and extremely tender, stroking my breasts, my neck while your tongue licking my cheeks behind the mango groves in the evening twilight.

Vinco, I don't know about you, but I still remember our very first night of wild caresses. I could still feel my heart racing inside my chest as you unlocked my legs and I opened up to you. I could still see myself breathing in the smell of your sweat. I held you and squeezed you in a desperate attempt to blend my body with yours. Love-struck, I never wanted to let go.

There, behind that giant mango tree, if you remember, we wanted to remain interlaced until dawn. But when the full moon pushed its way from behind the mountains to cast its glow on the valley floor and our shadows served as our sole companion in a universe of silence, we knew then it was time to leave. In the evening darkness, it was deathly quiet. The only noise to be heard was that of the occasional sounds of roosters crowing in the distance and that of the rushing current streaming down the shallow ravine, just a few feet away from us. The sky became starry, freckled with shooting stars that sent streaks of light across the sky, sending chill to our hearts in a serene atmosphere where we became dazed lovers, star-gazers, and instant witnesses of nature in action in the tropical night.

Later, when it was truly time to go our separate ways, we said goodbye more than a hundred times but still remained paralyzed under the weight of the intensity of our love. Locked in your arms, I couldn't ask for more. Paradise was reduced to the dimension of our bodies. This could go on forever. Only the faint cry of my mother echoing in the distance, searching for me, succeeded in forcing us to do what we would otherwise prefer never to have done: kissing goodbye.

So, we strolled back toward the house, resigned to an already factored-in sadness until we reached the edge of the hibiscuses and the crotons. There, I knew the moment would have to come to an end, for I could see the dim glow of the gas lamp beaming in the backyard, I could hear the murmur of my little brothers playing on the terrace, and I could hear the squeaking sounds of the Tap-Tap blaring from Main Street.

*The idea of leaving then started creeping up my mind without making a flutter, until it completely swooped down on me. In the end, I reluctantly let go, but not before you held me tight against your chest in an effort to subdue my tearless chagrin. All of a sudden, you released me **softly** to my worried mother and disappeared behind the palisades. I stood there for a few more seconds contemplating your silhouette fading in the darkness before I finally walked down the path leading to the back gates of my house.*

It was a good old time. I must admit. But if our love story fades with the passage of time, I will surely understand. I don't know about you. I will always have those memories to cherish...

Love, Régine.

After such a rollercoaster ride, I folded the note back into the envelope. Without any serious thought, I found this note to be very disingenuous, very deceptive. This note, to me, bore the trademark of a foxy young woman playing a two-sided love game. She completely disregarded my note and pressed on with her secret game, hoping my continued feeling of guilt would ultimately trap me, keeping me very close to her love nest as a sweet plan B, should she lose her current game with the gentleman she was supposed to marry in a few weeks' time. She had no clue of my knowledge about her relationship with her husband-to-be, the man with whom she had already committed to sharing her life.

I then became convinced she was no longer the girl I knew back in Saint Louis. I also knew I shared part of the blame and, perhaps, I was the trigger behind her sudden craft of manipulation. Still, I also understood using insidious means to deceive others was not part of her character. Her reference to our intimate moments had the opposite effect. Instead of trapping me on the hook of her deceptive bait, the move only strengthened my resolve. To me, Régine no longer matched the profile of the immaculate girl I had always dreamed of. I shredded the note, walked out, and threw it in a trashcan in the kitchen. I then went back to my room convinced I was in total control of my feelings, and whatever was left of our love story had come to a close.

Chapter 18

In sharp contrast with the clear blue sky and the fevered moment of earlier in the day, it was hot and gray when I left home, driving west down 62nd Street. A few crepuscular rays pierced through the thick clouds in the distance as the day pushed its way toward the twilight zone. Although the parishioners were long gone, the Haitian atmosphere was hard to ignore. Tiny homes coated in blue and red, the color of the Haitian flag, set the tone for this part of Miami rightfully called Little Haiti. In every open courtyard, groups of men and women congregated under giant mango trees and around domino tables, discussing the latest news from Haiti. Nearby, children roamed aimlessly, speaking Creoglish, an astonishing blend of Creole and English. It was a kind of home-grown vernacular that only Haitian Americans understood, and which for some time had become the trademark of this part of Miami. A few cars rolled by, and konpa music blared out of their open windows, splintering the air.

The music and the loud chatting in Creole grew distant the farther west I drove. Soon, Little Haiti faded from sight, and I went on, passing scores of decaying buildings, starving stray dogs roaming around, and poorly maintained housing projects. Farther down, inside a public park, a block party was in full swing. Kool & The Gang's "Get Down on It" rocked the atmosphere where shirtless young men leap-frogged and flexed their acrobatic abilities in a display obviously meant to lure young women.

The theatrical scene, in a flicker, took my mind off the uncertainty that lay ahead. Daylight was fast disappearing, but the stubborn waves of heat persisted, quite unusual for late January. I drove on, increasing my speed as I passed mounds of garbage, weed-infested lawns, and armies of carnivorous flies to reach 27th Avenue, the main artery in that part of town that intersected 62nd Street. The light turned red, and a whirlwind of emotions wrapped my soul. The music at the park was now behind me. Michaela's parents occupied my mind once more. Traffic slowed to a halt. My worries and anxieties now morphed into full-blown fear. Being late was the last thing I wanted at a historic meeting. The first impression can be bold if well done, my mother used to say.

The light turned green, and, relieved, I drove on, moving away in full speed to the very last stretch where the street died at the gate of Spanish Miami. I veered left, driving south and at last I was rolling down a busy street, not far from where Michaela lived. Cuban restaurants, Dominican beauty shops, and a multitude of small businesses set the tone for this section of town, and the Caribbean ambiance suited me well. I never felt out of place any time I drove Michaela home from school. The food, the music, the laughter instantly aroused my dormant melancholy; the everlasting nostalgia for Haiti. Although Haitians and African Americans had long found the brotherly ground in the constant fight against social and racial injustices, a

Caribbean ambiance, whether Jamaican, Dominican, Cuban, or Puerto Rican, was more likely to thrill a Haitian heart.

About five minutes later, I turned right to a narrow residential street that seemed a world away from the bustling atmosphere I had just left behind. As soon as I made that turn, I saw her in a floral dress, walking quickly up the street. I became worried. I stepped off the accelerator and slowed nearly to a stop. Her face was contracted, forehead wrinkled, and when she reached the car, she halted her march; and I stopped.

"Baby, where are you going?" I asked.

"To meet you," she said. Her voice vibrated.

"What's wrong, Mica. Is it because I'm late?"

She did not reply. Instead, she instructed me to join her at the curve of the street near an oak tree, away from the view of her parents' home. I slowly backed up the car and parked by the side of the road.

"Mica, can we sit in the car? It's getting dark," I said, imploring her to get in the car.

She refused. Until then I thought that change of attitude was the result of being late, and I knew how she wanted that first impression to be the signature mark of our relationship in the eyes of her parents. So, I got out of the car and joined her. I noticed she carried her purse, which was slung across her body. She avoided my embrace when I stepped up to her.

"Today may be the last time you and I have a conversation," she said bluntly, unzipping her purse, retrieving two pieces of paper, and handing them to me with a cold, resentful stare.

"What *is* it, Mica?" I became nervous.

"Don't *Mica* me. I want you to read these notes." Her eyes now brimmed with tears.

My heart sank as I took the notes. I immediately knew trouble was afoot. One note was the original version of Régine's last reply to my last letter, which was in French. The other was its English translation. My hands and feet hung limp. I trembled in fear and in embarrassment, and I began to sweat.

"There's no need for me to read them, Mica, since you already know what's in there," I said in total remorse like a prisoner admitting his guilt.

"How dare, Yrvin? How *dare?*" Her voice roared. "You've been using me as one more toy in your deceptive collection, lying your way to the innermost part of my life, pretending I'm the one and only while you're hard at work trying to rekindle the love of your life with this *Régine.*"

"Baby, can we go inside the car?"

"I'm *not* your baby." Her eyes were enflamed. "You must have promised this girl the world. It took me great courage to read this note. This girl's words were so clear, expressing her nostalgia for a time when she and you lived in paradise, and that after reading your note, she 'spent the whole night thinking of you' because these words have 'rekindled moments I thought were long buried in the shadow of my past.' And she went on to describe in explicit details some of the moments that will forever remain in her heart and mind." Mica paused for a moment, sizing me up in repudiation. "Oh, Yrvin," she continued, "I thought you were not one of them. You said you could never live without me while secretly rebuilding a romance with your childhood sweetheart." I could see her boundless anguish; she looked like she wanted to smack her head against the oak tree.

"Mica, why don't you give me a chance to confess my guilt?"

"Yrvin, there's nothing to confess. I was too naive to trust you, ready to give up my life for you, to follow you blindly anywhere. Little did I know that you were none other than a sneaky coral snake, even deadlier."

"Mica, I'm sorry for letting you down. But the story is not as it seems. Yes, I once was in a relationship with Régine. But that was long ago in Haiti when I was only seventeen. I don't know how you got this note and who translated it for you." She stopped me right there.

"Does it matter? What do you think I am? An empty-headed floozy?"

"Oh. Mica. I know I love you, and I stand by my words. I simply got carried away and was about to fall into the trap of a childhood fantasy. I'm not here to defend these words." She stopped me again.

"Yrvin, what do you mean by 'childhood fantasy?' The words from this Régine do not express fantasy. They are the expression of a love, pure and profound, describing the deepest of emotions, which clearly indicates that our relationship never existed. You were using me as a staging area, a sweet pastime while waiting to be reunited with your soulmate—*Régine*. And now I understand why that girl named Laurette always sizes me up each time I'm alone in the cafeteria. Oh, Yrvin, how could you do this to me? I speak so highly of you to the point my mom thinks I'm going crazy. But one of my cousins warned me about the reverse effect of love and the pain of betrayal." She broke into tears. I tried to take her hand to calm her down. "Don't *touch* me," she snarled.

"Mica, like I said, I'm ready to take the blame and full responsibility for my actions. There's one thing in this note, however, that cannot be ignored: Régine ends her note with the understanding that our story has been lost with the passage of time."

"And what are you defending now? Your stinky behavior?"

"Mica, could you please give me a chance to present my side of the story? I know I'm no longer worthy of your choice. But please reconsider."

"You seriously think I can still be fooled? Can a man genuinely love two women? Oh, I hate you and I hate myself even more for caving into your charm and your words full of hypocrisy."

Before I had a chance to say one more word, she was gone, and I stood there, feet anchored to the ground, totally shaken, watching her moving in swift steps until she reached the front gate of her home. She surprisingly turned around and walked back toward the car. "Yrvin, just so you know. It's over between us. Don't even try to talk to me when you see me at school." She then left.

Long after she pulled the latch from her front gate and faded in the darkness, I was still there under the oak tree, shaking and sweating. I felt trapped in my own selfish game, the game of dishonor, the ignominy of an egotistical loser. I should have spoken plainly to Régine, not leaving her any room to write her disingenuous letter. I sensed a big chunk of my life had suddenly been extracted. I could not foresee a life without Michaela.

Finally, I sluggishly walked back to the car, unsure of my own ability to safely navigate through the heavy traffic on the way home. I even began to question whether home was the safest place to be now in this moment of crisis. So, I decided to go see Pedro. I knew he should be home on a Sunday evening. He lived on the north side of town, about twenty minutes away.

When I arrived, I saw him standing in the front yard, speaking to a neighbor. When he noticed I was getting out of the car, he drifted away and moved to meet me. I apparently looked tense, and that alarmed him. Besides, I had never visited him on Sunday nights.

"Vinco, what's *wrong?*" he asked, edging closer to shake my hand.

"We need to talk. I need your help," I replied, breathing heavily.

"Why don't we go inside?" he suggested.

"No, I don't want your folks to overhear us. Can we talk in the car?"

"Yes." We both got in at once.

"Man, Michaela just dumped me," I stammered, stuttering in anger, hitting my head against the steering wheel.

"What did you *do?*"

"She found a note Régine wrote to me."

"The Haitian girl you told me about?"

"Yes."

"*What?* And how did she get the note?"

"I don't know."

"We need to find out. But more importantly, we need to temper Michaela's emotions."

"How? I can tell you, man. She was one angry wolf tonight. She confronted me with the original note written in French, and she had the English version as well. She took them out of her purse and threw them at me." I handed them to Pedro. He read the English version and he was stunned.

"Ped, you gotta help me. Exam's coming up next week. I need time and peace of mind to concentrate."

"Vinco, I can tell you, turning Michaela around won't be an easy task. She trusted you too much. She felt you let her down, and according to some of the words written in this note, she doesn't even exist. These words show you're desperately trying to lay out the foundation for a life in a union with Régine."

"Ped, don't be like Michaela, now. This was what she just told me."

"But that's true, Vinco. These are copies, right?"

"I have the original."

"It doesn't matter. Your action is repulsive. Put yourself in her shoes. Imagine if you were to find Mica cheating on you? Think of it for one second, Vinco."

Pedro's words—firm and frank—punctuated my heart. Truth hurts. He was right. "So, what do we do, Ped? We need to find out how she got the notes."

He stared at me with the look of an older brother disciplining his younger one. "Do you truly love Michaela?"

"What kind of question is this? Ped, I've been trapped in a dishonest game. Yes, we've been communicating, but I never gave her any hope that she and I can get back together, although I recognize I was too weak to push back at her deliberate advances. And I have my last note to prove to you."

"Vinco, I understand what you're saying, but I'm not convinced. And if you can't persuade me, how can you persuade Michaela that your love deserves a second chance? How can you? Does it matter how she got the notes? The most pressing problem to solve right now is to find a way to convince Michaela that your love deserves a second chance. I know she still loves you."

"You think so, Ped?"

"I know so because love doesn't disappear overnight."

"Ped, can you talk to her tomorrow at school?"

"Of course, I will. As you know, she and I have an early class in building nine. I usually get out first. Don't worry, I'll wait for her. But let me tell you something." He paused for a quick moment, eyes seeming to take aim at an empty field across the street. I had never seen him so serious. "Vinco," he continued in a firm tone. "If you really want to get Michaela back, you will. And I'll do everything to help you make it possible. But if you want to get her back just to satisfy your personal ego while persisting on playing the secret game with Régine, it won't work."

"I hear you, Ped." I became remorseful.

"That's why you have to make a choice. If you think Régine is worthy of your trust, and you're prepared to maintain a serious relationship with her, now it's the time to do it."

"Ped, I'm confused. What do you mean?"

"I mean now it's the best time to let go of your relationship with Michaela, however painful it might be. Michaela is *not* Judy, and you know that. And that would be the same for Régine." Pedro's words pounded my heart. "And I can add this, Vinco. It might be harder, if not impossible to get Régine back, because you told me she's engaged to marry someone. Right?"

"Yeah. Ped, believe me. I have no intention of going back to Régine not just only because she is getting married, but because of my love for Michaela and my deep commitment to that love. If I were to play this game with Régine, I would have violated my own principle. You just mentioned Judy, and you know why I could no longer continue in that relationship."

"I'm glad you understand that. You're right, between now and May, we need peace of mind to maintain our current grade point average. I'll do everything I can to help."

"Thank you, Ped. My good friend."

"I've learned the hard way. Remember at the beginning of the year when I told you Chen is now the one and only?"

"Yeah."

"At first I thought I could play her. Oh, man. I was wrong, *so* wrong."

Pedro smiled, a smile that catapulted into a bizarre laugh, like catching an aberrant chulo in the act of deception.

"I can't lose Mica, Ped. You know it."

"So, let's meet in the cafeteria tomorrow at noon after I talk to her. Drive safely." He got out and walked inside. Then, I drove off. When I got home, I found Nana lying on the couch watching *The Jefferson's*, her favorite Sunday night TV show. She muted the volume as soon as I stepped in. "I've been waiting for you. I'm anxious to know how the visit went," she said, rising from the couch. A big smile beamed on her face.

"I never got to meet her parents. When I arrived, they weren't home," I lied.

"*What?* Where did they go?"

"Mica told me they had to leave for an important church meeting."

"Oh wow!" She sighed. "You'll catch them next time."

"I'm so tired and sleepy," I muttered, dropping the keys off the table, rubbing my eyes, and going to my room. Feeling depressed, I took off my clothes and lay face up, trying to grapple with the consequences of my own misdeeds. What I did was so deceitful, and I could only hope for forgiveness. My main task was to repair my relationship with Mica. Still, I felt I had to find out how Mica got the note. The more I thought about it, the more confused I became. Someone must have given it to her. If this were true, some folks were hard at work to destroy my relationship with Mica.

No one I knew was a close enough friend of hers for her to accept such a note. I could see Laurette behind the coup, but I had no proof. She was slick, conspicuously eccentric, and as Régine's close friend, would do anything to make sure that Mica stayed away from me. In any event, I felt it was necessary to walk my way out of this mess, this self-inflicted blow. I had to focus on school, for failure was not an option. But losing Mica would certainly guarantee academic failure. I loved her too much. My future was at stake. Unable to concentrate, I left the room and went to join Nana on the couch. "My head hurts," I said, leaning on her shoulder, desperately seeking her sisterly love.

"You want some Tylenol?"

"No. I'll be fine, I think."

"You'd better go get some sleep, little man," she said, giving me a little nudge on the cheek.

"Not yet, Nana. I miss Manman."

"Me, too. But I don't talk about it as much as I used to."

"Why?"

"Because it'll deepen my nostalgia. The best thing for us to do is to work harder to help Papa so that he can save enough money to speed up the process of getting the rest of the family here with us." From the couch, she squinted, chasing the glow from the lamp table that was brightening an old family picture posted on the wall.

"You're right. In the Bahamas, things are rough."

"Maybe next year, you'll get a better job."

Although my sister did not mention the word "graduation," her high hope for that day remained an unmistakable desire and unavoidable necessity. I had to deliver. Above my personal yearning and my self-centeredness lay my family's pride and the hope they had bestowed in me. A week earlier, she told me she was going to start a graduation vigil.

"I know God will never abandon us. I have faith He will be there for you until graduation day as He has been over the last five years. He will be the conductor of your train of success,"

Nana said, getting off the couch while pulling me along to go to my room.

That night was as long and painful as the night before, an unpleasant agony I felt powerless to mitigate. Michaela's last words of rejection struck deep in my heart; and every time I dozed off, I could see her standing in front of me with the same cold stare of earlier in the evening, an infliction of pain I could not bear. I deceived her, and she had every right to be angry.

The next day, I made it to the cafeteria shortly after my late morning class. Pedro had not arrived yet. Outside, near the bookstore, a group of Haitian students flocked, chatting. Chantale and Laurette were among them. They then left the group and came to join me.

"How was your night, Vinco?" Laurette asked, like that schoolyard slicker always in the hunt for new gossip.

"Fantastic," I replied with an enthusiastic smile that left them clueless about my deteriorating situation with Mica.

"Vinco, you wanna treat me for lunch?" Chantale asked, teasing me.

"Sure, why not. Let's go." Ecstatic, Chantale grabbed my hand, ready to go, but Laurette seemed uncomfortable, even disturbed, unable to suppress her uneasiness, something she had not displayed before when we were together. She did not move until I said, "You, too, Laulau."

So, we went in, and I chose a table next to the main entrance, eyeing the hallway. I ordered sandwiches, and though I had a tightening heart and a complete loss of appetite, I chewed and swallowed with no sign of any struggle.

"I delivered the note to your *princess* as I was ordered to," Laurette vented like she was broaching an embarrassing subject.

"Otherwise, you would've been in trouble," I teased, playful and sarcastic.

"I was there, too, Vinco. Laulau is such a great fixer," Chantale affirmed.

"Really, Chantale?"

Laurette said nothing but threw a sly, cunning smile.

"Honestly, after I read that letter, I felt such an urge to go meet her. So, I drove by the house in the hope of seeing her."

"Do you know where she lives?" Laurette asked, eyes wide open, looking flabbergasted. Chantale turned her face away and took a giant bite of her sandwich.

"You know I have friends in town. But how I know is not the most important thing. I found out she's seeing someone."

Laurette looked stunned, not because she did not know, but because it was a secret she was unprepared to share. Chantale's mouth froze on a bite.

"First time I heard," Laurette cried, deceitful. I did not reply. I knew she was lying. As we chatted, I spotted Pedro coming with restless eyes, looking for me.

"Here comes your friend!" Both girls exclaimed.

"I see him. See you girls later." I ran to meet Pedro.

"Hey, Vinco!" Chantale called to me, and I turned around. "Can I call you tonight? I need some help. Have a math test this Friday."

"Sure, I'll be home after eight."

When Pedro saw me coming, he retreated toward the exit. "Let's go outside," he said.

We walked to a little table outside the cafeteria. I was tense. "How did it go, Ped?"

"Not good." My heart dropped. "But there's hope, Vinco."

"Tell me."

"Vinco, her class was dismissed, and she and a couple of her friends walked out, laughing and chatting, but when she saw me standing in the hallway, a few feet away, her mood suddenly changed, but it didn't bother me."

"Really, Ped?"

"Yes. Because I expected that reaction. I approached her and asked for a few minutes of her time."

"And she sensed why you came to see her."

"She didn't sense it, she knew it. Still, she said she was sorry, she was running late for a group study session in the library. I told her it wasn't going to be too long. I was courteous but firm. She then let her friends go, and we walked outside and sat at a small table under the pine trees. Before I opened my mouth, she said she knew why I came but it wasn't necessary because now there isn't anything anyone can say or do to make her love again."

"How did you react to such a statement?"

"I was calm, letting her speak, providing her another opportunity to release her frustrations. She went on to describe the depth of her love for you, and until yesterday, she thought she was born to love you, and she always had you in mind in everything she did, including her school, her church, her desire to be a great professional, to be a better person each day, everything... And when someone gave her the note late yesterday afternoon, she couldn't believe it at first. She thought it was a hoax, but when she returned to her senses, she then realized how much of a traitor you were. She called you a vicious liar. She said you kept telling her how much you couldn't live without her while you're romantically involved with Régine. She said she felt the greatest misfortune came crashing down on her. She said since last night, life as she knew it has ceased to exist. Her eyes were full of tears. She said she will never love again."

"And what did you say after listening to her?"

"I reasoned with her, asking her to reconsider. I expressed my disapproval of your actions, recognizing she has every right to be angry. But I told her you still love her more than anything, more than anyone, besides your parents. She didn't buy it. She flatly rejected my words, saying you yourself admitted to the secret love affair. I then said I also read the note. It's clearly damaging."

"Did you ask her how she got the note?"

"Yes, I did. She said it was Jahaira who brought it to her at home. Jahaira said she got it from Laurette."

"Is that right?"

"That was what she said, and I was visibly shocked. Then, I said, 'Laurette gave the note to Jahira without asking her to give it to you, Mica, but with the firm conviction that Jahira was going to take it to you. She's your cousin.' Then I pointed out that Laurette's intention was to destroy the relationship, 'not because she wanted to save you from the sinkhole of betrayal, Mica.' But still, she remained unconvinced, saying Laurette's intention may be mischievous, but we cannot deny the truth in this well-written note. Finally, I asked her to think deeper because she was down in darkness, unable to concentrate."

"Ped, I can't lose Mica. If there's anything powerful enough to derail my graduation process it's the loss of Michaela. I will have to make a formal apology and promise to prove my love and honesty once given an opportunity."

"That's right, Vinco. Don't give up. I think this will be the best way to convince her you truly love her. And I'll continue to talk to her and try to facilitate a meeting between the two of you."

"And also, Ped, I have to deal with Laurette."

"No, Laurette's plan can easily be unraveled."

"How?"

"Because what she sent was a note written by Régine, not the one you wrote, which would have been pretty damaging. I don't know why she sent Régine's reply. Maybe she's waiting to see how things develop before introducing a much bigger weapon. If I want to use the analogy of war, no conventional army goes to war with everything it's got in its arsenal. I'm sure Laurette can get her hands on the rest of the documents. For now, she may believe she's winning. Let her think that way, and it's obvious you and Mica are not walking around campus hand in hand today."

"Okay, Ped."

"Don't worry. Laurette can't be smarter than we are. Let's get to class. After all, life must go on."

"That's easy to say."

He laughed, and we went to our separate classes. Pedro's words of encouragement were not enough to ease my pain, but his insistence and promise to help me restore my relationship with Michaela was just sufficient for me to remain hopeful.

Walking around campus with a broken heart was agonizing. I missed Michaela, but her violent reaction had taught me one of the greatest lessons in my young life: never play with someone's emotions and dignity, for the reaction can be as brutal as the action that provoked it. We used to spend two hours each day studying side by side at the library. I did not go that day. I could not go alone. Instead, I went home to my room, studying for the test on Friday. It was a crucial week. Besides the test, two research papers were due on Friday as well. I worked hard to focus. In trying to make up for lost study time, I did not realize it was time for work. At three p.m., I called in sick and used the extra time for the research papers. I stayed in my room, getting them done.

Nana came home from work but did not bother me, for I had been complaining all week about the amount of schoolwork and deadlines I had to meet. She only pushed the door open a little and stuck in her head.

"Bonsoir, my little prince," she tittered, and I threw kisses to her. She then shut the door and I refocused on my study. I only took a break when Chantale called around eight-thirty.

"Hey, Vinco. I didn't see you after school as usual."

"I had to leave early. I figured going home and being alone would help me concentrate better. Two research papers and a test are just enough to make my head spin."

"I hear you. I'm taking Algebra II, and I don't know where I'm heading."

"Some of the concepts might be tricky, but not too difficult to grasp with adequate practice."

"That's what I need. I have an exam coming up this Wednesday, and it's an early class."

"Sorry, Chantoutou. I won't be able to help you, but I can start working with you beginning next week, for a couple of hours each week, and you'll be fine. I'm sure."

"Vinco, I wish I were you. You're so focused."

"Do I have any other choice? For those of us in this country, graduation is not an option. It's a must."

"I'll be a senior like you next year. So, I have to boost my GPA, which has fallen below 3.0. A 'C' in Algebra will drop it further."

"Mine is currently a 3.75. I'm working hard to secure a scholarship for graduate school next year."

"I admire a lot your passion and ambition. Yes, a master's degree in software engineering will suit you well."

"But for now, I'm taking it one step at a time."

"Vinco, I'm gonna share a secret with you, but you need to promise you'll keep it between the two of us."

"You know me, Chantoutou." The word "secret" triggered a frenzied scare. My heart raced compulsively.

"Don't trust Laurette in the story with Régine. She was the one who gave the note to Jahaira and encouraged her to take it to Michaela with Régine's approval."

"Does Régine know who Jahaira is?"

"Does it matter? She still loves you, despite everything. And she believes Laurette can help her realize her dream."

"How could that be? I know Régine is seeing someone."

"How do you know, Vinco?"

"I saw them kissing under the mango tree in the front yard of her home. Last Saturday, I drove by in the hope of seeing her. I was devastated. Does Laurette know about this?"

"She does, but she doesn't like him, obviously. He's uneducated, a brute in the manner of the wild players in town."

"What's his name?"

"Adler, the son of a sea captain from the Dubisson clan. They're very rich landowners in northern Saint Louis. He doesn't go to school, but he's the co-owner of Labelle Boutique, a clothing store on the corner of Northwest 59th Street and 7th Avenue."

"Really? I know that store."

"Régine doesn't like him, but under intense pressure from Augusta, Adler's older sister and the owner of the house where she's at, she feels she has to go along…"

"Well, I can wish her good luck. Don't get me wrong, Chantoutou. I still like Régine and I can only blame myself for her predicament. As you know, but more and more it's becoming almost impossible to patch things up. I know I treated her badly, and that's why I was unable to categorically tell her that our love story was over. I respect her dignity."

"Well, Vinco. Things happen, like I said last week when we were returning from the rally on 54th Street. But don't feel bad. You have your Michaela—pretty and smart, I'm told."

"Not anymore. Laurette has succeeded in destroying the relationship."

"You're *kidding*?"

"No, I'm not. Jahaira took the note to her. She read it, and she was furious, calling me a traitor, a cheater who no longer deserves her love."

"And you gonna let her go just like that?"

"What can I do?"

"There're plenty of things you can do. But first, you'll have to admit your guilt, and then focus on repairing the damage. Michaela still loves you, and that's why she's so angry. She's paralyzed right now, unable to find the way forward. I can't think of any girl at school who would remain passive after catching her man with someone else."

"Chantoutou."

"Hold on. The only thing that's keeping you from finding the right strategy to patch things up with Michaela is that you still love Régine, whether you want to admit it or not, even after you watched her kissing another man. If you really want Michaela, I can help you meet Régine, and you'll soon find out the task to reclaim her won't be an easy one."

"Are you sure you can do that?"

"I have her phone number, and we talk from time to time. Let's meet this coming Saturday at Rendezvous Restaurant on Dixie Highway. I'll bring Régine. If it's true what you're telling me now, when you meet her, you'll have to find the courage to let her know that you know she's getting married, and you're not interested in destroying that."

"What time you think it might be?"

"Let's say tentatively at four p.m. I'll have to check with Régine. Between now and then Laurette might call you to get the pulse of the situation with Michaela. Don't share anything."

"I'm not stupid."

"Let me let you get back to your studies. Be yourself. You'll soon find out if Régine is truly the person you would like to spend the rest of your life with. See you tomorrow at school."

"Have a good night, Chantoutou."

Chapter 19

The last time I set foot in Rendezvous Restaurant was two years ago with a group of childhood friends from Saint Louis on a Friday evening. Then, popular folksinger Manno Charlemagne put on an impeccable show, performing his latest revolutionary songs to dozens of fans. Located near a busy intersection where the city of Miami ended and North Miami began, Rendezvous Restaurant was a casual dining venue and one of the best places to be in this immigrant community, especially on weekends.

On that Saturday afternoon, traffic was light, and I arrived ten minutes before four. What used to be a modest house had been converted into a cozy resto with its own parking area, a backyard terrace with several sets of outdoor tables and umbrellas to shield diners from the harsh midafternoon sunrays. Inside, behind a little bar, two busy servers were selling Barbancourt, a famous Haitian rum and cremas, a popular Haitian party drink. Tables were arranged in rows of five with the menu du jour nicely displayed over beige tablecloths. Though it was not a fancy place, it offered estranged lovers the perfect spot to rekindle and weld the bonds that once underwrote the signature of their romance which had been lost and splintered with the passage of time. Two waiters dressed in red shirts and blue pants took orders from a few couples scattered around the room, speaking in low tones amid acoustic guitar music.

To be comfortable, I chose a table in the front corner near a window through which I could easily see who came and went. A young waiter then approached me and readied to take my order, but I asked him to come back because I expected a couple of more friends. He left, and my eyes glued to the window, waiting with elevating uneasiness for the girls to show up.

Five minutes later, a taxi pulled into the driveway, and Chantale and Régine waltzed out, gliding along a narrow walkway that ran up to the main entrance. Chantale wore a short-sleeved crewneck tee over high-waisted stretch jeans. Régine, hued in buttery-brown caramel, bore a ribbed pima cotton shirt stretching over knee-length denim jeans, moving along in graceful strides. An odd bittersweet feeling, impossible to explain, took hold of my heart. I did not know what to make of this moment. A pair of silver hoop rings adorned her flawless face, which was enhanced by lustrous and thick afro hair styled in small bantu knots. Purse in hand, she seemed confident of herself, showing the same impressive posture I remembered back in Saint Louis. Immediately I rose from my seat, checking my jacket to make sure it was wrinkle-free and well-suited over my Paco Rabanne pair of pants in a pure, gentlemanly fashion.

I stepped out of my seat and met them halfway. I greeted Régine with two small *bisous,* one on each cheek, and she reciprocated with a casual hug, like the ones I usually exchanged with my female friends around campus, as if it had not been five years since the last time we met. Chantale and I also exchanged kisses, but warmer and friendlier.

252

"Vinco looks so sharp," Chantale said, chortling teasingly.

"You both look lovely," I stated, struggling to regain self-confidence. Régine only grinned, holding her purse tighter, as if searching for a point of comfort. I led them to my table. Régine and I sat facing each other, and Chantale, hyper-happy for having been the friend who had made the meeting possible, promptly requested the menu. I handed it to her. She glanced at it and passed it on to Régine.

"I'm going for deep-fried, seasoned fish over mixed rice and beans," she said with an excited chuckle.

"You'll never change, Chantoutou. Ever since I've known you, you and food always sleep in the same bed," Régine said, mocking her.

"And you, Ginou?" I asked.

"I'm not hungry," she replied bluntly.

"Listen, guys," Chantale intervened, "as I already told both of you, I'll have to go as soon as the food arrives, leaving you two to make up for lost time. When you guys are done, I'll be at home."

"And how are you going back home?" I asked.

"Don't worry. A friend is already waiting for me outside."

"And I'll drive Ginou to you safe and sound," I said in a throaty laugh.

"You'd better..." Chantale warned playfully.

"But Ginou, could you at least order a drink?" I asked with a playful smile.

"I don't know. I'm not good enough in English to read menus."

"Me, I'm ordering passion fruit."

"Which is passion fruit?"

"Grenadia, I remember that was how we used to call it back home."

"I'll do the same. I love grenadia, especially if it's well sweetened."

"Look at you two!" Chantale said with a high-pitched, silly laugh. "Away from Saint Louis, face-to-face in a foreign land."

That did not seem to please Régine. She had gone subdued as if Chantale, in a priori assumption, had just forced on her the painful weight of bitter souvenirs she knew were going to be part of our conversation. While chatting, the food arrived, and Chantale abruptly got up, grabbed the food, and said goodbye, leaving us to sort out our problems. Then, it became all quiet. I did not know how to begin.

"You've grown quite beautiful," I said suddenly.

"And you're still the handsome young man I fell in love with long ago." Her lips quivered, and she burst out laughing, stirring the juice in her glass with her straw, and taking a timid sip. "How come you didn't reply to my last note?" She asked briskly.

"Ginou, I didn't know what to say."

"What do you mean?" She adjusted herself, grinned a little, and her Creole elegance magnified.

"I believe in my last note, I said that I will always cherish those unforgettable moments."

"You know, Vinco. When I was in Saint Louis, I thought Miami was as small as Saint Louis, a town where everybody knows your name. I was *really* wrong."

I avoided that subject. "Ginou, please tell me. How do you think I should have replied?"

"Not sure. Let's not focus on this."

"But it's important to me because the damage I've caused after five years of silence, in my view, is irreparable. I'm not trying to justify unjustifiable behavior." My eyes now fixated on hers, yearning for an answer.

"I don't know either. All I know is that although love never goes away, true love cannot be tested unless it undergoes the test of faith, like my mother used to say. Sometimes, you may have to fight to preserve what you cherish. I know life was not easy for you when you first came to this country. I can speak with absolute certainty now that I'm living such a reality, one of the most difficult times of my existence. It's an irony. I'm finally in America, where life was supposed to be a rosy journey. However, I strongly believe you could have done otherwise."

"I know I'm all to blame. I gave my education and other means of survival priority over our love, and I'm sorry."

"No need to, Vinco. It wasn't meant to be."

"But, Ginou."

"*What?*" Her face contracted and eyebrows raised in anger.

At that point, I became convinced she was about to reveal her upcoming wedding; but she said nothing. Instead, she went on to describe her ordeal of trying to get a job and her desire to be a nurse. I soon recognized I had to bring up the issue. I understood that was an uncomfortable subject, but one that could not be left unraised. Otherwise, our meeting would have been meaningless. I remembered what Pedro and Chantale told me about the difficult and perhaps impossible task of having Régine back into my life.

Throughout our conversation, her resistance slowly evaporated, and my anxiety gradually waned. We now had morphed into estranged lovers unable to relinquish the past. By then, more people started coming in, and their chats and laughter had become an annoyance we could not ignore. So, we decided to vacate our seats and strolled to a table outside, even though the sweltering heat had not gone away.

"I understand you're engaged to be married," I said, avoiding eye contact.

"Yes," she replied coldly. "Laurette must have told you."

"No. But, Ginou, although a wedding is private and sentimental, it is always executed in public before eyewitnesses and well-wishers."

For failing to tell me with her own words about her wedding, she seemed to realize she had made a major faux pas. "I was going to tell you, of course, but I didn't think this was the right moment."

"This was one of the reasons why I made the decision not to reply to your last note. By then, I knew you were seeing someone else." The last three words shook my heart: 'Seeing someone else,' an act for which I can only blame myself.

"Are you trying to say I'm dishonest?"

256

"No, Ginou. I'm myself seeing some else at school. The dishonest person is me because I'm the man who didn't keep his promise."

"And if I find myself in this predicament, Vinco, it's because life has not treated me fairly." She paused for a moment. Her eyes turned watery. "Vinco, never in my wildest dreams did I think you could treat me the way you did. The last evening you left my parents' front porch, I cried all night, afraid it was going to be the last time we held hands. The days that followed, I felt I was the most miserable girl on this earth. I spent most of my days in seclusion, crying and praying that you arrived safely at your destination. And one afternoon, the mailman showed up and handed a letter to my mother. I was sitting in the backyard, but I could watch her glancing at the envelope and smile. My heart jumped. She then called to me and I came. She handed it to me. I said nothing. I went straight to my room to savor your beautiful, poetic words. For weeks, I slept with your letter under my pillow. You said you would never leave me stranded in Haiti because the pain, the loneliness, and the lovesickness were mutual. My hopes and dreams grew stronger, and I was confident you would someday return. Not only did you never return, but you stopped writing me after a few short missives. And I felt belittled and betrayed."

"Ginou, I'm sorry, sorry for having caused all this pain."

"No need to."

"I'm truly sorry."

"I'll leave if you continue to say you're sorry. Sorry may be an acceptance of guilt, but it can in no way heal pain. As you're now living your American dream, it's impossible for us to reconcile our differences." Her face slanted, and she retrieved a

257

handkerchief out of her purse to dry the teardrops streaming down her cheeks. She had gone mute and seemed resigned and powerless in the face of unrequited love.

There, at the table, I wished I could turn back the clock and be with her again in Saint Louis, walking hand in hand along the sandy riverbed of the Saint Louis River on a Saturday afternoon, or dancing at the Coquillage, cheek to cheek, at a Sunday afternoon party, away from all entanglements and intricacies of life. But we both had to face reality. It was no longer possible. My heart belonged to someone else. I grabbed her hands and she held mine, and we began to sob into each other's arms. Long after the sun retreated and disappeared from the horizon, we remained interlocked and in tears.

Finally, she said, "Vinco, let's go."

We got up and shuffled to my car. We cried all the way to Chantale's house. When we pulled up to her front door, she was standing there on the front step, waiting and nervous. Before Régine walked out of the car, I had her wipe the tears off her face. Then, she pushed the door open and slowly walked toward Chantale. She did not look back. Later at home in my room, I could not stop thinking of Régine's words, so touching and soulful, words of her unfortunate ordeal, living with relatives she barely knew, away from her parents, her beloved siblings, and all that made her who she once was. Now, her days were languorous and sultry. Like marriage and loneliness, sunrise and sunset had equal meaning as she sat idly by, day in, day out, watching her high hopes and dreams now suppressed and distant, helplessly dying. I wished I could do otherwise.

Monday morning on the way to class, I met Laurette sitting on a remote table outside of the cafeteria, just off North Miami

Avenue. "Vinco, can you stay with me for a minute?" She asked. Her eyes moved restlessly, cannily alert.

"What for? I'm late. Don't you have a class?"

"I do, but I'm waiting on your friend."

I knew she was waiting for Ronel, her secret boyfriend with whom she was madly in love, although her parents had recognized an inoffensive lad named Ferdinand, the son of a well-known preacher in the community, as her official boyfriend. The Ronel affair had been a wild romance since our senior year in high school. In fact, her truant behavior had left no doubt in the minds of many classmates that the affair was nothing but *un secret de polichinelle*, an open secret, with which she seemed to have been quite comfortable. Despite our longtime friendship, she never openly revealed to me that secret romance, even though she was mindful of my friendship with Ronel.

Pecan-brown skinned with impressive and impossible-to-overlook curves, Laurette always dressed in the cutting-edge of fashion, even at school. High-heeled footwear, Chanel glasses, and Jordache jeans that stretched and swung at every step when she walked around campus. Laurette was conscious of her charm, and she used it as a magnet to trap Ronel. More importantly, she had become quite skillful in the art of deception and manipulation. That Monday morning, however, when Ronel pulled by the side of the road in his brand-new Datsun, calling to her, she had to tell me.

"Vinco, I'm going somewhere with Ronel, but don't tell anyone," she said, moving away in a hurry and nearly falling when her shoe hit a rock on the sidewalk.

"You'll have to pay for that," I replied, raising my voice to make sure she heard me.

"Is that a trade-off or a quid pro quo?" She laughed, easing her way into the front passenger seat.

"However you want to call it," I yelled, but I wasn't sure if she heard me, for the echo of my voice seemed lost in the air as she slammed the door, and Ronel sped away, laughing amid heavy traffic on North Miami Avenue. I stood there, watching the car zooming down the long line of vehicles going south until its silhouette faded out of sight. I could not help thinking how selfish this girl was. So, I ran up to class, ever determined to stave off her attacks against my relationship with Michaela, for whom the depth of my love had never been tested—until now. More and more, I could not see myself living happily in this cruel world without her.

Mondays were particularly heavy in my schedule. Subsequently, I had Software Engineering and Operating Systems class. Passing these two courses was key to my graduation, for they would push me ever closer to the finish line, and the last major course before the Big Day would be Seminar or Integrating Experience. Software Engineering was my preferred course among the three, not because it was an easier course, but because of the teaching style of Professor Jose Ariate.

He was one of my favorite professors. He was slim and straight with a hairy face and a simplistic chevron mustache that seemed at odds with his untrimmed cheeks. An Afro-Cuban American with a distinguished attitude, optimistic about even the most critical task, Professor Ariate commanded a lot of respect and admiration among his students. I never missed his class, and my punctuality and my progress in class impressed him. "For a young man whose first language is not English, I'm amazed," he would say in front of the class after I answered one of his trickiest questions. Others in the class dubbed him the coolest professor, whose hands were always thrust deep in his pants pockets as he paced back and forth, lecturing the class. That morning, when I did not show up on time, he was quite worried, because on Friday before he dismissed the class, he urged everyone to be on time on Monday for a midterm review. When I walked in, I saw Pedro standing near his desk, trying to stall him, engaging him in a conversation about Cuba, the beauty of the island—a land so close but yet feeling so distant—its politics, and history. Immediately after I came in, Professor Ariate glanced at the clock hooked into the wall and smiled.

"I told you Lacroix wouldn't miss this important review," Pedro said gaily, going back to his seat, which was next to mine in the back of the room.

"Let's get started, folks," Professor Ariate addressed the class.

"Mr. Lacroix, are you ready?" he asked me—only me, and that surprised me. His eyes turned wide and unblinking.

"Yes, sir," I replied, changing my demeanor.

Until then, I did not realize whether my nervousness had had such a visible impact on my face. I quickly relaxed, throwing a couple of bright smiles, enough to appease Professor Ariate's worry. He now turned his attention to the entire class. Pedro moved closer and said discreetly, "Vinco, we have to talk after class. I met Mica over the weekend."

Although Pedro had yet to tell me what the two had discussed, his news was just enough to temper my edginess. I gave him a thumbs-up without replying, and before Professor Ariate zeroed in on me again, I was ready, notebook and pen in hand. When the class was dismissed, Pedro and I crept out of our seats and weaved through the surge of students swarming out of the classroom. We ran to the cafeteria for the talk. On the way, I met Chantale near the main entrance. A boy in khaki pants held her hands as they talked.

"Vinco," she cried, snatching her hands off the boy and rushing to me. Her lips quirked upward in a jubilant smile. "I have news for you," she said, pulling me from Pedro.

"Not now, Chantoutou. Let's talk later after class," I said, laying a couple of *bisous* on both cheeks and quickly moving away.

"Okay, Vinco."

Pedro and I then rushed up to the line to order sandwiches. "Vinco, on the way to class this morning, I saw you with Laurette. What was that for?"

"You won't believe it, *man*. She was waiting for Ronel."

"And she wanted you to be with her?"

"She tricked me, and I didn't see that until Ronel showed up in his brand-new car. She then left with him."

"She's so selfish. She wants you to cover for her shady moves while she's destroying your relationship with Michaela."

"Don't worry, Ped. She's not smarter than us. I know her plan is to hit Michaela where she knows it hurts the most: her heart." We got our sandwiches and found refuge in a corner in the back.

"Vinco, I can tell you. Régine and Laurette seem to be winning the fight. In the long conversation we had yesterday afternoon, Mica did not budge. I tried my best to reason with her, telling her she needed to have faith and that your world is different from hers, and you were already a teenager when you came to this country."

"And what did she say?"

"She said you've already told her about your upbringing in Haiti, but that Régine's story was one well-kept secret she would have never known if it weren't for Jahaira. Then I reminded her as I already told her that I also read the note and nothing in it suggested you were about to leave her for someone else. I told her this incident has wrecked you."

"And she didn't seem to buy your argument?"

"I did my best to soften her emotions, but she was still angry."

"Ped, was she the one who called you?"

"Yes, to my big surprise. And that's why I think we have a chance. She still loves you. You can't give up this fight, and I understand my critical role and I'm willing to be the go-between."

"Ped, can you ask her if it'll be possible to give me a chance to meet her Friday afternoon after class?"

"I will. I may call you this evening to let you know. Let's get back to class, man."

"Why don't I call you instead? I might be home late. I'll be in the lab working with some classmates on a Cobol project."

Pedro and I went in the opposite direction. On the way to my next class, my eye caught Mica and Jahaira rushing to their classes in the south building. She turned around when Carmelita, one of my friends, called to me out loud. We did not make eye contact. She went on with her cousin and they disappeared behind the building.

"I know why you're walking so fast," Carmelita said, snickering.

"No, you don't," I replied.

"Never mind, Vinco, but she's not at the regular spot."

"I know."

"How so?"

"She's busy, running late for her class. I'm also late for class. Later."

"*Wait.*"

I made a U-turn, going back to her.

"I was gonna tell you something, but I don't think now is the time. You can go. We'll talk whenever…" Her red cinnamon face narrowed like an anxious big sister. So, I joined her anyway.

"Can I get a *hug*?" I pirouetted and bowed.

"You got it!" She held me tight. "Go *now*." We both laughed into each other's embrace. She then ran and I hurried to class, but when I reached the little bench where Mica and I always held our last morning chat before kissing goodbye, a thirst to be with her suddenly took possession of my mind and my legs buckled. I missed her enormously.

Standing a few steps away from my classroom, I fell into deep thought about how rosy that Monday could have been. We would have clutched to each other, hands clasped, refusing to let go. Now, I was alone and afraid that our romance had truly been dissolved, lost into nothingness. Before the last few students entered the class, I took out a sticky notepad from my folder and I wrote this quick note. "I was waiting for you, Mica. And as long as my mind, body, and soul permit, I'll be right here waiting. Bye, Mica." I left the note on the bench and used two marble stones from the flowerbed to protect it against the wind. I went in, but, later, on the way out, I stopped by the bench, and the note was gone, only the two little stones remained. So, every morning, I wrote the same words on a different color notepad. I never told Pedro about the note, although he had already told me that Michaela had agreed to meet on Friday afternoon.

Thursday night, I came home tired after a long day. My sister was on the phone, wrestling with her boyfriend. As soon as she saw me, her face, dried and unsmiling, quickly returned to her natural expression.

"You ought to do away with this guy," I said. I was filled with anguish, not only against her inability to protect herself from her playboy, but also against my own powerlessness to help her see clearly.

"Don't start it again, Vinco," she replied, hanging up the phone so Lucien would not hear our quarrel over his misdeeds.

"I'm not starting anything. I just don't want you to be taken advantage of."

"The world is not a perfect place, Vinco. It's best to try to change him if I can instead of going back in the market for yet another imperfect person."

"Nana, that's the point."

"What's the point?" She obstructed me, becoming quite apprehensive. "Remember the famous passage from the Bible, 'He, who never sins, casts the first stone?'"

I said nothing more. Her words resonated deep in my egotistical mind, for her shameful predicament bore the symbol of my own maladaptive quirkiness and melodramatic behavior. Until then, I thought I could rule over an imaginary kingdom, leading a two-pronged love game without paying attention to the consequences. I became pensive and retired to my room, leaving the door ajar. She remained in the living room, sitting at the table with a little face mirror, fixing her hair as usual, readying for the next day's work. "Listen, Vinco, Uncle Tony is in town. He called an hour ago. He's staying at Uncle Philippe's and wants to see you."

"Really? I can pick him on Saturday afternoon."

"Why wait that long? You know he always hangs out with you when he's in town."

"I have a big exam coming up, and he always wants me to be his chauffeur, driving around Little Haiti, visiting old mistresses." Uncle Tony was my father's youngest brother. He lived in New York but came down periodically to visit relatives.

"I know school is above and beyond everything. Just be prepared to squeeze him into your busy schedule, even for a few hours."

"I have to think about it. Can you help, Nana?"

"Me? You're kidding," she laughed.

"No, I'm not. With a major exam coming up and all the sleepless nights that come with it... Nana, please help."

266

"I have an idea. Why don't you pick him up early Saturday and drop him off at Rosalie's house?"

"Rosalie? That woman who lives on 48th Street and who sells soup *joumou* on Sunday morning?"

"You got it. I'll call him and let him know you'll pick him up."

"Why would he want to go there? What's the connection between the two?"

"You can ask him. I'm sure you're not a dummy."

"Oh, Uncle Tony. He'll always be the eternal player."

Nana burst out laughing. "Manman said when he was born, his umbilical cord was cut and dropped on a white sheet of paper with multiple women's names written on it."

"And what does that mean, Nana?"

"He would grow up to be a womanizer, running wild after every fat-butt woman who lived in Saint Louis."

"*What?* Nana, you're exaggerating."

"No, I'm not." She edged closer, lowering her voice as if some gossipers were behind the door, eavesdropping. "He had a whole bunch of them all over town. Some of them I can still remember like Danise, Georgette, Silficia, Magréellle, Antoinette Gro-Bounda…"

"Antoinette Gro-Bounda? That big woman who lived in lower Saint Louis?"

"Yep. She lived with a skinny man named Laurencio who walked like a bowlegged fellow with a huge *madougou* inside his pants."

267

"Madougou? You mean a hernia?"

"Of course. You know in Saint Louis, everybody calls it *madougou*."

"But in Port-au-Prince, they call it *maclouclou*." She laughed. "You always try to speak like those folks from Port-au-Prince. But Antoinette was not Uncle Tony's biggest prize. He was a sweet-talker like a libertine, a seducer, and most men in Saint Louis knew that. So, they forbade their women to interact with him."

"Really?"

"Yep. But other feckless, good-for-nothing men, who had no skills in the horrible game of love and deception, hired him to do their bidding. Sometimes, he ended up going to bed with many of these women."

"And what did the men do? Didn't they pay him for the job?"

"They got angry and wanted to cut his throat. Uncle Tony was a complete mess." We both cracked up laughing. Nana then went to the kitchen to make some tea, and I walked to my room, thinking of Mica.

I was totally afraid I had lost my girlfriend. I became restless. The phone soon rang, and I picked it up. Her voice was clear and unequivocal. "Vinco, it's me," she said.

"I know, Mica," I answered. My heart jumped.

"I spoke to Pedro on Monday, and he said you wanted to speak with me after my last class tomorrow afternoon."

"Yes, Mica. I'd like to present my side of the story."

"I won't be able to stay after school."

"I thought at least you could give me an opportunity."

She said nothing.

"Maybe school is not the perfect place. Mica, I'll go anywhere to meet you," I continued. Still, she said nothing, and in the silence that followed, I made a bold attempt to win that meeting. "Can we meet at the Bayfront Park this Saturday afternoon at four? We can meet inside that little coffee shop where we went on our first date."

Still, she did not answer, and the silence persisted. "Mica, are you there?"

"Yes. I don't know. I'll see." Her voice softened like a chirping bird in distress.

"I'll take it as a yes," I said.

"Bye," she said, hanging up the phone.

That call uplifted my spirit to a new high. Even though I was cautiously optimistic, Mica's phone call, I believed, provided me one more chance to win back her heart. Immediately, I felt a sense of urgency to go get Uncle Tony the next day, ahead of my Saturday date with Mica. Not only would this clear my schedule, but it would also provide me an opportunity to learn new tricks from Uncle Tony in this courtship game.

"Vinco, is there anything wrong with Michaela?" Nana asked as I was about to go for a couple of hours of sleep to get ready for another night of study.

"No, we're fine, Nana," I mumbled, trying to avoid the conversation.

"I watched your demeanor. Your voice was changed, sounding like a child begging for food." Her face was drawn and plainly concerned. She had a fond admiration for Michaela and would have been devastated upon learning about what I had done.

"No, no, Nana. She simply wanted to go somewhere tomorrow, and I told her I'll be busy," I lied, but she didn't seem to buy it.

"I know you guys from the Lacroix family. You're a bunch of cold-hearted, ruthless men in dealing with women," she said, walking to her room.

"You're overreacting, Nana. We're A-okay." She didn't seem to pay attention to my inexcusable, ill-founded explanations. She shut the door, and the house went silent.

I now layed on my bed in my room, thinking of Michaela, of how much she meant to me, to my sense of happiness and optimism. Her voice that night, although not reassuring, had brought a much-needed boost to get me through the night, and I now could not wait to meet Uncle Tony, a savvy love catcher, for some guidance.

Chapter 20

Uncle Tony stayed at Uncle Philippe's place every time he came to Miami, and visiting Uncle Philippe had been a joy, a place that had always reminded me of my first night in America when the taxi driver dropped me off at his front door. The difference between then and now could not be sharper.

"You're an American boy, now. My proud *nephew!*" he would shout out, bragging.

He was wifeless, and ever since Nana and I had moved out of his apartment, he had been living with Philippe Junior, his younger son, chubby and cinnamon-skinned. He was as short as my dad, but a bit thinner, with a shiny bald head. His neighbors liked him for his cordiality and his unique sense of optimism in the face of the hardships Haitian immigrants encountered in this country that was so different from the one they had left behind. An impromptu feeling of joy seized us each time I went to see him. He would tell me stories of long ago, of how he watched the community grow before his eyes, of his many concubines living in his neighborhood, of an old priest caught in a gay bar on Biscayne Boulevard, and many more. Lately, I rarely stopped by to share a moment with him. Between school, work, and my ordeal with Michaela and Régine, I had little time to visit Uncle Philippe.

When I showed up Friday afternoon to pick up Uncle Tony, I met him standing on the front step in his usual white polo shirt and short pants, drinking a Michelob Light and smoking a cigarette. "Hey, Vinco. I haven't seen you in years!" he joked.

"Not years, Uncle. It's only been a few weeks. I came to see you on New Year's Eve."

"I know why you come," he said, laughing.

"I've been busy, Uncle. In three months, I'll be graduating, and that has kept me on my toes," I replied as we hugged. He patted me on the back and scratched my hair, making a mess out of it. Uncle Tony was upstairs but soon came down upon hearing my voice outside.

"Vinco, I knew you were coming. You're my *best* nephew," he said, wearing a blue suit without a necktie with typical Caribbean machismo, overconfident and never admitting his wrongs.

"But my cousin Adolph told me you said the same to him the last time he talked to you on the phone."

"You know Tony is a sweet-talker," Uncle Philippe deflected, and then walked a few steps away, going back inside. "Vinco, I know you're not coming in. Tony is in a hurry. I was delighted to see you. Come back again."

He shut the door as Uncle Tony and I drove away, going east to North Miami Avenue, the main highway leading to downtown Little Haiti. He told me he was elated to have escaped the Brooklyn winter, where the crisp air made walking into snow felt like cruising into hell, and the nostalgia for the warm tropical

272

climate of Haiti grew to an intense sadness. Miami was the closest he could get to Haiti, he said, and for that he was overly thrilled. We stopped at a traffic light, and his eyes caught a woman in ragged garments selling peeled sugarcane pieces from a trolley. The woman quickly stepped off the sidewalk and approached the car.

Uncle Tony lowered the window. "How much are the pieces?" he asked.

"Seventy-five cents each," she replied, offering a bite-sized piece to Uncle Tony. He took it, and then pulled a five-dollar bill out of his wallet and handed it to the woman. The light soon turned green, and we sped away.

"Don't you want the change and the sugarcane?" the street vendor cried out.

"You keep it," Uncle Tony said with an empathetic grin. So, we drove on, rather slowly as we entered the shopping district on 62nd Street, where the Creole ambiance had always been a thrill. No skyscrapers were in sight, but low, shingle-roofed buildings that lined up the streets filled with shoppers speaking Creole. All things Haitian were omnipresent, from nail salons to record stores to barber shops to grocery stores to bakeries and more. Suddenly, a man in a convertible Oldsmobile drove right by us, his konpa music blasting away.

"Now, this is Brooklyn in the summer," Uncle Tony chuckled, "especially in the Utica and Flatbush neighborhoods." He stared, unseeing and lost in thought, until he caught a red-haired woman and her blond boy crossing the intersection near the Notre Dame Catholic Church, both drinking Cola Couronne and holding mahogany crafts.

273

Farther out on the pavement near the coffee shops and the bakeries, smiling European tourists, all fragile-looking and wearing tropical outfits, roamed the streets in search of, presumably, internationally renowned Haitian paintings. They were mostly older folks who had gone nostalgic to the good old days in Port-au-Prince of the 1950s when the *Bicentenaire* esplanade near the city harbor gained fame for its casinos, fancy nightclubs, and restaurants.

"To me, it looks more like the lower Port-au-Prince," I said. Until then, Uncle Tony did not realize if Little Haiti had become a miniature replica of Port-au-Prince.

"You're right, Vinco."

By then, we had arrived at my apartment, but Nana was not home.

"When will Nana come home?" he asked.

"Not sure, Uncle. Sometimes, she stops by her church for some prayer sessions before coming home. Other times, she would go to the fish market to buy groupers."

"Groupers? I'd love to get some, especially breaded and deep-fried." His eyes darted around, agitated.

"On Sunday, she'll cook it for you. She already told me. She knows that's your favorite."

He laughed, but a quick one. He began to glance at his watch. I sensed he wanted to leave. Rosalie had stolen his frivolous mind, and the short stop by the apartment felt like an obligatory detour to his real destination.

"Vinco, let's go," he said, leaning on the front door, ready to step out.

"Already? Nana could be here any moment, Uncle."

"I won't be able to wait. Rosalie is waiting on me."

"How about getting something to drink?"

"No. Rosalie has everything squared *away*." He seemed irritated but changed his mood a bit when he saw the disappointment on my face. "I'll be in trouble if I don't eat," he said, wrapping his arms around my neck. "Don't worry, Vinco. I'll spend all day here on Sunday."

But he only noticed part of my disappointment. I had hoped he would stay a little longer. As a pro, his advice would have been extremely important. As we shut the door behind us, I decided to tell him.

"Uncle, there's something I'd like to share with you," I said gravely, which seemed to worry him, and he stopped his march. We were both grounded in one spot.

"What is it, Vinco?" He became startled. I filled him in on my predicament, a young man torn between two charming young women.

"Ah! This is no big deal, nephew," he said dismissively, and that terrified me.

"How come, Uncle Tony?" I was alarmed, thinking my problem could be the result of far-fetched emotions, clumsy steps, and mismanaging my true feelings.

"It's getting late. Let's go and we'll talk in the car." While in the car, I noticed he had gone meditative.

"Uncle, don't forget I need your opinion and suggestions before we get to Rosalie's, and we're almost there."

"Yeah. I'm trying to find the simplest way to make you understand the complexities of life," he said softly, stroking the remaining, shrinking hair on his increasingly bald head. "You see, Vinco," he continued, "contrary to women, one's habitual disposition is not always how a man's love can be measured. However, we must agree on the important role it plays in building the foundation of a love story."

His words of wisdom left me bemused. "Translation?"

"Vinco, you say Régine is about to marry someone else, right?"

"Yes."

"And how do you plan on repairing the damage?"

"I don't know, Uncle."

"Then you need to be realistic. The only way to heal her pain would be to go back to her and try to win her back. But I don't think it's now possible. That girl has moved on. If that girl was genuinely interested in you or in reviving the relationship, she should have confronted you before making such a deep commitment to someone else. You may still be the one she will always love, but I'm afraid it's too late."

"To ask for forgiveness, you mean?" I preempted him.

"Vinco, I'm pretty sure a part of you will always love her, just like if you and Mica ever break up, a part of you will always love her too. That's why you feel guilty, but that doesn't mean she's the right person for you now. That girl doesn't need your forgiveness. You see, love isn't a fairytale. True love I mean. How many things in your life you so desire, but you can't afford them?"

"Lots of things."

"And I suppose Régine's love is one of them. So, you're going to have to learn to live with the sad reality. Vinco, you have nothing to offer this girl right now in exchange for canceling her wedding, breaking another man's heart, and disappointing everyone involved in the process."

"Uncle, I have no intention of destroying her upcoming wedding. In fact, we met last week. I raised the wedding issue because she didn't want to tell me."

"And then what did she say?"

"She acknowledged it reluctantly."

We were now a block away from Rosalie's. I slowed my speed almost to a standstill. She lived in a triplex across the street from which lay an unpaved parking lot dotted by mango trees. Aside from some hungry stray dogs roaming the lot, few cars parked there. Realizing my fear, he instructed me to pull into a spot near the sidewalk.

"Vinco, I'm assuming Michaela, just like Régine, loves you unconditionally. I'm also assuming she doesn't have Régine's baggage and she's committed to one man."

"Uncle, I'm not sure if the commitment is still there. I don't know if she still loves me."

"And why are you saying she's angry, very angry? If it's true she no longer loves, this means she never did. Learning from my own experiences, she's mad because she's now reeling from the raw pain of betrayal, and as long as the pain is there, the love is very much alive."

"We'll see, Uncle."

"And you say she called you last night and agreed to a meeting tomorrow?"

"Yes, Uncle."

"There is your chance to patch things up."

"I'm not as optimistic as you. But like you, I would say it's a golden opportunity to let her know once more how much she means to me."

"One good advice, young man." He leaned forward and looked me straight in the eyes. "When you meet her tomorrow, don't be defensive. Admit your guilt and let her talk. It's all part of the healing process. When she's done, when she runs out of arguments, you make your pitch." I nodded in agreement. Then a cheerful, plump woman in a red dress strolled by, pulling a young boy along while scolding him for being naughty. "*Rosalie,*" Uncle Tony called to her.

She abruptly turned around. "*Tony,*" she shrieked. "I've been waiting for the *longest time* now," she said, beaming a bewitching smile.

Uncle Tony then stepped out of the car and met her midway. They soon fell into each other's arms, exchanging a prolonged, emotionally charged hug. "Vinco, you may go now. Rosalie will drop me off at Philippe's home later."

"Okay, Uncle." Before I drove out of the parking lot, he retreated back to me. "Call me tomorrow night after you meet Michaela." He and Rosalie then crossed the street and disappeared behind a concrete wall.

#

It had been two weeks since Michaela and I shared a simple smile. It ached every fiber of my heart. The pain, so harsh and limitless, ran deep in my heart, an immeasurable soreness for which I had no remedy. Only Mica held the key to that evasive cure. I longed for the moment when she and I could once again find common ground, to clear the fog standing in the way, dimming the light of our promising romance. I made it to Bayfront Park thirty minutes ahead of time, shortly after a quick shower that had drenched the boardwalk along the Biscayne Bay Marina. I took it as a bad sign. But the rain did not seem to have much of an impact on the coffee shop located near the north end. From a distance, it looked busy and noisy, and therefore would not be the perfect venue for that special moment. Unfortunately, it was our meeting place, and having one more chance to be with Mica was golden.

I wandered down a walkway leading to the coffee shop's main entrance, passing through a myriad of young men and women ambling about, hand in hand, eating ice cream like lovers do in wonderland. There, I waited near one of the benches facing the shallow water. Shortly afterward, I saw her coming in a floral, buttoned dress, clutch bag in hand, waltzing with ease like a heroine on a mission to win a hotly contested battle. Midway, she paused as her eyes scanned the area around the coffee shop, searching for me. When our eyes caught each other, she strode on, and I left the bench, walking in her direction. When we met halfway through, I hunched for a hug, but she avoided me, rather politely.

"Good afternoon, Mica," I said in the most dovish manner.

"I don't know how I got here. I wanted to call to cancel, and I had been thinking about it since last night," she said, standing

279

firm and holding her head high; but in the well-trimmed crease of her brows, her pain was obvious.

"So, we go in?" I suggested.

"Can't we talk here?" she asked.

"Why, Mica?"

"Because I'm not comfortable being in a restaurant with you."

"Mica, if you choose to stay here, I'm fine with it, but I think it would be better if——?"

"If *what*?" she cried in resentment. The curves of her lips stretched out, and she smiled, a short smile she quickly repressed into a smirk. So, we decided to sit side by side on a small bench near a tree-lined pathway.

"Mica, I know you have the right to be angry. I know there isn't much I can do to reverse the damage I've caused to your heart. However, if you can listen to what I have to say, that might help save what we're now about to lose."

"What are we losing? *What*? As far as I'm concerned, we have nothing more to lose because whatever we had, if any, has already been lost in a stew of lies, deceptions, and betrayal. Now, I'm trying to find a way to free myself from a shameful past."

"Oh, Mica. Our relationship was in no way shameful," I said with teary eyes. "Can I please present my side of the story, Mica?"

"What side, Vinco? You've already admitted to being in a relationship with that girl," she growled from the base of her throat. I had never seen her so disagreeable.

"No, I've only admitted to having been, not to *being*." These words pained me so much. I paused for a moment. I knew I was not telling the whole truth. "You see, Mica, like everyone else, I have a past, and the relationship with Régine is part of that past. I never thought it was necessary to share that story with you. Honestly, Mica, I'm not comfortable talking to you about Régine. I thought it would be disrespectful to you. Now I realize I've committed a grave mistake. Please, forgive me, Mica."

She listened attentively and inquisitively, making no attempt to stop me.

"Yes, Mica. She was a childhood sweetheart who now lives in town. I've only met her here twice. One was only for a few seconds at Laurette's home when I went to visit her. Shortly after that, I sent her a note to explain why I could not return to Haiti and to also acknowledge the pain that may have caused her. But nowhere in that note did I make a plea to rekindle that relationship for obvious reasons that I don't wish to enumerate." I handed her the note to prove my point, but she refused to take it, and even seemed offended. She sized me up with a disgusted gaze. So, I continued. "The second time was last week when I invited her to a restaurant on the east side of town."

Her eyes widened in horror. "You invited *her?*"

"*Please*, let me finish, Mica. Yes, I did because Laurette is now working hard to undermine our relationship in the hope that Régine and I could get back together. If Laurette thought I was still in love with Régine, why would she have to fabricate baseless accusations to get her wish? Régine is getting married in a few weeks. Both Laurette and Chantale know that. But Laurette, a spoiler, is determined to destroy the girl's opportunity to have some stability in her life, and she wants to use me to achieve her goal. So, I felt the only way to stop Laurette was to meet Régine and to express my best wishes as well as let her know that I myself have moved on and am now seeing someone at school."

"Why would Laurette want to use you to destroy the girl's upcoming wedding, as you say?"

"Because she knows Régine still loves me. She also thinks I might still be in love with her, but my relationship with you would make this impossible." I then stopped, ready to make a plea, but she stopped me.

"Vinco, lately I've been doing a lot of soul searching, trying to find the way out of my ordeals. But in my thought process, every possible solution leads to one direction: you. So, my resentment grows to a level I'm afraid I may not be able to control. I will never trust you again, or any man for that matter. I was too naïve to believe in this fairytale. Ever since we met, I had been living only for you, making sure that I didn't do anything that would disappoint you. And look what you've done to me. I feel trapped in a trench of disloyalty and now I'm struggling to regain the energy I need to climb out of this sinkhole of endless pain. I'm fighting to learn how to live without you, without the memories, and it makes me angrier that I still have to think of you, the man who has perforated my heart and broken it into pieces. It's so true they say anger is a tie to the past, but I wanna be free from the shadow of this *terrifying* past." A well of tears streamed down her cheeks now reddened by the drops, and she made no attempt to wash them away.

"*Oh*, Mica." I wailed and sniffed under the sharpness of her words.

"It's true. You never loved me. I was only the shadow of a love you cherished for someone else."

282

"Not *true*, Mica."

"What do you mean 'not true?' Cheating and love are incompatible. When infidelity occurs, it reveals the missing part of a lopsided love." She shifted in her seat, now facing me with unblinking eyes fueled by rage. "You're just like one of *them*."

"Mica, how could Régine be a threat to our relationship? She's getting married in two weeks."

"Her marriage may be the boundary that keeps you…"

"Keep me from what, Mica? From going back to her?"

"Vinco, do you think you can still fool me?" And the tears kept coming. Her words, so punchy, struck deep in my heart, producing incalculable angst, inestimable guilt, and an immeasurable shame. Then, I remembered Uncle Tony's words, *Let her release her anger. Don't be defensive.* But Mica's demeanor did not foretell any reconciliation. On the contrary, it portrayed the hardening resolve of a young woman determined to beat back waves of anguished thoughts and be freed from the venom of unfaithfulness and romantic deceptions.

"Mica, could you please give our love a second chance? We should not allow Laurette's manipulations to stand in our way, to shatter our dreams, destroying a love that continues to be a wonderful example to many of our classmates. I agree that meeting Régine was a stupid decision, but I can speak with absolute certainty that in no way did I seek a secret love affair with her. It was a way to show empathy that I'd decided to meet her. Mica, I know how it feels to be left alone, helpless, and scared." I stopped for a moment, trying to carefully choose my words. "You know, Mica, you're the girl I will forever be in love with. Besides the natural chemistry that exists between us, you have many traits that impress me immensely, and chief among them is your ability to understand and sympathize with others' problems. This is a trait I'm proud of, for it showcases your good sense of humility and humanity. You've always lived in the comfort of your parents' love and shelter, but as immigrants themselves, I'm sure they had lived through uncertain moments like most immigrants away and alone in an unfamiliar country, deprived of any social support, and therefore unable to prevent waves of humiliations. Ask them, and they'll be more than happy to share their story with their lovely daughter."

She adjusted herself and swung a bit, taking fearful aim at my face, her unsaid words charged with scolding. "Vinco," she said suddenly. "I'm discovering a side of you I thought never existed. You lie with such a cold stare, trying to transform your wrongdoings into tales of compassion. It's hard to imagine you went to see Régine only to show empathy. Empathy for what? Isn't she getting married? What do you think I am? A naïve, childish girl?" Her eyes swelled with tears.

She joined me again on the bench. I had never felt so ashamed. I dared not to utter a single word. So, we sat, wallowing in a silence of grief. A happy couple soon strolled by, hands around each other's waists. The man, tall and coffee-colored, seemed to have found the key to the front gate of paradise, holding blissfully his pale-skinned woman as they exchanged kisses along the way. Mica's eyes squinted and she took a quick glance at the couple, who were weaving through bushes of multicolor flowers.

She stood right up, fixing the long, golden hair that curled around her chin. "I have to go," she said, straightening her dress.

"Can I drive you home?" I asked, standing up while pulling the car key from my pants pocket.

"No, thank you."

She walked away without looking back and I remained there watching, defeated, as her frame undulated between clusters of happy people perambulating the park, chatting, and laughing in the afternoon breeze, until she faded from my sight outside the park entrance. I knew then how clumsy I had been and how tough were the consequences of my clumsiness. I should have found a way to speak to Régine in the clearest fashion possible, to let her know our love story was over, to leave her no room for misinterpretation, no space to write her damaging letter, providing Laurette the weapon she needed to strike her fatal blow. But could I really do that without trashing Régine's dignity? If we could not revive our past romance, I thought, I owed her at least the respect she deserved. Obviously, Régine was getting married. Our past was an adventure I could not go back to, a past Régine herself had already left behind.

Days after the meeting with Michaela at the park, I continued to feel the weight of her words pounding at my heart. At school, I struggled to put forth the same jolly face my classmates had come to know me for, the face of a young man full of optimism, a young man passionate about intellectual discussions and maintaining his GPA. Only three people knew about my ordeal: Pedro and Ronel, whom I considered my adopted brothers, and Chantale, who was extremely concerned about my loss of appetite for any form of activity around campus, including students association meetings in which I commanded a lot of respect.

Chantale kept me company, staying with me in the library during study sessions, and I helped her with her math problems. She loved to cook and she, like my sister, cooked like a pro. She lived with her lovely parents a few blocks from my apartment. She knew I craved rice and beans mixed with coconut milk. She would bring the dish to school, hot and tasty, in an aluminum bowl that we shared, eating in my car. She would cheer me up during intervals of sadness.

"Mica will come around, Vinco. She will, like I did when Alain cheated on me." She would poke my cheeks and sing old Haitian folk songs. She would not stop until I laughed and began to sing along. Alain was her boyfriend, a smart young man, very extroverted and popular around campus. Chantale watched Laurette's every move to make sure she did not pull another trick. Laurette and I had become friends, and she later conveyed to Chantale her deep remorse for her actions.

These three friends had suddenly become a much-needed support system at school on which I heavily depended while going through my last semester as an undergrad student. The day after I met with Michaela at the park, I told Pedro about her hardening heart and my failure to persuade her to change her mind. Pedro told me to keep trying, but trying required extra time, something I did not have. Still, I tried, but she had chosen avoidance as her new way to deal with me. Several times, I waited for her after class, hoping to have a chat. She would return to the classroom as soon as she saw me standing in the hallway. One Saturday night, I called her at home, and she picked up the phone, not knowing if it was me.

"*Hola*," she answered.

"Mica, it's me," I said.

"*Oh*, Vin—*co*," she replied, stuttering in a way that was unlike her. "Listen, I'm sorry. We can't talk right now. My mom is about to use the phone."

She then hung up, and I began to accept the reality of losing Michaela. Her refusal to talk to me struck deep in my veins, as for the first time, she was explicit in her rejection. I figured if she wanted to exchange a few words, her mother would not have objected. Since that night, I started thinking it was the price to pay for playing the dangerous game of love and dishonesty. I only wished she would accept my apology for having hurt her in one of the most vital organs of her body: her heart. I now realized how much I loved her and how much I hated my bizarre behavior. Too much shame had befallen me.

There were days it was hard, too hard to walk around campus. Redoubling my effort to graduate on time would spare me the unsustainable, daily embarrassment. I assumed the alternative would be a major setback. I would betray the trust my sister had put on me, as having a college degree was our only ticket out of poverty. Pristine love never guarantees a productive life, Manman used to say. I never shared my decision with any of my close friends, knowing how much I would disappoint them, especially Pedro who, from time to time, would tell me about Mica's own struggle to recover. Although I stopped trying to win a chat with her, every day before class, I left a new note on the bench held by two small stones. "I waited, and you didn't come. No matter how long it takes, I'll still be waiting."

Chapter 21

Love is *such* a complex issue and can be hard to express sometimes. It has the ability to cripple someone's heart. It can provide the ability to bear the most powerful feeling of affection with an equal potential to inflict the clearest, most pathetic form of pain. When I was younger, love was, to me, the final frontier before leaping into paradise.

When Régine and I exchanged our first kiss, something unimaginable happened. Instantly, I had become a prisoner of my own feelings. Whenever we were apart, there was a constant fear of losing her. That fear waned months after I left Haiti, only to reappear when I learned she was in Miami. I worked hard to get rid of that fright and, for a while, I thought I had conquered it the day I watched her kiss that young man in her courtyard. This conviction was reinforced when I shredded her last note and trashed it. What Régine and I shared, however, was deeper than what I was willing to admit, and to let those childhood reveries die was one of the most painful acts in my love story. This was a lesson I learned three weeks after I had read her last letter.

288

It was a Friday afternoon, the last weekend of January. I was on my way to the gym to meet my Haitian buddies for our regular workout when Carine, a tall, honey-brown, slim girl, called to me.

"Vinco, I need a ride home," she said cheerfully.

"Sure," I replied, interrupting my stroll to wait for her.

Carine was Régine's cousin and the only member of her family who remained my friend after Régine and I broke up. Carine was always on the go when she was not in class. She was known for her brand of high-heeled boots and black jeans, and boys at school seemed to have lost their minds over her confidence and happy demeanor. I admired her for her exquisite *franc-parler* (her outspoken manner.) Although prudish in the way of most Haitian girls, she grew up in Miami, adopting more of an American lifestyle, obviously different from the traditionally reserved young ladies one would find in the tropics. Perhaps this was the reason why she always told me she well understood the rationale behind my separation from Régine. She spoke her mind, telling it like it is. She told me stories of how she used to go head-to-head with her sisters and cousins when they criticized her for our continued friendship.

"Tica, you'd better watch out for the hawks before they take a nosedive on you," I teased her as we met. Tica was what all her friends called her.

"You *stop* it. I wanna go home now." She shrugged off my shallow warning.

"At your command, madame," I laughed derisively. So, I forewent my afternoon exercise with the boys and strode together to the parking lot. While in the car, I could not help but ask about whatever happened to her car.

She owned a red Corolla. "Reynold has it," she said, referring to her boyfriend.

"Does he?"

"He was late for work, and his car was at the shop for repair."

"Tica, you're still seeing that loser?"

"I'm *ready* to dump him now."

"You've been holding this line for over two years now."

"Vinco, I have to be honest with you. I haven't had the courage to do so. I still love him, despite his so many wrongs… I know he's nothing but a basket case. I feel trapped, and he knows it."

"You mean love is such a hell of a trap?"

"Yes, that's my personal experience."

I could feel the pain coming out of her shaking voice. We rode in silence. Although our stories were different, the effect of an agonizing love story always felt like a riverbed going dry. In the absence of affection and the renewed sense of trust, it was almost impossible to rekindle a moribund romance, and that was why I was convinced Régine and I were done for good.

An old French song from the radio suddenly broke the silence. It was France Gall singing *"Ella, elle l'a."* (Ella, she has it.) Carine hummed a few lines. She had learned the song from her sister Marie-Lourdes who, like most Haitian girls in town, shared a passion for French ditties, a delicacy they could still enjoy while listening to Haitian radio in Miami. But that song also brought back the bittersweet memory of the very first night Régine and I danced at the Coquillage. Too painful to bear, I switched off the station.

290

"Why did you do *that*?" she asked.

"Because you're almost home," I replied.

Between chatting and singing, we drove past the Haitian clothing stores and the flea market without realizing it. By the time I switched off the music, we were already near her place. She lived on a dead-end street by the Golden Glades traffic circle on NW 7th Avenue. Before she had a chance to switch back to the song, we were already in front of the townhouse apartment she shared with a roommate. She exited the car and strolled toward her front porch. I was ready to drive off when she turned around and called to me.

"*Wait*, Vinco. I almost forgot. I have something I want you to see."

I backed up a bit and pulled into her driveway. It was a mixed neighborhood, but no one was in sight when she held the door and let me in. I soon followed her to the kitchen where I came face-to-face with Régine sitting on a highchair by the kitchen counter. She immediately jumped off the chair and edged closer to me, wearing a blue buttoned-up dress opened from her breast line and up. My lips went numb. Carine stood a pace behind us. She made no effort to try to justify what she had just done. She then stepped away from the kitchen and strolled to the living room where she turned on the television to get the latest news from Haiti.

"Good job, Tica. It was well *planned*," I let out. I was angry. I felt she had lured me into a trap. But out of respect for Régine, I had managed to control my demeanor. She did not reply, but Régine, dovish and submissive, threw a capricious grin.

"By the way, are you spending the weekend here with Carine?" I asked her, looking straight into her eyes, searching for any remaining sense of humility from the girl I knew back in Saint Louis.

"Yes," she replied, raising her lips gently to display a flirty smile.

Carine then walked upstairs, leaving us alone in the kitchen. Régine stood erect, hands on hips, taking aim at my developed upper body. I did not know what to say. She moved even closer, holding both of my hands. Intertwining her fingers with mine, she began to scratch my palms. In Haitian tradition, scratching your lover's palm is a request for lovemaking. "Vinco, I was hoping to hear from you after our meeting," she said timidly, coy as a turtledove.

"I wasn't going to do that. I suppose you know why," I said, contracting my face to show my displeasure.

"No, I don't," she chortled, still holding my hands.

"Ginou, the last thing I want is to be a spoiler, a heartbreaker once more," I said. I was blunt.

"Vinco, don't be sarcastic." She threw a cunning look loaded with deception. "I got some things I want you to see, Vinco."

"What are they?"

"*Come*," She instructed me with her index finger.

I was hesitant, but still I followed her to a bedroom behind the kitchen. The room was arranged in the neatest fashion, the way she knew I would have liked it. Photos of Barbara, our favorite French singer back home, were posted on the wall. A historic photo of both of us taken on a white sandy shoal against the backdrop of a verdant landscape by the Saint Louis River was displayed over the lamp table. She then handed me a bowl of cashew nuts. She knew I loved cashews.

"For you, Vinco," she muttered in her old whimsically waggish manner, twinkling her puppy eyes.

Michaela's face and piercing words flashed across my mind, and my heart leaped in horror. "Ginou," I uttered suddenly.

Her eyes widened. "Yes, Vinco."

"You didn't have to do all this. Like I stated in my notes to you, I will always cherish our good old time back in Saint Louis. But I want you to understand that I can't be the villain who destroys your up coming wedding."

She stopped me right there. "I've got enough of your senseless *preaching*," she meowed, a kitten cuteness, feline in all its form.

"No, Ginou. I thought back at the restaurant last week, we both understood the impasse that we're now in. You're marrying someone..."

She did not reply, but instead she pulled me down to sit next to her. She then began to talk about our upbringing in Saint Louis—the way we were, running wild in our parents' backyards, moonlit promenading along the unpaved street of our neighborhood. I quickly understood this was all a scheme to fill my heart with remorse. She then released my hands and lay face up, her legs spread, her firm, honeyed breasts exposed, and her dress now completely unbuttoned. She raised her index finger and rested it on my lips, letting me know it was no time for romantic questioning.

"I heard footsteps," she said suddenly, but I didn't hear anything.

"Maybe it's Carine in the kitchen," I said. My heart pounded heavily.

"Let me go see." She got up discreetly and, with a sensuous slink, walked to the kitchen. She came right back, lying face up again. Her head leaned on my lap. "She's upstairs, now," she uttered softly.

Still, I sat there on the edge of the bed, evermore convinced that Régine was no longer the girl I knew. Now, I understood that in the game of courtship and deceptive romance, she had become quite skillful. And this latest move, shrewdly crafted in such inexpressive, unimaginable adroitness, mixing feminine charm and sexual advances, left me no doubt about my immediate reaction the minute after I read her last note. But how could I resist such beauty displaying in front of me—*just* for me?

"*Ginou.*"

"*Vinco.*"

I did not reply. I could not. The heat of the moment had carried me away. I soon crept my hand toward her legs, spreading them now even wider. She eased her body to help me get rid of her dress, and beneath see-through panties, her pristine vagina burst into full view, sending my head to spin. Irresistibly, I began to stroke her breasts and she responded in waves of moans and groans. I shed my clothes without knowing it. Soon, we entered the forbidden land. After prolonged lovemaking, we emerged from under the bedsheet soaked in sweat.

"Ginou," I said briskly, "what can this wonderful moment do for us?"

"I'm not sure, but I know one thing."

"What, Ginou?"

"It will always give me the sweetest of memories."

"Ginou, why are you marrying someone you...?"

She pulled away from me. Her face suddenly drawn. "Don't even go there. How dare you? No one else has the answer, but you."

"When is the wedding?"

"In three weeks."

"Really?"

"Vinco, I'm ready to give it all up..."

"No, no."

"What do you mean? You think I'm a slut?"

"Oh, Ginou, how could I think so of you? But..."

She preempted me. "No need to explain. From today on, I'll be like a mannequin with moving limbs until it's my time to fade from this cruel world. And for you, I wish you all the best with your Dominican girl."

"Ginou, Ginou..." She no longer paid attention to my inexcusable verbiage. With teary eyes, she got out of the bed and walked to the shower, leaving me dumbfounded and still naked. Until now, I had not known if she was aware of my story with Michaela. I felt so used, like a piece of trash on top of an overflowing dumpster. After this moment, I expected some words of irrefutable reproaches, tales of her intimate experiences, moments of painful solitude, and her parents' struggles to send her here to America. I heard none of that. Instead, it was a subliminal coup that pushed me down, a fall from grace, an agony I will forever endure.

Michaela's sincere words now invaded my mind, strumming my pain even deeper, like the hardening scars from the strings of an acoustic guitar. Guilt crippled my heart. How could I look at her in the eye, knowing how dishonest I had been, betraying her trust? In the darkening room, it became icy cold and deathly quiet. From the bathroom, the rushing shower pierced the serenity.

"Vinco, you can come join me," she called to me.

"Don't worry. I'll wait," I replied, shaking.

I moved to the bathroom and grabbed a towel from the rack with which I wrapped my body. There, I waited, and as soon as she exited the shower, I went in. When it was all over and we had our clothes on, together we walked out of the room, no longer talking to each other, like two warriors after a bitterly contested fight and she was the winner. When we reached the center of the living room, she left me standing there and, without saying a word, she walked upstairs to join Carine.

"Régine, you can't do this to me," I said with a subdued tone of voice, full of remorse. That plea seemed to have emboldened her feeling of dominance, and in a stunning reversal of thoughts, she decided to face me head-on, heaving out of her consciousness everything she had consumed within her broken heart, for over four years.

"You know, Yrvin," she began. Her eyes brimmed with tears. "When we kissed for the first time at the Coquillage, I was shaking, if you still remember, not because I was afraid of what my friends might have said, not even because of my parents; I was shaking because I was afraid of losing you, I was afraid of romantic betrayal." She paused for a moment and, with a disgusted stare, wiped away the tears that swelled her eyes. She stood tall, strong and firm, but despite her effort to dry the tears off her face, they kept on coming, streaming down her cheeks. These were not tears of sorrow, but rather tears of anger and of an immeasurable thirst for revenge.

"Ginou, you know I've always loved you…"

"Don't Ginou me. Don't you *dare*," she growled. "You're talking about love. You don't know what love is. You're just a trailblazer who cruises shamelessly in the land of vulnerable hearts, those hearts so weak, like mine, that they easily fall prey to your deceptive charm. You don't know what love is. You're a vicious liar, a razor-sharped, multiple-edged knife. You don't care whose heart gets hurt, whose heart you've shredded, and whose dignity that has been shattered because of your *misdeeds*." Her voice rose and quivered on the last word. She then took a quick pause to catch her breath as Carine from upstairs, hands on the railing, watched her cousin with amused eyes. I glanced upward, and my eyes met hers, but she quickly averted her gaze to avoid mine.

Régine grinned a little and soon took aim at the wall behind me, as if her fierce and indescribable gaze were passing through me. "For four years, I waited, watching the passage of time and the fading of my hope to ever see you again. And every day, I would wake up thinking this would be the day that brought the end of my suffering. The day would come and go as dreadful, painful, as the day before. I could not escape the humiliation and the gossip spreading around Saint Louis, especially when they spread vile rumors about how you no longer needed me. I dreamed and cried in silence. Some days were tougher to go

297

through. These were the days when the haunting memories were too vivid in my wretched mind to ignore, and I would go near the river mouth to watch the sailboats and their captains and their passengers buying fish from the fishermen in Nan Figue, pretending you were the invisible ghost strolling along with me like we used to. Other times, I would go near the riverbed, spending hours, shedding tears of hopelessness. My nights were as agonizing as my days. Sometimes, I wrestled with my eyes to fall asleep. But I couldn't. The minute I started dozing off, it's you I could see, and I would wake up in the middle of the night, having nightmares."

"I waited and waited. You never came. But you know, Yrvin, it wasn't the wait that hurt. It was the indifference. As the song says, 'Indifference is what slowly kills.' Life has no meaning for me anymore. From now on, everything I do will not be because of some self-centered, egotistical ambition. I will do it because of some family obligations." She then left me stranded near the door and climbed up to join Carine.

I was a totally broken man. From a loft upstairs, both girls watched as I struggled to open the door. In a final gesture of sympathy, Régine stepped down and walked toward me for one last time. "In case you forgot. Today is the last day I share my love with someone, not with you or anyone else. *Goodbye*, Yrvin." She released my hand and shut the door. She then broke into tears, and I could hear her scream from behind the door. My heart broke as I walked to my car and drove home.

Chapter 22

My sister was not home, and I felt lucky she was not. I did not know how I was going to face her, for the devastation was written all over my face, and there was no way I could hide it. Fearing she might walk at any minute, I decided to get in the car and go straight to my cousin, Constance. She lived with her parents on 44th Street, at the entrance of Little Haiti coming from downtown Miami. When I made it to her street, she was in the front yard leaning against the gates of a chain-link fence that enclosed the property of her home. I hurried and parked by the side of the street and walked out, moving in uncertain steps like a loser. She had never before seen me in such a desolate state.

"*Vinco*, Jesus, Marie, Joseph, what's wrong?" she asked, spluttering in an explosive, shocked voice. She pulled the gates open and let me in.

"I can't *talk* right now. I need some tea with a grain of salt. I need it *now*," I stuttered.

She grabbed me by the arm out of fear I might stumble and fall. She was a mahogany-colored girl, a bit taller than I was, and she had a commanding stare that I admired. I trusted her. She held all my secrets, and her advice was golden to me. She knew

299

my agonizing story and had kept it under wraps. That afternoon, however, she could not conceal a thing. I was shaking so much that she had to literally carry me to the door, passing by her younger brother Smith. He was a short boy nicknamed Ti-Mimit, hued in a chocolate tan with an omnipresent tinge of shaded brown in his tawny face, especially after his regular morning jogs. Her older sister Priscille, and Kesner, another of our cousins. He was a boy with an ebony complexion and squinting eyes nicknamed Soyons, together with Ti-Mimit sat on a couch in the living room watching a music show on the television. Suddenly, they all stopped watching and directed their eyes on me. Constance soon dropped me into their arms. The boys carried me to Constance's bedroom where I lay face down on her bed. Constance ran to the kitchen. Priscille followed her.

"Vinco, you got us all scared. Please, tell us what's wrong," Both Soyons and Ti-Mimit raised their voices in horror.

"*M'paka pale, m'paka pale,*" I answered rather faintly. (I can't talk right now.)

The boys remained stupefied and resigned to sit by my side, creating a buffer to protect me, should I decide to jump and fall. I was losing my mind. The pain was too raw. Soon, the girls burst in from the kitchen. Priscille carried a cup of tea while Constance brought in a wet towel tinged with green alcohol to rub my forehead. Priscille was an older, introverted russet girl, quite reserved, and who, like Constance, had a special affinity for me, knowing my precarious life, living without my parents in the hectic city of Miami.

"Vinco, here, drink the tea and tell us what is bothering you," she commanded. I felt compelled immediately to tell it all to my beloved cousins. Priscille and the boys knew about my story with

Régine but had no clue about Michaela. So, I turned around, sat up, grabbed the cup of tea, and gulped it down.

I rested my head against the headboard, facing them. Their worried eyes were fixated on me. I filled them in on the story. I told them how Carine trapped me and led me to Régine's love nest so she could strike her fatal blow. I told them how it was impossible to resist as I sat in front of her elegant outline, legs widened and undressed. I told them how her face turned cold and became like an unhinged Madonna after our wild lovemaking. I told them how she admitted to having purposely staged the coup, using me as her favorite toy to satisfy her gratifying lust for the last time in her life, and that from now on she no longer needed me or any other man for that matter. Priscille's jaw dropped in horror. Constance moved closer and wrapped her long arm around my neck as if she wanted to shelter me from further danger. Soyons looked dazed, totally astonished. Ti-Mimit's face hardened in anguish.

"I'm disappointed in Régine, although I recognize she has a point. She's right to be angry, but seeking revenge in such vulgar fashion will serve her no purpose," Soyons whispered.

"What kind of girl morphs herself into a bimbo to make an ex-boyfriend pay?" Ti-Mimit let out.

"Be careful, Ti-Mimit. Her act is not that of a bimbo, nor does it mean she no longer loves Vinco. She still does, but she understands Vinco's love is now out of her reach, and the one waiting for her is the one she doesn't want. You all know why she's marrying this other man…"

"Let's not get into that. What you're doing now is like hitting Vinco's heart multiple times with a double-edged knife. This is too painful," Constance said, straightening herself in bed to take a direct aim at her sister. I lay there, guilt-ridden, for everything they were saying was true.

"Vinco, man up. Be strong. Dilemmas like this are part of growing up in this complicated world, so cruel sometimes. And if you think Régine walks away victorious, think again. Victors don't cry. They rejoice. They celebrate. There's no winner here. You just said how you heard her crying behind the door as you were leaving," Constance added.

"If I was you, Vinco, I would make her pay," Ti-Mimit inserted.

"You're a man of God, Ti-Mimit. Don't think that way," Soyons reminded him.

"Soyons's right, Vinco," Priscille conceded. "The pain will go away. Roll up your sleeves and take it with a grain of salt," she added.

"And then," Constance intervened. "Vinco, be yourself, your old self, cousin. You still have your Michaela, so pretty, so charming. Don't seek revenge. And even if you wanted revenge as Ti-Mimit suggested, against whom? Carine, that sleazy girl? Régine who lost it all? Listen, Vinco, in romantic backstabbing, vengeful pleasures always lead to self-destruction. Remember that," she concluded, standing up while asking everyone to take me home. She handed me a handkerchief to wipe away the tears welling down my cheeks. She instructed Ti-Mimit and Soyons to drive my car, following her while she and Priscille would take me in her car. I thanked them with many hugs after they dropped me off at home. They waited for me to get inside before they left.

\#

One cold windy morning in early February, I arrived at school earlier than usual. The campus yard was empty, as it was a very chilly day. The few students outside rushed to their classes. The chill, however, had a reverse effect on me. Reaching the bench, I felt grounded and alone. I wanted her. That little bench behind the chapel was now a shrine for our forgotten and buried love, from when Mica and I, at the prime of our time together, would hug and kiss, oblivious to our surroundings. That morning, I decided to write a different note.

Mica,

I want you to know that I'm cold, and only your soft, tendered hand can chase this wintry air away. I need you more than ever before. Please, forgive me for all the pain I've caused. I wish I could undo the suffering; but I hope in your heart there's still room for love, and if there isn't, I understand. I'll simply have to learn to live in this endless continuum of bitter chagrin. If there's still a trace of that love that I so desire, I implore you to reconsider. Love dies when and only when all the windows of hopes and desires have been closed. Mica, I want you to know that I'll never find the strength to reclaim my old self without you. Bye, my love.

I folded the note in a white envelope and pinned it down with two marble stones. Then I went to class. When the class was dismissed, I made a hasty run to check on the note. There, she was standing by the bench in a winter jacket, pair of jeans tucked inside high-heeled boots.

"*Mica?*" I exclaimed.

She smiled without reciprocation. I held her hand, and she made no attempt to pull away.

"I'm cold, Mica. I want you to know I'm suffering."

She turned her face away but her hands still rested in mine. "My pain is deeper and greater because it bears the story of betrayal and the shattering of love, dreams, and hope," she uttered timidly.

I pulled her into me, and her timorous eyes slowly blinked. "I believe, *amorecita*, we can rebuild from a stronger foundation."

"Vinco, I come here because I love you beyond reason."

"Mi amor, there're reasons that perhaps you and I can never explain, certainly not with words."

"But despite my uncontrolled emotions, I continue to feel betrayed, and I'm still fighting the clouds standing in the way."

"Mica, not all clouds can prevent the full moon. And every time we stumble and fall, the moon rays, ever-present, shine on us again, heralding a new dawn. If all that we've been through over the past few weeks was a test of faith, I can now speak with absolute certainty that our love can endure any hardship. I can't picture myself in a world without having to share my love, my laugh, my hope with a wonderful person like you."

She looked at me as if searching for a rejuvenated Vinco, the one she's always loved, the one whose flaws and cleverness have been the essence of her journey in this long chain of human existence. Michaela knew as humans we are not perfect, and our good moral character lies in our ability to build strength from our weaknesses and imperfections. The sun rose timidly, but it had no effect on the cold wind gusting on our faces, forcing us to vacate the bench. We retreated to a reading den near the chapel, where it was cozy and warm.

"Vinco, can I ever trust you again?"

"This is a question for which I can't answer with words. But I know I love you. Though it has yet to be written, our story seems so natural, with conspicuous evidence manifested in our inexpressible, ineffable feeling of everlasting love. Because of that, I'm confident, Mica, you and I stand ready to weather any storm, any unforeseen misfortune that might befall our shared existence. Mi amor, I'm truly sorry."

She wrapped her arms around my neck, rested her head on my chest, and threw a lacerating cry. I could see her reluctance. In agreeing to revive our shaky romance, she was unsure whether she was surrendering her dignity and all that made her such a respectful young woman. I lurched for her lips, and she now reciprocated in kind. Under the sway of our emotions, we hugged, squeezed, and kissed.

"Can I drive you home, Mica?"

"Uh-huh."

My hand wrapped about her waist and we walked out of the den and sauntered down the parking lot. On the way, twin voices echoed from behind. We turned around. There stood Pedro and Jahaira on the front step of the library, celebrating.

"Best day of the week. Happy for you, guys!" they shouted in unison.

We grinned as we walked hand in hand and soon vanished amid rows of cars in the parking lot. While in the car, I made a bold plea.

"I can still visit your parents if you want me to," I said softly.

"Yeah, you can come Sunday, same time as last time."

Chapter 23

Michaela was waiting on the front porch, assertive as always, but visibly anxious. A sudden glint of elation animated her face the minute she saw me coming, driving sluggishly. Her long golden tresses floated about her face as she stepped down, making long swinging strides toward the fence. Gracefully, she unlatched the gates as soon as I pulled into the driveway and walked out. I edged closer, and she grabbed my hands.

"What took you so *long*?" She whispered.

"An unusual traffic jam on 27th Avenue," I replied , landing a kiss on her sensual lips. I glanced past her, taking aim at the freshly trimmed shrubs behind which was a blooming rosebush glowing under the early evening light. In a quick gesture, I freed my hands from hers and went adrift, sauntering toward the rosebush where I picked up a stem. She was gleeful, molded inside a knee-length dress, hands on hips, watching with tenderly awed puppy eyes as I retreated to her. "Mica, would you accept this rose?" I asked in a subtle gesture of chivalrous romance.

"Of course!" she exclaimed in an upwelling of affection. She took the rose from my hand and then led me up the porch where she opened the door. Soon, I faced her mother, sitting on a loveseat in the living room, crocheting a patchwork quilt.

"Mama, this is Vinco." Mica grinned, still holding my hand in which I could feel the rapid pulsations of her heart. She was nervous, maybe more than I was.

"*Como estas, muchacho?*" (How're you, young man?) Her mother uttered, stirring in her loveseat while throwing a cautious smile.

"Fine," I answered with frozen lips, exposing the blush growing inside of me.

"Come have a seat, young man," she commanded in a very thick Spanish accent. She stopped crocheting abruptly, resting the hook on a lamp table near her. She then wrapped the unfinished quilt into two folds but left it on her lap.

"Thank you," I replied. Michaela released my hand, and I paced to the center, wondering where I should sit. To ease the embarrassment, Michaela followed me, and we took a seat on a brown leather sofa adjacent to her mother.

Her name was Lucrecia. She bore an impressive posture, and was staring at me with sweet, expressionless, indigo eyes. Soft black haired, she must have been in her late forties. She had a fairer complexion than Michaela, almost like a white woman. Well-mannered, she too wanted to appease my discomfort. So, she adjusted her dress and shifted to one side to make room for me to sit next to her, motioned for me to come, and I obliged. I rose from my seat and went to her, touching my shirt to make sure it was still nicely tucked inside my jeans.

"Mica, aren't you serving Vinco something to drink?" She urged her daughter.

"Yes, Mama. *Tengo jugo de naranja.* I made it!" (I have orange juice.) Like an excited puppy, she bounded out of her seat and rushed to the fridge in the kitchen.

"Especially for *him?*" Lucrecia giggled, grabbing my hand gently and pulling me down to the seat.

A couple minutes later, Michaela returned with a glass of fresh-squeezed orange juice. "For you, Vinco," she tittered, like a hummingbird in the backyard garden.

"Oh, this is so kind of you," I thanked her and took a couple of sips.

"Don't be a stranger. Make yourself at home, Vin...co? Is that how you say it?"

"Yes, but my real name is Yrvin Lacroix."

"*Como La Cruz?*" (Like the Cross?)

"*Sí.*"

"Ah, you speak Spanish?"

"A little."

"I'm teaching him, Mama," Michaela interjected. She apparently did not want to be left out of the conversation.

"Are you a good student?" Lucrecia teased me.

"I *think* I am," I replied.

She pulled me up closer to her. "Relax, Vinco. Make yourself at home."

Then, she glanced across the living room with pride— ecstatic, euphoric, as if she had just entered a state of crimson delight, inviting me to survey her well-furnished little place, which was decorated with imposing Dominican artwork, pictures of towns and villages in golden frames, and countless snapshots of relatives and friends still living in the Dominican Republic. All this showed a strong sense of patriotism and nostalgia for the old country.

Soon, a tall, slim young woman dressed in a velvet garment burst out of her room which was adjacent to where we sat in the living room. Her slender legs were anchored by a pair of high-heeled shoes. She was of her mother's complexion, but her nose was a bit pointier. Her hazel eyes slanted, and she noticed me sitting next to her mother.

"Hi," she greeted me.

"Gabriella, don't be late. You know it's Sunday evening," Lucrecia reminded her.

"I know, Mama." She gesticulated, opening the front door. "Bye, Mica," she added, waving her velour-gloved hand. She then shut the door behind her.

"She's my first baby," Lucrecia proudly said.

"She's very pretty," I said.

Michaela then got up and strolled toward me. "What about *me?*" she asked.

I said nothing, but I simply smiled. She sat on the carpet, her head resting on her mother's lap.

"I think she's the baby." I grinned, teasing Michaela.

"Stop it, Vinco," she castigated with a little pinch in my leg. Her mom did not notice, and Mica kept stroking my leg under the loveseat. I worked hard to conceal my discomfort.

"Vinco," Lucrecia said, turning to my side, facing me. "Do you live with your parents?" She was quite focused, the depth of an interest that could only be found in a mother's eyes.

"No, I live with my sister," I replied, rather timidly, avoiding eye contact.

"Where're your folks?" She picked up her crocheting again, still facing me.

"My mother lives in Haiti, and my dad is a businessman. He travels back and forth. He has businesses in the Bahamas."

"Like many of us Dominicans. We go home a lot, visiting old friends and family members."

"Michaela told me," I replied, trying to stave off Michaela's secret teases. From under the chair, she poked me again, stroking my leg. Discreetly, I resisted.

Suddenly, there was a squeaking noise from the back door, and then I heard rapid footsteps clattering into the room, but soon dwindled as the steps meandered away. I could see a man standing by the kitchen sink, manning a garden tool. He was a tall, mustachioed, rawboned man who wore a patched pair of blue jeans held by a large cowboy belt with a golden buckle, and he had large puffy bags beneath his eyes. Hearing our chatter, he leaned into view and waved, then came over.

"How are you, young man?" He asked in a deep voice.

"I'm fine," I replied timidly.

"Emilio, what were you doing in the backyard this late?" Lucrecia demanded.

He shrugged off the question. Instead, he threw a disengaged grin. He then turned around and wandered down the dark hallway leading away from the living room. Michaela followed him, mumbling words in Spanish that I could not understand. About a couple of minutes later, she came back and took her seat right next to me again. Lucrecia suggested that Michaela turn on the television. She did, and the latest news from Haiti was on the screen. Pictures of defiant Haitians demonstrating against the Baby Doc regime in Haiti kept my eyes glued to the screen. All three of us were thrilled to watch these images of people finally finding the courage to stand up to the tyranny that had victimized our beloved island.

Emilio returned and took a seat on a backless highchair next to Michaela, and we all watched together. He looked refreshed after taking a shower. He was in his pajamas. "That reminds me of the good old days," he said with a grin, facing me.

"*Papá*, you mean when generalissimo was assassinated?" Michaela inquired. He cleared his throat, head bent down, deep in thought.

"You're right, my dear daughter," he replied, wrapping his arm around Michaela's neck. "Festive moments like these are always short-lived," he added stoically.

"And why do you say this, Emilio?" Lucrecia questioned.

"It's not and never will be easy for deprived and exploited people of the world to rise to power and take their destiny into their own hands. If we want to learn from our own history as Dominicans, we'd see how happy the masses were to finally get Trujillo off their backs, only to run into Balaguer's roadblock."

"You mean the downfall of a dictator is not a cause for celebration?" I asked him with glaring eyes, hungry for an answer.

311

"My son, yes we all should celebrate with our Haitian brothers, but with an understanding that the real fight for profound changes still lies ahead. What's going on in Haiti right now is a historic opportunity to push for long-overdue changes that will better the lives of the people down there. But those who're working behind the scenes are not doing so in the best interests of the Haitian masses. They have their own agenda," he said, his voice full of deep emotion.

"Really, Emilio?" Lucrecia intervened. Michaela, proud of her father, leaned on his lap. Emilio did not reply. He just nodded to affirm his point. Michaela then shifted her head and rested it on the frame of the loveseat closer to me as her father went on to tell me the story of his life.

Emilio descended from a family of romantic fighters. His great-grandfather was a revolutionary who lived in Southern Haiti shortly after Haitian independence in 1804. There, he met Simon Bolivar on his way to Colombia. So distasteful of Spanish rule, he left with the general and died in 1818 in the battle of Rancheria River near Rio Acha. His grandfather fought with Maximo Gomez in the Ten Years' War for Cuban independence against Spain in 1870. His father was a devoted Marxist who staunchly believed that only a national liberation struggle could free his country from the grip of the powerful elite, who were oblivious to the plight of the Dominican people. Back in his native country, Emilio himself was a brilliant lawyer, who lived off his family's fortune to work pro bono on behalf of the exploited masses. He met Lucrecia, then only nineteen, in 1965 in a secret cell after he went underground to join the *Constitutionalists* led by Francisco Caamaño. He fled with Lucrecia to Puerto Rico after Caamaño was defeated. Growing disenchanted with the politics of his homeland, he took Lucrecia and their two daughters to Miami, where they had been living ever since.

Watching the Haitian story unfold before his eyes, Emilio's face grew pale, his lips were drawn and puckered, though he still clearly kept his strident form of revolutionary fervor. To him, the account of those brave men and women in Haiti was the latest chapter of what came to be known to many as a bloody feuilleton, an elusive prize almost impossible to grab in the struggle for social justice. Through the lenses of his big black eyes, I could see an unspoken assertion of endless nostalgia for Hispaniola, the island to which he held a deep and patriotic commitment.

The room went still after Emilio spoke. Lucrecia's eyes brimmed with tears as she listened and relived moments of her youth, episodes of her life she was committed to cherishing to the very last minute of her existence on this earth. From outside somewhere, a bird chirped and brought everyone back to the reality of the moment.

Emilio rose from his chair, patted me on the shoulder, and strode off. The news from Haiti had long been over. In the evening stillness, I peered through the shuttered windows only to discover the slanted traces of light down in the garden turning wet and drooping after a quick drizzle. I too rose from my seat.

"I think it's getting late. I have to get going," I said weakly. I then paced over to Lucrecia and gave her a warm hug. "I hope the quilt is done when I come to visit again," I teased her.

"It will be, my son," she laughed. Michaela walked me outside.

Hand in hand, we strolled toward the car, two doves from Hispaniola flying in perfect enchantment. Michaela felt a sense of liberation. She wanted to get in the car and go for a romantic ride.

"Don't spoil the moment, *amorecita*," I pleaded.

"I know, baby," she whispered in my ears.

"We have plenty of time to celebrate this major breakthrough," I whispered back, almost touching her lips.

"Tomorrow at school?" she begged.

"At school and beyond. By the way, what did you tell your dad when you ran after him in the hallway?" I added.

"I told him you were the boy I talked to him about yesterday."

"What was his reaction?"

"Well, no need to tell you. By now, I'm convinced you know. My parents have always trusted me. Before you came into my life, I knew nothing about love. Its pain, its joy."

She reached for my lips, but I refrained from meeting her halfway. "Baby, the light is on in the front window."

"I know, my folks are in there, in the master bedroom."

"And you're not afraid?"

She then released her hands from mine, turned around, and leaned against the driver's door. We now stood side by side, facing the window just when someone from inside the bedroom flicked off the light, and the driveway went dark, serene once more. I was as feverish as she was, but I understood parental vigilance does not end with the presence of darkness. So, we settled for a couple of French kisses. I was hesitant, and she set me free. I got in the car and she retreated toward the house. When she reached the front door, she turned around to take a last glimpse of me. I was doing the same thing. We threw kisses to each other. She stepped back inside, and I left.

Chapter 24

The next morning, I arrived at school earlier than usual. I had to meet some classmates in the library for a final review for my philosophy class. I avoided the cafeteria. It was too early, and I wasn't hungry. My mind was on the exam. I was walking fast, weaving through bikes and cars parked along the way. A few students strolled down the walkway parallel to the courtyard, empty and still, except for Cecilia, a heavyset Spanish woman with a muscular frame, who was sweeping the pathway leading to the library. When she saw me coming, she halted her sweeping and faced me with a broad smile.

"How are you, *muchacho?*" she asked.

"I'm fine." I grinned.

When I reached where she stood, short-haired, good-natured, and both hands resting on the broom, she moved to one side to make way for me to walk through. As many times before, she was ready for a couple of minutes of chatting, but I walked right by, quickening my steps. Her curious stare followed me as I scampered toward the library. I was one step away from the front door when she yelled, "I just saw *la chica*. Oh, she looked gorgeous!"

"*Where?*" I asked, turning around to face her.

"In the cafeteria."

I then made a U-turn, stepping away from the front door. I ran down the walkway and onto the cafeteria, searching for Michaela under the astonished eyes of Cecilia. The second I walked into the cafeteria, vast and empty, there she was in the far end, our usual spot, wearing a v-neck, burgundy velvet wrap mini dress and eagerly waiting.

"Baby, how can you be here so early?" I asked her, peering into her bluish eyes, they were like ocean waves at sunrise.

"I couldn't sleep last night," she admitted.

She rose from her seat as always and leaned forward to meet my lips. With a smile, she collapsed pleasurably into my arms but quickly regained her composure when she noticed some familiar girls entering the cafeteria. The girls then vanished, and she rose again. I held her by the waist as she reached for my lips, arms around my neck. Eyes closed, we caressed each other unhurriedly. When it was over, my lips were coated in rouge, which she wiped with her index finger. She wanted to sit down, but I held her still and firm. With utmost pleasure, we stood there, locked into each other's arms. I had never felt such extreme emotions. I wanted to climax. A flicker of sunlight crossed her face and it sent her cinnamon tan aglow. She was softly coy in my arms. She was my princess, and I once more discovered her beauty—voluptuous, exuberant, coquettish, and prudish. I felt I was lucky to be the proud recipient of her pure and honest love.

Slowly, the cafeteria began to feel alive again as students arrived for their breakfast. Soon, the noise swelled to an intolerable pitch, and we walked out, passing groups of students rushing to get to their early morning classes. As usual, I walked Mica to her classroom. We chatted for about a minute or so, kissing each other goodbye. She walked in, and I reclaimed the path that led to my class, meeting my Haitian friends along the way, chatting and laughing in their acoustic Creole.

"Hey, Vinco, come join us at Élodie's corner after class. She has hot Haitian pastries!" exclaimed Antoine, a chubby boy in a red and blue cap.

"I don't think so."

"Come on, *man.*"

I didn't reply. The exam was once again at the top of my mind. My classmates were already there when I snuck into class, but Dr. Cassini was not in yet. I had seen him on the way in, wearing his usual trench coat and stroking his hair while chatting with Sister Jean.

"Hey, Vinco. What happened to you?" Asked Marco, my best friend in class. He was with Alfred and Carmelita doing a last-minute brainstorming for the exam. They were worried since I didn't make it to the review in the library.

"So, sorry. I had a last-minute emergency."

"Yeah, right," Carmelita smirked. "You were too tied up with the princess in the cafeteria."

Nicole and Roberts hastily vacated their seats in the front row and crept to the back to join us. They all counted on me to come to the rescue, for since the day of my questions about the Russian revolution and the subsequent classroom discussions about class antagonisms in a bourgeois democracy, my classmates had been looking to me for clarifications when Dr.

318

Cassini raised confusing and complex issues on dialectical materialism and other Marxist theories, especially when he made references to teachings that outline nuances and complexities in societies where greater emphasis is placed on the accumulation of wealth and too little on the have-nots and their misfortunes, which always shake the deepest of human emotions.

"Did you get everything ready?" Whispered Marco.

"What?" I whispered back.

"The answers to the questions from the study guide."

"Yeah," I replied. I passed the guide with the answers to Alfred, who was closer to me.

"Can I go make the copies in the cafeteria?" inquired Carmelita, who sat ahead of me.

"Shut up," Roberts interjected. "How the hell you gonna get back with the paper?"

Nicole stepped in. "Roberts is right. Since the exam is multiple choice, everyone has to have their papers on the right side of their desk, visible enough for us to verify answers. And you, Carmelita, come sit to the left of Nicole. You hold the study guide with the answers."

"Why me, Roberts?"

"Because you're taller and bigger than us. You can easily provide the cover."

"Hey guys, don't worry about me. I prepared the guide. I can survive," I reassured them.

While the rest of the class was busy making a last-minute review, we took up our positions as planned. I sat in the tail end of the last row, in the corner next to Alfred. Just then, Dr. Cassini walked in, taking off his trench coat and rolling up his sleeves. Before he had a chance to say anything, Nicole rose from her seat.

"Dr. Cassini, I have something for you," she uttered loudly, to the amazement of the rest of the class, myself included. Moving in strident steps, she approached and handed a book to the professor.

"What is it, Carmelita?" Dr. Cassini asked, a bit startled.

"It's the book you told us about last week, *Between Existentialism and Marxism* by Jean Paul Sartre."

"Ah, you found it?"

"Yep. Can I pass out the test papers?" Carmelita asked capriciously.

"Sure." With his eyes buried in the book, he handed the test materials to Carmelita. He then went back to his desk, consumed in the narrative of Sartre.

I soon understood the ploy. I was overjoyed, not so much for me because the class was never a challenge. I was happy for my classmates, who struggled daily to understand theories that were way beyond the level of their thoughts and certainly out of touch with their existential realities. Within minutes, I was finished with my exam. I waited fifteen minutes to see how my classmates were doing, and when I realized everyone was on track, I rose from my seat, walked toward the desk, turned in my paper, and discreetly walked out.

I stepped out onto the porch, and Michaela was not there, standing just below the steps waiting for me as usual. I took aim at a small chapel bench behind a low pine-edge where many

320

times before she waited for me, reading her novel. But she was not there either. The atmosphere was serene. No students perambulated up and down the pathways in the courtyard. Eyes glancing wildly, I sat on the bench like a hungry, home-alone child yearning for Mom.

I was so lost in my lust that I did not realize it was too early. Suddenly, the classroom door squeaked, and rapid footsteps followed. I got off the bench, gleeful, strolling out of the pine-edge to surprise her.

"Baby!" I exclaimed.

"You got it all wrong, Vinco. It's me."

"Oh, Carmelita. So, sorry. I thought it was…."

"She's not here yet." She laughed.

"How did you do?" I asked, referring to the test.

"I think I did pretty good. And you?"

"You know I passed it. How about the rest of the crew inside?"

"They're having a field day. Dr. Cassini is still reading. His big gray eyes are glued to the pages." She was ecstatic.

She took my hand and we walked to the cafeteria. I wished I could share her elated state of mind. My mind was on my ladylove. My anxiety had lowered a little, for now I knew she was still in class. Instead of getting into the cafeteria where a few diehard, hard-headed students were already having lunch, I got Carmelita to follow me to the terrace facing east, where Michaela would be coming from. There we sat on high backless stools.

Carmelita was a blonde girl with stunning azure eyes who wore nothing but plaid tops over blue jeans to class. She had a sharp mouth and was never afraid of speaking her mind. Students said her upbringing was the reason behind her idiosyncratic manner, for she was born and raised in the uptown world of aristocratic, suburban Baton Rouge, Louisiana. I never knew her class of origin until Marco told me one Friday morning before class. One would mistakenly think she was arrogant. But getting closer to her, one would find a heart as tender and as dovish as that of a turtledove.

"Vinco," she said, raising her eyebrows.

"Yes, Lita," as we all lovingly called her in class.

"That girl really got you in her nest."

"*Who?*"

"Your Spanish girl."

"Why do you think so?"

"Because she has such an overbearing attitude that I find hard to comprehend."

"I'm not sure I understand."

"Yes, you do. I mean, unless you're in class, she's always with you on campus, all over you. Is she insecure?"

"What a stupid question!" I laughed.

"Vinco, this is no laughing matter. I think you're too young to have a girl get you in such a box."

"I'm not in a box. Believe me, Lita—"

"So, is this the way Haitians are when they fall in love?"

"I can't answer that. All I know is that she deserves my heart and my full attention."

"No doubt. She's pretty, too." Then, there was a brief silence.

I sensed she had more to say, but she must have refrained for fear I might misunderstand her cautiousness and the honesty that had always been the solid foundation of our friendship. In the brief interval of quiet that followed, I remembered my mother, who, in the sincerest fashion of her boundless love, never let an opportunity go by without reminding me of the power of self-confidence and the ability to follow one's principles. She used to tell me to always be frank, to never lie, and that God always stands on the side of those who speak the truth, for those who live in the shadow of infantile emotions easily fall prey to unwanted advances of the devil.

The silence persisted, now taking possession of the terrace, the emptiness, the rising sunlight, and the shrubs and flowers that gave aesthetic pleasure to the schoolyard. A breeze swept through. The dry leaves cracked, flew, and splintered in the air.

"Let's go inside," Carmelita suggested. As we were about to, Carmelita turned around. "There she comes, Vinco." She then wanted to leave me on the terrace.

I held her hand. "You can't leave," I commanded.

We both stood on the terrace, waiting for Michaela, who was exuberant as she strolled toward us. She stepped onto the terrace and hugged and kissed me. I then pushed her forward, presenting her to Carmelita.

"Hi," Carmelita said in a feeble voice.

"Hi," Michaela replied but quickly turned her attention back to me. "Vinco, give me another hour. I stepped out just to ask you to wait a bit more because I have to stay for a midterm review. Give me an hour, baby."

"You got it."

Michaela returned to class, and I walked inside with Carmelita. We went back to the cafeteria as a few more students started to come. We ordered burgers and I paid for both of us.

"You have such a commanding, macho attitude..." Carmelita teased.

"You think so?"

"I just witnessed it," she said. "If I were your girlfriend, I would do away with your Caribbean machismo."

"I myself hate macho men. Lita, you're a friend. You have to heal me." I poked her rosy cheek with a brotherly admiration.

"We're friends for life, Vinco. Honestly, I'm worried about you and this girl...."

I did not reply, but we chatted for a few more minutes then hugged each other goodbye. Knowing Michaela was not going to be out of class for another hour, I seized the moment to rush home to change clothes. I did not know Michaela was going to dress in such fancy attire, and I wanted to sharpen my look; to dress for the occasion as she had.

I drove home as fast as I could and I got dressed, wearing my best Yves Saint-Laurent and Pierre Cardin outfit. I returned to school just in time to greet Michaela as she was walking toward the terrace behind the cafeteria.

"Vinco, where did you go?" she asked, taking a closer look at my outfit.

324

"Can't you guess?" I quizzed.

Ignoring my question, she edged closer and we joined hands. From the terrace, we walked straight to the parking lot. It was my intention not to pass through the cafeteria because I knew my Haitian friends were already there. I could hear their chatting, their laughter, and their gossiping that would have undoubtedly gotten louder if Michaela and I were to be spotted strolling hand in hand in fancy clothes. As we reached the car, I opened the passenger door to let my princess in and gently closed it back before I paced to the driver's seat. Just when I was about to turn on the ignition, she stopped me.

"Baby, we need to have a destination," she said, and I agreed.

"Let's go to *Brucci's* for lunch."

"That's fine."

From the parking lot, we drove east. Because this was going to be a special moment of our love story, I did not want to drive the conventional way, speeding down Northeast 2nd Avenue, where Miami Shores cops kept a hawkish eye on university students violating the speed limit in this affluent neighborhood. So, I circumvented the avenue and took a narrow street where poorly maintained, built-off-the-ground homes lined both sides. A few minutes later, we arrived and parked, then walked out of the car, and, like an amorous twosome, we went inside. Michaela leaned on me; my arm wrapped around her waist. We stood firm in front of the greeting stand where a chubby young woman in a white-and-blue uniform greeted us.

"How many?" she asked.

"Two," I replied.

"Wait a minute." She narrowed her eyes and smiled, glancing around the room full of Italian cuisine lovers, looking for a table for two. "It'll be about five minutes."

Resigned and frowning, we retreated to a tiny den adjacent to the hostess's stand. By then, it was past eleven a.m., when *Brucci's* entered its busiest time of the day. I held my sweetheart tighter, her head resting on my chest. An aroma of Italian food filled the air, pushing our hunger to an uncontrollable pitch. Finally, the hostess called to us. Wide-eyed, we rose and followed an ebony young man in uniform. Tall, slender, and exuding an old-fashioned gaiety, he guided us to a two-seat table in the corner. Thrilled, we took our seats and quickly surveyed the menu. Notebook and pen in hand, the young man waited for us to make our choice. "Take your time. Meanwhile, what would you like to drink?" The young waiter asked.

"We're ready to order," Mica and I answered with one voice.

"Okay," the waiter smirked, witnessing the agony of making a choice when selecting among delicious sustenance. It did not give great comfort to food lovers like Michaela and me who bore a special fondness for such fancy gastronomy. In the end, we ordered chicken pesto paninis with sweet lemon iced tea. The young man jotted down the order and soon disappeared in a discordance of cutlery sounds. Up and down the pathways, young men and women in uniforms staggered, passing each other under loaded trays.

"Baby, I can't take it anymore," my ladylove said faintly.

"Me too, darling," I softly replied, injecting a kiss on her sexy lips to lower her anxiety. My eyes and mind were not on the food. I wasn't as hungry as she was. I wanted to move beyond, past the restaurant to set the stage for what would be coming next.

Chapter 25

At last, lunch was behind us. Back in the car, we were ready to hit the busy Biscayne Boulevard again, but before I turned on the ignition, Michaela stopped me. "Mi amor, where do we go from here?" She asked abruptly, eyes fixed on me as if searching for the answer that led to a forbidden land.

"To a place where we can be alone, away from the rest of the world," I told her. She said nothing more, but her facial expression, full of undeclared love and wild romance left me no doubt that deep within her heart lay a mutually inclusive, unbound longing to make passionate love.

"Let's go to the Omni International Hotel," I urged her.

"No, baby. I won't be comfortable being there."

"Why, amorecita?"

"Because this hotel is only a few blocks from my job, and my coworkers shop there in the mall near the entrance of that hotel."

"Uh, okay. Let's go to one at the beach, then."

"Which one?"

"Earlier, when I went home to change clothes, I called two places: Omni and Fountainbleau by the ocean."

"Really?"

"Yep. I've reserved a room for one night."

She flinched, like her heart had leapt in her chest. "One *night?*" she asked with a concerned stare.

"Of course, we won't spend the night there, baby. But this is a five-star hotel. They don't book for only a few hours. We can leave or check out whenever we want." I poked her glowing cheek out of admiration.

"No, no, baby. I know you would never ask me to spend a night with you." She grinned.

"Why would I? We're not married. And what would you tell your parents who trust you? What would I tell my sister, who is so overprotective?"

In order to soften my fear and sudden change of tone, she moved to placate me. "Making love with you has always been my dream," she said shyly.

"And it might be done under the right conditions," I responded.

By then, we had already left *Brucci's*, driving north, passing Biscayne Boulevard and swinging east toward Miami Beach, taking the 36th Street Causeway under which ocean waves rolled, surged, and swayed by the wind gusts from the bay area. She leaned against my shoulder as we drove. As soon as we left the causeway, we rolled into Alton Road, a stretch of a boulevard that ran through the heart of a wealthy South Beach suburb of million-dollar mansions. Alton Road led directly to A1A, Miami

Beach's most famous boulevard, where fancy hotels and restaurants could be found. When we reached the eastern edge of Alton Road, we drifted into the parking lot of a Shell gas station.

"Baby, are you running out of gas?" she asked, looking startled.

"No, darling. I just wanna ask you this specific question."

"*Di me.*" (Tell me.) She appeared anxious.

"Mica, are you sure you wanna do this?"

"Do *what*, Vinco?"

"Be in a hotel room with me."

"I'll follow you anywhere, baby."

"No, Mica. I want you to walk *with* me, not follow me. Love is the rawest expression of a shared existence. Like you, baby, I've never been—"

She halted my words with a soft kiss on my lips. "You know me. If I didn't want it, I wouldn't have come this far. Come on, let's continue, Vinco."

So, we got back on the road just as the sky was turning gray. Above the high rises in the distance, thunder broke with a crash. We had to hurry. Finally, we made it to the hotel lobby seconds before heavy raindrops began to pelt the cars outside. I held her hand and we strolled in harmonious rhythm toward the concierge. A woman in a business suit greeted us with a welcoming grin.

"Are you the newlyweds?" she asked.

Michaela and I looked at each other. "Yes," we uttered both at once.

The receptionist surveyed the reservation list. "And your last name?" she asked. She was rather sarcastic.

"Lacroix," I replied, holding Michaela tighter. My arms wrapped about her waist. The lady then asked us to wait for few minutes to ensure that our room was ready. We retired to a remote corner in the lobby where we waited on a sofa for them to call us. She rested her head on my shoulder and I lay my hand over her chest. Beneath her velvet dress, her heart throbbed. She was no longer smiling, nor did she seek words of assurance from me. Being in unchartered terrain seemed to scare her to the core, just as it paralyzed me.

She shifted her head to one side in a ponderous, capricious manner. She was thoughtful and appeared ready to start speaking, likely in one-syllable words, like she usually did when she was not happy. Those were the words that used to shake my consciousness and made my stomach churn. She then shook her head, and part of her golden-honeyed hair covered her face, but she quickly pulled it back and smiled. She sighed and then buried her face in me. She seemed crippled by fear not because she was afraid of being with me, but because of the breathtaking venue in which we were and in which we felt totally out of place—a five-star hotel with dazzling corridors filled with Renaissance artworks, an imposing lobby floor of waxed marble over which wealthy business folks wined and chatted cheek to cheek as crystal chandeliers sparkled overhead.

Soon, the woman from the concierge called to us. "Sorry for the wait," she said, smiling. "Here you go. Room 1218," she added, handing us the electronic card for the room door.

We then made our way to the elevator and onward to our room. The minute we stepped in, we were blown away. We felt as if we had just entered paradise. It was too exotic to be real. Rectangular-shaped, it was a room built with golden accents and meticulously decorated with fancy artworks and cherry furniture. The colonial windows were dressed in velvet draperies. A lush divan sat across from a king-size bed dressed under crisp, white sheets that were at least three hundred thread count. Instantly Michaela and I were drawn to lie down and make love. All worries and anxieties were gone.

"Baby, you did all this for me?" she giggled.

"For both of us, Mica." I held her by the waist and drew her closer to me, and she began to stroke the nape of my neck, licking my face.

The place was too dazzling, and we found ourselves lurching into an unexplained, indescribable excitement, a kind of romantic merriment that could only be satisfied by lovemaking. On the lamp table, a tiny radio played Frédéric Chopin with an acoustic, filtered sound that soothed our hearts. With our clothes on, we went under the bedsheets.

"Baby, you got me scared earlier," I muttered.

"For *what?*"

"When I watched your change of attitude after the woman from concierge told us to wait."

"Are you trying to make me feel guilty for being here with you?"

"No, *no.*"

She didn't reply, and I realized the unforgivable blunder I had just committed. The last thing she wanted to hear was a replay of a question she thought she had overcome. Her jolly mood completely vanished. She seemed lost in a fog of thoughts. She was silent for a minute or two with her eyes half-closed and her face drawn. Chopin no longer played from the radio as if an invisible hand just shut it off. I made no further move for fear of exacerbating her pain. Sounds of music, acoustic or romantic, did not fit anymore, and in the soundless air that followed, she turned on me, stretched out her faultless legs, and pulled the sheet tighter about her body.

Then, in a brisk move that made my heart vibrate, she pushed the sheet from her, got out of the bed, and strode toward the divan, facing me. I wanted to shoot myself in the mouth for committing what appeared to be an irreparable bungle. I had blundered every attempt, and now another wave of fear had descended in her mind and heart. I was afraid she might start questioning my ability to match her love and affection. I soon got out of the bed and joined her on the divan, and I began to caress her face, stroking her breast and kissing her lips. She offered no resistance. Then, we began to kiss. The heat started coming back as we glided from the divan to the bed.

"Undress me, baby. *Acaricia me, te necesito, te quiero, mi amor.*" (I wanna feel your soft hand undressing me.)

She moaned and whined in my arms as she unbuttoned my shirt. I took the clip that held her hair, dumped it on the lamp table, and settled her head onto the pillow. Tenderly, I undressed her as she undressed me. Our naked bodies intertwined, and suddenly she became nervous, for she had never been unclothed, exposed, and lay next to me before. She closed her eyes and started breathing softly. But it was a quick blush that soon vanished as I began to stroke the tail of one breast while sucking the other to heighten the vibe, the priceless moment that pushed us to the paroxysm of our desires. To me, it was a dream come true. The woman I loved was now folded in my arms as we went under the bedsheet, savoring the thrilling sensation of lovemaking.

We were drenched in sweat when it was over. But we remained interlaced, not wanting to let go, knowing from then on, we had crossed the point of no return. Within me, there was an indescribable blissfulness, a triumphant feeling which was sweet and everlasting. The girl I cherished whose trust I fought so hard to earn was truly mine. In this genius and profound act of explicit romance, Mica had shown to me that love can endure and thrive if stemmed from the deepest of emotions.

Despite my flaws, she was able to make me feel real and holistically loved. There in that bed as our bodies interlocked, I felt evermore resolute in my devotion to telling her every day, not just in words but in actions, that I was equally dedicated to sharing my life with her.

"Baby," I said softly, tipping to one side, reaching her lips for a slurpy smooch. "You can't imagine how lucky I feel to have met you."

"Me too, *amorecito*," she replied with a smile loaded with the purest of affection, revealing the love that dwelled in her heart. "And I'm committed to keeping my words until death, Vinco," she added.

"Me too, *amorecita*."

There in that fancy hotel room, we wanted to stay until nightfall. But we understood this was not possible. We had to go home. So, I got out of bed and walked to the shower room. From the rack, I grabbed a towel with which I wiped away the sweat from her face. We then fell into each other's arms again.

"Baby, I'm scared," she said.

"Why, Mica?"

"What if I get pregnant?"

"Don't think of the worst while we're still enjoying this incredible moment."

"Vinco, you're the best thing that's ever happened in my life. I have to admit I feel vulnerable when I'm with you. I love you so much."

"Baby."

"Huh?"

"Whatever happened to the stain of honor?" I teased her.

"I don't know. You tell me. This has been your favorite toy ever since we met." She pulled my hand down and dragged it into her *secret* part.

"You *quiet.*"

"As you know, no one has ever touched this forbidden part of my body, until I met you. Do you remember that first time at your place on the sofa? You sneaked your finger between my legs and started stroking. This was an inexplicable sensation, painful but sweet, where awesomeness and dreadfulness merge to create such an odd feeling."

"You stop it. Will you?" I poked her smiling face. We started again exchanging French kisses to further sweeten this timeless moment of romantic affection.

"You know, Vinco. A baby from you would be a gift from God," she said, awkwardly sarcastic.

"*No*, no, baby. A baby would be a setback. We have plans, remember?"

She said nothing more, and we redirected our attention to the fancy surroundings, living the best moment of our love story. I got the sense she had come to realize that romance at its purest is the finest thing a human being could ever experience, even if it is for a short moment. Like her, I too felt I was living in the most gratifying moment, not only because I had the girl of my life in my long brown arms, but because I was the guest of a venue in which I thought I could never set foot in my lifetime. This hotel stood against the backdrop of the same beachfront on which I was dropped as a deprived young refugee to find my way along the unforgiving streets of Miami.

Haiti suddenly felt so close. In this luxurious and lavish hotel, Mica and I were treated with utmost dignity. No one asked us who we were or what our upbringing was. Every human being, if allowed to live to his God-given potential, could achieve great strides, especially in the quest to restore human dignity. Right here in this room, this idea dawned on me. Michaela and I were at the spring of our lives. We were hopeful and ambitious. I held her tighter in my arms, and she started dozing off, and her sleep deepened when I began to rub her shoulders. After a while, we both fell asleep.

It was midafternoon and getting late when we woke up. We jumped out of bed and rushed to the shower, naked. After cleansing our bodies, we put on our white guest robes and strolled to a sliding door that opened to a balcony from which the ocean view was magnificent. Hand in hand, Mica and I stood there for a moment, contemplating the coconut palms tossing in the wind down on the white sugar sand beach. A pair of gulls flew by but soon vanished. The beach looked vast and empty, except for a lone beachgoer walking in the distance. At the shoreline, the waves were surging against the foaming sand. In the sky above, mushrooms of clouds billowed. Mica and I went back inside and shut the door. It was truly time to leave, but not before we went under the bedsheet again for a second round of lovemaking. We had to shower once again and get dressed. Afterwhich, we took the elevator and made our way to the parking lot without checking out from the front desk. There, we got into the car and drove off into our shared, bright future.

Chapter 26

Since the day of the demonstration at the Notre Dame, the Haitian community had been on edge in anticipation of the Duvaliers' downfall in Haiti. Father Guy, as well as Father Karl Levèque, were long gone. Rumors spread daily like wildfire. Every afternoon, hundreds of Haitians swelled 54th Street outside of the Haitian Refugee Center, awaiting the latest news from Port-au-Prince. Local news organizations, including all local television stations, had picked up on the news, which kept changing, sometimes by the hour. For a while, the Haitian story was no longer a portrayal of ragged Haitians reaching the shores of Miami, handcuffed and hauled off to detention centers.

At school, the rumors reached the university campus. The Haitian Student Association of which I was a part, was not immune to the debate. Every Thursday afternoon, we held our regular meeting in a small room behind the cafeteria. Usually, the agenda was dominated by school-related activities or a weekend party at a student's home. Politics rarely took center stage. In part, this was to avoid offending some of our fellow students whose parents were functionaries in the Duvalier regime.

One Thursday afternoon, during a regular discussion, I purposely raised the issue. I and another student named Lucille led the meeting that day. Just before the start, I made a motion to revise the agenda to include a discussion about the latest development in Haiti. Lucille seconded the motion. Four students in the committee opposed, saying we should remain above politics because what was going on all over Haiti was not their concern. I looked at them with barely controlled rage. I wanted to get out of my seat and, like a hungry hawk, grab them by the neck and throw them out of the room. Lucille, however, noticed how my body was shivering, wrapped her arm around my shoulders.

"Calm down, Vinco. Let me handle this."

Lucille was a tall, ebony girl who was never afraid to speak her mind, despite her class of origin. She came from the top echelon of Haitian society, the daughter of a wealthy landowner who belonged to old-fashioned cliques. So these mixed-race students did not impress her, for she, like them, was part of the same tiny elite of whom many, if not all, harbored an unimaginable disdain for their fellow, lower-class Haitians, who'd been fighting and dying for freedom and democracy after having to endure twenty-nine years under the most repressive regime in Haiti's modern history. She did not share their arrogance and social prejudice.

With a commanding stare, she rose from her seat and cleared her throat. "Listen, guys," she growled. "How could you be so cold-hearted? How could you be so indifferent to the suffering of your fellow countrymen? The whole world is watching how innocent people in the streets of Haiti are being beaten, arrested, and killed, and that doesn't seem a cause for concern to you *Haitians?*"

338

One of the mixed-race girls from the back of the room raised her hand, requesting a rebuttal. I asked Lucille to take her seat and allow the girl to speak. "Lucile, contrary to what you may think, we're Haitians and proud of it, too. We just don't think this is the place to discuss politics."

"And if this isn't the place to talk about Haiti, tell us where. Where should we go, mademoiselle? Where should we go to talk about our country now facing its greatest challenge yet?" I asked her, peering into her eyes, searching for any remaining traces of humility from her cold and cruel heart.

"Martine is right, Yrvin," said a young man named Richard Coles. "If you want to talk about politics, go to 54th Street by the HRC," he added in a hideous display of cynicism.

"Shame on you, Richard," echoed a chubby boy who sat next to my friend Laurette in the middle of the room. "Lucille is right. Everyone has been touched by the violence against the people in Port-au-Prince. Everyone but a small group here on this campus," he added. His face turned red. His name was Calixte Nadal of Arabic origin.

"Calixte, I couldn't agree more. And I think what Richard said was very disrespectful. The refugees are Haitians just like us. It's very sad for him to think that somehow he's superior to other Haitians. I know their Haiti is far different from the one you and I live in. It's a Haiti that's stuck in outright misery…"

Calixte turned red under the weight of his emotion, but he had hit the nail on the head, seeming to trigger soul-searching among many of us. He went on to remind his friends, Haitian children from the upper-class, that their arrogant lifestyle formed the basis of others' misfortunes, and if thousands of Haitians were braving shark-infested waters to seek a better life elsewhere

339

it was not because they were unpatriotic, but because they saw no future in a land that offered them nothing to better their lives.

In my heart, there was a sense of renewed confidence that I was not alone in the room. I then raised my hand and requested a vote on whether or not we should move forward and include a discussion about the latest development in Haiti. Everyone agreed with my motion except for the small group of recalcitrant individuals who apparently could not hide their personal prejudices against their own compatriots. They were six of them, obnoxious in nature, who never had anything to do with what they called "dirty foot" Haitians. All at once, they walked out, and the meeting went on with Haiti as the main item on the agenda. At the end of the meeting, a resolution was unanimously adopted to create a committee to raise money in support of the cause. It was one of my happiest days at school.

Although the meeting was adjourned, Lucille and I remained in the room, talking about our worries and hopes for the future of our country. We stayed there until it was time to go to our separate classes.

I was on schedule to work that day, and after class, I threaded down the path to the financial aid office. Michaela was still in class. Usually, when Mica was not around, I would go to the cafeteria just to have a sandwich and walk right back. I did just that. As I stepped into the office, Pablo was behind the counter. He seemed worried.

"Man, you've just saved my life."

"How so?" I asked, moving over to the sign-in sheet.

"Selena and I broke up last night."

340

"You think I'm surprised. She got tired of you cheating on her."

"No, Vinco. That's not what you think. You know how much I love her."

"I also know how much she loves you, too."

"That's what she always makes me believe."

"And then what, Pablo?"

"I discovered her secret love affair with a gentleman named Javier."

"Javier Molina?"

"No, no, Molina is my cousin."

"This Javier is an Argentine boy. His parents are wealthy business folks. They own several clothing stores downtown. They live in Coconut Grove by the ocean."

"How do you know she's involved with this man?"

"At Sofitel Hotel last night on Brickell Avenue downtown, my friend Francisco caught her in the arms of Javier as they danced, laughed, and squeezed like lovers do. Francisco alerted me immediately. He then secretly followed them to a back door that led to a tiny alleyway where they began exchanging wild kisses. Francisco told me they then ran outside, and through some glass window he watched the boy get her into a black limousine…"

"Are you kidding?"

"Why would I kid you about something so serious. As proof, Francisco showed me a picture of them that he secretly took while the bitch was kissing him." Pablo's face turned scarlet red like that of a ripe cherry tomato. He then pushed the door and was ready to walk out.

"*Pablo,*" I called.

He turned around and raised his sinking eyes. "Vinco, I have some good advice for you. Never invest your love one hundred percent in a girl. You may pay a heavy price," he said and slammed the door behind him.

Pablo's meltdown left me puzzled, and so did his advice. The images of Régine molded in the arms of the gentleman flashed across my mind. It was the second time in less than a month a friend had warned me about love beyond reason, and that was how I had felt for Régine. So, Pablo's advice only strengthened my understanding of human behavior in this complex world.

With Michaela, however, I could only see a romance at the spring of its blossoming. I also knew that despite the undeniable relativism of all things in life, human relations have always produced more good than bad. My parents were a clear example of this. They were not perfect, by any stretch. But within the scope of their own interpretation of how we should interact as humans, there was always a persistent, recurrent theme each time they had to discipline me or any of my siblings. "I know you're not perfect," Manman would say. "But you should never stop trying to be the best, and at each try, you make yourself a better person. Remember this."

I cherished this advice to the depths of my heart and I used it as the light that was guiding me through one of the most uncertain moments of my young life. I spent the rest of the afternoon quite disturbed. So much so that Sister Joanne, who had never seen me in this state of gloom, could not help but ask what was wrong with me. I lied, telling her I was not feeling well due to an unexpected flu. She then sent me home early. I left the financial aid office and made my way toward the cafeteria.

Halfway there, I met Michaela. She was breathless. She held my hand, asked me to walk her to the parking lot. I became anxious, but she quickly reassured me that she was fine and that she had to leave early because her mother, who was not well-versed in English, had a doctor's appointment, and that she had to go with her. That day she had driven her father's car, so I walked her past the library building, crossing North Miami Avenue to the south parking lot near the newly built gymnasium.

There we met her mother, Lucrecia, sitting on a bench by the gym. I was surprised. Mica did not tell me she was waiting there. It was the first time I had seen her since my home visit, and she was happy to see me. We hugged each other, and she lovingly poked my cheeks like one would do to a baby, while Mica watched in awe. We chatted for a couple of minutes and they left in a beige Toyota Corolla. I made my way to my car and drove home.

Along the way, I struggled to stay the course. To make matters worse, the traffic on North Miami Avenue slowed considerably and soon grew to a halt near 82nd Street. While stranded in the car, my unwanted melancholy returned. Deeply pensive, I felt powerless against waves of painful nostalgia, a burning stew of nightmarish thoughts in my mind. I was worried about my parents in Haiti. Deep in my thick fog of reverie, a teenage driver blundered his car into a row of vehicles trailing behind me. This triggered a dissonance of yelling, bitching, and horn blowing. A middle-aged woman driving a BMW took a direct hit that pushed her car upward and almost landed on my rear bumper.

Like a lightning strike, the commotion brought me back to reality. Before the cops arrived to block the road, I managed to swing my way out of the traffic and headed west. Soon, I came to a housing project. This neighborhood was unknown to me, until now. Young black males in baggy pants and unkempt hair, young women and their children roamed the streets as groups of old black men congregated on front porches. I drove in silence. Then, I turned east, reclaiming North Miami Avenue. At full speed, I drove down, and within minutes, I was home.

My sister was still at work, but there was food on the kitchen stove. It was my favorite, *diri kole* (rice mixed with beans) and stir-fried chicken. Yet, I was too consumed by my gloom to contemplate putting food in my mouth. I was about to walk to my room when the phone rang. I hurried and picked it up. It was my mother on the other end of the line. In an instant, all feeling of sadness vanished.

"*Manman!*" I said, ecstatic.

"Vinco, I missed you," she said, excited.

"Me too, Manman."

"When are you coming to visit, Vinco?"

"I would love to, Manman, but I'm waiting for my green card to travel. Otherwise, I won't be able to return here once I get to Haiti."

"I see, my son. You know Régine is in Miami, now. Don't you?"

"Yes, Manman, I heard that."

"You mean you never saw her."

"No, Manman."

344

"Vinco, I heard she's getting married."

"Really?" I lied. I quickly changed the topic of conversation. "Manman, how are my brothers and my little sister doing?"

"Guyto couldn't go to Port-au-Prince to school because of the riots. This morning, he went up to Nan Dubourg with a group of friends from the neighborhood. Compa is struggling with school work and I can't help him. Royo is doing fine, shaping up to become a beautiful young lady. All her teachers still like her."

"Manman, why did Guyto go to Nan Dubourg?"

"My son, I'm in a public phone booth. I can't explain, but you know...." She lowered her voice substantially. But I got the message.

"*Pitit mwen* (my son), things are tough here. There's nothing to feed the children. Your father hasn't sent anything in three months. I'm totally in debt, and I can't pay the people back. Every day, people keep coming to my front door, angry, like dangerous wolves, to claim their money. They threaten to storm the house..."

This account was too much for me to bear. "Manman, I understand. No need to explain any further. Go home. I wouldn't want other people to overhear our story. You know how folks in Vertus are nosy?"

"There's nothing to hide anymore, Vinco."

"Manman, you can go home now, and you'll hear from me later. I just got a little job. I'm going to talk to Lorna and see what we can do. Bye, Manman."

"Bye, my son. Stay safe."

We hung up the phone. I was terrified. I could hear the scratching sigh of her voice. I could feel the agony, the sense of despair that escaped her mouth as we talked. I knew my mother, a proud woman who sheltered her children under the weight of her dignity, now found herself powerless in the face of barrages of insults from lenders to whom she was unable to pay. In an environment of nosy neighbors, shame had befallen her. Adding to the humiliation was the feeling of impotence that was eating her inside as she watched my brother flee to unknown places to fend off the fatal paws of the Duvalier henchmen, who were aggressively hunting down all young men of fighting age in a desperate attempt to put down a popular rebellion.

From the Bahamian island where my father lived, all communications with Haiti were shut down during the final days of the Duvalier regime. He too had to be under extreme stress. My mind was in turmoil. A self-inflected guilt now weighed on me. I had to act. I knew a sleepless night awaited me unless I found a way to send some money to my mother. My brother in hiding was also a cause for concern, even though he was not in the hands of the *tonton macoutes*—the Duvaliers' brutal police.

It was past four o'clock in the afternoon, and finding my sister was my top priority. For more than a month, my sister had been coming home late from work. She had joined a group at her church called "The Ladies in Crisis," made up of young women in their late twenties who, despite countless sentimental overtures, had yet to find their groom-to-be. They met every afternoon in a back room of their small Haitian Baptist church on the corner of 36th Street and Northeast 2nd Avenue, on the southern fringes of the Little Haiti neighborhood, just north of the fancy business quarter where the Palm Beach rich came to squander their money.

346

I grabbed my car keys and was ready to go find my sister. I was about to push the door open when the phone rang. "Hello," I answered. My voice swelled in anxiety.

"Baby, it's me," Michaela said from the other end of the line. "Vinco, you sound preoccupied. Is there anything wrong?"

"No, Mica. I have to go pick up my sister from church. Are you home already?"

"No, my mom is still here at the doctor's office. My sister is with her in the consultation room. Just wanted to hear your voice."

"Me too, *amorecita*. My sister is waiting. We'll talk later tonight. *Besitos*..."

"*Besitos*, bye."

I ran to the car and drove east toward Third Avenue, a narrow stretch of road, just off the railroad, that snaked down to uptown Miami. Traffic was light. Few cars swept by. Like a trailblazer, I sped down and, within minutes, I was at the church. The front door was unlocked. Stealthily, I went into a room that was dark and empty. There was a distressing cry of female voices echoing from the back. The deeper I advanced, the louder the voices grew, which led me to a tiny glass door separating the church building and the small room where the women congregated, all lying face down and wailing in profound communion with God. My sister lay near the door on a small oriental rug, her Bible by her side. I knocked on the door and she lifted her head, on full alert, and saw me. In a quick move, she was up and walked out.

"Vinco, *what* brought you here?" she asked. Her voice and body shivered like a frightened child in a damp, foggy cold.

"I just got off the phone with Mom…." I filled her in on the story.

"So, what do we do?" she asked, startled.

"I don't know. That's why I came to get you."

"Do you have any money on you?"

"No."

"We have two hundred dollars at home as you know, Vinco. But that's part of the rent money. Rent is due on the tenth."

"Nana, I get paid on Friday."

"Let's go home, Vinco." She went back inside, picking up her Bible amid cries of tears and fervent prayers.

No one noticed when she gently walked out and closed the door behind her. We drove back home and got the money. Still, the problem was far from over. We had yet to know how to get the money to Manman. There were several places in and around Little Haiti that offered such service, but in the chaotic days that preceded Baby Doc Duvalier's downfall, sending money to Haiti was as risky as playing the lotto. Many desperate Haitians lost their money to men who preyed on innocent people by giving them false hopes and then robbing them. The legitimate services shut their doors, for it had become impossible to transfer money to Haiti.

My sister then remembered a woman from her crisis group who knew someone from our hometown of Saint Louis who was still in the business. My sister called her over the phone, and she gave my sister the person's name and address, but she warned that dealing with this person was just like gambling. Only if you are lucky would the money arrive at the destination. The information was far from reassuring. So, my sister and I pondered our options.

Manman's cry of hopelessness suddenly came vibrating in my tormented mind. I told my sister that it was a risk worth taking because doing nothing would make us feel like accomplices to the corruption and misery that had tightened its grip over a nation hungry for freedom and democracy, a collective lamentation of which Manman and my siblings were an integral part.

"I know the way. Let's *go*," she commanded, pushing the door open.

I followed her. We got into the car, and I drove us off. By then, it was already five-thirty p.m. To temper my anxiety, my sister told me the woman on the phone had promised her she was going to call the place to let the receptionist know that we were coming. So, we pushed on, driving through downtown Miami as luxury high rises swept by. Before reaching the old Du Pont Plaza on Biscayne Bay, we turned right and headed west on Flagler Street as my sister directed me. Her face was pinched with worry. I could see it, although she tried as hard as she could to conceal it.

"Are you sure you know the way, Nana?" I asked. Both of my hands were on the steering wheel, my eyes fixated on the road.

"I think so," she replied between tight lips, narrowing her eyes to fight off the piercing, late-afternoon sunrays that beat down on the windshield.

"Nana, do you have the physical address?"

"No, but the lady told me on the phone it's on the corner of Red Road and Calle Ocho."

"So, let's turn left on 12th Avenue and head for Calle Ocho, which will put us on a direct path to Red Road."

"You're right, Vinco."

We rode on in silence, crossing several boulevards until we made it to the intersection between Red Road and Calle Ocho. My sister instructed me to cross, and I did.

"Don't go fast. We've arrived."

I pulled behind a blue Volvo parked on the right side of the street. A sticker of Haiti's blue and red flag was tagged on its rear bumper. This was a busy intersection. Traffic increased, and Cuban shops and restaurants framed all sides. Just as in Little Haiti, sounds of English seemed scarce. Street vendors paraded their merchandise on sidewalks and were ready to bargain their products to prospective buyers. All this took place in the midst of an amalgam of salsa, meringue, and bachata. Michaela came to mind, for she had been teaching me how to move to the beat of hot and wonderful Spanish music, not too distant from that of my Haitian konpa music. It was no time for me, however, to think of my ladylove. Manman needed my help, and that was the most important task at the moment.

We got out of the car looking perplexed and lost. From a Cuban bakery, a young woman in tight blue jeans and a white t-shirt emerged, walking two steps down and strolling toward us. She was of a cherry complexion and slim posture, with long, dark hair that floated in the wind as she walked. I thought she was a Spanish girl until she reached us.

"*Ou se* Lorna," she asked in perfect Creole. (Are you Lorna?)

350

"Yes," my sister replied.

"Follow me," she commanded.

Without hesitation, my sister and I trailed her down an alleyway that led to a wooden fence behind which was a small white house built off the ground in the center of a concrete courtyard. A gravel pathway led to its front door. A young mango tree in full bloom with sprawling branches tossing in the wind shaded our way. The girl knocked, and a robust boy swiftly opened the door. All three of us entered at once. The room was empty, except for two high chairs placed in the far corner of the room.

"Where's Snake?" the girl asked.

The boy was shirtless and wore strange red trousers like those of lower Port-au-Prince street jongleurs. "He's in the back room," he replied while opening the door.

He motioned his index finger, gesturing for us to enter. The room was crowded, full to the brim. I was astonished. More than a dozen people, men and women with worried stares, waited. Some were standing, others simply squatted on the concrete floor.

A tall, slim gentleman sat behind a tiny wooden desk. He was the man of the hour, everyone wanted his service. He wore only a white undershirt and khaki pants held by dirty suspenders. His head was triangular shaped, like that of a water-moccasin, the venomous snake commonly found in the Florida Everglades, and I concluded maybe that was why they nicknamed him "Snake." His hair looked filthy, uncombed, and spiky. Despite the sudden crack from the door as we entered, he was unmoved, making no acknowledgment of our presence. He seemed deeply lost in a prolonged search on the desktop, digging into a mountain of wrinkled papers, old business cards, and messy folders.

"We don't have a chance," I whispered in my sister's ear.

"Have faith, Vinco. God is in every detail," she replied.

After about two long minutes of digging, he raised his head. "*Suzel*," he yelled.

"Here, I am," the girl replied, shaking rather subserviently.

I recognized his face, though I was not sure from where. I knew someone who looked like him back in Saint Louis. "Emilus?" I asked.

Without hesitation, he replied, "Yrvin?" He was suddenly gleeful, which caught everyone in the room by surprise. The young man who stood behind me later told me he had never seen him smile.

"Yes, it's me," I answered.

"Look at you! You've grown tall, and handsome."

All eyes were on me and my sister who, until now, had never met the man with the snake head. Suzel, the young lady, was also stunned. She worked for Snake as a shadow receptionist, the person who led the people to Snake's backstreet business.

"Yrvin, are you sending some money to Aunt Anne-Rose?" he asked, referring to Mother's maiden name, Anne-Rose.

"Yeah, my sister and I want to send two hundred dollars. Emilus, do what you can. She needs the money before the sun goes down."

"Don't worry, Yrvin. Aunt Anne-Rose should get the money as soon as I can reach Saint Louis over the phone."

My sister's optimism grew, but she was still cautious. She, who had spent most of her time in Port-au-Prince prior to immigrating to Miami, did not know the man. Back in Saint Louis, Snake had lived in the same neighborhood where I grew up. His mother, a starved-looking woman named Aséfie, was a laundrywoman who worked for my mother and other families in the neighborhood. Back then, Snake was a rawboned boy with hollow cheeks, a boy on the brink of collapsing from starvation. Manman used to have him come to our backyard every afternoon to share our meals with him. He seemed to have remembered that.

He pulled away from the desk, turned around, and grabbed a wired phone from the top of a file cabinet on the corner behind his desk. Soon, he was on the phone with some middlemen in Haiti. I heard him ordering the person to take the money to my mother as fast as he could. That was how he operated his lucrative underground business. He collected the money, charging twenty percent for each transfer with guaranteed delivery the same day. To many people, however, delivery was assured, but not on the same day. They did not mind, as long as their money arrived at its destination, for Snake was their only hope.

A woman who stood behind my sister whispered in her ear, "Don't believe him. It might take three days before your mother sees that money." My sister grew nervous again. Sweat dripped off of her skin like droplets of water after a shower.

"*Sir*," she raised her voice a little to get Snake's attention. "How can we know when she gets the money? This is a life-and-death situation."

He did not reply to my sister's question. He simply turned to me. "Yrvin," he said, "I waive the fee. Just give me the two hundred dollars and wait here. I'll have you talk to Aunt Anne-Rose to confirm," he added with a broad smile.

Suzel then took us to the empty room to wait, promising us that Manman would call to talk to us. Meanwhile, other folks kept coming, passing right by us, led by Suzel on their way to Snake's office. Soon, the office was overcrowded, and Snake had to order Suzel to have newcomers wait in the first room where my sister and I were. What struck me the most was that none of these people lived in Little Haiti. I had always thought all Haitians in the Miami area lived in and around Little Haiti. I was wrong.

A middle-aged man with stooped shoulders leaned against the wall, facing me. He said he was from Cutler Ridge where he worked as a handyman. He told me he had left his wife and three children in Haiti, and he had not heard from them in two months. He was hoping Snake would help him the same way he helped my sister and me. In the far end of the room, two couples waited with visibly mounting fear. They were tomato pickers from Florida City near Homestead. Heads bowed, they, like everyone, were hoping for a rapid Duvalier downfall so they would no longer have to come to Snake. They told my sister that their children, to whom they spoke a day earlier, told them they had not eaten a hot meal in days. We all were in the same predicament. We immigrants had a burden far greater than any other group in society. After waiting for about fifteen minutes, Suzel opened the door and called to my sister and me. In haste, we went back in.

"Your mother's on the phone," she said, handing me the telephone.

354

"*Manman*," we both cried, shedding tears out of emotion.

"*Yes*, my children," she replied. Her voice was distant but strong.

"Do you have the money?" Lorna asked.

"Yes, thank you, my kids. May God keep you safe. I love you more than anything. Say thank you to Emilus for me."

"We love you more, Manman. We'll call you tomorrow."

We hang up the phone. Suzel, who stood in front of us, seemed humbled and admiring of our passion while we talked to Manman. Snake was busy, taking care of the long line in front of him. He barely noticed when we thanked him, said goodbye, and walked out. My mother's voice, confirming she got the money, was the best of all gifts, knowing she was going to be able to pay the people back. Oh! I was happy.

#

Friday morning of February 7, 1986, I woke to the sounds of horn blowing and cries of joy. It was six in the morning. I ran to my sister's room to ask what was going on outside. She was clueless, so we then turned on the television. The breaking news reported that Haiti was in a festive mood. Dictator Jean-Claude Duvalier had fled the country along with his wife, Michelle, under the cover of darkness. I could not believe my eyes. Dramatic pictures aired on CNN showing the dictator behind the wheel of his BMW, his wife by his side as they navigated through the streets of Port-au-Prince on their way to the city's international airport.

By the time we pushed the door open and stepped outside, my neighborhood was fully alive. It was 6:30 a.m. Everyone stood on their front porches, hands in the air, chanting, "*Ayiti*

Libere!" Hispanics, Arabs, African Americans—all were celebrating along with the Haitians for this moment in history. A brutal, twenty-nine-year reign had come to an end. At last, the fascist regime was gone. It was the first time since the story of Esmeralda's failed wedding that I witnessed the neighborhood so unified in such a cohesive way. From the street, I watched Mr. Hakimono, the retired sumo wrestler dressed in a Santa outfit, herding the schoolchildren down toward the Notre Dame Catholic Church, dancing and singing "*Ayiti Libere.*" (Haiti is free.)

On the corner of Northeast 2nd Avenue and 63rd Street, I saw Mohamed, the grocery store owner, giving away fresh produce and yellow bananas to happy customers. My jaw dropped when I saw Fosia moving down from 66th Street, leading a group of women, Susana included, on their way to 54th Street in front of the Haitian Refugee Center for an impromptu celebration. Mr. Jackson was not in his blue robe in the courtyard that morning. Nor was he chewing on his tobacco. Instead, he and Travon were running toward North Miami Avenue to walk along with other neighbors in a long procession leading all the way to the refugee center. Mrs. Jackson had already joined Fosia and the rest of the neighborhood women.

Public schools in Little Haiti were forced to close because few students showed up that day, and the teachers were jubilant. The Haitian blue and red flag floated in every car driving up and down the street amid horn blowing and loud music blasting in the air. Even Fatty Henri, an overweight Haitian man with stooped shoulders and swollen limbs, who walked as slow as a turtle, was following in jubilation the rest of the people making their way to 54th Street.

Lorna and I decided to join the procession. Then, we realized we had not taken showers. We hurried back inside, but as soon as we got in, the phone rang. My mother was on the other end of the line.

"*Manman!*" I cried.

Lorna ran up to me, dropping a towel off her hand as she was about to get into the shower. I had to put the phone on speaker mode so that we both could talk with Manman.

"*Nou libere!*" (We're free!) she replied with unmatchable elation. I could also hear the voices of people in jubilation in the background. Then the voices of my siblings joined hers to sing along with other euphoric Haitians at the phone center where she usually came to call my sister and me. "*Ayiti, Ayiti, Ayiti!*" they kept on singing.

"*Manman,* when did you get the news?" my sister asked.

"Around five a.m., there was a knock on my door. We didn't know who was knocking, and Guyto was just back from the mountain. We were afraid. We all joined each other's hands lined up in the big bedroom. 'Zazou, open the door! *Nou delivre, Duvalier ale!*' (We're free, Baby Doc is gone.) Aloudres, my sister, cried, knocking harder. Then we walked out. There were already some neighbors outside. I saw Palto, the fisherman leading a group of more than twenty men. They were going after Dorgélus."

"*Dorgélus?* You mean the *tonton macoute* who lives by the seaside?"

Manman could not reply. She could barely hear us, but it did not matter, for the joy was holistically mutual and, more importantly, Guyto, who went into hiding, was with her at the phone center. Manman wanted to celebrate with us over the phone as many of the people at the phone center were doing, celebrating with relatives overseas. After a few minutes of this, we hung up the phone. Now that we knew our family was safe, we were ready to party.

By the time we took our showers and walked out, the neighborhood was emptied, the procession was gone. We made our way east on Sixty-second, passing by Notre Dame Catholic Church, and soon reached Northeast 2nd Avenue to get to 54th Street where the celebration was taking place. As soon as we passed Notre Dame, I saw a Metro Transit bus stationed by the bus stop. Then, I saw Michaela and a group of other students from the university getting off when they saw me. Michaela was dressed in blue jeans and a red t-shirt. Her cheeks were painted in blue and red, like the rest of the students who were with her, including the aristocratic ones who wanted no part of the earlier anti-Duvalier demonstrations near the Haitian Refugee Center.

During the Duvaliers' twenty-nine-year reign, the Duvalierists used a black-and-red flag to promote a perverse form of racism called *noirism* under the false pretense of protecting the vast majority of Haitians who were dark-skinned blacks against the mixed-race minority population. When I arrived in the United States, I found out that the blue and red flag, the historical color of the flag, was the symbol of the anti-Duvalier opposition.

Michaela moved in and kissed my sister, then wrapped her arm around my waist. "Baby, I'm so happy for you," she giggled in an explosion of joyous laughter.

"Oh, sweetie, only you can bring this joy to my heart," I replied, reaching for her lips.

We formed a long line, walking down. When we got to 55th Street, it became almost impossible to move closer. We had to fight our way through a thick crowd. My sister moved ahead of me, and I held Michaela's hand. She didn't speak Creole and she had never been in such a large Haitian crowd before. We made it to Northeast 1st Avenue, a few feet away from the center. Then, it became too dangerous to go any farther because groups of young men were taking on the business leaders who had been accused of being Duvaliers' spies. Phil Dorcéans, a record store owner, was grabbed by the neck and dragged out of his store. Soon, another group jumped on him and started hitting his head against the building walls. Police intervened and saved his life. The record store was ransacked. Fifty-fourth Street was one of Little Haiti's busiest business districts filled with shops, boutiques, and restaurants, and like all fascist regimes do, the Duvalier regime had collaborators throughout the Haitian diaspora.

Suddenly, Father Gérard Jean-Juste, the center's director, ordered the violence to stop. He was a balding man of distinctive stature who had risen to prominence because of his charisma, his commanding voice, and the respect he earned for his tireless work on behalf of the refugees. Stepping in front of the center and holding a microphone, he reminded the crowd that the day was for celebration, not for revenge. He went on to say that we had suffered enough under the Duvalier regime, and not a single drop of blood should be shed in vain. His voice was echoed throughout Little Haiti. The mood quickly changed, from vengeful to dancing and chanting in unison amid loud music.

I saw Rony, Gérard, Maxo, Patrick, Hervé, Tipous, Philo, Abel, and the rest of the revolutionary group stood next to Father Jean-Juste, raising their hands up in the air and making the victory sign. They all played a leading role in the struggle for refugee rights and against the Duvalier regime in Haiti. My childhood friend, Rose-Philippe, was also with them, wrapping her body with the Haitian flag, crying out of emotion. Tears sprung out my eyes. I never thought that I could live to see that day. Mica held on to me. She also was visibly moved. When the group saw me and Mica, they invited us to join them.

"You can come with your princess," Patrick shouted in total elation. He was tall with salt-and-pepper hair. His Romanesque profile seemed to tower over his revolutionary comrades.

"We can't, Pat, as you can see."

We wanted to go, but to do so, we had to fight our way through the crowd, too thick to penetrate. We stood on the other side of the street. Rony, tall and slim, left the group and shoved his way to get to us.

"This is the girl who has stolen your heart, Vinco, huh?" He said with a funny form of sarcasm.

"Yes, she is!" I boasted, pushing Mica forward. They shook hands.

"You're truly beautiful. He never stopped talking about you," Rony said, pulling away to go talk to some other folks in the crowd. Mica smiled.

After about three hours, the students left the party, and so did my sister who had to join her Sisters in Crisis group at the church. Michaela stayed with me until sundown when the party was over. Then, I drove her home. On the way, I took pleasure, teasing her. "Amorecita, who made the Haitian costume for you?" I asked, tickling her.

"You won't believe it," she giggled. "My mom *did!*"

"Really?"

"Yep."

Exhausted, Mica leaned on my lap in the car while I drove. As we drove through town, we quickly realized the festive mood of earlier in the morning did not disappear. We witnessed more horn blowing, Creole music-blaring, and flag-waving. In this joyful atmosphere, Mica, feeling tired and beaten, could no longer hold herself together. She fell asleep. While driving, I managed to push her passenger seat backward and ease her body to make her feel comfortable. Halfway home, she briskly woke as the car stopped at a busy intersection.

"Baby, I forgot to tell you. As you know, June eight is my birthday. My parents are having a party in my honor, and my mom has asked me to give you this," she announced, straightening herself while handing me an invitation card.

"Thank you!" I said with mixed emotion, taking the card from her and putting it inside the glove compartment. I had never received a formal invitation from any girl's parent before in my young life.

"Vinco, are you coming?"

"Of *course*," I replied, pulling her closer to me. "She's sending invitations already?"

"That's the way my mom is. She likes to plan ahead." She was now fully awake and gleeful. "Baby, be careful. Drivers are crazy today..." she reminded me.

I then redirected my attention to the road. As usual, I drove her right up to her front gates. She got out of the car, and I watched my princess, dressed in a Haitian custom, her purse slung around her neck as she stepped up to her front door. Then

I drove off. After that festivity, all of my effort had been concentrated on my last semester as an undergraduate student. Duvalier was gone, and Mica and I were living the best of times.

Chapter 27

May had arrived—at last. I had successfully completed all my courses and was now on track for graduation day, which was scheduled for the second Friday of the month. Mrs. Dickenson, a coffee-colored Jamaican woman with a thick afro hairstyle, could not hide the elation that escaped her heart when I went to see her for the last time. She had been my academic adviser since the beginning; watching every step how my worries changed into calm, reassurance, and contentment over what had been a challenging journey. My academic achievements stood like her personal triumph over the uncertainty of life. The high-spirited and exultant gladness she could not conceal that day thawed my heart. I felt Manman's arms in our embrace as I was leaving her office.

"I will forever be grateful to you, Mrs. Dickenson," I said appreciatively.

"No need to, my son. I have no doubt you'll be a successful professional."

I invited her to the graduation ceremony. She assured me she was going to be there as she took part in the event each year. I walked out of her office with a wild jubilance like a conquistador at the zenith of his glory. I wanted to jump all the way home, but reality set in. I was still on campus ground. So, I stepped down and followed the path to one of the small benches in the courtyard. I sat, feeling like a young man overwhelmed by an indescribable exuberance, a young man who had just crossed a key milestone on the road to realizing his dream.

There on the bench, I glanced across the vast university campus with restrained excitement, knowing all presentiments and forebodings of yesterday had been conquered. My relentless devotion to academic ardor had paid off. Reviewing the last four years, I could not believe I had fought and won against the odds in a world that could be quite unforgiving in the absence of social and moral courage, which was imperative for wading across the uncertainties that too often pin us down, morphing us into timid, tired, sluggish souls.

A few students walked by on their way to the cafeteria. Soon, classes would be dismissed, and the commotion would be unbearable. I got up and went to look for Pedro, who was also graduating, but I could not find him. Meanwhile, waves of students had swarmed the yard, giggling, chatting, and gossiping. My elation abruptly stopped, giving way to some odd mixed emotions. Already I missed the undergrad world. Up until that morning, my sense of belonging was in that world. But now, it was becoming distant and estranged. I thought of Mica. I wanted to share the moment with her, but she was still in class.

I dawdled back to the yard and onward to the chapel. I went in, and it was empty and quiet. A few candles shed dull, dim light. I kneeled, thanking God for protecting me, for guiding me along that difficult journey. Then, I walked out, wandering around, passing groups of former classmates. Some of them I barely knew, but I waved, and they all waved back. Angel, light-skinned and short, was beardless when I met him as a freshman four years earlier. Now, his boyish face had been replaced by unkempt, hairy cheeks, a reminder of how we all had aged with the passage of time, and with enchanted, irretrievable moments of college life, moments that forever remained engraved in my heart.

I roamed campus, touching every building, every section of this entranced university, a home away from home, including the dormitories where many of my Haitian friends had stayed, the gym where Ronel, Pedro, and I worked out in the afternoon stillness, and under the coconut palms near the flowerbed where Mica and I exchanged our first kisses. The merriment of college life seemed destined to forever live in my memory. But I knew that college life was only transitory, a passageway to an unknown future that awaited me.

However, this newfound self-assurance could not prevent new worries from creeping into my mind. My part-time job at the financial aid office expired soon, which was a major concern. For now, I had to beat back this new wave of uncertainties, avoiding dwelling on the way forward. Unable to find any of my friends, I drove home, thinking it would not have been fair to my sister, my biggest cheerleader. My success was also hers. When she came home later, I gave her the news while throwing a big *bisou* on her forehead. "It's *official*, Nana. I'm graduating this month!"

"Hallelujah, hallelujah. Glory to God, the Almighty!" She kept on saying. She then got on the phone, calling her friends from church, who had been in a prayer vigil with her, to deliver the news. She made rice pudding for me that day. She called Manman in Haiti and then Papa in the Bahamas to give them the great news. Her jolly mood reminded me of the night I arrived from Haiti. In the days preceding my graduation day, I spent my time reading, searching for a new job, helping Nana with the house chores, talking on the phone with old school friends, and being with Michaela.

Chapter 28

Graduation Day

We all gathered in lines inside a great hall outside the convention center in downtown Miami. There, hundreds of us, soon-to-be alumni all in long black gowns and green caps, were ordered to wait. Soon, members of the faculty came in and ordered us to follow them into the vast convention floor where we were all assigned to prearranged rows of seats. I was assigned to a seat in one of the middle rows next to students I did not know; but I could see Pedro sitting in the front row, chatting with some other students. Relatives and friends sat on the stand with cameras in hand to capture the historic moment when their loved ones' names were called to walk across the stage.

I could not see Nana and Michaela. I thought the large crowd had submerged them, but suddenly I heard someone scream from the lower stand. I peered through the crowd. There, they were, well-dressed for the occasion. I could not scream back, but I waved in acknowledgment. A few minutes later, it became all quiet. The formal ceremony had begun. Sister Jean, the Dean, in a brief speech, spoke of the significance of the moment and took frantic aim at the top academic achievers. I was among them. As my name was being recognized, I glanced toward the stand to get Nana and Mica's reaction, the two most important women in my life. When our eyes met, they burst into an explosion of laughter, beaming with exaltation. Following Sister Jean, two other speakers made some serious remarks. One of them, a community leader, a tall man in a business suit, sent accolades to students who stood out in various community service programs.

Immediately after he spoke, Professor Jose Ariate rose to the microphone and began to call the name of each student to come and walk across the stage and shake the hands of high-end guests before they reached Sister Jean, who gleefully awaited them to present an empty folder symbolizing their degree. At each name being called, cheerful relatives burst in uproarious laughter. When Professor Ariate called my name, the noise was a solo, high-pitched one because my crowd was rather small, but the piercing sound sent my heart vibrating. Both Nana and Michaela, brought their cameras to capture on film that historic milestone in my life.

"Go, Vincooooo," they shouted as I walked past Dr. Ariate, one of my favorite professors who also could not hide his joy, on my way to meeting Sister Jean who handed me my folder. I threw kisses out of excitement to Nana and Michaela while they took pictures of me stepping down, returning to my seat. About a half hour later, the ceremony was officially ended. The new graduates poured out of their seats to join their relatives. I scanned the crowd for my Nana and Mica, but I could not find them. I pushed my way through, trying to find them until I heard Pedro calling me from behind.

"Here, we *are*, Vinco!" He cried.

I turned around. There, they were. Nana, Mica, Pedro, and his parents wrestling against waves of cheery people. I got to them in a couple of giant leaps. With teary eyes, Nana and Mica and I hugged and kissed. Pedro and his parents stood there doing the same thing. Then, he grabbed me by his long arms.

"We made it, *bro!*" he bragged.

"Oh, yes, we *did*," I boasted.

He then left with his parents for a graduation party. Likewise, for me, my day was not yet over. Pushing through the throng, we finally made it to my car. As we were leaving the busy parking lot, Nana asked me to avoid Interstate 95.

"We're going to *Chez Moy*," she proudly said. Mica laughed and tickled me, stirring up my body.

"Please, Mica, don't start," I begged.

"You guys can do this when we get to Chez Moy," Nana commanded.

Mica did not seem surprised on Nana's Chez Moy announcement. She later told me she and Nana planned it all. For the first time in my life, I felt so profoundly loved. I never questioned Nana and Mica's love, but never did I feel it so demonstratively.

"Let me see the diploma," Nana cheerily asked.

"What they gave me was a fake one made just for the occasion. The real one will be mailed in a couple of weeks," I said. The food was on my mind.

Chez Moy was a cozy Haitian restaurant located in the heart of Little Haiti, a short drive from downtown Miami, not far from the refugee center. There was no outside terrace, no music bands, but there were plenty of happy faces that early afternoon when we stepped in. Nana's entire group from her church showed up for the occasion. They all stood and clapped to greet us, showering us with hugs, kisses and "Congratulations!" Even the restaurant staff joined in the festive atmosphere. Enthralled by the moment, my lips went numb.

In some quick remarks, Nana, in her broken English, presented Michaela to the group as my girlfriend and fiancée-to-be. Mica felt flattered by Nana's loving words. We then ate, chatted, and laughed. Mica sat next to me and was visibly moved by the genuine welcome. We spent over two hours at Chez Moy. Then, the group dispersed. Nana and I drove Mica home. But we did not go in.

The next morning, Saturday, I woke up to the voice of my sister's humming. She was in the kitchen, making breakfast. Soon, the phone rang, and I picked it up.

"Baby, are you going to the Hialeah Flea Market today?" Michaela asked from the other end of the line.

"I don't think so. But, let me ask my sister. Hold on."

I turned around. "Nana, are we going to the flea market?"

"No. I have to go get my hair done."

"Mica, I'm sure you heard my sister," I teased her.

"Yeah, but I didn't understand. I only heard No."

"That was exactly what she said."

"Listen, Vinco. Are you gonna be home?"

"Yes, are you coming to see me?"

"Yeah."

"Okay."

We hung up the phone. By then, my sister was already dressed up and ready to leave, still in a jolly mood. "You'd better eat that egg before it gets cold," she said with her usual big-sister commanding voice. I didn't reply. I simply threw her a smile. She shut the door and left. I then went to the kitchen and ate my breakfast.

I hurried to take my shower, then sat on the couch waiting for my princess to show up. Meanwhile, the phone never stopped ringing. Friends, cousins, and classmates were all calling to congratulate me and to discuss the latest events back home. The night before, some old friends in Little Haiti came to my house to personally commend for what they called my devotion to staying in school and graduating.

What I liked the most about Little Haiti was the Creole atmosphere. Everything was in close proximity, including many of my friends and cousins. We could literally walk to each other's homes. Soon, my friend Ronel showed up, wearing blue jeans and a red shirt with a blue and red scarf wrapped around his neck.

"Where were you yesterday?" he asked, hands in his pockets.

"Where did you think I was? Yesterday was graduation day."

"Really? I forgot. There was a huge demonstration near the refugee center. Gertrude and Adeline were both with me."

A week earlier, news reports out of Port-au-Prince had confirmed mass demonstrations had returned to the streets of the Haitian capital. Duvalier sympathizers had refused to accept reality and went on a rampage, going around at night in popular neighborhoods, massacring scores of innocent civilians. This had prompted mass rallies in the community. Haitian immigrants had accused the military junta of trying to reinstall Duvalierism without Duvalier himself.

"What time did the rally take place? After the graduation ceremony, Nana and Mica treated me at Chez Moy. When I drove by Little Haiti, I didn't see anything."

"It started shortly after eight o'clock."

"Did the girls ask for me?"

"You know Adeline. Her eyes were all over, looking to see whether you were gonna come."

"I know. She has an algebra class that's giving her the hardest time, man. I promised to work with her. Last time we talked, she seemed lost in that class, and Dr. Knudson doesn't play. She was struggling with linear equations, exponential and logarithmic expressions. But, what about Gertrude? I'm sure she was all over you, huh?"

"Man, that girl is not what you think. You remember how hard I worked to have a date. I begged her for a special moment, but she refused categorically. By seven p.m., I managed to convince her. She reluctantly agreed, though. So, she and I left Adeline with her little sister and went to Joceline's apartment on the back street behind the refugee center."

"Where was Joceline?"

"She was about to go down to join the demonstration when she saw us coming. She simply let us in."

"Did you guys make love?"

"Nope, I only got a few kisses. She is a dignified young woman, and I respect her for that."

While we were chatting, someone knocked on the door. Ronel glanced over and swiftly turned around. "Your Dominican girl and another one I don't know."

Ronel opened the door, and Mica waltzed in with her usual agile gaiety. A slim, walleyed, brunette girl I had never met before was with her. Mica lurched forward, landing a kiss on my lips and saying hi to Ronel, who answered with a nod.

"This is Josefina, my little cousin. She and her parents arrived yesterday from Europe to visit," Mica said, presenting her cousin to me.

The girl offered her hand, which I grabbed with welcoming laughter. She reciprocated in kind. She seemed very friendly. She had an ivory, oval face dotted with few freckles around her forehead and her thin upper lip.

Ronel headed for the door. Mica tried to hold him back, but he refused, saying he had to go meet his older brother Herold, who was having a party later that night. I then offered both girls to take seats near me on the couch. Josefina's eyes, crystal and blue, scanned the room with a strange prudishness. She held a leather purse while moving with an effortless saunter toward the couch. She took her seat a bit away from Michaela and me, and then buried her eyes in a book she yanked out of her purse while my girlfriend and I chatted.

"Baby, I have something we need to talk about," she said.

"You wanna talk now?" I asked.

"Yes."

"But, your cousin...." I lowered my voice.

"Let's go to the kitchen, Vinco."

We both got up at once and walked to the kitchen. She held my hands, which suddenly started shaking. "What's wrong, Mica?" I inquired in concern.

"Baby, I think I'm pregnant," she whispered.

"Mica, don't overreact. You're fine." My heart leaped and began to race. I struggled to conceal my fear.

"No, I'm not. I haven't had my period since we made love in that hotel at the beach."

"Really? It's been two months already." My face grew pale, and she collapsed in my arms. She was fearful, and her fear could not be hidden from her virtuous face, from the obvious crease across her brow and around the curve of her sensual lips. Her eyes were orbs of ferocious fire, and before the tears started splashing down her cheeks, I pulled her against my shirt and wiped them away. "Mica, to put this to rest, we're going to schedule a visit to my cousin's gynecologist. You're gonna have a pregnancy test. If it's true, baby, I'm ready for whatever the consequences. While I'm looking for a software engineering position, I'll be ready to take up any job..."

"Baby, if it's true, I won't know how to face my parents. My father would probably not survive such a reality. He always uses my innocence and my progress at school to motivate my older sister, who chooses her boyfriend and partying over education. My action would be interpreted as an act of betrayal, or at the very least a gross and unacceptable violation of parental rules. And my sister would have a field day. Vinco, I'm not sure I'd be able to survive this humiliation." In her uncontrolled sob, she melted against me.

"Mica, let's put this on hold until Monday."

"Mi amor, if it's true I'm pregnant, I will keep my baby no matter the consequences. A baby from you would be a manifestation of our love. God would punish me..."

From the couch, Josefina called to her. "Mica, I'm hungry."

"Be right there, Josie. We're going to Jade Garden, a little Chinese buffet, and you can choose your favorite. Vinco is going with us." We walked back into the living room. I joined Josefina on the couch while Michaela went to the bathroom to wash her face.

While on the couch, I noticed it was a French book Josefina was reading. She had been speaking in Spanish with Michaela, which was normal to me because I knew, like Michaela, she was Dominican, and when she had to address me, she did it in broken English. "Do you know French?" I asked, trying to maintain a normal composure in front of the girl, for inside of me, there was a mounting fear after Mica's revelation.

"*Bien sûr*," she replied, putting the book aside to talk to me. (Of course.)

"Did you learn it at school?"

"I live in France."

"I thought Michaela was referring to Spain when she said you came from Europe." We now switched from English to French, for she was having a problem expressing herself in English.

"I lived in Spain for two years when my parents left the Dominican Republic."

"And then?"

"Then they decided to move to Alsace where my father had a job offer. So, I grew up in France..."

"Alsace has always been to me the most intriguing region of France. Where in Alsace do you live?"

"In Strasbourg, now, but when we arrived there, we lived in Colmar."

"I can see that you love reading."

"Of course. Reading is my favorite hobby."

"Mine too. Do me a favor, Josefina."

"What is it?"

"Practice French with your cousin for me."

"As if you knew. She's been bugging me to teach her since I arrived yesterday. She said she wants to please you." Josefina shed a self-assuring smile and laughed, just as Michaela came out of the bathroom.

"What are you guys laughing about?"

"*You*," Josefina and I answered almost with one voice.

"I was just asking her to practice French with you," I added, pulling her down to sit next to me. Josefina reiterated again that she was truly hungry. So, we got up, closed the door, and left for the Chinese buffet.

The restaurant was in North Miami Beach at the entrance of a busy shopping plaza on 167th Street, right off Dixie Highway. It was a place I knew too well, for Mica and I had eaten there several times before. Off to eat we went. I took Biscayne Boulevard North. The traffic was surprisingly light for a Saturday morning. When we reached 125th Street, Josefina glanced to the right and saw a business sign in French that read *Le Chocolatier*, a

Canadian bakery, which was very popular among my Haitian classmates.

"Can we go there?" she asked.

"I don't think it's a good idea," I replied.

"Why?"

"Because what they serve there won't be enough to fill you. Besides, there's a parking problem. Look how people are crisscrossing each other."

"Josie, I know you. The buffet will fill you. Let's not change course. French bakeries are plentiful in Strasbourg. We want to please you with some Chinese American food," Michaela said.

Josefina agreed, and we drove on. A few minutes later, we pulled into the Chinese restaurant parking lot, and luckily, we found a spot right outside the front door.

Jade Garden was unique. It was the only Chinese restaurant in town I knew that served a cuisine so nutritious. There was a salad bar that had pleased Mica immensely during our previous trips there. She was a control freak when it came to watching her weight. When we walked in, it was almost eleven a.m. The place was packed, and more people were arriving. We managed to break through the unsteady line of hungry folks. A young lady with almond-shaped eyes greeted us at the entrance with a welcoming smile but quickly asked us to wait to be seated. "We have a table for three in the far end," she told us.

"Okay," I replied, but Josefina became restless. The aroma was irresistible. "We'll be seated soon, my girl." I tried to temper her impatience.

Michaela laughed. Soon, from the back, a waiter called to us and directed us to our seats. Josefina did not sit. She twisted around and headed for the buffet. Michaela and I watched with amazement. She grabbed the food like a starved young tigress, picking up a few pieces out of every item on display. She staggered to carry her plate to her seat.

"If you eat this much, how come you look so thin?" I asked, teasing her.

"I don't know. Maybe God wants me to be this way," she retorted, chewing on the food.

Michaela and I then got up and strolled toward the buffet. As we approached, Mica told me she wasn't interested, her appetite was at its lowest point, and the food smells seemed to have worsened it. Behind us, there was a window where two chefs in toque blanche hats and double-breasted jackets stood for customers who wanted their service. They chose their own ingredients and handed them for cooking while they waited for the chefs to prepare it.

"Why don't we go there. I know you like salad," I suggested, and she agreed. Michaela was paralyzed by fear, and her terrified attitude had taken hold of me, too.

"What if it's true that I'm pregnant?" She muttered into my ear. I could not answer. I simply held her tighter. We then ambled along, grabbing our plates. Still, she did not want the food.

"Baby, don't do this to me," I said. "Your demeanor is abnormal, and the last thing you now want is to raise suspicion in your cousin's mind."

"What do you mean?"

"She might think I'm hurting you."

378

"Baby, I'm scared for two reasons."

"What are they, Mica?" I held her even tighter.

"Pregnancy and losing you."

"What do you mean by losing me?"

"I don't know."

I grabbed her hands and walked back outside with her while Josefina was busy eating. We headed for the car, away from the crowd. "Mica, do you think I will abandon you? I want you to know that whatever the outcome, I'm committed to staying with you, to sharing your pain, your joy, and any unexpected obstacle. Your life is my life. Losing you, to me, would feel like losing the most vital organ in the human body: my heart, my sweetheart, and because no one can live without a heart, my life would be doomed the very moment of such eventuality. So, let's enjoy the moment."

"Oh, Vinco! I love you more than I can ever describe."

She turned, facing me, and I searched for her lips upon which I landed a fresh kiss. We then strolled back inside. Josefina was still lost in the food. So, we went back in line. Behind us, a young couple stood waiting. The lady, a tall brunette, was all over her man. She was licking his face, scratching his neck.

"Look behind us, Mica," I whispered.

"I think she suffers from an acute form of *lovinjitis*," she uttered feebly with a grin, pulling away from the insane couple.

"What's *lovinjitis*?" I asked.

"It's lovesickness, the disease that puts us in this predicament."

I cracked up laughing, picking up some bean sprouts and some bell peppers, dumping them in both of our plates over which I sprinkled a little Romano cheese. We then walked to our table.

Josefina was already on her second plate by the time Michaela and I returned to the table, and she was getting ready to go back to the buffet. "Josie, don't tell me you're going for more," Mica teased her, adjusting herself in her seat.

"Stop nagging her, Mica, will you?" I riposted.

Josefina grinned and whirled around. "No, I'm going for dessert now," she chuckled.

A couple of minutes later, my jaw dropped when I saw her coming with two slices of carrot cake and a full cup of strawberry ice cream. I was tempted to ask her to stop, but I refrained myself out of fear of embarrassing her.

"You know? I wouldn't mind living in Miami," she said, taking her seat near Michaela. She nearly choked herself while swallowing a heaping spoonful of ice cream.

"It wouldn't be a good idea to live in this town," I told her instead.

"*Why?*" She mewled, giving a small whine like a little puppy.

"Because you'd lose your flawless, God-given pretty-girl outlook, so petite and assertive. I'm sure you don't want to trade this all in exchange for food."

Mica smiled but said nothing.

"You sound just like my dad. He always watches what I eat for the same reasons you just mentioned," she voiced guiltily, becoming quite pensive.

"And he's *right*," Michaela interjected.

"At home in Strasbourg, my parents use portion control at the dinner table," Josefina told us.

"You mean everyone gets a little bit?" I asked her.

"Vinco, you'll be surprised to know how these Dominicans-turned-Europeans watch their diet," Michaela said, wrapping her arm around my neck.

"My older brother was obese, and Papa bought special plates," Josefina explained.

"Tell us, Josefina. How does Strasbourg look?" I asked, changing the conversation.

"A bit like Paris, but a lot smaller. It has a central district that is always full of tourists and local shoppers. But things are very expensive there."

"So, where do your parents shop?"

"In Germany, in a town called Khel, across the Rhine River."

"In Germany?"

"Yes, Strasbourg is a border town, fifteen minutes away from my house. Things are much cheaper there. What I like about Strasbourg is that if you live there, several countries are near."

"Which ones are you talking about?"

"I just told you Germany. And there're Luxembourg, Switzerland, Belgium…"

"Does it snow in Strasbourg?"

"Of course. It's a very cold place."

"But you get used to it, now, huh?"

"I'm Strasbourgish, now. And I love the snow and skiing. My brother takes me to ski on the Vosges every winter." She unzipped her purse and took out a photo of her and her brother side by side, both in their ski gear, standing on the platform.

"Baby, we'll spend our honeymoon there," Mica whispered in my ear.

"I hear you guys!" Josefina exclaimed, spreading her long, skinny arms like a flying eagle.

We stayed there for about an hour, joking, talking about the past in our respective old countries and about life after immigration, the struggle to learn a new language, to adjust to a new culture, and in the end, to immerse completely. On the way back to the car, Josefina, tired and feeling full, fell asleep in the backseat. Mica and I could hear her snores, even as my konpa music blared.

A few blocks from her home, Michaela asked to go out later that night. She wanted to dance to Haitian music. "Would your folks let you go? You've never been out at night with me."

"Don't worry. My sister is going to Las Palmas, a club near County Line Road, about a mile from Interstate 95. I'll leave with her, and you'll pick me up from there."

"Baby, I don't wanna see you get in trouble…"

"Don't tell me that, Vinco. I wanna dance with you tonight."

On the main road two blocks from her home sat an Eckerd Pharmacy, where Mica wanted to get off. I hesitated because I had never done this sort of thing.

"Baby, I don't want my folks to think you were with us the whole time."

"Josefina was, and I'm sure she'll tell."

"I'll manage her."

I pulled into the pharmacy's parking lot and let both girls exit the car. I watched them go in, and I drove back home, wondering about the accuracy of drugstore pregnancy tests.

Chapter 29

It was a gorgeous day. The sky was cloudless and blue, and the neighborhood was fully alive when I pulled into my driveway. Mr. Jackson was outside, hosting some friends in the backyard. I waved to him as I was shutting the car door.

"Hey, Vinco, whatever happened to you, my boy? I haven't seen you in two days!" he cried, pulling away from the visitors and drifting toward his fence to talk to me.

"You know, with all the festivities going around town, Mr. Jackson, I've been busy celebrating," I replied with a hearty laugh, crossing the street to go meet him by the fence.

"Listen, I saw two girls walking to your door earlier this morning. Was the older one your girl from school?"

"Yes, Mr. Jackson."

"She looks like an angel. She's pretty like those mixed Creole girls in Baton Rouge. You really have good taste, boy."

"Thank you, Mr. Jackson. But there's something I'd like to share with you."

"What is it, my son?" He lowered his voice and edged closer.

"I think she might be pregnant," I muttered in a feeble voice.

"What makes you think so?"

"We went out, and things got out of control. I didn't use protection. She hasn't had her period. We're both scared to death. She's adamant about keeping her baby if she's pregnant."

"Don't jump to any conclusions. Take her to a private doctor, a gynecologist, and ask him to run a pregnancy test. Don't go to Borinquen clinic. You'll need to protect her reputation and yours, too."

"Mr. Jackson, I try not to think about it. But my situation is so bad. My sister and I can barely make ends meet. How can I provide for a wife and a baby? I love her to the core. I would sacrifice anything for her. But I have nothing to sacrifice. Besides, my sister will kill me." My eyes began to water.

Mr. Jackson then unlatched the gates and stepped out on the sidewalk to be nearer. "Be a man. You've been through worse than that. I have no doubt you'll survive this one. But, let's not bury the cat while it's still alive."

"What's that, Mr. Jackson?"

"Don't agonize over things that may or may not be true." He turned around to take a glimpse at his fellows still chatting in the backyard just as his wife stepped out of the back door. He turned to me again and gazed upward. "Are you sure you love this girl?" he asked. His piercing, gray eyes fixated on me.

"Yes, why?"

"If your heart beats for her and her alone, now is the time to prove to this girl that together you can weather any storm. I've been through that with my wife when we were dating. Travon was born before we got married. So, if it's true that she's pregnant, you know she's gonna have a hell of a time with her parents. You should have a game plan in case she's thrown out."

"I don't think her parents would throw her out of their home if she was pregnant. Folks from the island aren't so cold-hearted."

"Then, roll up your sleeves and redouble your effort to find a new job, now that you've graduated, as your sister told me yesterday. Proud of you, though. That way, you can marry her sooner."

"But should I go home now and talk it over with my sister?"

"No. Why do you want to inflict pain in your sister's heart for something that may not be true? Wait until after the test result."

"Thank you, Mr. Jackson."

"You bet." He gave me a hug and he went back to join his friends. I then crossed the street and walked to my apartment.

When I arrived home, I met my sister with her entire crisis group. Onès, the sacristan from the church, was also there along with another bald-headed, robust dude. It was the first time I saw this man. He sat by the window near the dining room table. One of the women, a lady named Claire, the leader of the group, stood next to him, her head leaning against his chest. Onès was in the kitchen speaking to Clautide, whose desperation was boundless and who dwelled in deep hopelessness because she was the oldest of the group and time was running out. I was shocked because Onès was reputed to be an inoffensive, worthless loser in the game of love, and on top of that, he was said to have a myopic attitude toward women.

My sister was about to lead them in prayer. My presence created a sudden disturbance, and the women had to pause in their meditation. When Claire and Clautide saw me, they tried to change their demeanor, tightening their dress a little closer, hands folded inside their legs. I went straight to my room and gently shut the door, evermore convinced these women might really be in crisis.

Five minutes later, the prayer was over, and the chatting and the testimonies began. Lavanette, a tall woman with bulging breasts, who spoke with a deep and almost masculine voice, revealed her surprising breakthrough. The day before, her on-and-off boyfriend had proposed to her. Her voice rose from the center of the room.

"God has spoken," she uttered in pure Haitian tradition.

"*Amen*," the group roared.

"My prayers have been answered and the grace of God has come down," she added.

"*Amen*," the group cried, filling the room with joyous laughter.

This may have played well for Onès and his clumsy attempt to win Claudite's heart, but it seemed she was resisting his advances. A thin wall separated them from my bedroom, so I heard them speak to each other.

"You just heard Lavanette, right?" Onès asked her.

"Yes, and then what?" She riposted.

"I want you to be the next one in this group to make this announcement this afternoon," Onès countered.

"Announcing what?" Clautide asked him again, her voice deepened.

"That you and I are next in line," Onès clarified.

"Onès, you think I'm a sore loser like you? Your impotence is well-known. Two women left you because you couldn't perform. Louise, the wild turkey, was one of them. And I was told you were nicknamed 'Minute Man' because Louise told everyone you climaxed even before she suited herself for you. She had enough, and she dumped you."

"That's what you think, Titide. Why don't you let me try?" Titide was how Clautide was lovingly called.

"Onès, show it to me then." Her soft, tender voice confirmed my suspicion; her resistance was shallow at best. Titide was in crisis. She did not have much of a defense. From my room, I listened with utmost attention. Their conversation stopped, and the silence that followed was soon replaced by the clinking of glasses, sweet laughter, and low moaning. Then, it became deathly quiet in the kitchen. About five minutes later, I heard a creak on the front door. I then peered through a tiny hole in my bedroom door. I saw them all exiting the living room as my sister stood by the porch, waving goodbye. Onès and Titide walked out hand in hand, smiling in affirmation of their newfound solace after a mutually troubled existence in the game of love and the painstaking life of immigrants.

My sister then closed the door. As soon as she was back in the room, I stepped out. I noticed a bit of disappointment on her face, and I sensed why. She was one of the few women in the group who did not cheer when Lavanette made her grand announcement. From my room, I watched her demeanor. She simply stared and threw a smile with concealed chagrin.

She had been in that crisis group for almost a year, and the romancero of her dreams had yet to cross her path. I sometimes watched her with worried eyes and hidden dismay as she went from cycles of hope to the unraveling of empty promises. She would be thirty soon, and the prospect of transitioning to womanhood with an unsettled life terrified her. To her, not having a husband at thirty would be an unbearable pain. "If I don't get married next year, I don't know what I'll do," she would say in a low voice to her groupmates to make sure I did not hear her.

"Nana, Onès and Clautide want to get married?" I asked, joining her on the couch.

"It looks like it," she replied vaguely.

The subject did not please her. I switched the conversation. "Listen, I have an invitation for you."

"From whom?" She asked, looking surprised.

Without answering, I got up, went to my room, and walked out with Michaela's mother's invitation card. I handed it to her. She read it intently. "Who's Lucrecia?" she asked.

"Michaela's mother. She's having a party for Michaela, who turns twenty-three next week."

"How does she know you have a sister?"

"Michaela told her that I live with my sister and when I visited them the last time, I confirmed it for them. I told both of them that you play the most important role in my life. You're Mom, Dad, and sister."

She laughed but made no comment. She got up and walked toward the kitchen, pondering the invitation. She then returned to the couch. "I could go, but I have a Saturday evening prayer meeting with the group. So, I'm not sure."

"Please, Nana. Go with me. Michaela's birthday would be spoiled if you don't show up with me. She's dying to have you there," I begged.

"Okay," she sighed. "I'll go."

I jumped to my feet in delight. "I'm gonna see her later," I told her.

"Where?"

"Chico and I are going to the YWCA club. Mica wanted me to take her to a Haitian dance."

"Be careful. Make sure Chico is with you."

"You know who I am." I edged closer and landed a kiss on her rosy cheek. I purposely did not mention Las Palmas, the Spanish club. She would have opposed the plan.

#

It was nine-thirty when I pulled into the parking lot of Las Palmas, located near a Winn Dixie supermarket at the edge of a strip mall, just off Countyline Road, the main artery that divided both Miami-Dade and Broward counties. Finding a parking spot was not a problem because the supermarket was closed at nine p.m. and its vast parking lot was available. I found a spot not too far from the entrance of the club, then walked out of my car just to face a long line of partygoers at the front door. I had no choice but to join the line. I grew quite edgy, trying to pinpoint where my girlfriend would be coming from. I had never been to any Spanish club before, but I was sure I would be quite visible to her, for being the only dark face in a slew of brown faces. I looked in every direction, but she was nowhere to be seen. I started to worry.

When I reached the front door, two robust gentlemen both asked at once for my identification, which I provided. They glanced at it and let me in. I went in, totally lost. The room was packed like sardines with people. The music blared with such a powerful force that I thought I was going to lose my sense of hearing. Johnny Ventura was on display, and *bailadores* went crazy moving to the beat of a Dominican merengue. Young men held their ladies by the waist as they stirred to the rhythm of what sounded very similar to fast Haitian konpa music. I could move to it too. I soon realized why Mica had been telling me that my Haitian music was like a merengue in slow motion, and that she preferred the Haitian version because it was sweeter.

I searched in vain for my girl. Finally, someone pulled me from the back. I turned around. It was her older sister Gabriella. "*Vinco*, Mica was going crazy looking for *you*," she cried, elated. A tall gentleman with thick dark eyebrows was with her.

"Where is she? I already searched the entire room."

"Mica went outside, looking for you. She said she thought you might get lost in this big old place."

Without replying, I ran for the door and headed toward the parking lot and the entrance of the strip mall. There, she was in a red, long-sleeve tee tucked inside blue jeans. A Salvatore golden-silk scarf was wrapped around her neck. She was fashionably noticeable.

"*Mica*," I twitted like a starving bird. Arms spread, she jumped on me.

"Mi amor, where were you?" She asked. She was delirious.

"I've been around, looking for you," I said.

"Look at you, my prince. Your leather jacket and blue jeans suit you *so* nice," she tittered.

"Thank you, my sweetheart."

"Do we leave now, Vinco?"

"No, your sister was also worried. We need to go back inside and let her know that we're together."

"Yes, *mi corazón*." (My heart.)

"By the way, Mica, did you tell her you won't come back here after we leave?"

"Yeah. You'll drop me around three a.m. at her boyfriend's place. Then, we'll go home."

So, we rushed back inside to Gabriella. As we stepped in, squeezing our way amid alcohol-intoxicated partygoers, we spotted her on the floor dancing with her boyfriend. We did not want to disturb them. We strolled to the table where they had been originally seated. Folding into each other's arms, we felt like we were at the zenith of our love. Then the DJ switched to a softer, romantic, old classic by Juan Bao, the great Spanish singer.

Tu no comprendes
Que tu amor es mi destino
Mi esperancia mi camino
El fin de mi soledad…
You don't understand
That your love is my destiny
My hope, my way

The end of my solitude…

Irresistibly, we walked to the dancefloor, arms folded about each other, and started dancing. Her sweet fragrance teased my nose. I pulled her hips in close to me, and our lips met and brushed against each other. She laughed, and I responded in kind. The music ended, but we remained in each other's arms, until there was a little knock on my head.

"Stop it, you two crazy lovers," Gabriella chattered with an outburst of laughter. "You're my two adorable birds who fly regardless of the spot."

Mica and I grinned but did not reply as we followed Gabriella to the table where her boyfriend sat. We did not sit. I hugged Gabriella goodbye and I gave her boyfriend a handshake. We then rushed to the car and soon took Interstate 95 South, which was swamped by fast-moving vehicles on both sides on our way to the YWCA in uptown Miami. She leaned on me as always while I drove.

"Baby, I'm curious. What's the name of Gabriella's boyfriend?"

"Hector."

"He seemed very polite."

"Yes, he is. My mom is praying."

"For what?"

"So Gabriella doesn't scare him away. He's her second one in thirteen months."

"Is he Dominican, too?"

"Yes, but he was born in New York. The boy is madly in love."

"What about her?"

"She seems in love, too, but that's the way the stories always start. There's always a euphoria in the beginning, and when she's no longer festive, you know it's already over."

While talking, we nearly missed the exit ramp that led to Thirty-Sixth Street. Then I became more assertive while driving. A few minutes later, we pulled into the YWCA, a small building on the corner of 5th Street and Northwest 3rd Avenue. The place offered a variety of services for disadvantaged youth, marginalized individuals, battered women, etc. On the weekends, Haitians used it for Saturday night parties.

A gentleman named Harold D'Or, a master DJ, entertained the partygoers with the latest vibes from the most popular bands. As Michaela and I pulled into the parking lot, young men and women flocked to the front, chatting. We recognized some of them. They were classmates, but we paid little attention to them. It was a windy night and a bit cold. Hand in hand, my girlfriend and I walked inside after I paid the entrance fee, which was ten dollars.

It was almost eleven o'clock and the place was packed. There was a pause in the music, and because the place was so full and there were not enough seats to accommodate everyone, many of the folks remained on the dancefloor, chatting, laughing, and buzzing like chirping birds.

All my estranged Haitian female friends were present, including Carine, who was in a burgundy dress and sitting at a table with three other girls I did not know. Her lazy boyfriend

Reynold, a fat boy with a pimpled nose, who was wearing a coonskin hat and a patched jacket was also with her, taking swigs off what appeared to be Haitian rum in a plastic cup.

This guy thinks he's in Siberia, I said to myself.

When Carine saw me, she turned her face away, seemingly embarrassed. It was the first time I had seen her since she lured me to her apartment to meet Régine.

I held Mica by the waist while she walked ahead of me as we fought our way to a remote corner where, in a stroke of luck, we miraculously found a tiny table for two. I wanted to order a piña colada, but she stopped me, saying it was alcoholic. So, we sat side by side, her head leaning on my chest while I stroked her hair, which sprawled about my shoulders.

A few feet away was my cousin Mimit engaging his estranged girlfriend Lonise, a tall, chocolate-colored girl with a punchy, knockout stare, in what seemed to be a plea for reconciliation.

"Please, honey, give me one last chance," he begged, poking her flawless cheeks while trying to cozy up to her. He did not realize that I was eavesdropping. In a shadowy corner, I spotted Gina, a slim, peach-skinned girl, very drunk, cooing in the arms of a muscled, tattooed fellow. I was stunned.

"*Vinco*," some girl chirped from the back suddenly.

"Hey, Laurette," I replied. Michaela sat up and took aim at the girl calling to me.

"Vinco, I haven't seen you in a while," she said, advancing toward me. With mounting dread, I rose to stop her. She opened her mouth to speak again, but I preempted her.

"Look, I think Ronel was looking for you," I told her.

"Where?" She asked, rolling her eyes to see where Ronel would be coming from.

She secretly liked Ronel, though she had her own boyfriend, a weak-minded young man, the son of a wealthy pastor who could not even dance to the chair, let alone the sweet konpa music. I never saw Ronel, but he was a good friend. He would have understood why I said so if nosy Laurette were to find him. Mica did not understand. The music now started again, and my favorite song, "Love to Love You" by the iconic New York band Djet-X was playing. I grabbed Mica's hand and we strolled down the dancefloor. She was nervous. She had never danced to the beat of konpa.

"Vinco, my legs are shaking," she said softly in muted tones.

I tickled her, and she stirred in my hands, giggling. I leaned forward and kissed her. She laughed and smooched back with parted lips.

"Baby, let me show you," I purred, holding both of her hands and folding them around my neck. I reached out for her waist to pull her into me, just like earlier in Las Palmas. There on the dancefloor, our bodies stood still. "Let me lead you, Mica."

"Yes, baby," she muttered.

She was a great dancer, far more skillful than I was, and her weaves transcended all genres, except for the Haitian konpa. For some reason she was afraid of committing a faux pas, even when she was molded in my warm and comfortable arms. As we moved together, she quickly regained her self-confidence. The sweet konpa had taken hold of her soul. Now, like a pro, she began to whirl in my arms, and when the music attained its sweetest moment, like everyone around us, the steps were no longer followed. What came next was what they called the "slow-dragging time," the moment for lovers on the dancefloor to get "plugged-in," their bodies wired in an indescribable heat, and the thirst for lovemaking at its peak.

When the music was over, we sauntered back to our table. A cluster of classmates ambled by on their way to the bar where a tiny woman in a white apron was busy serving alcoholic beverages. "*Vinco nan setiyem siyel!*" (Vinco is in seventh heaven!) was shrieked in Creole by a nosy girl named Élodie, who had a crush on me and to whom I never paid the least of attention. I held Mica tighter and turned my face away. Next to her was her friend Solange, beautiful and assertive, rebuffing a young man's overtures. I watched her holding her ground.

"I don't date sluggards or shameless SOBs," she growled, and he pulled away, dropping out of sight. Michaela laughed, for she understood the whole conversation, which was in English.

In the next dance, Mica and I were on the dancefloor again, but the inquisitive Élodie and her friends now congregated a few feet away from us, gossiping.

"Marcelin," I called to a friend, and in Creole asked, "Can you get those girls out of here?"

"Yes, sir," he replied, asking the group to follow him to the bar once more.

"Baby, what did you just say?" Mica inquired, pulling me tighter as the music got more romantic.

"I told him to get these girls out of our space."

"You're *so* bad," she laughed.

So, we danced, we kissed and breathed in each other's soft fragrances, like romantic wayfarers on a voyage to conquer paradise. Around two a.m., we decided it was time to leave because her sister was waiting. Arms entwined, we walked down the path that led to the parking lot where we boarded our car and left.

The night seemed still as we rolled through the empty streets under the black velvet sky. Nothing stirred. Exhausted, Mica straightened her passenger seat. Her arm went around my shoulders. "Baby, I'm tired," she muttered.

"Me too, mi amor."

"One day, Vinco, if it's God's will, we'll only take one road home. We'll share a bed together, and in the morning before you go to work, I'll make you breakfast, just like my mom does for my dad." We then reached an intersection. The light turned red, and I stepped on the brakes.

"Baby, that day will come. I have faith," I replied, searching for her lips, voluptuous and sensual, to which I landed a kiss that seemed to calm her emotion.

She started dozing off. I lowered her seat. She then fell asleep and did not wake up until I pulled into the driveway of the house where her sister was waiting. We both got out of the car, and I walked her to the front door. I had to make sure her sister was indeed there. She knocked, and both her sister and her boyfriend stepped out. I kissed Mica goodbye and drove home.

Chapter 30

I picked Mica up from school early on Monday morning to go to the doctor's office, which was a small cottage roofed by Spanish tiles located on the northern fringes of Little Haiti. It was late morning, but it was still gray. The atmosphere looked serene, and that serenity had come at the worst of times, for it deepened our fear as we drove in silence from Miami Shores to the tiny community of El Portal and on to Little Haiti, where the doctor's office was two blocks away. I was afraid we could be spotted by some of my nosy Haitian friends, so I shielded my girl as we went in.

The reception room was near empty, except for a pregnant woman with a swollen belly who bowed her head, reading a magazine. We walked past her down a hallway that ran up to a half-open glass window, behind which sat a short lady with a strange, goofy face and bulging chest. She was wearing a tight pink shirt and biting on a juicy whopper from Burger King. She startled like an obese madame caught cheating on her diet and put the food aside, straightening herself while wiping away the tiny pieces of the bun splintered about her face.

"How can I help you?" She asked as she swallowed.

"We're here to see Dr. Jean-Claude. My wife has to have a pregnancy test," I replied with a pale face. Mica pressed my hand and wanted to laugh, knowing it was a lie.

"Do you have insurance?"

"No. I'm paying for it."

"Here, fill out this form. You can go sit down on the couch. They'll call you."

It was a long form held on a clipboard. So, hand in hand, we strolled to a loveseat in the corner. The pregnant woman was still reading, so we communicated in low tones. Shaking, I struggled to fill out the form.

"If you don't understand something, leave it blank," the receptionist said from behind the window.

Mica did not want to see the form. I could tell her heart was racing. She leaned against my chest with eyes closed. I only wrote her first name down, checking a few boxes without paying much attention. I too was fear-stricken. I did not dare to show it because Michaela would have collapsed. A Caribbean man does not display his weakness in front of his woman. Inside of me, however, there was a strange, unexplained feeling. Entering the twilight zone of my young adulthood shook me to the core, and premature fatherhood would ultimately do just that, wearing off the spring of my life. I truly loved Michaela, every bit of her. I knew neither of us at that stage of our lives would desire a baby. Still, we were hopeful that our fear was nothing but a false alarm.

Suddenly, the door opened, and a young lady wearing a nursing cap stepped out. She called to Michaela. My girlfriend got up, legs clearly shaking, and walked up to the lady. I rose from my seat and readied to follow Mica, but the lady stopped me, saying I needed to remain seated. When Mica reached the nurse, she turned around and faced me. "Baby," she said.

Though paralyzed by anxiety, I got up and joined her. "Go, baby. Whatever the result, we'll deal with it." I hugged her, squeezed her. Then, we let go. She regained her step, following the young lady. From the glass window, I watched her trail the nurse down a hallway that led to the consultation room, and I lost sight of her. I returned to my seat, biting my nails compulsively, restless.

About forty-five minutes later, the double doors reopened, and Mica walked out. Her face was no longer drawn, but she was not smiling either. She walked right up to me and collapsed in my arms. I did not have to ask. I knew then our worries had been confirmed. The silence that followed was spine-chilling. Before our agony was spurred into an unwanted scene, we stepped out and walked to our car.

"Baby, I don't think I can go back to school," she told me in an exasperating sigh of despair as soon as we entered the car.

"Me, too," I said with suppressed desperation. "You wanna go to my place? My sister is not home."

"No. I'd rather be some place neutral."

"How about going to school? We can go to the library and sit in the back."

"No, baby. We wanna be some place where we can be together to plan the way forward."

"*Amorecita*, my place can offer that, at least for a few hours."

"Vinco, why don't we go to Morning Side Park?"

Without saying anything further, we took off, turning left toward 79th Street where street vendors and hungry buyers swelled the walkways on both sides. I wished I could be one of them. They seemed so happy. We then drove east toward Biscayne Boulevard. The park was a mile away from the main road on the western edge of the shorelines. I worked hard to put on my best face. I had never been so scared in my life. Her eyes were closed, and she held my hands. I wanted to reassure her, but I restrained myself. I was thinking of my parents, too, my sister in particular. I did not know how I was going to face her to deliver such scandalous news.

Like Michaela, I refused to even think of an abortion. It would demean her pristine character, call into question my Catholic faith, and throw out the most sacred element of our love: our dignity. Michaela was my life. I had no clue how I could ever live without her. Keeping the baby had its own nightmarish complications. She was the pride of her parents, the jewel of their union. I began to rub her shoulders.

"Baby, we'll make it through. This is our first test of faith," I said.

"I know, mi amor," she replied, adjusting her body, tilting toward me. "Be careful, Vinco," she added, poking my face lovingly as we reached the park entrance.

We rolled in, passing a grove of careworn trees with scaly branches, crinkling in the ocean breeze. Hundreds of woodpigeons cooed overhead, dropping splintered Spanish mosses over the well-kept green lawn. Sluggishly, we drove on, and a few yards down pulled into a parking lot, and exited the car. We stood alone, except for a few quacking ducks that flew away as soon as we stepped into a narrow trail that ran straight to the seaside benches facing the water, blue and motionless, the other side of which the skyscrapers of Miami Beach rose in the distance.

"Mica, I never expected us to get this far so quick, but it looks like we were destined to tie our lives sooner than we thought," I said feebly.

"Love doesn't always bring happiness, though. Does it?" She uttered suddenly.

"Oh, Mica. This is *so* true."

"Vinco, I need you more than ever before."

"Mica, don't tell anyone yet."

"I know, *amorecito*, or my birthday party is ruined, as well as the lives of everyone in the house. But, at some point, I have to tell my mom, at least, before she finds out herself."

"So far, baby, how do you feel?"

"Fine. I'm a little light-headed in the morning. That's all."

"Mica, I have something in mind."

"Baby, tell me." She stood up and turned around, facing me and lowering herself on my lap, spreading her legs. I held her by the waist as her arms rested on my shoulders. I searched for her moist and sensual lips on which I landed a slurpy smooch.

"Tell me, *mi vida,*" she said, recovering from the kiss.

"We're gonna tell our parents that we're taking full responsibility for our actions and that we're prepared to face the consequences. I'll ask you to marry me. If you say yes, we'll get married. We'll rent an apartment on the eastern side of town. I'll find a job, and you'll continue with school. We'll take precautionary measures to avoid another baby until you graduate."

She turned her head back as if to rediscover once more the man who wanted to marry her. "Vinco, are you sure you want to sacrifice all this for me?"

"Mica, this is not a sacrifice. You're a part of me."

A river of tears welled down her cheeks, and I began to lick her worried visage to wipe away the drops amid scores of seagulls flying under the turquoise sky.

#

I came home that day thinking about Michaela's sacred words: "Love doesn't always bring happiness." Unforeseen pitfalls can swiftly destroy one's jolly mood. I was also learning how to be a man; and to be a man, I thought, was to muster the strength necessary to overcome fears that usually cripple the mind. I should have known better. I failed to protect her. I should have resisted the urge to make love unprotected. As a result of our action, our bright future that seemed so certain a day earlier now appeared in doubt.

Premature marriage tasted like a bitter pill for a young immigrant living outside of the sheltered arms and guidance of his parents. My sister needed me just as I needed her at this critical time in our lives, and delivering such news would be a betrayal. I knew my sister wanted a husband, and that man had yet to come, and her hope of finding that husband could be in serious jeopardy if I moved out. Adding to the dilemma was the precariousness of our financial situation. Without me, there was no way she could hold onto the apartment. My problems were overwhelming, but I was not in a fog. I knew what to do to secure and preserve the dignity of Michaela and that of my dear loving sister. The odds seemed insurmountable. For now, I kept my secret to myself.

Michaela and I spent the week agonizing over how we were going to tell the devastating story to our respective parents. We spent several sleepless nights talking on the phone. Sometimes, she fell asleep in my ear, only for a brief period, for the phone rang again as soon as I hung up to take a nap. "Vinco, are you there?" She would whisper to my ear.

"Yes, *mi vida*," I would reply.

Saturday evening came at last. I was dressed in my best outfit. I had gone shopping a day earlier just for the occasion and now wore a navy-blue, three-button suit jacket over dark-blue trousers with no tie, a style I knew Michaela loved, especially when it was just the middle button that was fastened.

My sister was inside getting ready, taking forever as usual before going out on special occasions. I was in the dining room, nervous and impatient. After a long wait, she walked out of the room in a beige, sleeveless gala dress. She stood tall in her elegant high-heels. She had gone to a professional hairdresser earlier in the day and she looked beautiful.

"I've never seen you so pretty, Nana!" I shouted. She smiled.

"Let's go before we miss the party," she commanded.

I grabbed the car key, and we hurried and locked the door. I had an impressive bouquet of red roses I bought from a florist shop. Lorna had a gift-wrapped present for the birthday girl. Though I pressed her, she refused to tell me what it was. We lay everything gently in the backseat, driving through the streets that led to her home. It was sunset, and the traffic was light, quite unusual for a Saturday evening. When we arrived, she was there on the porch, wearing a glamorous red velvet dress with a V-neckline and high front slits held by spaghetti straps. She was eyeing the street to pinpoint the direction where my sister and I would be coming from. The minute she spotted us coming, her face beamed like a mellow crepuscular ray at dusk. Indescribable awe soon chased away all my anxiety. She moved two steps down with grace and nobility.

Josefina cheerily stood by her side and soon dashed off to come crashing on me as I got out of the car. *"Beau garçon!"* (You're very handsome!) she exclaimed in French.

Lorna, stunned, followed me. We reached the porch, Mica hesitated a bit, and I threw kisses on both cheeks in part to avoid messing up her lips coated in rouge, but also because I desired no unwanted attention. *"Te amo tanto,"* (I love you so much) I said softly in Spanish, handing the bouquet of red roses.

"Mi tambien, mi amor," (me too, my love) she replied in a voice like that of a cello, sensual and romantic.

My sister then handed Mica her gift with an emotionally charged, sisterly hug. Michaela widened the door to let us in, and Lorna and I stepped into a myriad of rosy cheeks that were chatting, smiling, and laughing in the middle of a living room meticulously decorated with multicolor balloons, piñatas, and a conglomerate of Dominican party favors that I never knew existed. Merengue played in the background at a low volume. The attention quickly turned to our two strange faces, and the cacophony of joyous laughter abruptly stopped.

Michaela strolled to a gift basket and placed Lorna's present there, but still held the bouquet of roses in her arms. Then came a barrage of kisses, hugs, and shallow inquiries about health and life in general. Emilio and Lucrecia seemed happy to see me and my sister, whom they were meeting for the first time. Emilio, in a straight leather jacket, stood erect near his wife, who was wearing a wide, padded-shouldered dress, nipped at her trim waist and knee-length, like a dignified, prudish Dominican queen, as pretty as any woman in her late forties.

My sister, who was not well-versed in either English or Spanish, found solace in Josefina, who dragged her into a frantic conversation in Strasbourgish French. Then it was time to transition to the dining room where a sumptuous dinner was ready. Dressed in white velour fabric, the table was garnished by fancy silverware along with several crystal serving bowls filled with *arroz con gandules y pollo frito* (fried chicken over rice mixed with pigeon beans), a sizable bowl of salad made exclusively with tropical greens marinated in an in-house vinaigrette, clearly designed to showcase delicious Dominican gastronomy. Several bottles of *Presidente*, the famous Dominican rum, were on display along with bottles of red wine and scotch whiskey.

Everyone took their seats, except for Michaela, who remained standing to deliver a formal thanks to everyone for coming to celebrate in harmony another milestone of her bright and promising future. She took time to welcome each person sitting at the table, including her uncle Antonio, his wife Camelita, and their daughter Josefina, my sister Lorna, her sister's boyfriend Hector, and other guests. Then she turned around, adjusting the straps of her beautiful dress and taking aim at me as everyone looked on.

"Vinco, you don't understand how happy I am to have you and your sister here celebrating my birthday. You make me feel so special. When I met you, Vinco, I had no idea if our friendship could hold this long. They said Dominicans and Haitians can't be friends forever, but tonight you make me feel empowered to reject this claim. I also know Haitians and Dominicans have long intermarried, and my own grandfather André Dimanche is a clear example. Oh, I miss him tonight." Her eyes turned moist while I was blushing in embarrassment. She quickly wiped away the tears before they started dropping down her rosy cheeks, and glanced across the room. Everyone's eyes were glued on Michaela, who then turned to me and my sister again. "Vinco, Lorna, *muchísimas gracias* for coming," she said before taking her seat near me. (Thank you so much for coming.)

Then I rose to speak. "I have to say thank you, Mr. and Mrs. Monsalve, for allowing my sister and me into your lovely home to celebrate your daughter's birthday. Thank you, my dear friend Mica for inviting me. I totally agree with you. We, Haitians and Dominicans, have more in common than we may be aware of. At schools, I have had friends who were the products of Haitian-Dominican parents, ordinary people who understood they could not be held hostage by historical wrongs that were committed by both sides of Hispaniola. Their unions and their children had symbolized the eternal coexistence between two peoples: one Creole, one Spanish. It so happens that the recent history of Haiti is not one any Haitian can be proud of. It is a history clouded in mismanagement, anti-democratic governance, and a complete disregard for honesty in public affairs. This has resulted in an endless continuum of suffering. Dominicans also had their own fair share of fascism, something they got rid of in 1961. Today, it's Haiti's turn to seek justice, to be free at last after twenty-nine years of a brutal, repressive regime. I'm confident Haiti will someday land on its feet like many other countries that had fallen before. More importantly, ladies and gentlemen, Haiti will catch up, and Mica and I and others will march in harmony, not just with the full knowledge of our tumultuous past, but with the strongest desire to shape a successful future together. Thank you." I took my seat near Michaela as she trembled out of emotion under a shower of applause.

"I'm so proud of you, my love," she said discreetly. I remained tightlipped. Then, dinner was served. The delicious rice and beans and the chicken stew proved Lucrecia had mastered the culinary art of Dominican cuisine. Even my sister enjoyed the dinner.

We still talked politics as we ate. Mica's uncle, Antonio, recalled his revolutionary years in 1960 fighting alongside his older brother Emilio against the repressive regime of Trujillo. He told me how he was arrested and sent to prison. He stopped eating then and lay his fork on his plate, which was still filled with rice and beans. His recollection was too painful. He began to tell me about his dark nights in a prison cell, the psychological torture, the forced labor, the daily deaths at the hands of Trujillo's henchmen that came to characterize the sadistic nature of the regime. He then turned to both Mica and me. "You both could make a great couple."

I was stunned. Mica looked thawed. Her eyes morphed into those of a hungry puppy. "Baby, change your demeanor. People are watching," I said in her ear.

"You think they're stupid?" She laughed.

It was an evening to remember. As the guests were busy chatting and savoring the delicious meal, Mica could not help to drag my hand under the table and rest it on her still flat belly, knowing somewhere in there, the seed of our love had already been planted. In the end, amid shaking hands and hugs, my sister and I reiterated once more our sincere appreciation for having been invited to that special occasion. Michaela then walked us outside and down toward the car where we kissed goodbye.

My sister and I came home like happy souls. She only kept saying how proud she was of Michaela, whom she hoped someday to be her dear sister in-law. For a moment, I forgot about my predicament. I stopped thinking of myself as the father-to-be. The next day was Sunday. I slept most of the day, and Mica and I did not talk on the phone. This was normal because it was not the first time we did not chat on Sunday. Monday morning, I got to work at the financial aid office earlier than usual. This was normal, for we always had a chat before class, and I wanted her reaction to the Saturday night dinner party. I waited in vain. There was not a single sign of her. I went to work unable to concentrate because I sensed something was wrong. I thought she had either gotten sick because of the pregnancy or she was late for class.

After class, when the students started invading the courtyard, I walked out of the financial aid office, hoping to find her below the steps as usual. She was not there. I seriously began to worry. I walked back to the office and called her home. No one answered the phone. Then, I told Pablo about my worries. He encouraged me to go find her, and he would cover for me. I went and located all her friends. They all told me they did not see her at school. I spent the whole day waiting for a call or some sign of her. I placed several other phone calls after my first one earlier in the morning. I left messages. There were no replies.

I came home that day a troubled young man. Still, I tried to be positive, for I knew my girlfriend, wherever she was, should be okay. So, I went to bed with the firm conviction I was going to see her at school the next morning. I even had plans to drive to her house if she did not show up for school again. By five-thirty Tuesday morning, I woke up to a loud knock on the door. I jerked right up. My sister too was startled.

"Who is knocking this early?" she asked.

"I don't know," I replied with mounting apprehension. I jumped out of bed and looked through the window. There she was, standing on the porch in a flower dress. She looked tense, like someone who was in grave danger. I hurried and opened the door.

"*Mica*, come in," I uttered, trembling.

"No, baby. I can't."

"What do you mean, Mica?" I glanced across the street and I saw a minivan parked by the roadside, and there were people in it. "Who are these people? Why are you here this early?"

"Baby, I know you won't approve of it. After you left Saturday night, I had a frantic conversation with my mother."

"And?"

"I told her that you and I have plans to marry."

"And?"

"She asked me why so soon?"

"And?"

"I had to explain why. Then, there was a crisis meeting in my parents' bedroom. My uncle Antonio was also there. Although they like you a lot, they didn't think you and I should get married now. Although they know you've just graduated, they think I need to finish school. So, they decided to send me to Strasbourg to stay with my uncle and have the baby there. I'll learn French and finish school there. The baby will be multilingual like you.

Meanwhile, you can continue looking for a better job, thinking I'm safe and, more importantly, our baby will be safe."

"And you decided to go along with their decision. Is that *right*?"

She broke into tears. She tried to land in my arms, but I avoided her embrace. "You decided without me because you thought my opinion didn't matter, Mica."

"Baby, don't say that. You know how much I love you. I'll put my life on the line for you."

"*Prove* it now, Mica."

"Oh, Vinco. If I stay, you would feel compelled to abandon your sister to take care of me and the baby."

"Mica, isn't that what men do? We had a plan at the park, and you agreed to it. You were the one who told me at the library that you could never live without me, 'and the day I leave you will be the day that you love no more.' You told me you were born to love one man, and one man only. And that man was me."

"*Baby*."

"Don't baby me, Michaela."

"That's not what you think, Vinco. You're my whole life, mi amor."

"And you decide to go living two thousand miles away from me? And then you expect me to believe you?" I too broke into tears, but swiftly wiped them away. "You know what I think?" I continued. "I'm almost convinced your parents believe I'm not worthy of your love."

She winced, appearing to be in lacerating pain. My sister, who was eavesdropping from her room, leaped right out, took Michaela in her arms, and got her inside. Michaela then collapsed on the couch.

"Vinco, *forgive* me. I feel I have to make this sacrifice, so you won't feel pressured to make big sacrifices because of me. I'll write you every day. We'll talk on the phone every Sunday. I'll send pictures of our baby. My love for you will never die. You're the only one I've ever loved, and I'm committed to loving you until death. When we meet again, which I hope will be in a year or two, we'll get married."

"Really?"

"Vinco, *mi amor, mi vida.*"

Her sweet, filtered voice nearly melted me. "Mica, I don't deny the truth in your words, but there's only one thing."

"What, baby?"

"You never taught me how to live without you. You call me your sweetheart. How can one live without a heart? And I remember I made reference to this at the Asian restaurant last weekend."

She then jumped on me and started licking my face. A river of tears soon sprang out of her eyes and flooded her rosy cheeks. I remained numb, erect like a statue. My heart turned cold. She held me by the waist and began to stroke the nape of my neck. I was unmoved.

The front door was abruptly opened, and Josefina walked in. "Michaela, *Papá* is waiting on you. We can't miss the flight," she urged and went back to join her parents.

413

"Baby, baby, speak to me. Walk me outside."

I put on my robe and walked her all the way to the minivan, struggling to find the strength. When we reached the van, I tried one last time to talk her out of the decision to the astonishment of the people in the car.

"Until we meet again, my love," she kept on saying. "Until we meet again…"

She then got in, and the van drove off. I started touching my surroundings to see if I was not in a wild dream. When I regained my senses and realized that indeed it was true, the girl I love was now out of my sight, out of my reach, I ran to the corner, trying to chase the van, but I could only see her silhouette facing the back window for a last glimpse of me. I kept on running until the van sped under the overpass that led to Interstate 95.

I was alone.